About the author

Geoffrey Blackstone was born near Stamford, Lincolnshire in 1910. Educated at Uppingham School, he worked for the family engineering company, before joining the London Fire Brigade as a Direct Entry Officer in 1938. He won the George Medal during the Blitz, when he was the Divisional Officer responsible for London south of the river. An auxiliary fire station was bombed at Woolwich, and he worked for four hours with his bare hands, rescuing several people while more bombs fell and the building was in danger of collapse.

Later, he wrote *A History of the British Fire Service*, published in 1957.

LONDON BURNING

G.V. Blackstone

LONDON BURNING

Vanguard Press

VANGUARD PAPERBACK

© Copyright 2020
G.V. Blackstone

A CIP catalogue record for this title is
available from the British Library.

ISBN 9781784657 08-6

Vanguard Press is an imprint of
Pegasus Elliot MacKenzie Publishers Ltd.
www.pegasuspublishers.com

First Published in 2020

Vanguard Press
Sheraton House Castle Park
Cambridge England

Printed & Bound in Great Britain

Dedication

Dedicated to the memory of Geoffrey Vaughan
Blackstone CBE GM by his loving children.

Chapter 1

"Now may God bless you all and may he defend the right. For it is evil things that we shall be fighting against, brute force, bad faith, injustice, oppression and persecution. And against them I am certain that right will prevail."

Neville Chamberlain's flat, sad voice had stopped speaking as the telephone began to ring in the Kensington house.

"That must be my call to Mrs. Carew-Finch," said Kitty Farrow to her maid. "The exchange couldn't get through before and they promised to ring me. Oh dear, Alice, isn't it all terrible," she added as she hurried to the telephone.

"Is that Brandon 29? Oh, it's you Betty; I tried to ring you before. Have you heard his speech? Isn't it terrible? What are you going to do? You know that Claude has joined up. Isn't he wonderful? All the men in the office joined together last week in an ack-ack battery and, my dear, all as ordinary privates or gunners I think they call them. But they'll all get commissions; they've practically been promised that. What will Janet do? My dear! The sirens! they're blowing. I must find my gas mask and get to the shelter, goodbye." She put down the telephone and hurried from the room.

Elizabeth Carew-Finch, tall and grey-haired, could

hear the London sirens in her Norfolk house over her cousin's excited voice. She put down the telephone, walked to the French windows and looked out into the September sunshine. She looked over her trim lawns and well-kept flowerbeds, across to where the roof of the red brick stables showed above the shrubbery.

So, it was war again after twenty-one years and London was already being raided. He would have been forty-three now if he had survived. She crossed the room to her desk, picked up a silver-framed photograph and held it in both hands. The handsome young face she remembered so well looked back at her from behind the glass; Sam Browne belt, Grenadier badges, the ribbon of the Military Cross upon the tunic, the fine light brown hair with the slight curl near the forehead, wide-spaced eyes and sensitive, smiling mouth, brought back her memories with a new bitterness that broke the spell of healing time.

It was on 3 November 1918, that she had hurried to Victoria station to meet the hospital train that had brought back the shattered wreck to England, to the bride of four months who had nursed the stubborn suppurating wounds and the gas-damaged lungs for two years of mingled hope and fear as recovery followed relapse and relapse followed recovery. He had died by her side a few weeks before his daughter had been born.

She put down the photograph and opened the desk's drawer. All the sad and happy memories were there; his letters and her own, the hurried field postcards, the long and cheerful letters from rest billets, and the wristwatch that he had worn. She picked up the three medals; the MC with its white and purple ribbon, the General Service and the Victory medals. 'The Great War for Civilization 1914 – 1919'. She read the words again on the reverse of the General Service Medal. Where was civilization going now, she asked herself — what would he have done? Kitty's words came back to her. "What will Janet do?"

She stood for a moment deep in thought; the Carew-Finches and her own family had fought in England's wars for generations. Her mind was made up. She acted with her usual incisiveness and went to find her daughter.

Janet was leaning against the lower half of a loose box door watching Harvey the groom attending to her mother's hunter. The nineteen-year-old girl was dressed in jodhpurs and the yellow polo-neck sweater, which her mother thought was far too tight, and which showed off her youthful but full breasts to advantage. Glossy brown curls framed a face with big brown eyes and the fine features of her father. Tall and long-legged she made an elegant picture framed in the stable doorway and she drew the covert, sidelong glances of Jack Hart the stable hand as he shovelled straw and droppings towards the pile in the stable yard.

"I'd never go to war with horses again," said Harvey. "Too hard on the creatures. Outside Gaza I saw their tongues swollen for want of water and still we had to keep them working."

"Janet! I thought I would find you here." Her mother's voice made her turn. "Please come with me I want to talk to you."

The tall woman and the tall girl set off towards the

house, Mrs. Carew Finch talking as they walked.

"London is being raided already. I was talking to Aunt Kitty on the phone and I actually heard the sirens. I should have discussed this with you before but with the evacuees arriving and everything else, I don't seem to have had the time; very remiss of me."

"It's a question of what you should do in the war. I'm tied here with all the village and county work but you're not. London and the poor souls in it must need all sorts of help. Lady Dorothy Henshaw will advise you. She's at WVS Headquarters and she is a very old friend of mine. You can take the car. Pack some things and leave after lunch. Wear your blue suit; it's smart and serviceable. Ring me as soon as Dorothy Henshaw has fixed you up in some suitable post. Lots of organisations must need drivers. What a good thing you passed your test."

Two hours later, Janet took the blue Alvis down the drive and out onto the road to Norwich and London. Assailed by doubts, Mrs. Carew-Finch stood on the porch steps and watched it go out of sight. Her eyes misted with tears.

News had reached the village that the alert in London had been a false alarm. Had she been right to play the Roman matron so precipitously? Not only was Janet so young she was utterly inexperienced; an expensive boarding school, the finishing school in Switzerland and then the outbreak of war.

She wondered if she should have told her something of the facts of life before she had left but decided that with Kitty Farrow and Lady Henshaw in London, Janet would know where to turn for advice if needed.

The Alvis wound through the Norwich streets and out onto the Newmarket road. Janet watched the speedometer move up to sixty miles an hour and as she sped through the September sunshine, she let her racing thoughts move with the tempo of the car. She was half afraid and yet very excited.

She was going to war, where she would do great things. The bombs would drop out of the sky and she would tend the wounded and rescue the children. She would be wounded herself, but she would carry on as though nothing had happened and gain universal admiration. She would meet the king who would pin a medal on her.

But first she had to drive alone right into the middle of London with all its traffic and confusion of streets she did not know. It was rather frightening too.

She reached Newmarket and took the road to Royston and then the long straight Roman Ermine Street to Ware. The Hertfordshire villages dozed in their Sunday peace on this first day of war. She wished that the journey would last longer, but soon she was in Enfield and passing through the shabby streets of north east London.

At five o'clock she parked the car in Grosvenor Crescent, relieved to have found her way, and she went into the WVS headquarters to report her arrival and to offer her services to her mother's old friend.

She went through the double doors into a lobby crowded with waiting women. They sat on benches, leaned against the walls or stood disconsolately in small groups talking in undertones.

Janet stood indecisively and after some minutes she saw a door marked 'Enquiries'. She knocked nervously, heard an answering 'Come in' and, on entering, saw a woman in a green uniform sitting at a desk.

She was told that Lady Henshaw had left for the day; that they had more applicants than they could find posts for, but that the London Fire Brigade was still recruiting auxiliaries. It was suggested that she visit Manchester Square Fire Station where her enrolment would probably be welcomed.

After negotiating her way up Oxford Street, she found Manchester Square and drove twice round without seeing a fire station. She was finally directed to Chiltern Street, where the red brick building with four big red painted doors dominated the narrow street of shabby Victorian shops and flats.

Outside the fire station four grey trailer-pumps, their towing bars lashed to rear bumpers of London taxis, stood by the curb, attended by groups of men in the double-breasted tunics and peaked caps of the Auxiliary Fire Service. The bodywork of the taxis gleamed and reflected the sunlight and the glinting silver buttons on the men's uniforms.

When she had parked and approached them, Janet thought that the polish must have reached the peak of perfection. Yet the rearmost vehicle was still being gently wiped with chamois leather by a tall and languid young man who turned at her approach and said, "Looks good, doesn't it?"

"Yes."

"It ought to, you know, I've been polishing it since Friday."

"Really," said Janet, and then in a rush, "I've come to join. Who should I see?"

The young man straightened himself up and from his full height of six feet two inches, he looked her slowly up and down; taking in the pretty ingenuous face, the smart navy costume, the silk stockings and the expensive black shoes.

"My dear, you should have more sense. Do you really want to be shouted at and buggered about all day and night by a most uncouth collection of ex-lower deck sailors? You must be very innocent. Do you come from the country?"

"Yes, I come from Norfolk."

"Very flat Norfolk," he replied in a clipped mimicry of Noel Coward, and added, "you go through the side door there and up the stairs. I'll buy you a drink in the Wallace Head later." He nodded towards the pub on the corner.

She thanked him, went through the door indicated and up a steep linoleum covered stair to another door marked 'WAFS Recruiting, Walk In'.

A pale, middle-aged woman in a blue uniform confronted her. She had two red stripes on each shoulder, and she sat at a table littered with forms, teacups and stub-filled ashtrays.

"Yes?"

"I've come to join."

The woman leaned back in her chair and she looked

severe.

"We've been appealing for volunteers for the past two years and now that war has broken out and two pounds a week is being paid you come to join. We shall probably be raided tonight; you've had no training. What do you think you can do?"

"I can drive," said Janet, feeling very small.

"What about your topography?"

Janet looked blank.

"Topography," said her interrogator severely, "is most important. My volunteers who joined in 1938 can drive by the shortest route to any street in London. Can you?"

"No, I'm afraid not."

The woman shrugged her shoulders and called through a door behind her.

"Carter! Bring me some more enrolment forms."

"Yes ma'am," said a voice behind the door and a young woman in blue with a single red stripe on her epaulettes brought in a sheaf of papers, which she laid on the desk. Her senior took the top one and handed it to Janet.

"Fill that in at the table over there," she said.

Janet did as she was told, using the thin nibbed scratchy pen and ink provided, and returned it to the older woman who read it through aloud.

"Janet Mary Carew-Finch, age nineteen, driver. I suppose you want to serve in the West End?" she said, looking up.

"Yes, please."

"Well, I'm posting you to Whitechapel."

Carter interrupted respectfully to the effect that there were no further vacancies at Whitechapel Fire Station or any of its substations.

The woman looked annoyed and then she picked up the telephone; obtained a number and said, "I've a woman called Finch here, driver aged eighteen, no other experience, can you fit her in?"

She apparently received an affirmative answer for after some generalities she put down the phone and said, "Report to station 69, Bermondsey. It's in a cul de sac called Piper Place off Grange Road. Take a 16 bus in Baker Street to Victoria; number ten to Lambeth Bridge; get the tram there to Old Kent Road; ten minutes' walk past Bricklayers Arms station. Good evening."

"Well, are you in?"

"Yes, I'm going to station 69, Bermondsey."

He whistled. "The old cow! So she's sent you to Bermondsey. Do you know where it is? South of the river is very unfashionable you know."

"I was told to get there by bus, but I've got my car."

"That yours?" he said, looking at the Alvis. "Very nice too." He gave her instructions for the journey and then said, "You can give a week's notice, you know."

"I came to do a job, so I don't think I'll do that."

"A very pretty sentiment from a very pretty woman. Now what about that drink I promised you?" He nodded toward the Wallace Head.

"It's very kind of you but I don't drink," said Janet truthfully, hoping that she did not sound too prim. She liked the tall young man and she would have enjoyed his company.

"Besides, I was told to report to Bermondsey, so I had better do so."

She let in the clutch and drove off, turning left into Baker Street, as she had been directed and finding her way without much difficulty to Westminster Bridge, which she crossed.

Somewhere in the maze of mean streets beyond, she lost her way. Months later, she tried unsuccessfully to retrace her wanderings of that September evening, which three times brought her back to the busy, confusing, five-road junction of the Elephant and Castle.

As darkness fell, the little red, green and amber crosses of the almost blacked out traffic lights winked in the dusk at the confusing intersections. The friendly, helpful people she asked and who called her luv and duckie seemed to expect of her knowledge that she did not possess.

"Turn right at the Elephant luv, straight on past the Rialto, turn left into Old Kent Road, second left past the World Turned Upside Down."

Finally, a middle-aged man she asked, noting the pricking panic in her face, opened the door with a "Let me show you, duck" and he sat beside her while he directed her to Grange Road and Piper Place.

"There it is luv, in the cul de sac there. You're all right now ain't cha? Ta-ta!" And he opened the door, stepped out and walked away in the direction from which Janet had brought him, a mile away. She sat in the car, feeling for her handbag to offer him something for his trouble, but he was gone.

She looked down the short cul de sac, which was Piper Place. In the gathering gloom the red brick fire station faced Grange Road, with its glass-panelled scarlet doors, a patch of colour in the drab surroundings. She had noticed petrol pumps a hundred yards back and in a sudden impulse, turned the car round, drove back to the garage and she arranged with the proprietor to leave the car there.

Then, carrying her leather suitcase, she walked back, looking up occasionally at the starry sky and wondering if the bombers would come that night and, if so, what duties would be assigned to her.

Piper Place was quiet and deserted. She walked up to the red doors and, shining her electric torch on the shoulder-high glass panels, she peered through, seeing her face reflected in the glass backed by a blackout curtain.

A voice from Grange Road shouted, "Put that light out," and with nervous guilt she hastened to obey.

There was a wicket gate in one of the doors with a latch, which did not yield to her nervous fingers and at the side of the station beyond a single window there was an ordinary street door above two steps.

She climbed the steps and turned the handle, but the door was locked. The door had a letterbox, which she rattled nervously and ineffectively. She stepped back on to the pavement, wondering if the only way to gain entry to this strange building was to stand in the street and shout when she noticed, in the dim starlight, an unmistakable bell knob, large and brass and highly polished.

Irritated at her previous lack of observation she went

to it and pulled. A loud continuous ringing echoed from the building.

The wicket gate flew open, a hand seized her arm and an urgent voice in her ear said, "Where to?"

Before she could reply the big red doors folded with a crash into the sides and the startled girl saw a large garage dimly lit with blue lights and she heard the engines of two big fire engines roar into life.

In a corner, figures were sliding down a polished pole, which disappeared into a circular space in the ceiling. The heavy lanyards that operated the door gear were swinging to and fro; shoes were being kicked off as men leaped and clambered on to the vehicles, from one of which the driver leaned and shouted, "Hurry up Brusher! Where to?"

The hand on her arm drew her from the street into the dimly lit station and she saw a pleasant faced young fireman with brown curly hair and eyes of the same colour, who said: "Hurry up, Miss, where to? Where's the fire?"

It was only then that Janet realised that the big brass bell knob she had pulled was the station fire alarm placed outside for the benefit of members of the public who were near enough to run to the station to give the alarm.

Her face flushed and she said, "I'm awfully sorry, there isn't a fire, I've come to join."

A fireman with a single brass epaulette on one shoulder had joined her interrogator. He turned towards the red machines and with a wave of his hand, palm turned downwards, he silenced the revving engines. In the contrasting quiet, ten pairs of eyes turned to the embarrassed Janet.

"You'd better explain to the guvnor," said the Sub-Officer, nodding towards an approaching figure.

Station Officer Brewster, in charge of station 69 was tall, thin and greying, with the lines of dyspepsia in his lantern-jawed face.

"What is it, White?" he said, turning to the young fireman.

"False alarm, sir, the young lady here rang the alarm bell by mistake, sir."

"Is that true?" he turned to Janet.

She admitted that she had, and she explained how it had happened.

"Come with me," said the station officer. He stepped outside, took a small shaded torch from his pocket and shone it on the jamb of the side door where a very small bell marked 'Enquiries', in very small letters showed up in the feeble beam.

"When you want to get into a fire station, young woman, that is the bell you ring. Only station officers and above are allowed to turn stations out for drill!"

She followed him back into the station, where the appliance room was now mercifully empty.

"You Finch?"

"Yes sir."

"My superintendent station rang through about you. My woman officer's there now or she would see you. You're to report to Y substation. I wouldn't have sent you there myself. It's in Augur Street, about a mile and a half; bottom of Grange Road, turn left, third right and it's on the left, halfway down. Report to Sub-Officer Davies; there's a women's section officer there who'll look after you. Don't lose your way now."

He turned on his heel, and then he turned back.

"That your case?"

"Yes sir."

"You tired?"

"I am rather. I came from Norwich this afternoon."

He turned to the well-lighted watch-room and walked in.

"White, I'll send your relief to take over. Take this auxiliary firewoman to Y sub in the spare taxi." He turned back to her. "You'll be all right now. You can't turn them out for drill, no alarm bell there!" A flicker of a smile played around the grim mouth and he was gone.

The young fireman stepped out of the watch-room and gave her a friendly smile.

"What's your name?"

"Janet Finch," she said. "What's yours?"

"Brusher White."

Janet thought that, as hyphenated names were apparently acceptable in the London Fire Brigade, she might have given her own as Janet Carew-Finch, but the memory of the woman officer's scornful rejection of it at Manchester Square had made her chary of using her full surname.

"You've done me a good turn," said the fireman. "It's stuffy in the watch-room with the blackout up and a run in the old taxi will be a nice break, come with me."

He put on a round, peakless cap and picked up Janet's case. They walked through the station to a yard at the back and he took her arm as they emerged into the darkness. In the corner of the yard the shape of a prefabricated hut loomed dark against the sky.

"Women's quarters there, they're all right; proper beds and lino. Seven women here and the officer. They won't let them take over the watch-room on their own though. Us firemen still have to do it. Pity they didn't post you here. Y sub's not much of a place."

"Why not?" asked Janet.

"It pongs."

"It does what?"

"You know, pongs — stinks. It's in part of a tannery, rough old place, and they've got rats."

By now, he had groped around the yard to a taxi and switched on the sidelights, dimmed with several thickness of tissue paper inside the glass. Janet could see other taxis alongside, to which trailer pumps were lashed.

"Want to sit in the back or hop up alongside me?"

She chose the latter, only to find that there was no seat beside the driver's, and she had to squat uncomfortably on her suitcase. The taxi ground slowly out of the yard; first into a back street and then into Grange Road, where its front wheels bumped the opposite curb.

"Coo, ain't it dark?" said the fireman. "Almost impossible to drive with only dimmed side lights; the stores van nearly drove into the dock at Pageants Wharf last night. How'd the old man take your turning the station out?"

"What old man?"

"The guvnor, Station Officer Brewster."

"He seemed rather severe at first."

"He's all right, got woman trouble. One woman, his missus, she's a real cow. When she takes it out on him, he sometimes takes it out on us, but he's all right — good fireman."

"Are you in the Auxiliary Fire Service?" asked Janet.

"What me? No, of course not. I'm a regular, see! round cap."

She noted the indignation in his voice and in the reflected glimmer from the sidelights she could just see his hand go up and touch the peakless cap he wore.

"Been in three years, driver, passed BA last month."

"You mean you went to university?" said Janet, much impressed.

"No, BA. Breathing apparatus, special gear, selected men wear at smoky fires or in gas. You carry your own oxygen in a steel bottle on your back and you have a special breathing bag fixed on your chest with tubes leading to your mouth. You can live in any atmosphere; only selected men though, special medical, special training course. Make you stay in smoke for an hour on end and walk all round the training school blindfolded. When you've passed you get the letters 'BA', after your name in the brigade list."

The taxi bumped a curb again, which on investigation proved to be an island in the middle of the road at a junction.

"Cor! Gone right past our turning. We're in Dunton Road. Old Brewster won't half give me a going over if I'm late back from this trip."

He turned the taxi round and found the right turning a few hundred yards back.

"Taff Davies is in charge of Y sub; nineteen years' service, passed over for promotion years ago, but they've made about three hundred temporary sub-officers for the war so that one can be in charge of each substation, with a regular fireman deputy to be in charge if the sub's away. Taff's all right, but a bit slow."

"Didn't they make you a sub-officer, then?"

"No, only three years out of the drill class; not enough service, see! But there ought to be some accelerated promotion skulking around when the raids start."

"Do you think there'll be a raid tonight?"

"Can't tell, can you? We had an alert this morning, but nothing happened; reconnaissance planes I should think, here's Y sub."

The taxi had come to a stop opposite open gates in a mean narrow street. In the gateway stood a steel helmeted auxiliary fireman with a gas mask on his chest wearing rubber boots and oilskin leggings.

"Who's that? What do you want?" he said, as the pair jumped out and walked towards him.

"White from station 69. Where's the sub?"

"He's in the watch-room."

They passed into a narrow, cobbled yard where taxis and trailer pumps were parked. A pungent, acrid smell of half-cured hides filled the air as, guided by the gate-duty man's torch, they walked into the building. As they opened the door the stench increased so that Janet caught her breath and felt her gorge rise fit to vomit.

"Somebody wants you, Sub!" shouted the auxiliary fireman.

A door opened in the whitewashed passage where they stood and a stocky, middle-aged man looked out.

"Get back to the gate. 'Aven't you been told not to leave it for one moment until relieved? What would 'appen if someone on my station's ground 'ad a fire and ran into my station to give the alarm and nobody there to accept it. Do you want to get me broke? 'Ullo young Brusher. What do you want?"

"Brewster sent me down to bring you some reinforcement: extra fireman for you."

"Cor! What am I going to do with 'er? I've already got five splits 'ere; no beds, no proper accommodation and no ladies lav! Good evening miss. You trained for watch-room duties?"

"I'm afraid not. I'm a driver."

"Bloody 'ell! A driver? That's the sort of thing they do. I've got AFS firemen drivers for all my appliances. They're trying to get me broke!"

"Sense of responsibility weighing you down, Taff?"

"Now then, young White, none of your lip. Don't you Taff me, I'm Sub-Officer Davies to you and your like. You'd better get back or you'll cop it."

"All right Sub, goodnight," and turning to Janet; "Goodnight, be seeing you."

"I've left my case in the taxi."

"Go an' fetch it and then report to me 'ere," said Davies.

She followed her escort out into the darkness where

he took her arm, guided her to the taxi and handed down her bag. She held out her hand.

"Well, goodnight Mr. Brusher-White and thank you."

"Where d'ya get the Mr. Brusher-White from? My name's Bill White but they call me Brusher. All Whites are Brushers same as Clarkes are Nobbies, Wrights are Shiners and Taylors are Bucks. Don't ask me why."

"Oh, I see. Your name is just White and Brusher's a nickname".

"That's right, be seein' you".

The taxi slewed round in the narrow road and its dim rear light disappeared into the distance.

Bracing herself to the smell and feeling lost and unhappy, Janet returned to the station where Sub-officer Davies waited for her.

"Bring your bag into the watch-room. You'll have to doss there. The section officer will tell you what to do."

He led Janet into a small room that had once been an office of the hide warehouse. It was brilliantly lit by a single unshaded electric lamp, which hung over a table against a wall. There was a single large sash window which was open, displaying sandbags piled up against the outside, completely blocking the opening. The wooden floor had been freshly scrubbed and the smell of soap competed with the smell of hides. The air was frowsty and cold.

A gas ring with a kettle on it burned on the floor in one corner, surrounded by a teapot and cups. In the other corner were a mattress and a pile of neatly folded blankets. On the table was a telephone, an inkwell with a pen in it and a thick foolscap book.

Sitting on hard wooden chairs were two women in AFS uniform, one of whom had two red stripes on each shoulder. They stood up as Davies walked in.

"Sit down, this is Firewoman Finch just joined. This is Section Officer Casey and Firewoman Brown. Now Casey, I want you to take this recruit in an' show 'er the ropes so if anything, 'appens tonight she can give you girls an 'and in 'ere, see. I got to get on with my returns."

He left the room and the elder woman turned to Janet.

"You just joined?"

"Yes, this afternoon."

"You from up West?"

"No, East Anglia. I come from near Norwich."

"Want a cuppa tea?"

"Yes please, and do you think that I could get some supper?"

Janet had just realized how hungry she was for she had been too excited to eat much at lunch and she had had nothing since.

"Brought anything to eat with you?"

"No, I'm afraid not."

"The broadcast announcing mobilisation told everyone to bring at least two days' rations. We've been here since Friday but those who've run out of food have been given short leave to get some more in. There's no cooking or canteen facilities here yet. You'd better go to the fish and chip shop up the road. It's only a hundred yards away. Brown, ask Sub-officer Davies to come to the watch-room."

Davies returned, "Now, what is it?"

"Can Firewoman Finch go and get some supper? She's had nothing to eat since dinner time."

"Book gone for supper. You 'aven't been in the station five minutes. Don't you know we're on continuous duty? Don't you know there's a war on? I can't take responsibility for dishing out leave ad lib."

"No Mr. Davies," said the section officer, "and you can't take the responsibility of having a half-starved Firewoman on your station and refusing them food."

"I shall 'ave to ask Station Officer Brewster. Get station 69 on the blower."

"Now Mr. Davies you know he got annoyed with you this afternoon for ringing him up about anything and everything, as he called it. You're perfectly entitled to give one of your own firewomen half an hour's short leave to get some supper."

He hesitated. "I suppose so, don't be more than 'alf an hour and come back at once if the siren blows."

He left the room.

Section Officer Casey said, "Poor man, for nineteen years he's been trained to take orders and not to think for himself and now the war comes and they put him in charge of this station with more men in it than the regular stations had in peacetime; no wonder he worries. Brown take Finch to the gate and show her from there how to get to the fish and chip shop. You needn't bring your supper back here, eat it in the shop. The smell here puts most of us off our food."

Janet followed her guide out of the watch-room and

into the yard.

"You'll be all right at ol' Ma Judge's. She serves good stuff. Used to be on the knock you know. Bought the business out of the profits. 'Ere you are; turn left out of the gates, keep on this side, thirty doors up, keep on the left and count 'em as you go along, or you'll go right past it in this bleedin' blackout."

Janet thanked her and she did as she was told. The fish and chip shop was one, of a mean row of houses, with the window of its front room knocked out and enlarged. A blanket hung inside the door and the brightly lit interior was hot and full of the smell of frying fish and batter.

Between a small zinc-covered counter and the oven stood a stout woman with black hair greying at the roots. She wore a dirty white overall. Her lips painted in an exaggerated cupid's bow, parted in a friendly smile that displayed ill-fitting teeth.

"Evening, ducks."

"Good evening. Could I have some fish and chips please?"

"That's what I'm 'ere for ducks, though you wouldn't think so, this time of night. People won't come out in the blackout, what with the bloody slops running them in for shining a little flashlight. You want a two and one?"

"Just some fish and chips please."

""That's right, a two and one, two penn'orth of fish and a penn'orth of chips. You're new round 'ere ain't you?"

"Yes. I'm in the Auxiliary Fire Service just down the road."

A newspaper wrapped packet of crisp brown chips and steaming cod was placed on the counter.

"That'll be three pence."

Janet looked around nervously.

"I was told to eat it here. Can I have a knife and fork please?"

"Bless you ducks, you don't use knives and forks 'ere. You eat it with yer fingers, there's salt there. 'Ave a drop of vinegar on it."

She took a bottle from the counter and shook it vigorously over the contents of the newspaper.

"Now you just make yourself comfortable on the stool and enjoy it."

Janet did so. She was hungry and she found it delicious. When she had finished, she sat on her stool, reading the greasy newspaper that had been her plate. It was a sheet from the News of the World, a copy of which had once been left in the stables at home by Harvey. Her mother had snatched it from her hands when she found her casually glancing at the headlines.

'Cornish choir master on serious charge', said the caption and though she read and re-read the paragraph below she could not make out what the charge was. She looked at her watch. Her half hour was ticking away. Having noticed a pillar-box en-route from the station, she took a stamped postcard from her handbag and scribbled a note to her mother. She wrote that in Lady Henshaw's absence, she had been advised to contact the London Fire Brigade and she was now an auxiliary firewoman at fire station 69, Piper Place, Grange Road, London SE1, at which address she could be contacted.

Having posted the card, a few minutes later she stumbled against one of the taxis in the yard, bringing subdued giggles from its dark interior and she realised that she could not find the door to the substation. She felt her way back to the gate and asked the way.

"Put your hand on that wall," he said, "and follow it along to the corner. I'd come and show you but you 'eard how I was spoken to for leaving the gate before. That's the LFB that is; four hours at a stretch standing at this bloody gate in case there's a raid or somebody wants to give a fire call at this lousy dump when there isn't one; that's how they speak to volunteers. Jim Newton's my name and they're going to remember it when I've done with them. I'll be writing to my MP and to my County Councillor."

Janet thanked him.

Section Officer Casey turned in her chair as Janet entered the watch-room.

"All right Finch? Now I am going to leave you here with Firewoman Brown while I go and help Sub-Officer Davies with his returns. Brown, book Firewoman Finch back and see you do it neatly. Put that magazine away and you can spend half an hour giving her an outline of the brigade organisation."

Firewoman Brown looked indignant.

"'ark at 'er. See you do it neatly! I been trained on occurrence books since Munich. She's toffee nosed; she is. Talks posh same as you, but she ain't got no call to. 'Er dad's only a docker but she got some sort of scholarship and reckons to be educated. See this is 'ow it's done."

She picked up the pen and wrote in the foolscap book '22.03 hours, Firewoman Finch returned'.

"Everything that 'appens on a fire station's got to be entered in this book in ink and no rubbin' out's allowed. If you make a mistake in an entry you must cross it out so it can still be read and the officer in charge must initial it."

Janet sat on the hard chair while the knowledgeable little Cockney girl gave her a resumé of the London Fire Brigade organisation. She learned that there were sixty fire stations. Each one now had four to six substations manned by AFS in the charge of temporary sub-officers and that some twenty thousand AFS men and two thousand women had been mobilised three days before war broke out, and they were posted to the hurriedly commandeered substations.

She asked how many fire engines there were at the station and she was told that she must never refer to fire engines in the Service. Only the outside public called them that. To the firemen and their auxiliaries, they were called appliances and they were garaged in the appliance room.

She was told that there were different sorts of appliances called pumps; pump escapes; escapes and ladders; and now the AFS trailer pumps and self-propelled grey painted machines with their own engine and a proper chassis, a cheap mass-produced version of the big red peacetime machines.

She was also told that the brigade was divided into two divisions, one north of the river and one south, and each division was divided into three districts, commanded by a superintendent who had a district officer as his deputy. The superintendents had all been firemen in their time and they wielded great authority. Firewoman Brown related in awe how a visit to Y sub by the superintendent that morning with his district officer and Station Officer Brewster trailing in his rear, had reduced Sub-Officer Davies to a chronic state of nerves for the rest of the day.

The clock on the wall ticked on past eleven. Janet began to feel sleepy and she longed for her comfortable bed at home.

Firewoman Brown looked at her.

"You tired? Casey will have to fix you up with a mattress, but it's the rule that there must always be two of us together in a watch-room, never only one. That's in case the firemen get up to any tricks with us — daft isn't it?"

Janet agreed that it was daft, and she wondered if she would have to spend the whole night sitting in the hard chair when Section Officer Casey came in.

"All right Brown, I'll take over. You can go and rest."

Brown left the room and a few moments later, muffled by the sandbag wall against the window, a taxi door banged in the yard outside.

"You'd better try and get some sleep," said the officer. "You can stay in here with me and use my mattress and blankets. Put them under the table. You'll be out of the light."

Janet gratefully obeyed. She kicked off her shoes; took off her jacket and having moved the mattress crawled under the table. Beneath the blankets she lay and gazed at Miss Casey's black shoes and lisle stockings and she soon fell asleep. She dreamed that a visiting card lay on the silver salver in the hall at Brandon. It was inscribed William Brusher-White.

Chapter 2

Janet was woken at seven o'clock by the vigorous ringing of a hand bell. She sat up, hitting her head on the table as she did so, and momentarily dazed, looked around her and she saw a pair of legs that were slimmer than Section Officer Casey's and wore artificial silk instead of lisle stockings. The legs moved and a head appeared at the side of them.

"Hello, you under the Cainan'. Woken up at last? You've 'ad a good doss. Been snorin' somethin' lovely."

Janet crawled out of the blankets and looked down with dismay at her rumpled skirt. She found her shoes and put them on, uncomfortably conscious that she had gone to bed for the first time in memory without washing and without cleaning her teeth. The bare dingy room smelt damp and was still lit by the single unshaded electric light bulb, the sandbags blocking out light and air from the window. A tall good-looking blonde girl sat at the table, alternately looking at Janet and then at her own manicured fingers.

"You Janet Finch?"

"Yes."

"You the one who turned station 69 out for drill last night?"

"I'm afraid so. How did you know?"

"We heard it on the blower as soon as it happened. You hear everything in this show. All the stations are linked up by telephone and people stuck in the watch-rooms all day with Fanny Adams to do but wait for a call."

"I'm Molly Breaks; joined at the time of Munich. Been here since Friday, the day Poland was invaded. My ol' man's in the army. Don't know what he'd say if he saw this dump."

Janet looked at her and asked what she should do.

"Well," said Mollie. "All that noise was old Davies turning his station out for drill. He'll be here in a minute to put the times in the occurrence book so you'd better ask him. There's meant to be two of us in the watch-room all the time, so you may have to stay on."

Before Janet could reply Sub-Officer, Davies came into the room.

"First appliance out in twenty-six seconds. Put it in the book, Miss. Twenty-six seconds! Oh, my Gawd! What a shower! Call themselves auxiliary firemen! What'll the station officer say when he sees that in the book? And they bin on the payroll and on continuous duty for three days. Trying to get me broke. That's what they are."

Janet made her enquiry. Sub-Officer Davies looked perplexed.

"What'll you do? I don't know what you'll do. You enrolled as a driver and there's no establishment for women drivers on substations. You'd better see Miss Casey after breakfast and make yourself generally useful."

He jerked his head towards the door and Janet went out. From down the dingy passage she heard the sound of voices and she walked shyly towards an open door, to be greeted by Firewoman Brown.

"Come on in. Sit this end with us. You've met Molly Breaks in the watch-room I expect. Well this is Cissie Spence and this is Mabel Smith."

She nodded toward two young women sitting at a trestle table with her, who both said, "Pleased to meet you."

"The men'll be along in a minute so you'd better 'ave some char before they drain the pot."

A large brown enamel kettle stood on the table and from this Edith Brown poured a turgid brown liquid into a large mug she had placed in front of Janet.

"Only bull's milk this morning. Hope you don't mind," she said.

Janet, without knowing what was meant, said she did not mind. She later discovered that bull's milk was condensed and that the tea was made by putting all the ingredients — tealeaves, milk and sugar into the boiling kettle. It was very hot, very strong, and very sweet.

Her companions had produced paper packets of sandwiches and cake.

"You got no breakfast?" said Mabel Smith.

Janet protested that she had had a large supper and the smell of hides was putting her off her food, but the three girls insisted on sharing their food with her.

She was given bread and margarine with cold fried bacon and a piece of currant cake. As she ate, she thought of the dining room at Brandon with its polished furniture and gleaming silver, its windows facing out onto the lawns and the flowerbeds. The maids would be serving breakfast there soon.

She looked around at the dingy room. An old gas stove stood in one corner. Two long trestle tables with benches at each side occupied all the remaining space. In a corner, an old Bakelite wireless set stood on the floor. Two windows looked out on to a grimy brick wall a few feet away. The smell of carbolic soap with which floor, walls and tables had recently been scrubbed, mingled with the smell of hides that permeated the whole building.

A wave of nausea and homesickness swept over her.

She gripped the table and mouthed. "Oh God, get me out of here."

The door opened and fifteen men wearing rubber boots and blue overalls tramped into the room, followed by Sub-Officer Davies and Section Officer Casey, who briskly sent Mabel to the watch-room carrying her mug of tea and another for Molly Breaks.

Davies sat at the head of the table with Section Officer Casey on his right and Clarke, his London Fire Brigade deputy, on his left. The other men pushed their way in between the benches and the table while a new pot of tea was brought from the gas stove. Auxiliary Fireman Newton sat down next to Janet, jogging her elbow.

"Well what do you think of this for a set-up? Mess room, recreation room and what you will for twenty-five men and six women; ten of us still waiting outside for breakfast because there isn't enough room for everyone to sit down. I gave up a good job to volunteer for this lark. Three pounds a week they're paying us. Sounds all right doesn't it but work it out; continuous duty, no time off, a hundred and sixty-eight hours a week, four pence an hour, that's what it is."

"The LFB, they're all right. All but the newest recruits bumped into so called officers and even those who aren't officers getting fifteen bob a week more than us auxiliaries. They're used to these sorts of hours. You know why the LFB up to a few years ago would only recruit fuckin' sailors? It was because they were used to being shut up in ships for months on end and they wouldn't object to being shut in fuckin' fire stations."

"Cor!" said Edith Brown. "You still moanin'? 'E's done nothin' but grizzle and bellyache since we arrived 'ere on Friday. Don't cha know there's a war on?"

The argument developed but Newton got little support. The slow build-up of tension since Munich and the forecasts of immediate bombing, should war break out, had produced an atmosphere that had temporarily put discomfort and the lack of amenities into the background.

There was an air of tension as the morning newspapers were passed around. The facile optimism of the headlines were studied: Fleet Begins the Blockade; Winston Back; Winston Churchill enters the Cabinet as First Lord of the Admiralty; Fierce Fighting on two Polish Sectors; Gort VC to lead our Troops; Poles Cheer our Declaration; Warsaw Crowd Cry 'Long Live England'; France's Resolute Young Army of the Maginot Line. The stop press mentioned a big British liner torpedoed. The *Athenia* had already gone down with the loss of two hundred and seventy lives.

Breakfast over, the men left with Sub-Officer Davies exhorting them to get busy. Miss Casey turned to Janet.

"Now Finch I've got a job for you. After dinner you are to report to Mrs. Bridger, the Company Officer at 27. She is going to arrange a driving test and some preliminary training for you, and she will see about your uniform."

Janet, meanwhile, had been taken to the women's dormitory, a small green distempered room. It contained no furniture. There were five suitcases standing on end and five mattresses, which lay on the floor with blankets folded on top of them. She was ordered to remove the bedding into the passage outside; sweep out the room and then scrub the floor. She was given a broom, a large bucket of warm water, a scrubbing brush and a bar of soap.

An hour later, hot and flushed, with stockings laddered and the front of her skirt wet and soapy, she reported her task finished. Miss Casey was not impressed. Too much water had been used and where the floor was drying soap smears were visible. This was pointed out with some asperity.

"We shan't be able to put those mattresses on the floor again for hours. What will Sub-Officer Davies say if they have to be left in the passage all day? I'll have to get one of the other girls to mop up after you. It's a lovely day; you'd better go out in the yard and get some fresh air."

Chastened and despondent, Janet did as she was told. It was indeed a lovely day. The sun shone from a blue sky in which the barrage balloons reflected the light with a silvery sheen. The yard was cobbled, and it had been scrubbed each day since the fire brigade had arrived. It was enclosed on three sides by the grimy red-brick buildings of the hide warehouse and on the fourth by a wall with double gates, which were open.

The gate man stood there in full fire kit, with steel helmet, leggings and gas mask on his chest. Two taxis with trailer pumps lashed to their rear bumpers and one of the grey painted self-propelled pumps stood against the wall.

Janet walked to the gate and looked out along Augur Street. Opposite, the little red brick houses with blue-slated roofs had front doors that opened straight onto the pavement, their monotony unrelieved by any variations except for the double window of Mrs. Porter's fish and chip shop and the three-storey Carpenters Arms public house on the corner, where Augur Street joined the wider Rampton Road.

There were no trees, no grass nor greenery in sight except aspidistras between open lace curtains. The gate man was tall and past middle age, with a lined but cheerful red face.

He smiled and said, "I'm Charlie Pierce. What do you think of it?"

"I don't know," said Janet. "What do you think of it?"

"Oh, I'm all right. The kids are grown up and the Missus is staying with 'er sister. Three quid to come next Friday. My old rate was only forty-two bob a week and it's matey 'ere ain't it? Kind of exciting too or will be when the raids start. Funny thing they ain't been over yet. Some say they won't come; daren't fly through all them barrage balloons".

"Makes yer think, don't it? They'll 'ave to give us a

bit of time off though between the raids. Shut in a bit ain't we? Some of us went down the road last night to the Carpenters while the Sub 'ad his back turned. Made a nice break and we could 'ave answered the old siren almost as quick from there as from in 'ere. It ain't right though, disobedience to orders, that's what it is."

He glanced towards the yard. "Two of the pumps are out on a water relay exercise at the docks, Nice break for them crews to get away from 'ere for an hour or two. Y'ur the new one ain't ya? The one who turned station 69 out for a drill. Cor what a lark! We all 'ad a good laugh, all them regulars turning out on their red engines for a little old AFS girl. I expect you did it on purpose."

He looked at her quizzically.

"No, I really didn't," said Janet. "I felt very foolish afterwards."

"Ah, you're a deep one you are, but you look a bit down, duckie. Are you all right?"

"Yes. I'm all right, but it's all rather strange and I'm used to the country. Perhaps I'm a bit homesick."

"You'll be all right. It's matey 'ere. It's matey all around 'ere. Been 'ere fifty-five years. Born 'ere. Expect I'll die 'ere. You keep your pecker up, cos that's yer name ain't it?"

"My name's Janet."

"Ah, but your name's Janet Finch and a Finch is a bird and all birds are Dicky's round 'ere, so they'll call you Dicky, you see."

Molly Breaks, who had strolled across the yard, interrupted them.

"'Ullo Charlie Boy. 'Ullo Janet. Cor it's good to get out of that watch-room. Hardly anyone has got anything left to eat so they're allowing a taxi to go out and collect dinners. Shilling each. Expect it will be fish and chips with something for afters. You interested?"

Janet was and she produced her shilling. Charlie Pierce explained that his wife had called around that morning with a parcel of food for him.

Dinner was at one o'clock and as Mollie Breaks had guessed, fish and chips was handed to everyone in newspaper packages and jam tarts followed by tea.

Janet was told to report to Mrs Bridger at two thirty and, her absence having been put down in the occurrence book, she set off for Piper Place, walking along the drab streets that she had passed along unseeing, in the taxi the previous evening. She found the fire station and was directed to the hut in the yard.

Mrs Bridger received her in an office partitioned off at the end of the hut. She was a small, business-like woman with grey hair and glasses.

"Ah Finch, you're early. I said three o'clock but it doesn't matter. I expect you were told to report at half past two, weren't you? That's LFB procedure. If the chief officer wants to see a fireman at four o'clock, he tells the divisional officer to arrange it. The divisional officer tells the superintendent to have him there by half past three, the superintendent tells the district officer to have him there by three o'clock and the district officer tells the station officer to have him there by half past two. That way the fireman has to wait one and a half hours, but nobody in the chain of command gets into trouble because he was late.

"I have no room for you here, where the station's drivers are meant to do duty, so you will have to stay out-posted to Y sub. Not very nice premises I'm afraid."

"Here is an order for your uniform. Take it to Rego's. Any branch will do, but the one in the Old Kent Road is nearest. As a driver, you are entitled to a mackintosh and you can have it lined at your own expense for extra warmth. The form says skirt or trousers, but you must have the trousers. I don't like my girls wearing skirts getting in and out of vehicles with all these firemen standing around. When you get your uniform, you mustn't carry a handbag and remember no jewellery of any sort except rings."

"I'm sorry there are not enough mattresses or blankets to go around yet. You could buy your own if you have the money or get them sent from home. There is a short training course for new recruits starting tomorrow at 60 station, Southwark Bridge Road. That's F District headquarters."

"I have arranged for you to go on that course. You have to do sixty hours basic training. Report at nine o'clock tomorrow morning. Section Officer Casey will know all about it by then. I have to go there myself this afternoon. You can take me there. Then I'll see what your driving is like. You can take a little walk now but be here at half past three."

On her walk from Augur Street Janet had thought of giving the weeks' notice that was the only requirement to put substation 69Y and its strange inhabitants out of her life forever. She had decided that her first interview with the company officer would present the opportunity for resignation, but Mrs Bridger's brisk manner had overawed her.

She walked to the garage where she had left the Alvis and she looked long and earnestly at the sleek blue car. She had only to slip into the driving seat and drive away to the northeast, leaving London behind, to be back at Brandon soon after tea. Across the road a large red poster announced, 'Your Courage, Your Cheerfulness, Your Resolution Will Bring Us Victory'. She paid for a week's garage in advance and she then walked slowly back to the fire station.

"Do you know the way?" said Mrs Bridger.

Janet admitted that she did not, and she was told to make topography her special and immediate study. She was directed through Tower Bridge Road and Dover Street, across Borough High Street and into Southwark Bridge Road, where the red-brick Victorian fire station dominated the tram-congested street.

They turned under an archway and drew up in the large courtyard, partly fronted by a fine Georgian house that had formerly been the chief officer's quarters. Here, Janet was told that she could take the car to collect her uniform, thereby improving her knowledge of the district, and to return to pick up her passenger at five o'clock.

In the clothing shop in Old Kent Road she stood before a mirror and admired her new uniform. It consisted of blue skiing type trousers, fastened at the ankle and matched by a jacket done up at the neck with white metal buttons. The letters AFS were embroidered in red on the left breast. A blue skiing cap with red piping and a red badge was set at a slightly jaunty angle on the brown curls. She found the effect pleasing. There was a war on, and she was going to play her part in it.

She left the shop, carrying her blue suit in a brown paper parcel. She found a bedding store nearby and bought a mattress and blankets. She also stepped into a grocer's shop and bought a meat pie before returning to Southwark Bridge Road.

Mrs Bridger was punctual.

"So, you've got your uniform. Caps must be worn straight, not at an angle. When driving an officer, you can sit in the passenger seat while waiting, but when the officer comes to the car, get out and open the door. Now we'll go back to station 69 but you can drop off your bedding on the way."

Janet was dismissed after leaving Mrs Bridger and she parked the car at the station before walking back again to the substation.

Janet looked in at the watch-room and she was told that Miss Casey wanted to see her.

The section officer handed her a pair of rubber boots, blue dungarees, a steel helmet and a service gas mask.

"These are yours. They came with the stores van this afternoon. See that they are marked with your name. They are entered on your clothing card and if you lose anything you will have to pay for it. Let me have your civilian gas mask so that it can be handed in at the town hall. You had a nice break this afternoon, so you had better go and relieve Firewoman Spence in the watch-room for a couple of hours. Firewoman Smith will be in charge and I will have you relieved at once if the siren goes."

Janet sat in the watch-room for her allotted two hours before being relieved for tea in the crowded mess room. She noted with surprise that her companions were eating fish and chips, hardboiled eggs and meat sandwiches, and assuming correctly that this was the last meal of the day, she fetched and ate her meat pie.

The meal over, she was told by Section Officer Casey to wash up with Edith Brown. They stood together at the sink, rattling the cups in the brown-stained water, listening to the wireless and the hum of conversation from the men sitting at the benches with their elbows on the tables.

Edith, short and dark, with big brown eyes and a vivacious air, nudged Janet's elbow.

"You game for a lark this evening?"

"What sort of lark?" said Janet.

"Well, there's a message for old Taff Davies come into the watch-room. 'E's to report at station 69 with Casey at half past eight for some sort of exercise. Some of the boys have been going up to the Carpenter's Arms after dark, while 'e's been out. Nobby Clark, 'is deputy don't go skulking around, looking for trouble, see.

"Ernie Cliff, 'e's nice, 'e is, says they're going up tonight and 'e's asked me to go with 'em. I don't want to be the only girl there. 'Ow about you coming along?"

Janet looked over her shoulder into the crowded uncomfortable room.

"All right," she said, and she immediately wondered if she had not been very stupid.

"Nine o'clock then. I'll tell the others. We go out by the door at the back of the office. Don't want to give the gateman ideas. Don't look so worried!"

At nine o'clock, Janet went to the door that led from the office straight on to Auger Street. Standing by it were Charlie Pierce and two others.

"Wotcher Dicky. I 'eard you was coming with us to see the sights of little old London for an hour. You met Jack Adams and Arthur Clayton? Where's Edie and Ernie?"

"In the back of number two taxi as usual," said Adams. "They'll bugger up the springs of that poor old crock before it ever goes to a fire."

"Can't wait for 'em. They can come along later if they like. Quiet now, the gateman is only twenty yards up the road. 'E might like to try for promotion by splitting on us to old Davies."

Charlie opened the door and the four of them tiptoed out into the night and made for the corner where the three storeys of the Carpenter's Arms loomed darkly above the little houses. The door opened against a blanket hung from the top of the entrance and as Adams drew it aside to let them pass, they were greeted with cries of "Mind the blackout!" from customers and from a stout middle-aged woman who stood behind the bar.

"Sorry Mrs Barnacle, but we've got to get in," said Adams.

"That's all right me old china, but the police 'ave, been worrying me to death. They've been standing out there and every time a customer comes in, they say I'm breakin' the regulations and I've got to 'ave a proper screen round the door. Now, what is it?"

"Three pints of bitter and what'll you have Miss?"

Janet hesitated. She wanted lemonade but believed that beer was the cheapest drink available and did not want to put Jack Adams to expense.

"I'll have the same," she said.

The three men looked at her.

"Cor, that's the girl," said Charlie Pierce. "You're a real goer, Dicky. Be turning 'em out for drill again, I should think, before the night's out."

The four pints of beer were drawn and placed on the counter and handed round.

"Well 'ere she goes." And the three men each took a swig.

Janet drank with them. She gasped at the acid taste and hastily put the glass down. It reminded her of the quinine she had been made to drink by her old nanny to ward off colds when coming in from hunting. She had never forgiven nanny for that quinine and now here it was again but not in a little medicine glass.

The pint glass stood on the high counter near her with the amber liquid only an inch from the brim. She had heard of people surreptitiously pouring unwanted drinks into flowerpots at dances and she glanced round the room. There were no flowerpots, only the high bar, a bare floor on which sawdust had been sprinkled, three round tables and bench seats, all occupied, around the walls.

"What's it feel like on three quid a week?" said a soldier at Adams' elbow.

"What's it feel like on fourteen bob a week?" replied Adams.

"Cut it out," said Charlie Pierce. "It was seven bob a week when I was in the last war, but the married men got their allowances and we got our grub. We got to pay for everything in this lark."

The argument went on. Janet sipped her beer, trying not to pull faces, and she managed to keep pace with her companions by occasionally screwing up her courage and taking long swigs. She was relieved to see the blackout curtain parted and Edith Brown came in with Ernie Cliff.

Asked what they would drink Ernie chose beer and Edith a port and lemon.

"What's yours Dicky?" said Charlie.

Janet knew vaguely that port and lemon was considered rather common, but she had occasionally been allowed a glass of port after dinner and did not dislike it.

"You can 'ave what you fancy my old duck," said Charlie, putting his money on the counter. "Four pints of bitter, a port and lemon and a large port please."

The port was sweet and mellow after the bitter tasting beer. Janet leaned on the counter, surveying her strange surroundings, listening to the talk.

"Them tall towers on the coast, they're secret but d'you know what they are? They throw out an electric beam what interferes with the spark plugs and coils of petrol engines. Soon as an aeroplane gets near one its engine stops. That's what the sirens were yesterday morning. The Jerries got as far as the towers and crashed."

"There y'are. What did I tell you? They'll never get

through. You boys and girls in blue with the silver buttons better go 'ome an' join the friggin' army."

The airless room was very hot. The conversation buzzed and ebbed in her ears. I'm feeling a bit faint, she thought. She wanted to get out into the cool night air. Perhaps she could slip quietly into the substation. They would think her a bit of a prig. Besides customers hemmed her into the bar.

She looked at the pint glasses. They were nearly empty. She must return her companions' hospitality. She was dizzy now. I'm going to faint, she thought. Brandy was given to fainting people. It revived them. She took a ten-shilling note from her pocket and she caught Mrs Barnacle's eye.

"Four pints, a port and lemon and a brandy please."

The drinks were pushed across the bar to her. Her companions were deep in conversation. She touched Charlie's arm.

"Have another drink."

"Cor that's very civil of you, Dicky. You shouldn't you know; not the ladies. Still you are working girls with money to come on Friday and times do change."

They took their glasses and they drank her health. She drank the brandy with them.

It's doing no good. I'm still just as dizzy. She held onto the bar as the room swayed around her. The conversation ebbed and flowed; now very loud; now inaudible. Luckily there were hands under her armpits, or she would have slid to the floor.

"You all right? Cor you're pale. 'Ere give us an 'and.

Get 'er out of this."

The fresh air hit her face and the stars wheeled in the sky. She was sweating but cold and she felt desperately ill as she staggered against Charlie.

"Cor, she's pissed."

The stable term she half-understood permeated her wretchedness.

"I haven't," she said indignantly and then she fell in the road.

Charlie picked her up in his arms and he carried her effortlessly towards the substation. They got to the office door.

"We've got to get 'er up to the women's dormitory without Davies or Casey seeing 'er. Lead the way Edie."

She lay on her rocking, swinging, mattress and she vomited on the floor beside it. Section Officer Casey shook her by the shoulder.

"You, dirty drunken little beast. Get up and clean up your mess."

A bucket was thumped on the floor beside her. It contained water and a floor cloth. The smell of the vomit made her retch.

Miss Casey's voice was suddenly gentle.

"Lie down. I'll do it. If Davies hears of this there'll be a report sent up to station 69. You, stupid girl, what have you let them do to you?"

She went out with the bucket and returned with a cup of hot, strong tea and a wet flannel. Kneeling on the floor beside the mattress she wiped the young girl's clammy face. The tea was comforting. The room no longer swayed so alarmingly.

"What did you drink?"

"Beer, port and brandy."

"Good God! Don't you know that you shouldn't mix drinks? How many of each?"

"Only one. I didn't like the beer, so I had a port and then I began to feel faint, so I had a brandy."

"Are you used to drinking?"

"No, I'm not allowed to at home. Besides I've never wanted to."

"Well, let this be a lesson to you. You'll get quite a reputation you know, turning station 69 out for a drill your first night in the service and getting carried into Y station drunk on your second night."

"I feel so ashamed. Will everybody know?"

"Well, Brown knows, and you can't shut her mouth, but I doubt that it will spread to the top. It wouldn't be very nice to have to go home and tell your parents you'd been dismissed for that. Now go to sleep. You've got to go to training school in the morning. I'll tell the other girls to come in quietly so as not to disturb you."

"Thank you for the tea and for cleaning up."

"That's all right. I'm used to it. Most people know around here, so you might as well. My father's been carried home often. I hate drink."

The training school held its lectures in the old married quarters at Southwark Fire Station. Two small rooms had been turned into one by the removal of a wall. The floor was covered with new brown linoleum, which smelt strongly. On this were placed a dozen wooden folding chairs and an equal number of small folding tables. The instructor stood in front of a wall blackboard. He was a regular fireman who wore his small round hat while he lectured, to show his class that he was a real fireman and not a member of the AFS.

Janet sat at one of the tables, her aching head between her hands, a child's exercise book and small pencil in front of her. These the instructor had emphasised were for taking notes, but Janet's exercise book held between its open pages her mother's letter sent from station 69 that was handed to her as she left for the training school that morning.

"A station officer wears a hard-crowned cap with a gilt badge and a double-breasted blue suit. His fire tunic has two rows of brass buttons with full brass epaulette on the right shoulder only," said the instructor.

Janet made a pencilled note and went on reading.

How nice that you got fixed up so easily despite Lady Henshaw not being there," her mother wrote. *"I think that the London Fire Brigade will be very suitable for you and I am glad you didn't join the ATS* as there are some rather nasty rumours going around the village about their morals and the sort of supervision they get.*

I find Lady Pleydell-Bouverie is the head of the women's section of the LFB. She is Lord Redesdale's daughter — a very nice family. I don't think an introduction for you will be difficult. Nearly all the senior

---

* *Auxiliary Territorial Service — the women's branch of the British army.*

*officers come from the navy. My cousin Harry Clinton
served with two of them, a long time ago of course, in fact
before 1914.*

*They were Commodore Sir Lionel Wells who was
Chief Officer before the last war, and Commander Sir
Sampson Sladen, who was Chief Officer during the last
war. I rang Henry yesterday. Unfortunately, he doesn't
know anything of the present heads except that they are ex-
navy or army officers, but I feel sure that you will get to
know them.*

"We'll finish up with the principal officers," the
instructor was saying. "That is the chief officer, the deputy
cChief officer and the divisional officers. You needn't take
notes on their uniform. There are only seven of 'em and
you in your lowly walk of life you will never come across
any of 'em any 'ow."

The lectures ended at five o'clock and Janet was told
to return to her substation. She met Jack Adams by the
door, holding three of the brooms issued to the station.

"You know what Davies told me to do with these," he
said. "I'm to scrub the bleeding 'andles. And they was only
new last week."

Four men were scrubbing, the stairs and, through the
open watch-room door, Edith Brown and Cissie Spencer
could be seen on hands and knees at the same task on the
floor, while Mollie Breaks sat at the telephone, her shapely
legs bent back with heels resting on the chair bar.

"Don't put your dirty feet on the floor. You'd better
sit on the table. Don't let old Taff see you. He'll have a
scrubbing brush in your hand in no time. I'll book you

back."

"Davies won't see 'er. 'E's been polishing 'is LFB buttons for the last hour."

"What's happening?"

"What's happening? Haven't you heard? Officers are visiting at six o'clock and that doesn't mean old Brewster, and it doesn't even mean the superintendent. It's his nibs, the DO himself, one of the toffs, with all the others hanging on I expect.

"Davies is having kittens. The buzz is that he's going to condemn this dump and move us to the LCC* school in Rampton Street. All the kids are evacuated but some other department got it first and it's an emergency mortuary."

"Well, I should think this is a better place for the bodies."

Davies came in and glanced at the clock. It was a quarter to six.

"Come on, 'urry up and get that floor dried off. Breaks, you'll be on duty when 'e comes in. Don't forget, stand to attention and say 'Firewoman Breaks on duty in the watch-room. Sub-Officer Davies in Charge', and that's all you do say unless you're asked any questions.

"Brown, you'll be sitting beside 'er. Stand to attention when she stands to attention. Spence, you'd better be standing by your bed in the women's dormitory. Finch, you're meant to be a driver, so stand by the first pump in the yard and put your cap on straight."

---

* *London County Council*

Two big black cars drew up. Janet could see them through the open gateway.

The superintendent, grey haired and ruddy faced, sat in the back of the first car with his district officer. In the second was the divisional officer. They stood talking in the street a moment, and then they walked through the yard and in at the station door. Janet stood stiffly to attention but none of them looked at her.

She stood to attention for another five minutes until she heard Ernie Cliff on gate duty say, "You might as well relax, old china. They can't see you from in there."

She turned around to look at the station. Twenty minutes later, Sub-Officer Davies led his visitors back into the yard and she stood to attention again. She saw their backs as they passed and then the divisional officer swung around and he walked up to her.

"What's your job?"

"I'm a driver, sir!"

"What are you doing here?"

"I was sent here from station 69."

"What do you drive?"

"I'm still under training."

"Are you enjoying it?"

"Yes, sir!"

He smiled and to her surprise he slowly winked as he turned away and walked to his car.

"Well, what did you think of his nibs?"

"Bit of all right I should say."

"Fancy him ordering the little old superintendent about. Don't look a day over twenty."

"I don't care what 'e looks like so long as 'e gets us out of this fuckin' dump."

The conversation buzzed around the crowded mess-room. Janet sat at the end of the table with Edith Brown, Cissie Spence and Mabel Smith.

"You haven't heard this. This is ripe," said Cissie.

"I was standing in the women's dormitory and I hears the whole gang coming up the stairs. Davies throws open the door, walks in and says: 'This is the ladies' quarters, Sir'.

"Do you have fire gentlemen and fire ladies on your station?" says the DO.

"Old Taff looks puzzled but says 'No'".

"'Right,' says the DO. 'Get the senior woman officer and tell her to show me the women's quarters and don't let me hear of you going into a women's dormitory again without your senior woman officer with you'."

"Yes, and quite right too. I hope 'e takes it to 'eart," said Mabel.

"I was standing up there in my bra and knickers the other day and old Davies walks in. 'All right', 'e says, 'I'm a married man', and 'e walked out again, calm as you like."

"It's the married men that are the worst," said Edith enigmatically.

Janet wondered what they were worst at.

Nobby Clark, still wearing his round LFB cap, elbowed his way into a place opposite the girls.

"You still talking about 'im?" he said.

"Yes, is 'e married?" said Edith.

"No, 'e isn't, and 'e lives in one of the ten-roomed

flats at the top of HQ. Probably be phoning through to ask you there to tea. Do you as much good as Cliff does and more room than in the back of a bloody taxi."

Edith blushed. "You shut up Nob. There's no call to talk like that. Cooped up here for days on end you've got to do something."

"Or let somebody do you," said Clarke.

Newton's harsh penetrating voice came from down the table.

"There you are, a ten roomed fuckin' flat for one man; fuckin' great car; too tired to drive it himself, so 'e 'as a brigade driver and a brigade fuckin' flunkey on top of that, to wait on 'im."

"Not so much of the flunkey from you, Newton," said Edith. "You wouldn't like the job at a big fire. You'd find yourself along with the DO, in the hottest and smokiest part of it and having to stay there."

"Wonder when we'll go to a fuckin' fire. Joined this lot to go to great big fires and all I've done for four fuckin' days is polishing."

"You'll get your big fires when they come over."

"Ah, but will they come over? Look at all those barrage balloons."

"There'll be plenty of fuckin' fires when they come over", said Newton, "and fuckin' bombs dropping and it'll be you and me and the likes of us that will be putting the fuckers out; the AFS, you'll see. There won't be many LFB about then. They'll be directing affairs from the control room. Do you know what they're doin' at Lambeth? They're digging a dirty great fuckin' hole under

HQ. Working day and night, breaking the blackout with lights so as to get it deep enough and strong enough for the LFB to get into."

"Shut your big mouth, Newton," said Clark.

"Who are you telling to shut his mouth?"

"Me, Clark, the number two on this station."

"You're only a fireman, same as me, even if I am only an auxiliary fireman. Just 'cos I don't wear a fuckin' round cap and keep it on even when having tea opposite the ladies."

Nobby Clark got up slowly and he walked behind Newton, putting his big hands on the AFS man's shoulders.

"All right, I'm not the number two on this station; just another fuckin' fireman like you. Taffy's gone up to see Brewster at station 69. While he's not here you and I could go outside in the yard, just a couple of ordinary firemen and sort this out, couldn't we?"

"What are you talking about? Sort what out?"

"I told you to shut your mouth and to stop running down the LFB."

"Oh, don't get the 'ump so easy. I didn't mean the LFB firemen like you. I only meant the top brass."

"You meant the LFB. You goin' to say sorry."

"I'm sorry."

Clarke walked slowly out of the room, leaving Newton red-faced and the centre of all eyes.

"You asked for that, Alf Newton," said Charlie Pierce.

Chapter 3

"We're moving. We're going to Rampton Street School. We get out of here tomorrow." The gateman gave Janet the news as she returned from training school.

"Don't come back 'ere this evening," said Davies the next morning, "because we'll be gone. I'll see that your gear gets shifted for you. Nice for you going up to training school. It'll be 'ard work for everybody 'ere today."

The infants' school was built of red brick with the date 1907 on one of its gables. An asphalt playground enclosed by low brick walls topped by railings, stood between it and the road. The trailer pumps and taxis and the grey painted self-propelled pump stood in line there, when Janet walked back from training school that evening.

"Better 'ole this," said the gateman. "Room to move and no smell."

She reported back at the watch-room and Cissie Spence booked her return into the occurrence book. The watch-room was a teacher's room next to a classroom; the men were just completing a sandbag wall outside the windows and they had built it a few inches away from the wall so that a little daylight came in.

"Bit better, ain't it?" said Cissie. "Your gear's in the women's dormitory and the stores van called, and they delivered us each a bed. We've got sixteen lavs now for the women instead of one and sixteen washbasins. You go and take a look."

Janet went and looked. The washbasins were two feet high and the lavatory pans were also designed for children. A closet flushed and Edith emerged.

"Ullo Dicky, whad' d'ya' think of this? Like a bloody doll's 'ouse ain't it? Casey says it's just right, the natural position, good fer yer bowels, see? Seen yer bed? Come and look."

Six iron, folding bedsteads on six-inch legs stood in a classroom. Janet's mattress was on one of them with her blankets neatly folded on top and her suitcase at its foot. The room was over-large and chilly, even on a September evening.

"Got a big mess room and a recreation room combined," said Edith. "There's a piano in there and 'Arry Booth can play it. 'E 'ad a go at dinnertime. Smashing 'e is. Does syncopation sort of. Old Taff Davies says we can 'ave a moving in party tomorrow evening if everybody works well and gets the place shipshape as 'e calls it."

When Janet returned from training school the next evening, quart bottles of beer in crates were being delivered from the Carpenter's Arms.

"Can you manage 'arf a crown for the whip round, Dicky?" said Jack Adams.

"That'll make about three pints each as a start."

She handed him the money.

"You be careful tonight, my old duck; don't you get in the state you was in on Monday or you'll 'ave Mother Casey on your tracks. We got three bottles of port for the ladies. You'd better stick to that and not mix it."

Janet knew that she would never drink alcohol again and she hoped that nobody would press her to do so.

The party started at eight o'clock. The gateman was to be relieved every half-hour. Sub-officer Davies, greatly daring, said that he would, on his own responsibility, waive the rule that there must be two women in the watch-room. The watch-room opened off the recreation room and its door stood open, so that Mollie Breaks sitting by the telephone could both see and be seen. The quart bottles were passed around the men, who filled tea mugs and the few available glasses.

Janet was handed a mug and Edith Brown brought a bottle of British port wine and half-filled it.

'I needn't drink it.' she thought. 'Nobody will notice in an enamel mug.'

Auxiliary Fireman Booth sat at the piano and he began to play. He was a dark wizened little man of forty who supplemented his dock labourer's wage by playing the piano in public houses on Saturday nights.

He could not read music and he had the skill of the self-taught who played by ear. His long fingers, with black edged nails, fluttered over the yellowing keys giving the old upright piano the jolliness of a barrel organ.

'We're going to hang our washing on the Siegfried line, have you any dirty washing mother dear?' sang the firemen and firewomen. The beer and the port were passed around. The clock on the wall ticked away the minutes and the hours. The singing grew unrestrained and then ribald.

"Now! Now! Not in front of the Ladies," said Charlie

Pierce.

The beer ran out and they sent around to the Carpenter's Arms for more. 'Knees up Mother Brown' had five verses and when they had sung them all with the energetic actions required, Janet was hoarse and thirsty. She had drunk her port and she was flushed and excited. When Jack Adams went by with a beer bottle, she held her mug out to him. He winked at her as he filled it. She disliked the taste, but it slaked her thirst.

It was midnight when Taff Davies closed the party down and four of the girls went to their dormitory, leaving Section Officer Casey and Mollie Breaks in the watchroom.

"Cor! I enjoyed that," said Edith Brown.

"What did you enjoy?" said Cissie Spence.

"Why, the party of course. Old Harry Booth thumping the Joanna and the singing and the bit of dancing. What do you think I enjoyed?"

"I thought that you enjoyed-yourself more in the back-of that bleeding taxi with Ernie. Don't think everybody except Casey didn't see you slippin' off through the door into the yard with 'im."

"Oh, shut up Cissie; you jealous? I enjoyed the whole evening; didn't you Dicky?"

"Yes! I enjoyed it."

The light was out, and she lay on her expensive mattress that lay on the cheap six-inch high iron bedstead. She had enjoyed it, the noise and the skilfully played tinkling piano, the cheerful company. She lay in the dark in southeast London, waiting for the sirens to sound and listening to her companions' snores. If she gave a week's notice she could go back to Norfolk, to her well-furnished room and her easy sheltered life. You couldn't do that when there was a war on. They were nice people. Her mother wouldn't understand that. She slept soundly.

"What day is it?"

"Sunday."

"'Ow d'you know?"

"Paper says so."

"'Ow long we been in this mob now?"

"Eleven days."

"Cor! Eleven days on end and not an air raid yet."

"You only came last Sunday, Dicky."

"Yes. That's right."

"All right for some. You been goin' to training school every day. Any'ow this is better than the old ware'ouse."

"You girls complainin' about continuous duty?" Sub-Officer Davies stood in the watch-room doorway. "Well, fall in alongside the men. There's a new brigade order to be explained to you all."

Davies stood in front of his paraded station, holding a sheet of foolscap paper in his hand from which he read.

"The Brigade and Auxiliary Fire Service will be divided equally into three watches known as the Red watch, the White watch and the Blue watch."

Davies read out a list of names. Janet's name was read last, among the Blue watch.

"Anyone 'oo wants to change 'is watch may do so if 'e can find a fireman to change with 'im. Those 'oo want to do so can see me in my office now."

The Red watch gathered together near the gate.

"This'll be a surprise for the missis when I get 'ome."

"Not too much of one, I 'ope."

"Second thing I'm going to do when I get 'ome to the missis is to take these ruddy boots off."

"You can't go to the pictures. They're all closed."

"It says in the paper there's a cinema just opened again in Aberystwyth."

"Where's that? Somewhere up the West End?"

The men chaffed in the September sunshine, and were joined by Edith Brown and Mabel Smith, the two firewomen of the Red watch.

"Fall in," said Davies.

"Fall out the Red watch. All got your gas masks with you. Right then the best of British luck to you and don't be late in the morning." They streamed out through the gate.

"What you going to do on Tuesday, Dicky, with the whole day off?" said Charlie Pierce.

"I have an aunt who lives in London. I shall go to see her. My mother arranged it for as soon as I get some time off."

"Ah, that's all right then. Coming from the country I thought you might be all on your lonesome. If you are any time you come along to my little place and meet my missis. She'll look after you."

Janet thanked him, wondering what Mrs Pierce and her house were like and whether she could feel at home there.

Her week at the training school was finished, and she went into the recreation room to write letters, to her mother and to Mrs Farrow, telling the latter that she had twenty-four hours off on Tuesday and asking if she could come to lunch. Then she read the papers until dinner time.

One of the crews were going to the docks for an exercise and she stood in the yard to watch them drive off. Wearing their steel helmets and leggings, rubber boots and blue tunics with the khaki gas mask containers strapped to their chests and axes in their belt pouches, they looked competent and confident, standing on the sections of the self-propelled government issue pump, as it drove through the playground gate.

'When the raids come, they'll do well,' she thought, and she hoped that she would be worthy of them. Cissie Spence touched her elbow.

"You're wanted on the dog."

"What do you mean?"

"The dog 'n bone, the telephone, for you. Mollie's in the watch-room holding on for you."

Mollie Breaks handed her the receiver.

"Is that you Miss Finch? This is Bill White, you remember me, Brusher?"

"Why? Yes of course."

"You on Blue watch?"

"Yes! I am."

"Ah! I thought you would be. So am I." There was a pause punctuated by heavy breathing. "I just wondered if you'd like to come out with me on Tuesday? You know, dinner or something somewhere and tea as well, afterwards, if you could put up with me for so long."

"That's very kind of you Mr White, but I have an aunt

in London. I have already arranged to see her."

"Going to see her all day?"

"Yes! All day I'm afraid."

"Some other time then?"

"Yes! Some other time perhaps."

She put the phone down.

Mollie Breaks grinned, "Going to see your aunt all day? You must be a bit queer. Was that Brusher White? He's a nice chap."

Janet went back to the Sunday papers and her thoughts. It was one thing to live and work with such people when there was a war on, but to go out with them; what would her mother say? What would Aunt Kitty think? Aunt Kitty was a bore, always talking about her adored son Claude.

She didn't want to spend the whole day with her. She would like to spend some of it with Brusher. She smiled as she thought of the ridiculous nickname and she remembered a hand on her arm in the dark yard at station 69, a pleasant voice and a lively handsome face, crowned by curly hair which stuck out from under a round peakless cap.

She went back to Mollie Breaks.

"Do you think that I could speak to Bill White again on the phone?"

"Well we ain't meant to use it for private calls but he may be in the watch-room. That would be easy but if not, somebody will fetch him without old Brewster knowing. You changed yer mind; don't blame you. He's a nice bloke."

She lifted the phone and a minute later said, "That Brusher White? Here's Dicky Finch again."

Janet took the phone her heart beating hard.

"Oh Mr White, I just wanted to say that I think that I could get away from my aunt's by four o'clock on Tuesday, so I would like to have tea with you. I could meet you at Hyde Park Corner on the same side as the park, coming from Knightsbridge."

She left the substation at nine o'clock on Tuesday morning and she walked to the garage in Grange Road to fetch the Alvis.

"You want any petrol?" said the attendant. "It's going to be on coupons next week."

She had the car filled up and drove to Kensington.

"Well let me have a look at you," said Aunt Kitty. "I think that uniform suits you. It's rather smart, not very good material though. When will you become an officer? Fancy being posted to a place like Bermondsey. What's it like there? I suppose you've heard all the news from your mother. Isn't it awful? At least fifteen cases of scabies among the evacuees in one village. Those poor people: washing bed linen and blankets every day and all for 7/6 a week for each child."

"And isn't it dreadful? Income tax going up to 7/6 in the pound. We were talking about it at the first aid post. Everybody there thinks that the Government have done it on purpose, because nobody can possibly afford to pay that and so there will be a negotiated peace which is what they want. Germany must want it too because there haven't been any air raids yet. I hardly think it worth my while doing part time at the first aid post, but it is rather nice there and it's only just around the corner."

She paused for breath.

"And now my dear. I've got a lovely surprise for you. Claude has telephoned. He's got leave with a late pass and he is coming to see us both. He'll be here by teatime."

Janet apologised and said that she was sorry she could not stay to tea.

"Not stay for tea, but my dear child, you must stay for tea. You've got twenty-four hours leave and you're staying the night, aren't you? That's what was arranged. Poor Claude will be terribly disappointed. You know he fixed up his own leave especially to be here to see you. He will have to go back to Essex in the evening. He's terribly fond of you, you know."

Aunt Kitty looked arch.

"I think that you two should see more of one another; after all you're only second cousins. You would make such a handsome couple. Why can't you stay to tea?"

"I've promised to go out to tea with somebody."

"Well if it's Lady Henshaw, I'm sure that she'll understand if I ring her up and tell her that Claude is coming to tea here. I will ask her here to meet you both."

"It isn't Lady Henshaw. It's somebody in the fire brigade."

"One of the officers?"

"No. He's just a fireman."

"Well I know that there are some very nice young men in the AFS. At the Basil Street Fire Station, I hear there are several with titles. You must ask him to tea here instead of going out with him. I don't think that your mother would like it if you went out alone in London with a young man on what must be very short acquaintance."

The doorbell rang.

"That will be Neville Boyd. He's coming to lunch."

She opened the door.

"Come in Neville, my dear, and I'll get you a whisky and soda, even though they've put it up to thirteen shillings a bottle."

Colonel Boyd handed his hat and his gas mask to the maid. He was tall and grey with a clipped military moustache. He wore an ill-fitting blue battledress with the words 'Light Rescue' on the shoulder tabs. The two rows of medal ribbons on the left breast began with the DSO and MC.

"Morning Kitty. Morning Janet. How are you my dear? I heard that you were in the Fire Service. Very fine crowd. Good discipline there. How you've grown; quite the young lady. Nineteen is it now?"

"Still wearing that awful blue battledress, Neville" said Aunt Kitty, "and you used to look so handsome in khaki."

"Can't do anything about it, my dear. Rang the war office; wrote the war office; called at the war office. No good. I'm sixty-four you know. They said they might offer me a job as RTO* in London. I'd turn it down if they did; no good being a soldier if they won't let you go and fight.

_____

* *Reserve Training Officer*

72

Matter of fact I'm thinking of going full time in the Rescue instead of a part time volunteer. I could do with the three quid a week."

"Don't be silly. What difference would three pounds a week make to you? Janet dear, would you like to take your bag to your room and unpack?"

After lunch, Mrs Farrow left the room. Colonel Boyd looked at Janet.

"Well my dear, you seem to have upset Kitty. What's it all about? Wanting to go off to tea with some fellow in the AFS and leaving her darling Claude all by himself with his mother?"

"It's not an AFS man. It's an ordinary regular LFB fireman, one of the ones with a round cap. I said I would have tea with him, so I must go."

He raised his eyebrows.

"You won't have much in common you know."

"Perhaps not. I don't know him at all. He just asked me, and I accepted. Perhaps it was silly of me. I must go or he will be standing in the street waiting."

"All right. You go my dear. Perhaps he'll teach you some fire-fighting; but it won't please Kitty and I don't think that it will please your mother when Kitty tells her about it. You know that your father had a wonderful aptitude for being absolutely at ease with his soldiers, perhaps you've inherited that from him. You've inherited something else. You've got his looks. He was a damned handsome fellow was John Carew-Finch, besides being one of the best officers in my battalion."

He walked to the window and said quietly, "He'd have

been over forty now. God how time flies. We never thought then that it would all be starting again twenty years later. All the best were killed. I went to the funeral you know. Your mother was a very brave woman. I can see her now standing in the rain eight months gone, with you on the way.

"Do you remember when she brought you to London and I took you to the pantomime? I enjoyed that. I don't think you did. You were sick in your lap. Betty was very cross with me, said I had given you too many chocolates."

He walked back to her and he put his hand on her shoulder.

"Well, here you are again in London in uniform. If ever you want anything you know my address. I might be able to help if you get into any scrapes, even if only with an old man's advice."

"Thank you very much, Colonel Boyd."

"Colonel Boyd. You used to call me Uncle Neville. Go on calling me that even if I'm not a real uncle. Come to that, Kitty Farrow's not really your aunt either; just your mother's cousin. I believe she's been matchmaking with you on behalf of Claude?"

"Do you know what she asked me before lunch? Could I pull any strings at the war office to stop him being sent abroad to fight? I told her no I couldn't and that I wouldn't if I could. Found it hard to be polite. Well you slip off whenever it is your tea date. I'll prepare the ground with Kitty. You can easily be back by six and if Claude's got a late pass he'll still be here. Read the papers? The Hun's are making mincemeat of the Poles. Can't for the life of me see why we and the French don't do something to help them."

Janet drove up Knightsbridge to Hyde Park Corner. He was standing by the park railings when she drew up at the kerb.

"Coo this yours?" he asked, looking at the Alvis.

"Well it's mother's actually, but she lets me use it. Get in. I'm holding up the traffic. Where are we going?"

"Where would you like to go?"

"Well Mr White, if you ask a lady out to tea you should have that arranged."

He looked crestfallen and she regretted the remark.

"Shall we go in the Park? There's a café by the Serpentine," he said.

"That will do very nicely. Did you wait long for me?"

"Well, some time. Thought I'd have a swim in Lansbury's Lido, the Serpentine you know, but when I got there, I found it reserved for armed forces only."

"That seems rather unfair."

"Yes, it does a bit. I'd like to get into the army myself you know, since there's a war on. But I'd have to resign, and I like this job and there's a chance of promotion and a good pension at the end of it and anyway when the raids come there'll be our bit to do. My Dad was a regular soldier."

They drove slowly down the Carriage Road.

"He would like to see you in the army, I expect then?"

"I hardly remember him. He was killed at the Somme. I just remember a figure in khaki with sergeant's stripes when he was on leave and Mum crying after the telegram had come. There's the café over there."

She pulled into the grass verge.

"We have something in common, Brusher. My father was killed in the last war too, or rather he died of wounds just after it. I was born after he died."

"I am sorry. That was 'ard luck."

The words and the quiet voice touched her strangely. She took his hand and she squeezed it. It was a large dry warm hand and she thrilled to the answering pressure.

"Come on. We'd better get out." she said.

They sat at an outside table in the warm sunshine.

"There's only bread and butter and cakes on the menu," he said. "I hope you had a good dinner."

"I had a very good lunch and I shall be having dinner at eight."

"That's supper."

"No, it's dinner, but what a silly conversation. Let's change it. Tea and bread and butter will do fine. Now tell me about yourself."

He told her that he lived alone with his mother at New Cross and that he had a married sister who was evacuated to Kent with her two children. His mother eked out her war widow's pension with part time office cleaning. She had been in domestic service before she married.

He had done well at school and after leaving, he had gone to the Polytechnic and passed an exam in mechanics and engineering draughtsmanship. It was a triumph to be accepted by the London Fire Brigade, with its fifty applicants for every vacancy. The old naval preference was passing, but it was difficult for a young man to get in without some time in the armed forces or the merchant navy.

He had twenty-eight years to serve before full pension and he was determined to get a promotion. In his more ambitious moments, he thought that he would retire with the rank of superintendent, although there were only seven of them in the brigade.

They finished their tea and they walked down to the Serpentine and watched a balloon barrage section inflate their monstrous charge and winch it slowly into the air.

"Look, there's a lot more of them going up all over London,." said Janet. "Do you think a raid is expected? What will you do if there is one?"

"I'll make straight for station 69, leave or no leave and book on duty. I'm not going to miss any air raid fire-fighting experience that's going."

"What and leave me all alone in Hyde Park in an air raid?"

"No. I'd see you back to where you were going first."

"I think I'd go back with you and report to substation 69Y."

"That's my girl."

The balloons glistened in the blue sky and they took on the pink colours of the sunset.

"They look so pretty and there are so many of them. Will the Germans ever dare to fly through all those cables?" said Janet.

"I don't know. Perhaps not and when we attack the old Siegfried Line and go straight through it, it'll all be over and we'll have missed everything."

Janet shivered. There was a faint nip in the September evening and the denim uniform was thin.

"You cold?"

"A little bit, let's walk around the park."

"Number two station, Manchester Square is just up beyond Marble Arch. I've got a china there on Red watch so he'll be on duty. We could go and have a drink in the wet canteen and sit in the warmth."

"What's a china?"

"Why a china plate, a mate of course."

"But why?"

"Well, it's rhyming slang. Same as apples and pears for stairs or butcher's hook for look or Cain and Abel for table but you only say apples, butchers or Cain."

"I still don't understand what it's for?"

"T's just a way of speaking. Gets a bit complicated sometimes. An AFS chap at station 69 wanted to go off sick last week. 'What's wrong with you?' said Brewster. 'I've got a Kennington in my Newington,' he said. That foxed all of us until we found out that he meant he'd got a Kennington Lane in his Newington Butts or a pain in his guts."

"I don't think that's a very nice expression."

"Oh, I'm sorry Miss Finch. I didn't mean to be offensive."

"That's all right and you can call me Janet, not Dicky like the other firemen do, and I'll call you Bill instead of Brusher."

"Thank you. I'd like that."

"Good, now we'll get the car and go and see your

China."

While he went to look for his friend, he left her in the appliance room, a large enclosed garage with white tiled walls where five red machines of the regular brigade stood in line, polished brass and chromium at every metal point. At each end of the room, shining poles ran from openings in the ceiling to the floor. Everything was scrubbed and polished to a perfection of cleanliness. The place had an atmosphere; a keen alert atmosphere like that of a greyhound in the slips. Janet stood and took it in with her back to one of the polished poles.

Suddenly there was a thud behind her as two feet hit the mat at the pole's base. Startled, she turned and looked up at the smiling face of the young man she remembered the day she had joined up.

"You gave me such a jump. I thought you had dropped out of the sky."

"No just through the old pole 'ole. When I grow up and stop playing at being a fireman and have a home of my own, I'm going to have one of these installed. So much easier than running downstairs. What are you doing here? Have you got a transfer?"

"No. I'm still at Bermondsey. I'm on Blue watch so I've got twenty-four hours leave."

"Can't you keep away? Whatever are you doing coming to a fire station when you are on leave?"

"I'm with a friend. He's come to see a china here."

"I say! A china! You're learning the language fast."

"Yes, I can talk about apples, and butchers and Cainan's."

"And cobblers?"

"What are cobblers?"

"Cobblers awls."

"I still don't get it."

"I'm afraid it's rather rude my dear. It's balls."

"What's rude about balls?"

"Oh crikey, the errors of innocence. Don't learn too fast or too suddenly. Look, you can change your leave day, or I can change mine some time. We only have to ask someone on the station to swap watches. My people live in Kensington. Come and have dinner with me one evening or come to lunch and we can have a run out to Sunningdale. The name's Cartwright, James Cartwright. Strangely enough they call me Jim. What's yours?"

"Janet Carew-Finch. Strangely enough at substation 69Y they call me Dicky Finch."

Bill White hurried into the appliance room with a stocky red-haired and freckled fireman.

"Sorry to have kept you waiting. This is Tom Blake. We were in the drill class together. Now we'll get you a lemonade in the canteen."

"Are you going to take this nice girl into that poky little boozing hole?" said Cartwright.

"The superintendent's in his quarters and the guvnor's gone out visiting substations. We could all slip out to the Wallace Head for a civilised drink."

"That's all right for bloody AFS," said Blake. "If you get caught you only get a reprimand. If we do it's a charge and stoppage of pay and a note in your record file that's there for twenty-eight years. You go around to the Wallace

Head if you want to and stop pokin' your bleedin' nose in. Come on Brusher. Come on Miss."

"Oh, very uncouth people. Watch your step, dear girl."

"Who are you calling 'dear girl'?" said Brusher.

"Just a figure of speech," Cartwright shrugged his shoulders and walked away.

They sat in the corner of the canteen and talked about the war, and how strange it was that the air raids had not begun straight away as expected. In the West End hundreds of AFS men and women were already handing in their resignations.

It was eight o'clock when Janet got back to Kitty Farrow's house.

"Janet you are late. Claude has to be back by midnight. It will take him two hours in the blackout. Dinner is ready."

Claude Fanshaw was short and slight with pale blue eyes and sandy hair. Janet noted with regret that the acne, which had troubled him through his adolescence, still marked his slightly receding chin. His battle dress, ill-fitting and baggy, sat strangely on him for, since his school days, he had dressed meticulously and expensively. He shook her hand and pecked her hastily turned cheek.

His mother monopolised the conversation as she always did. She made arch reference to how happily he and Janet had played together as children; how well he would do in the stockbroker's firm when the war was over. She insisted that since they were now living less than thirty miles apart that they must see more of one another. Claude left at ten o'clock. Janet went gratefully to the bathroom and she luxuriated in her first hot bath for ten days.

She reported back for duty at eight forty-five the next morning.

"Keen ain't cha?" said Mollie Spence. "Quarter of an hour early. You'll get a good mark from old Taff. There's a letter for you."

The envelope addressed in a strange handwriting to Auxiliary Firewoman J Finch, lay on the watch-room table.

Bill White thanked her for coming out with him; was sorry that she could not stay for supper, hoped very much that she would come out with him again. And would she please let him know if she could say 'yes'. Tom Blake had said she was an absolutely smashing girl. He thought so too. The letter ended: 'yours respectfully and sincerely Bill'.

It was neatly written as though a final fair copy had been made after several laboured drafts.

"What a nice letter," said Janet to herself.

She went to the dormitory and she put it in her suitcase.

Another addressed to Miss J Carew-Finch arrived the next day.

"What's all this Carew-Finch about Dicky?" said Ernie Cliff, as he handed her the envelope. "Anything to do with mad Carew in the Green Eye of the Little Yellow God?"

Mrs Cartwright wrote to say that her son had asked her to invite Janet to lunch or dinner or both if she liked. If she could accept would she phone or write to fix a day, as James would have to change his leave day to suit hers.

"The Cartwrights," said Kitty Farrow, when told of the invitation. "Why? I've met them. Very nice people. He's something in the City and they've got a place at Sunningdale as well as the Kensington home in Victoria Road. I didn't know James was in the AFS. He's not really your type you know. A little bit airy-fairy, almost precious I would say. He hasn't got both feet on the ground like Claude."

James Cartwright greeted her standing behind the maid who opened the door.

"Hello! I'm glad you could come — for the whole day too. At the same time as changing my leave day, I've changed watches too so I'm Blue watch same as you. Come and meet my mother."

Mrs Cartwright was nearly as tall as her son, slim and well groomed. It was easy to see that in her youth she had been a noted beauty. She greeted Janet cordially.

"I was so glad you could come and that I could be here. My husband packed me off to Sunningdale on the third but I couldn't stand it, especially with him and James having to look after themselves in London. So, when some of the evacuees started drifting back to London last week, I drifted back with them. I suppose you are both free until tomorrow morning. Would you like James to run down to Sunningdale in the car? It would help me, as I would like some fruit and vegetables brought back. I hear that petrol rationing has been put off until next week and even then, we are to get ten gallons a month. We'll have dinner at eight."

They left after lunch in the Cartwrights' Bentley. Janet had never stayed as long as a fortnight in a big city before and she was glad to see the countryside again, stockbroker belt notwithstanding. The Sunningdale house stood alone in a big garden. A resident maid served tea on the terrace in front of a large croquet lawn at the end of which was a bank and an immaculately tended grass tennis court.

"Why did you join the AFS?" asked Janet. "You look and speak more like a commission in the guards type."

"The Wonder Book of the Fire Brigade. Did you ever see it? A great big book for boys with lots of coloured illustrations. It was an eighth birthday present and my favourite reading for years. There were pictures of brass helmeted firemen on top of those hundred-foot ladders squirting water into windows belching flame and smoke and there was one picture of a beautiful girl in a very coy flannel nightie being carried down a ladder on a fireman's shoulder.

"When I was eight, I wanted to squirt water into a high window. When I was eighteen, I wanted to carry a girl in her nightie down a ladder. When Munich came along, I joined the AFS like thousands of others."

"Are those the only reasons?"

"Oh, I suppose not. My family have no sort of service background although father was in the army, Artists Rifles I think, as soon as he was old enough in the last war. It seemed this one was different with modern air forces and that as soon as it broke out fire and destruction would rain down on London from the sky. Well, I'm a Londoner. I like London and I thought that I ought to be there to stop it being burned up. Turned out a bit differently hasn't it?"

"Yes, but I expect that it will still happen when the war really starts. Do you find it very boring waiting?"

"Not really. It's quite an experience living in a fire station. I was lucky I suppose being posted to a regular station rather than a substation. Except for the ones in schools most of them are ghastly places to spend days and nights cooped up in; garages, bits of warehouses and even railway arches. On a superintendent fire station like Manchester Square you get the atmosphere. Of course, the regulars hate the AFS. Can't really blame them. We crowd into their station where they lived their tight little life for years and the overcrowding makes life uncomfortable for them. Then they have to spend hours of what used to be their standby time training us, and they get no extra money for it.

"One thing I can't understand and that is that some of them seem to have an idée fixe that the AFS have come into their service to pinch their jobs or their promotion prospects. Can you imagine anything more absurd? Fancy any of us staying on after the war's over. I like them though. They're tough nuts."

"You didn't seem to like the one who I called at Manchester Square with on Monday evening or his china, Tom Blake."

"Purely incidental, my dear. I was just having an unexpected conversation with a charming young lady and they came and took her away to their pokey little canteen.

Anyway, what were you doing gallivanting around fire stations on your leave day with one of the regulars? You surely can't have much in common with him?"

"I've been told that before. I don't know whether I have got anything in common with him or not. I've only met him twice before, but I already know he's a very nice person. He's what my mother would call one of nature's gentlemen."

"Are you going out with him again?"

"I don't know. He's asked me to. I may do."

"I changed to Blue watch because I hoped that you'd spend your leave days with me."

"What all of them? We get two a week you know, three some weeks. You'd get tired of my company."

"I'd never get tired of your company."

He leaned over and he took her hand. She drew it away.

"Please don't be silly Mr Cartwright. Tell me some more about life at number two station."

"Not if you call me Mr Cartwright. Oh, I'm sorry, Janet. I didn't think you'd mind me holding your hand. What shall we do? I believe the Wonder Book of the Fire Brigade is still in my nursery here. Shall I find it and read it to you? It wasn't altogether accurate you know, at least the pictures weren't.

"There was one of a fireman holding a branch* and directing a stream of water right over the top of a blazing

---

* *hose*

warehouse. It was a very high warehouse. To put a jet of water over the top of it would have needed a pressure of about a hundred and fifty pounds per square inch, yet this chap stood there in a nonchalant manner holding the branch rather like someone holding a fishing rod. The back pressure would have been enormous. It would have taken two firemen to hold that branch, hanging on like grim death with one hand tucked on top of the nozzle and the branch hugged to their bodies, while the backpressure nearly lifted both of them off their feet.

"The regulars used to play a game with us. They'd stick two AFS men on a branch at a drill in the yard and then gradually raise the pump pressure until their victims were swaying and staggering about trying to hold the back pressure. Their victims knew that if they let go that the thing would whip and rear about like an outsize angry snake with ten pounds of brass and copper in its head. Get in its way then and, besides becoming wet through, you could end up with a broken leg or a cracked skull.

"I saw it get away once at a drill at the Regent's Canal. The pump was around the corner. The operator could not see what was happening in order to reduce pressure. 'Now what happens?' I said as I jumped to safety looking over my shoulder at the beastly thing thrashing about. One of the regulars took a sort of flying rugby tackle at the thing both feet off the ground and pinned it under his body. Next time I see a branch take charge I must try the technique.

"Anyhow it's interesting. The AFS chaps I am sorry for are the ones who were earning five to ten pounds a week before the war broke out and suddenly found their income cut to three pounds a week with a family to keep. They are simply resigning and going back to their old jobs until the call-up for their age group comes along. I shall stay on until something happens."

"You think that something will happen then?"

"I don't know. I'm not the war cabinet but if it doesn't happen soon there won't be many of the jolly old AFS left, not in the West End anyway."

They drove back to London and they were greeted by Mr Cartwright.

"Have you heard the news? The Russians have invaded Poland from the East. They've practically joined up with the Germans already and the remnants of the Polish army are trapped between German and Russian forces. Shocking isn't it? All fixed up apparently in the so-called Non-Aggression pact agreed between Ribbentrop and Molotov. Not much good our going to war to save Poland and then to let this happen. The evenings are drawing in."

He hurried to the curtains and he adjusted them to eliminate a gap.

"Damn the war and damn the blackout. It's the worst part of it, so far anyhow. I had to go to court today on the firm's business and while waiting for our case to come up, I heard one against three old dears, two men and a woman, pensioners who had been to a Salvation Army function. They were feeling their way in the blackout and a young policeman decided that they didn't have the required thickness of tissue paper in their torches. He ran them in, and the magistrate fined them ten shillings each. It made my blood boil; probably a whole week's money for each of them."

After dinner James Cartwright walked Janet back to Kitty Farrow's flat.

"Well, goodbye," he said. "I've enjoyed the day. Back to pump drill and scrubbing in the morning. What will you be doing back at substation 69Y?"

"A lot of hanging about I suppose. They might send for me from station 69 to do some driving job. I hope that they do. Please thank your mother for me and thank you for a lovely day."

"Since I can't hold your hand, I suppose that a goodnight kiss would be out of the question?"

"Oh yes, quite out of the question."

He turned and walked off into the pitch-black night illuminated only by the glowing cigarettes and shaded torches of passers-by.

His mother was sitting alone in the drawing room when he got home.

"Well, what did you think of her, Mama?"

"Oh, a nice young thing, Jimmy. Certainly, very pretty but such a bread and butter miss. Not your usual type, almost naive. What do you think of her?"

"I think she is absolutely adorable."

"Why, you, silly boy. Don't tell me you're falling in love. You've hardly met her yet. Did you make your usual passes?"

"Very tentative ones and so firmly and sweetly rebuffed."

"Well that must have made a change for you. Perhaps

it will do you good. I would like to see my little Jimmy in the role of the pursuer instead of the pursued for once."

She reached out and stroked his hair.

"Would you mind if I asked her here again?"

"Of course not, ask her as often as you like. You may ask her to stay the night. But if she accepts, none of your usual tricks, Jimmy, or you'll get a real rebuff. Besides your father is still furious over finding you in that awful Curtis girl's bedroom in June."

Chapter 4

Janet fell in with the Blue watch at nine o'clock the next morning. Sub-Officer Davies called the roll, dismissed the Red watch and detailed the drills and the station work for the other two watches. Janet was told to report to Company Officer Bridger at ten o'clock, as she had a driving job for her. She walked from the yard to the school building with Charlie Pierce.

"Been staying up the West End for your twenty-four hours?" he said.

"Yes. I stayed the night with my aunt, and I went to Sunningdale with an AFS man from number two station. It was nice to see the countryside again."

"Ah, AFS from number two. 'E'd be a young gentleman I suppose?"

"Oh, quite a gentleman. Why do you ask?"

"Well, perhaps I shouldn't tell you but young Mr White from station 69 was 'ere at ten past nine yesterday morning. Must 'ave run all the way 'cos 'e wouldn't 'ave bin dismissed before nine o'clock same as you. Seemed quite upset 'e'd missed you. You was off up the road pretty sharp when Blue watch was dismissed."

"Yes, I suppose I was, but it was silly of him to come running down here like that. If he'd rung me or sent a message, I'd have waited for him."

"Would you 'ave now Dicky? Well there's a thing now. I'd 'ave thought you'd 'ave very like given 'im 'is cards when you 'ad a young gent in the AFS at a West End station waiting for you. Like to like, that's what they say. You're a nice girl but you must find it strange livin' down 'ere with the likes of us; not used to our ways and talk I mean."

"No, I don't find it strange, Charlie. You've all been so nice to me although I talk la-di-dah as Edith Brown says. If there's going to be a real war, I can't think there would be a nicer substation to serve at than 69Y."

"There's a good girl, Dicky. You stay alongside us, my old china. We'll see you through come what may. We'll all see one another through. That's the way down 'ere."

She booked out at the watch-room, walked up to Piper Place and reported to Mrs Bridger.

"I want you to take the spare taxi to the LCC stores in Olaf Street. This street map will show you where it is. They will be expecting you. Give them this requisition. There'll be six parcels of stationery. Bring one back here and deliver one to each of our five substations. You'll find the taxi very easy to drive and it has a wonderful steering lock. Don't do anything silly. One of the men from W substation was sent out with a taxi and he started picking up fares. He's being prosecuted for plying for hire with an unlicensed cab. The meters and the Hackney carriage plates have been taken off."

Olaf Street was in Hammersmith and she drove off towards Lambeth Street. The traffic was thin in Borough

Road and she felt an irresistible urge to try out the taxi's lock. All clear in front; a glance in the mirror; all clear behind. She turned the steering wheel sharply to the right and the taxi swung around in a perfect U-turn and made its way south. She tried the manoeuvre again and was back on her route.

It began to rain as she went through the West End. Cabs were scarce after the requisitioning by the government of over two thousand to tow trailer pumps.

"Taxi! Taxi!"

She was hailed several times and she drove on with a regretful shake of the head. She collected her parcels and delivered them to the five substations that lay in a radius of about a mile around the regular peacetime station before returning to Piper Place.

The regular crew were at escape drill in the yard and she saw Fireman White among them. The big-wheeled escape was extended to its full height of fifty feet against the drill tower. A fireman with another on his shoulder was stepping from the top platform onto it.

"Still!" shouted Brewster.

The man froze, his heavy burden on his shoulder, one foot on the escape and one on the platform, his left hand grasping the top rung of the escape. It was the word of command used in the London Fire Brigade generally only when a recruit was in trouble high off the ground. It ordered him to stay quite still until instructions had been given him on how to extricate himself from trouble. Station Officer Brewster had used it because the way that the manoeuvre had been carried out did not suit him. His rasping tongue pointed out the fault.

He then ordered, "Carry on."

The fireman stepped onto the escape and he began to climb down.

"Cor! The old bastard,." muttered a fireman behind Janet. "Fancy leaving a bloke standing in that position while giving him a bollocking."

"I'll take the drill, Sub-Officer," he said, as he came down from his quarters, sucking one of his indigestion tablets.

The escape crew knew what they were in for then.

"They ain't 'alf been sweating. Slipped and pitched the escape four times they did, before 'e'd decided they'd done it fast enough."

Janet walked back to Y substation, hoping that Brusher was coming well out of the ordeal.

She found the station handy man Auxiliary Fireman Foster standing beside the gateman, a roll of wire around his neck, fixing something to the school playground's gate post.

"Hello Bert. What are you doing?"

"'Ello Dicky, my old duck. You wouldn't know, would you but I've managed to borrow a bit of wire and I'm fixing a little old electric bell from this 'ere gate to the watch-room. Then we'll be just like a regular station see. We won't want a gateman anymore and if anyone around 'ere comes running up 'cos there's a fire around these streets 'e just as to press the tit and the alarm sounds in the watch-room and you girls turn the little old pump out."

The bell worked perfectly and was surmounted by a

neatly painted notice: 'In case of fire, press', but hopes that the unpopular gate duty would be scrapped were dashed.

Station Officer Brewster visited at ten o'clock that night. He complimented Foster on his neat handiwork but said that it gave him no power to rescind the brigade order that a fireman properly dressed should stand at the gate of each substation throughout each day and night.

"The rotten old bastard,." said Ernie Cliff as they watched him get into his car and drive back to station 69.

When he got there, Brewster parked his car in the yard, booked in at the watch-room and went through the door that led to his quarters above the station.

"Where've you been?"

The whinging voice greeted him as he opened the door. It made the acid in his stomach curdle.

"I told you dear. I've been to a meeting at Southwark and I made a quick call to the substations afterwards."

He took an indigestion tablet from his pocket and put it into his mouth.

"Are you coming in now at half past ten at night expecting supper?" said his wife Doris. "Who was at the meeting? Some of those AFS women I expect. In the old days when things were decent, a woman wasn't allowed on the working part of a station. Now the whole place is full of them and its meetings all day and half the night. There's meeting and meetings in my opinion and wives left stuck in station quarters by themselves, while their men folk play around with a lot of tarts in blue uniform.

"Station quarters in Bermondsey of all places. If you haven't the gumption to get further in the job than station officer why don't you apply for a West End station or somewhere nice in the suburbs like Dulwich. Walking home alone in the dark around here gives me the creeps. I'll probably be assaulted one of these days and little you'll care."

"Now Doris, we've had this out before. You know that a fireman's wife walking home through Bermondsey at night is safer than one walking home through the West End."

"Oh, yes, we've had it out before, the public heroes and their families in a high-risk area. The station officers in line for promotion command the high-risk stations. Well I don't like living here and you know that I don't like living here. Why don't you do something about it? Aren't you in line for a promotion? You've been passed over already. There's Abbot, made District Officer last month. He joined a year after you and now Freda Abbott's talking down to me and playing Mrs District Officer to the station officer's wife."

His eyes wandered around the room.

"Any letter from Charlie?" he said.

"It's on the sideboard and that's another thing; why do you want to put the boy into the navy just before a damn war starts? He could have been living at home and getting three quid a week in the AFS if you hadn't done that, and I might have had a bit of company sometimes."

"You know that I didn't put him in the navy. He wanted to join up and then come into the brigade when he'd done his time."

"Yes. When he's done his time; if he does his time.

Sailors get killed in wars and you encouraged him to go."

"Don't talk like that, Doris. He's on a battleship, a big battleship. He'll be all right. There isn't a ship in the German navy that could take on the *Royal Oak*."

"Well let's hope so. Your supper's in the oven."

He walked over to the sideboard and picked up the letter; pulled out the wall plug of the telephone and carried the instrument to the bedroom, putting it on the bedside table and plugging it in there. He put his fire boots with the leggings draped over, ready to pull on in one movement, at the foot of the bed. His fire tunic he hung above them. He undressed, washed and got into bed and he began to read the letter from his son. The lantern jaws relaxed in a half smile.

October came and the nights grew longer. Janet was given a regular morning and evening job. She had to drive the spare taxi to each of the steel water tanks in the streets of her substations. In the evenings, she put down red reflecting oil lamps to warn traffic of the tank's presence. Every morning she took the lamps back to the substations to be refilled and to have their wicks trimmed.

Soon, the little patch of southeast London was as familiar to her as Brandon village and winter's advance was measured by the narrowing gap between dawn and dusk. On 8th October, she sat in the mess room after supper drinking tea and listening to the conversation.

"Do you realise," said Alf Newton, "that all the other

ARP* services: ambulance, rescue, the lot, get a leave day every other fuckin' day? They're on twenty-four hours off instead of forty-eight hours on and twenty-four hours off like us and for the same pay. It's fuckin' barmy us doing these hours and at six fuckin' pence an hour too. At some of the stations they're resigning and joining the ARP."

"Well, why don't you?" said Ernie Cliff. "It would save us all having to listen to your fuckin' moaning."

"That's not the point. If we stuck together and all resigned at once they'd have to do something about it. I don't know why we put up with it."

"I do," said Charlie Pierce. "It's because this old firm's got something about it. A bit of tradition and a bit of discipline. You may not go in for discipline, Alf, but it's necessary. It took me through the last lot on the Western Front and I hope that it will take us all through this."

"I wouldn't mind the hours," said Bert Foster, "if I could go to a fire."

"Cor! I'd love to go to a fire on a real red engine with the little ol' bell ringing an' all the traffic getting out the way and the crowd held back by the slops when you get there, and them all watching you when you get to work."

"If I could find some bells, I'd put them on the taxis so that we could ring 'em when we go to a fire, if we ever do get to a fire. Y'know station 69 went to a fire right down Rampton Road the other day, past this station and never even gave us the call."

---

* *Air Raid Precautions*

"It was only a chimney fire. I was in the watch-room at the time and I asked them where they was called to," said Mabel Smith.

"Still a little old chimney fire can be quite excitin'. Lots of smoke and all the neighbours watchin'. When I was a nipper, I used to go to all the fires, run all the way. I saw the fire at the Carpenter's Arms. That was a real goer. When the Crystal Palace caught fire, I got on a bus to Norwood, but the traffic was so thick with 'alf London goin' to look I couldn't get near it."

"Why didn't you join the old LFB in peace time?"

"Because 'e was too short, too fat, couldn't pass the education test, couldn't pass the strength test and hadn't been in the navy."

"That was about the sum of it," said Bert ruefully. "Still, I'd give up my leave day if I thought station 69 was goin' to 'ave a real goer on its ground and would call us in when the assistance message was sent."

"Well, I don't reckon I'd give up my leave day just for a fire," said Ernie Cliff. "Not if it was a Saturday one any 'ow. It says in the papers they're going to allow league football to start again but the gate 'as got to be regulated to eight thousand maximum, in case bombing starts and there's a panic. Cor, 'ow are they going to pay their way and pay the players on gates of eight thousand?"

"Well, they've let the pictures open again. I took the old woman last night and an ugly great commissionaire wouldn't let us in cos we weren't carrying our fuckin' gas masks. 'What would you do, madam?' 'e says, 'if you was caught in an air raid and they was droppin' gas bombs and you 'adn't got your gas mask. You'd ask some man to lend you 'is, I suppose and let 'im choke to death!' Makes you think though don't it?"

"Well, talking of the pictures, I know someone 'oo wouldn't want to give up 'er leave day in a 'urry, eh Dicky? I have seen you going into the old Trocadero cinema at the Elephant with young Brusher White and some other little dicky bird says you were seen going into a West End cinema with a long lanky chap from number two the leave day before that. Two strings to your bow eh? Pictures every leave day and six penn'orth of 'ot 'ands in the back row, I shouldn't be surprised."

Arthur Clayton pushed open the double swing doors that led into the yard.

"Oy! All of you lot come out 'ere. Just come and look at this lot."

They left the table at his summons and joined him in the open air. The northern sky was lit up by a lurid glow that was accentuated by the blackout.

"Cor, what is it?"

"What is it?" said Taff Davies. "You should know. That's a fire and it's a big one too. Brigade call I should think."

He went to the watch-room and spoke to Section Officer Casey.

"Ay miss, get on the blower to station 69 and ask what's come in and 'oos ground it's on."

She lifted up the phone and made the enquiry, writing down the answer as she repeated it.

"It's the Pantechnicon. They've made a brigade call

100

of it. The information message said a building of four floors and basement about one hundred and eighty feet by two hundred feet, ground and first floors well alight."

"The Pantechnicon," said Davies. "That's in Motcombe Street and about the biggest furniture depositary in London. It burned once before, back in the eighties and they had about sixty horsed steamers trying to put it out. They'll be there all night and most of tomorrow by the look of it."

Bert Foster was jumping from foot to foot in excitement.

"Shall we go and get rigged, Sub?"

"Go and get rigged, my arse. That's in fuckin' Northern Division off fuckin' Sloane Street. There's thirty regular fuckin' stations between us and that and about a one hundred and fifty fuckin' AFS stations. I suppose station 69 might be told to send their pump to Southwark to stand by, if they're making closing in moves, but you won't need to get fuckin' rigged."

"I can see the flames."

"I can see a turntable ladder."

"Balls! You couldn't see a turntable ladder from here. It's four fuckin' miles away."

"Let's get up on the roof!"

A trap door in a top floor classroom led to the loft and another to the roof, giving access to a small flat area between slated gables. They heaved and hauled one another up. Janet was thankful that she was wearing trousers and not a skirt. The glow in the sky was getting bigger and tongues of flame could be plainly seen.

"Cor, that's making a Charlie of the old blackout. I wonder if the rozzer's will run 'em in for showing a light. There you are Bert, now you can say you've seen a fire. Did you 'ear me Bert? There's a right fire for you. Where's old Bert Foster gone? 'As 'e stayed down in the yard?"

Four hours later, the bored gateman stamped his rubber boots in the chill October night as a figure sidled through the blackout towards him.

"'Oos that?"

"Don't let on. It's me, Bert."

"Christ! You gave me a jump. Where the 'ell 'ave you been?" He put his hand on a wet sleeve. "Blimey you're soaked through."

"Couldn't miss it," came the whispered reply. "I've been up to the fire. Caught the tram, then the tube. It was smashing. Does old Taff know? Don't let on if he doesn't."

"No, Taff never missed you, but the other boys did. You'd better creep in. Miss Casey and Mollie are in the watch-room, but they've got the door shut. Don't let them book you in 'cos you was never booked out."

"Thanks mate."

He made his way quickly to the men's dormitory, undressed in the dark, leaving his wet tunic and underclothes under the bed and shivering with cold, he slipped naked between the blankets. At nine o'clock the next morning, wearing underclothes and a shirt that clung damply to his skin he was dismissed with the White watch for his twenty-four hours leave.

Four days later, he sat in the mess room after supper blowing and wiping his red nose.

"You ought'er go off sick with that bloody cold of yours, Bert. You'll give it to all of us."

"Was it worth it?" said Jack Adams.

"Yes, it was worth it. 'Aven't I told you about it?"

"'Asn't 'e told us about it? Blimey 'e's talked of nothing since."

"Well Jack wasn't 'ere so I'll tell 'im. You 'aven't got to listen if you don't want to. I got the tube right to Sloane Street and when I came out, the 'ole street was lit up so you could read a newspaper. There was about forty regular red pumps there belting bloody great jets into it and God knows 'ow many AFS pumps what 'ad been sent for extra to give 'em a bit of experience. Those West End AFS boys was 'avin' a real night out. Well I got 69Y painted on my little ol' steel 'elmet and I thought some officer might twig I 'ad no right to be there, so I makes a beeline for the basement where I knew it would be dark. There was only regular crews working in the basement and cor, wasn't it 'ot and smoky. Suffocating it was and they was working without BA, and the water was pouring through on us from the jets upstairs and it was scalding 'ot.

"Well, after a while I thought I was goin' to die of 'eat stroke or suffocation, so I starts to feel my way out along the 'ose and was I glad to find the little ol' stairs. There was an escape pitched just outside the stairway door, so I nips up that onto the roof. That was grand. About twelve blokes was sitting astride the ridge holding branches, two blokes to a branch at full pressure, banging away into the fire below them and the old steam and sparks flying up like a Brock's Benefit.* I was up there a long time just watchin'. Then I comes down and 'as a walk round the 'ole building.

"Then I goes inside again on the ground floor. Furniture was piled right to the ceiling and it was then I got in the way of a two-inch nozzle. It 'it me right in the back and knocked me arse over tip and that water were cold, bloody effin' cold. There was a couple of regulars on the branch and one did 'ave the decency to say: 'sorry mate. Are you all right?' The other said: 'you want to watch where you're going'.

"So, I gets out the building and 'as another walk around and sees the turntable ladders at work and where the pumps was set in. They 'ad about forty hydrants opened up all around. There wasn't many AFS pumps at work. Mostly those chaps was just watching from outside, not like me 'ood been inside and on the roof.

"Well, some of the posh dames that live around those parts was dishing out cups of tea to these blokes. Then along comes the district officer, looking like a nigger minstrel with 'is face all black from smoke and does 'e tear into 'em for accepting refreshment from strangers against brigade orders.

"'You wait for the canteen van' 'e says, 'but as none of you 'as done a stroke of work, you'll be lucky then if you get a cup of tea'.

The spectacular fireworks display held at the Crystal Palace 5 November 1865-1938

"Well, after midnight they started to knock off pumps and got the AFS making up hose. It seemed to be mostly over, and I was anxious about old Taff Davies or someone missing me, so I caught the tube to Borough and walked back from there."

"Aren't you going to tell us how someone saw you strolling about like a lord's bastard and mistook you for the effing superintendent and 'ow you started giving orders that saved 'alf the building?"

"I didn't say nothin' of the sort and you know it. You is just jealous 'cos I've seen big fires which you ain't. All you can do, mate, is go sneaking out to the Carpenter's Arms about an 'undred yards away."

"There's one thing that makes me think," said Alf Newton. "Bert fuckin' goes to a fire and gets fuckin' wet through and catches a fuckin' cold, which he starts giving to all of us. What's going to 'appen if we get air raids in winter and fires like that all over the place. The regulars 'ave got two fuckin' sets of uniform and dry kit to put on when they get back from a fire. We've got one fuckin' set. 'Ow are we going to carry on? It will be sickness all over the fuckin' brigade."

"Let's wait and see if we're going to 'ave any bloody air raids. Any 'ow they're going to give us an escape carrier. That'll be something new to do. A bit of escape drill. X substation 'as got one. It's only a bloody great van with an escape stuck on the back. Not like the regular ones with a pump and 'ose reels and all the effin' lot as well."

"It 'as got an 'ose reel on it. When X substation got theirs, they drilled with it for two days under their own sub-officer. Then old Brewster came down from station 69 to put them through their paces. Crikey they was fuckin' lathering when 'e'd fuckin' finished and even then 'e wasn't fuckin' satisfied. If they didn't carry each other down properly 'e nipped up on the roof and said: 'Right carry me down' and all the way down 'e was nattering at them."

"If that fuckin' bastard tells me to carry 'im down the fuckin' escape, I'll throw the fucker off my fuckin' shoulder on to the deck when we're still near the top," said Alf Newton.

The escape carrier arrived two days later, and Sub-officer Davies started training his crews.

"Now you all reckon you can 'andle a pump and run out 'ose and 'old a branch but 'ere's a new piece of equipment you've got to learn about. And see that you learn it proper the way I'm going to teach you. And don't try and get me broke by actin' stupid because when I've got you trained the guvnor will be down from station 69 to put you through your paces."

Except for its grey paint, the escape was the same as those carried on the regular machines, but it was mounted on a van that had few refinements and reflected the government economy in the provision of AFS equipment.

"Now this is known as an escape and it extends to fifty feet. But it isn't no turntable ladder, which is mechanically extended. This 'ere works on the Armstrong patent 'ydraulic system and when you get on these winch 'andles to start extending it, I want to see 'em fly round real fast. And I want to see everything with this piece of equipment, done real fast: slipping, pitching, extending and mounting."

He divided his command into crews of four and he instructed the first in removing the seventeen hundred weight escape with its five feet diameter wheels, and from its vehicle, while the others watched.

Each crew repeated the manoeuvre in turn and then the escape was run up to the three-storey building and extended to its full height, just above the piece of flat roof between the gables. They ran up and down the ladder; lowered it and extended it till dinner time and again in the afternoon.

"Well you're beginning to get the 'ang of it now," said Davies. "So, I might as well tell you why this piece of equipment is called an escape. It 'as several functions such as giving firemen access to roofs and other parts of buildings when stairs are burning, or smoke-logged. It enables us to get the 'ose quickly to the 'ighest parts but it was primarily designed as a means of escape for persons trapped in tall buildings. Now, if those persons are unconscious, or in any other way incapable of coming down the escape under their own steam, they've got to be carried down, so we'll now start the carrying down drill.

"Now you should all have done the picking up drill on 'ow to pick up an' carry an unconscious person by means of the fireman's lift. But we'll just run through it again because I don't want any mistakes made while you're fifty feet above the ground with one of your mates on your shoulder.

"'Avin' got your load lying face downward," Davies

continued, "proceed to the 'ead, place the 'ands under the armpits of the person to be carried and bring 'im to a kneeling position, at the same time bending the right knee and letting the body rest against it. Bring the left foot up to the right; bend down and interlace your fingers be'ind the back and bring the body on its feet; take its right wrist in your left 'and with the back of your 'and on top, extended in line with the shoulder and let the body lean against yours with your right arm around its waist.

"Then bend down and put your right arm between the body's legs and using its right arm as a lever, pull 'im across your shoulders and get 'im balanced there. Transfer the body's wrist to your own right 'and and you will find you can walk easily with your own left 'and free to open doors and both 'ands free, as we shall see in a few minutes to come down an escape.

"That is the fireman's lift for male persons. Since it is in the drill book I also 'ave to make sure you know the lift for female persons. 'Ere the drill is the same except that you may not put your right arm between the legs which would never do with a female person, would it now? Instead you must put your right arm round both legs and then 'eave 'er on your shoulders. She won't be so secure and will probably fall off and break 'er bleeding neck, but at least she'll be knowing that she 'asn't 'ad a fireman's right arm between 'er legs. Now get fell in in pairs."

He sorted out the pairs, according to weight and size so that a small man would not have to carry a big one down and he sent the first pair to the roof. Ernie Cliff hoisted Jack Adams onto his shoulders, grasped the head iron of the escape and stepped up on to a round.

"Careful Ernie. It's a long drop," said Jack, and he received a grunt in reply.

The pairs made their precarious journey until dusk, their instructor sweating with nerves and constantly shouting, "Still!"

Station Officer Brewster arrived two days later.

"Right. I'll take the drill, Sub Officer, get the escape out."

He stood and barked his orders often followed by the command: 'As you were'. The escape was pitched to the flat roof.

"Now we'll try some carrying down. Newton, that's your name isn't it? Follow me up the escape and bring me down, the way you've been taught."

He sprang lightly over the levers and ran up the escape; stopped on the roof and turned around.

"As you were! You're using the escape as a superannuated window cleaner would. Get down to the bottom. Now run up it. Left foot left hand; right foot right hand. Hands on the rounds not on the strings."

The crews stood on the ground and watched as the station officer hoisted himself onto Newton's shoulders and the AFS man began to descend.

He stepped down two rounds when Brewster's voice rang out, "Still!"

Newton froze in position as instructed.

"Now I hear you've said that if you ever had to carry me down an escape, you'd throw me off near the top. All right throw me off. Carry on."

The two figures remained stationary at the top of the escape for a minute that seemed an age to those waiting below.

"All right if you don't want to throw me off, carry on descending and in future don't boast of doing things you've no intention of doing."

They gathered in the mess room after dismissal.

"The old bastard! 'E's got guts though. You got a nasty temper when you're roused, Alf, and I wouldn't 'ave liked to 'ave been in 'is place. It's a long way up there."

Newton glowered.

"All I want to say is you can't open your mouth on this station without everything getting back. Who's been tellin' tales? That's what I'd like to know. Oh, I know you don't mean it to get back there but someone tells Clark and Clark tells Davies and Davies goes around kissing Brewster's arse and tells 'im. 'E knows what I think of 'im and that doesn't worry me."

"You couldn't see what 'is 'and 'was' down there, but I could. It was 'anging just over the guy wire and if I'd tipped 'im off 'e'd have 'ung on to that and then run me in. 'E wants to get rid of me, see, because I stick up for my rights but 'is little plan didn't succeed."

"Still, I wouldn't like to be on an escape forty feet up with only a little old guy wire to hang onto," said Bert Foster.

The wireless in the station was no longer switched on for all the news bulletins. The second phoney war was on its second month and the announcements were as tedious as drill and scrubbing, not to mention the endless games of solo that occupied substation 69Y.

On the evening following the station officer's visit for escape drill, Jack Adams returned from duty at station 69.

"You 'eard the news," he said.

"What news? Little ol' 'Itler suing for peace?" said Clark.

"No. They've sunk the *Royal Oak*."

"You been listening to Lord Haw-Haw?"

"No. It's the real thing. It was on the nine o'clock news. Believed to be a submarine. Over seven hundred killed and practically no survivors."

Clark put down his cards.

"Is that true? Brewster's son was on the *Royal Oak*."

"Blimey. He lived for that boy."

"I know. That's what they say up at station 69. There 'asn't been no telegram for 'im yet though."

"Over seven hundred; not much chance for him then. Where was she?"

"In Scapa Flow."

"Crikey! Torpedoed in Scapa Flow and all the ex-sailors in this job keep telling us that there can't be any submarine menace in this war because this time we've got Asdic. Poor old Brewster. He'll take it 'ard. Charlie was his only kid."

"We'll take it 'ard too. It's not going to improve 'is temper."

"You shut the fuck up. That's no way to talk."

Station Officer Brewster went about his work. His lined face looked more lined but his harsh voice strangely softened.

Winter came early, with hard frosts and bitter cold. The water in the steel tanks in the streets froze solid and the crews were sent around each morning with large axes to hack out the ice and pour freshwater in. There was insufficient anti-freeze for the radiators of the self-propelled pumps and the taxis standing in the school playgrounds. Orders were given that the engines were to be started up and run for a minute every quarter of an hour, throughout the day and night.

In December, the deferment of over three hundred regular firemen who were reservists of the armed forces ended. The men were instructed to report to their units. Clark, a former regular soldier was among those recalled. The substation rallied together to give him a farewell party.

They sent to the Carpenter's Arms for beer and while they were waiting, they sat around the big coke stove at the end of the classroom that served as their mess and recreation room.

Conditions had improved since September. They now had furniture, which included some rather uncomfortable armchairs, dining tables, cooking equipment, plates and cutlery.

A stores van called regularly with food from an LCC depot, and each station now had a female cook.

Agnes Jenkins, who filled the post, was a short fat woman in her mid-fifties with a whole set of large white false teeth. They were uncomfortable and she often left them on the kitchen table while she worked.

"Fancy me being in uniform," she kept saying.

She was very proud of it and she wore her AFS cap at all times, even in the kitchen, where it looked odd above the white overall, which regulations insisted she should wear whilst working. She was not a good cook, but she was always cheerful and obliging. She blessed the strange fortune of war that had taken her from a damp back street room to the warm substation; from loneliness to companionship and from a widow's pension to the comparative affluence of two pounds a week.

Charlie Pierce poked the coke in the stove.

He said, "Well, where are you off to tomorrow, Nobby or is it 'ighly secret?"

"No. Nothing secret about it. Borden Camp's to join the Second Battalion."

"You glad to go?"

"Can't say I'm sorry. It'll be nice to meet some of my old chinas."

"Well, if the government 'as allowed all the LFB reservists to be recalled, they can't be expecting air raids. They can't want fuckin' soldiers much with little old Lord Gort and 'is boys just looking at the Siegfried Line and doin' sweet Fanny Adams else."

"Ah, and the effin' RAF doing fuck nothing but drop fuckin' pamphlets on Germany. If they fuckin' fly all the fuckin' way over there, why don't they drop fuckin' bombs on the fuckers?"

"They called all the reservists up in 1914 and when the Zepp raids started they 'ad to send 'em all back again."

"Ah, but there weren't no AFS then."

"Well, I don't know what we're all doing 'ere. There's

some good jobs skulling around in munitions."

"You 'eard the buzz that's going around?"

"No. What's the latest?"

"They're going to replace the reservists that 'ave been called up with temporary firemen. They're going to wear LFB uniforms and 'ave the 'ole issue, two of everything and they're going to get LFB pay and they're going to be picked from the AFS, whoever can pass the tests."

"What tests?"

"Same as the LFB: arithmetic and dictation, strength test, right 'eight and when you're accepted you've got to go a hundred foot up the tower at Lambeth on an 'ook ladder."

"Blimey. Count me out. All that for an extra fifteen bob a week and two sets of uniform with a round cap."

"You can fuckin' count me in," said Newton. "I'm applying for that. I can do it all better than some of them that are wearing round caps now."

"If we see you in a round cap, you'll be giving us fuckin' orders and throwing your fuckin' weight about."

"I may be giving you orders but I shan't be throwing my weight about like some people we all know."

"'Ere's the beer. Good old Ernie. 'Ow much 'ave you fetched?"

"As much as the whip round would buy of course."

"What you going to play us 'Arry?"

Harry Booth moved to the piano.

"You ask for it. I'll play it. Any tune you like."

The party ran its course like the one in September, but Janet did not drink British made port wine. When the beer came around, she held out her tumbler to have it filled. At midnight Taffy Davies made a short speech, wishing luck to Fireman Clark, who from then on would be Private Clark.

The big man thanked them shyly and leaving the gateman and watch-room staff to their vigil, the firemen and firewomen went to their dormitories and their trestle beds.

Agnes Jenkins sat on her bed, sleepy and happy.

"I enjoyed that. I 'aven't 'ad such a good time since me 'usband passed on," she mumbled.

"Where are your bleeding teeth, Aggie?" said Edith Brown.

"They're all right. They're in the kitchen."

"Crikey, they'll end up in the stew one of these days and we'll think we're eating sheep's 'ead."

"I don't know where my teeth'll end up but I know where you'll end up if you don't watch your step. When you start asking for second 'elpings, I'll know you'll be eating for two."

"You shut up you old bag. I can look after myself."

"Don't you call me an old bag, you little trollop."

"Now that's enough of that both of you," said Section Officer Casey. "If you have complaints about Firewoman Brown's conduct, Jenkins, you can bring them to me. Finch put out the light and open the window a little. We could do with some air in here."

Janet obeyed, and then she slid between her blankets. It was Blue watch's leave day tomorrow. She lay and listened to her companion's snores and the revving of the engines in the yard as the gateman went about frost precautions.

Blue watch on leave at nine o'clock. To Aunt Kitty's for a bath; a lazy morning, followed by lunch off a tablecloth; and at three o'clock she would be meeting Bill White.

They had chaffed her in the mess room about having two strings to her bow, but she knew now that she was only interested in one of them. Jim Cartwright was amusing and attentive and his parents were kind and hospitable; their home made a welcome break from the fussy atmosphere of Aunt Kitty's house each leave day.

But Bill was strong and kind and handsome. She lay and wished that he was not so respectful and that he would attempt the intimacies that she rebuffed so often when she was with his rival. His rival; yes, that was it. It really was becoming stupidly complicated and perhaps unfair. Unfair to Jim anyhow. He was so ridiculously jealous with his, 'what did you do last leave day? Out with that White fellow again. What can you see in him?'

While Bill would say, 'Did you enjoy yourself Thursday?' and 'Good, I wish that I could provide the same sort of things he can. I'll get promotion then there'll be a bit more spending money.'

He'll get promotion, she thought. Lying in the dark, she slipped into one of the waking dreams that were beginning to recur so often. Accelerated promotion — it was a term she had heard at station 69.

He would make sub-officer and one of the specialist posts at headquarters. Then he'd rise to station officer, the youngest in the brigade. He would look swell wearing the strange LFB undress uniform; the well-tailored double-breasted dark blue lounge suits that carried no insignia nor rank markings and that were worn with black tie and white shirt and were common to every rank from station officer to chief officer.

The war would bring casualties and more promotions. She saw him in the burning streets directing operations; his firm and phlegmatic bearing; his brilliant dispositions of men and machines. His gallantry would be noticed. He would be made the youngest district officer; the youngest superintendent.

She smiled at her own absurdity as she thought of the grey haired, hard bitten men, each with more than twenty-five years of service, that she had seen leaving a meeting at Lambeth headquarters.

'That is too impossible,' she thought. 'There's a better way. He must become a principal officer. The divisional officer must die in an air raid. They can't take an army, navy or air force officer in the middle of a war. They will have to look for a brilliant young man in a junior rank. Station Officer WR White to be promoted to divisional officer,' Brigade Orders announce; the first promotion from the ranks to principal officer.'

She momentarily regretted the death of the tall young officer who had winked at her last September, but nothing must stand in Bill's way. But there were no air raids, only the blackout and petrol coupons and the threat of further rationing and the dull repetitive news bulletins on the wireless.

Should she tell her mother about Bill? She stirred uneasily beneath the blankets. None of her family or former acquaintances knew about him. Kitty Farrow knew of Jim Cartwright and she had written to her mother. Her mother had written to her suggesting that she bring him to Brandon when she got her first week's leave.

Only Colonel Boyd knew of the LFB fireman with whom she was falling in love. Back to her daydreams; they were pleasanter than the nagging worry that she might be indulging in deceit.

When Bill was an officer it would be easier. Her thoughts raced to new absurdities.

Lady White was receiving in the big Chief Officer's flat overlooking the Thames at Lambeth Headquarters.

'Have you met Sir William, such a handsome man? You know he rose right from the ranks. Quite brilliant they say, but his wife must get a good deal of the credit you know. She brought him along so wonderfully. She was a Carew-Finch from Norfolk. They have such beautiful children. They say that her family was opposed to the marriage but are of course more than reconciled to it now.'

Perhaps it was too ambitious; too high flown. She laughed softly.

"You still awake, Dicky? What are you laughing at?" said Cissie Spence

"Just my thoughts."

"Penny for them."

"They're worth more than a penny."

He was waiting for her at Hyde Park Corner, his shoulders hunched against the cold.

"Hello Bill, you look frozen. Have you been waiting long?"

"Only about a quarter of an hour."

"But it's only just three o'clock and I did say three o'clock, you know."

"I like to be a bit early when I meet you, in case the bus gets held up or something."

"You are funny. If you were late, I'd wait for you, you know."

"I wouldn't like to keep you waiting."

"No, I know that you wouldn't. You're too nice. Now the film I want to see is, 'Gone with the Wind' but it's West End prices and you've got to be my guest today."

He protested and they argued as the bus went down Piccadilly. He held open the foyer door for her. She walked in past him straight to the ticket window and asked for two seats. He stood behind her and, reaching around, he put the money on the counter. But when they sat down, she slipped the pound note, which she held in her hand, into his overcoat pocket.

For three hours they watched the film of the civil war of eighty years ago, before emerging back into reality; the bitter cold and the blackout. They could see no moon above the low clouds and thin snowflakes fell on Leicester Square, around which the traffic crawled with dimmed sidelights, as the red, green, and amber crosses on the masked traffic lights winked their signals.

"Come on," he said. "Let's get out of the cold. How about Lyons Corner House?"

"That will do beautifully."

The pavement was crowded, and he took her arm and they felt their way by the light of other people's torches, occasionally bumping into those who also carried no means of lighting on the way. The Corner House, inside its double doors and blackout screening, was warm and bright.

"Well, what did you think of it?" he asked.

"I thought that Vivian Leigh was wonderful as Scarlet O'Hara, but I was never quite sure if it was Rhett Butler or Ashley Wilkes she was really in love with."

"Oh! It was Ashley. Rhett Butler was only an adventurer. Yes, it was Ashley all right, a man of her own class."

"Do you think class, as you call it, matters in these things?"

"Yes, it does matter."

"Then, how do you define it?"

"Just money or the lack of it; what you've been used to; family and those sorts of things; even the way you hold a knife when you're eating. Oh, I'm sorry about that. It's such a little thing. I should never have told you about it."

"Yes, you should because now we both do the same thing and I want to do things just like you. You see I've remembered, no longer the penholder grip as you called it."

"It's very sweet of you to have remembered, but it really isn't important because I've decided that what people call class doesn't matter at all, not if you really like somebody."

"And do you really like me?"

"Oh Bill, it's more than that, much more than that."

"Do you mean you love me Janet, like I love you?"

"If you love me, I love you like you love me, but you've never told me before that you loved me."

"I thought that you knew it. I never dared to tell you in case you laughed or something. I think of you all the time. I think I began to love you the moment I first saw you last September, when I took you from station 69 to substation 69Y and you were so shy and beautiful."

"Come on. Let's go and have a drink to celebrate."

"We haven't finished our supper and you surely don't want a drink after all that tea."

They finished their meal and sat talking and holding hands as the band played. The waitress brought the bill unasked and put it on the table. Later, she returned and said that people were waiting for tables. They left and stood together on the pavement.

"We'll have the drink now," he said.

They found a pub and went into the saloon bar crowded with khaki and air force blue.

"Would you like a glass of wine?"

She laughed.

"I don't think you'll get wine here. I'd like half a pint of bitter."

"You used to hate it."

"I know. It's an acquired taste and I seem to be acquiring it. Isn't it awful? They say it makes you fat. I never thought I'd drink it again or anything else after that awful night at the Carpenter's Arms. I expect you heard about it. I still blush when I think of it."

"Yes. I heard about it. I was very sorry for you. You don't want to worry though. That's all over and done with. Section Officer Casey never put a report in."

"No. She's a good sort. She was very kind to me, especially as she's TT herself. Look there's a table free in the corner."

They carried their beer over and sat down.

"Are we engaged then?" said Bill.

She held his hand on the cold marble tabletop and sat a moment deep in thought. Her careful upbringing and her mother's domination of an only child presented difficulties that she dared not face immediately.

"Bill, I don't think I like long engagements and we can't get married just yet. For the moment let's just say we're engaged to be engaged. It will be a secret between the two of us. I've got to get things worked out a bit, not with myself, but other things. I've got rather a formidable mother to contend with, you know, and I'm only just nineteen. You'll have to contend with her too. I'm afraid that she won't like it at first, but when she gets to know you, she'll be wonderful to you just as she has been to me."

"She won't approve because she'll know that I'm not good enough for you. I agree with her. But I'll work hard for you, Janet, and give you everything I've got. When I make station officer I'll try and get South Kensington or Basil Street or West Hampstead and then there'll be nice quarters in the sort of place you're used to living in."

"No, you won't. You'll try and get Whitechapel or Bishopsgate, one of the busy stations where the station officers in line for promotion go. You and I are going right to the top, Bill."

"Not right to the top. That's direct entry officers only."

"Things may change by the time the war's over."

"It'll be hard for you in the early days. Not what you've been used to you know."

"No, it won't. It will be wonderful with you. Besides my father left me some money, though he never saw me, and I don't come into it until I'm twenty-one."

"That wouldn't be right, living on your money."

"Oh, don't be absurd Bill. We wouldn't be living on it. We'd just use it to buy nice things for the flat and for the children."

They talked in their crowded corner, oblivious to their surroundings until closing time. He walked with her from the bus stop and they stood for a moment by the door of Kitty Farrow's house.

"We must say good night, Bill. It's been wonderful."

He put his arms around her, and he looked down towards her upturned face.

"May I?"

"Of course, you may."

His lips found hers and she thrilled to her first kiss. A wave of desire swept through her whole body and she pressed herself close and she hung on tightly, as she felt she would collapse. Regrettably, the door latch clicked, and they stepped apart.

"Good night," he whispered. "See you on Thursday."

"Yes, on Thursday. Goodnight darling."

He went away, light footed into the darkness as the

door opened.

"Come in quickly. The hall light's on," said Aunt Kitty, shutting the door as Janet entered.

"Goodness, you're late, child, and you look so flushed. I don't think your mother would like you to go out so late with young men. Do the Cartwrights approve? I heard talking outside so I thought that it must be you. Claude has telephoned. He's got forty-eight hours leave from Thursday. Won't that be nice for both of you?"

She resented the interruption of her ecstatic mood.

"I don't know. I've got an engagement on Thursday."

"What, all of Thursday? Oh, Janet if only you knew how much he was looking forward to spending the day with you. We've had such a long chat on the phone. They may be sending him to France. He doesn't want to go. He wants to stay in England, so that he can be with you more often. They aren't sending the married ones unless they volunteer. You know that he wants to marry you."

"No. I don't know. He's never mentioned it to me. I'm sorry Aunt Kitty. I can't discuss it now and I can't marry him. I'm not in love with him."

She turned and she walked quickly up the stairs to her bedroom. Leaving the light switched off, she drew back the curtains and opened the window.

There wasn't a glimmer of light below as she stared into the blackness in the direction that he must have taken. The night air chilled her hands and she withdrew them from the sill and plunged them into the pockets of her mackintosh. There was a crumpled pound note in one of them.

"Oh Bill, you proud, kind, generous darling," she whispered to the darkness outside.

Chapter 5

"Which watch will be off for Christmas Day?"

"Red, the lucky bastards."

"Well, Blue will 'ave Christmas Eve off and White will 'ave Boxing Day off. There's nothing in it."

"Yes, there is. It'll be the first fuckin' Christmas day I 'aven't spent with the missis and the kids and since no effin' bastard in the Red watch will change with me, there must be something in it."

"It'll be all right 'ere on Christmas Day. Dicky Finch's mum 'as promised to send us two turkeys. Be all right if old Aggie doesn't fuckin' burn the fuckers."

"Is that true, Dicky?"

"Yes. They're on the way."

"Well, I call that very civil of your mum. Very civil. Turkey for dinner and a little party in the evening with a drop of the old pig's ear. You'd be worse off in France or at sea you know."

Blue watch reported for duty at nine o'clock on Christmas morning. After roll call Janet walked into the mess room, decorated with paper garlands and Christmas cards.

Fred Mason dismissed with the Red watch followed her. He was a C class auxiliary fireman, too old for firefighting and he was assigned to driving duties only. He said that he was sixty, but he was so grey and wizened that everyone doubted his word and they accused him of faking his age to supplement his old age pension. It was part of his duty to collect and distribute the lamps on the street water tanks when Janet was on leave.

"I've filled your lamps and trimmed the wicks for you, Dicky. Thought I'd let you know before I went off. Nothing for you to do except take 'em round at blackout time. The postman's been. There's three for you in the watch-room. One's registered."

She collected two small parcels and a letter addressed in her mother's handwriting. The registered parcel bore the label of a west end jeweller with the address typewritten. The other was addressed in Bill White's handwriting. She went to the empty women's dormitory and sat on her bed to open it first.

It contained a marquisate bracelet and a Christmas card signed 'with all my love from Bill'. Dear Bill, she had been with him yesterday and she had handed him his Christmas present. His must have been already in the post and he had said nothing. She unbuttoned her sleeve, put the bracelet on her wrist and buttoned the sleeve back over it.

She then opened the other parcel. It contained Jim Cartwright's card with the words 'Happy Christmas' scrawled across the back and a diamond brooch.

"Oh God, you opulent fool, I can't accept things like this from you."

Vaguely disturbed she put the parcel in the bottom of her suitcase, underneath her clothing and she opened her mother's letter.

My Darling,

Thank you for your good wishes and your Christmas present, which will be most useful. I hope that the turkeys have arrived safely. Well this will be our first Christmas apart for nineteen years, but I simply couldn't get to London, being Chairman of the Committee, that is arranging the Christmas festivities for the evacuees or rather for those of them who still remain with us. Over fifty per cent have now returned to their homes. Goodness knows what will happen to all those children if air raids ever do start.

I thought that the Fire Service would surely be arranging some sort of Christmas leave like the other services do, and then you might have been able to come home, though I agree it would not be worth the journey home and back for twenty-four hours.

I have heard from Kitty again that you seem to be spending most of your leave days with the Cartwright boy. I really must get to London to meet him and his parents as soon as the WVS, and other work give me the opportunity. She seems to be rather hurt because you don't pay more attention to Claude when he's on leave. I'm sorry about this because I think he is a nice boy and, after all, our two families are very old friends, as well as being distantly related.

Well you have been nearly four months away. I am rather disappointed in what you tell me about your prospects of promotion. Surely, with your education and background there must be supervisory posts that you could fill, even if it did mean that you had to give up driving duties.

I still think that you should apply for a position at HQ, where you would be under the eye of senior officers and would soon be noticed. Also, whatever you say, I think that Bermondsey is a most unsuitable neighbourhood for a girl of your standing and upbringing.

I know I have written about all this before and you must think me very tiresome and repetitive, but you will know that I only say these things because I love you and am anxious. I will let you know as soon as I can get away. In the meantime, Happy Christmas.

From your loving Mother.

Mollie Breaks walked in and sat on the bed opposite as she finished reading the letter.

"You heard about Edith Brown?"

"No."

"She's got a duck in the oven."

"How nice."

"What do you mean? How nice?"

"Well, two turkeys won't be all that much for twenty-six of us."

"Are you trying to be funny?"

"No. I'm sorry if I'm being stupid. I thought that you meant she had given a duck to the mess and was cooking it."

"No, I didn't. Don't be so daft. I meant she's in pod. Don't look so dumb. She's going to have a baby."

"But she can't. She isn't married."

"Oh, can't she. You just watch the front of her for the next few months, if they don't throw her out, you'll see if she can or not."

"Well, she'll get married then."

"She might if Mrs Ernest Cliff was prepared to agree but she doesn't even know about it. Look we've got to help the poor kid out. She's got a swine of a father and a bitch of a mother. They take nearly every penny of her wages, although she's only home one day in three and they're the sort who'll chuck her out in the street over something like this. Ernie's got three kids evacuated along with his wife and he sends her most of his little lot. Some of us are going to sub-up for her to get her out of trouble. You ever heard of an abortion?"

"Yes, one of our mares had one last year. We lost the foal."

"Oh, my Gawd! Did the bloody animal slope off to a back street, quack vet for it? Listen, animals can have abortions and it's neither here nor there. Women can miscarry if they're lucky or unlucky, as the case may be, but if a woman is landed with a baby on the way she doesn't want, she isn't allowed to have an abortion. It's an illegal operation, and because it's illegal it costs money, because those who do it go to the jug if they get caught.

"We got to raise twenty-five quid for Edie. I've stuck a fiver in because I've got my pay and my army marriage allowance and we're still ten quid short. Will you help towards it? They'll pay it back bit by bit when they can."

"If it will help Edith, I'll give her the ten pounds."

"Dicky Finch you're a sport. The fewer of us who know about it the better. We'd do the same for you, you know. Blimey how much do you know? Hasn't your mother ever given you a book to read or anything?"

"No, and she's never discussed those sorts of things with me, nor has anybody else."

"Hasn't Brusher White ever tried to get a bit fresh with you or anything?"

"No, never."

"Well there you are you see, he's a real nice bloke; but they aren't all like that and it's early days with him yet."

"Sometimes when I'm with him, I think that I wouldn't mind if he did."

"That's just it. Listen kid, you're all on your own here in London. It's just about time you were taught a thing or two."

Mollie Breaks sat on the low bed, her knees hunched almost to her chin and methodically gave her lecture. When it was over, her embarrassed but grateful pupil thanked her and walked to the mess room, to join the group, who crowded round a flustered Agnes Jenkins and gave contradictory advice on the cooking of turkeys.

A week later, Edith Brown went on leave and reported back for duty twenty-four hours late. She claimed the one-day's uncertificated sick leave allowed, and she satisfied Section Officer Casey that she had had a severe migraine.

She stopped Janet in the yard.

"Don't forget to ask me anytime I can give you an 'elping 'and."

On payday, Ernie Cliff put two crumpled ten-shilling notes in her hand.

"Keep it Ernie. You needn't refund it as a loan. It was a present."

"We're grateful but we've got our pride you know."

She put the money into her pocket.

The days lengthened and her round with the lamps became minute by minute later each evening and earlier each morning. The first winter of the war was slowly passing and March came with cold sunshine.

"Take the spare taxi to Olaf Street Stores; pick up the gear that's waiting there and take it to 60 Southwark."

Sub-Officer Davies gave Janet the order and she went about the task with alacrity, for it was pleasant to get away from the substation on a spring evening and drive through London's streets. She heard a shout of 'Taxi' as she drove along Bayswater Road and a moment later, she was held up as the traffic lights turned to red. Feet pounded along the pavement and the rear door of the taxi was flung open.

She turned in her seat and said, "You can't use this one. It's AFS."

The heavily built bowler-hatted man walked to the offside. He leaned his head into the driving compartment.

"Can't use this one. It's AFS. No and nobody can get a taxi because they're nearly all AFS. It's time all you useless bastards were given the sack and were stopped wasting taxpayers' money. What's the good of you anyhow? You're about as much good as the bloody blackout."

His whiskey-charged breath filled the cab.

The lights changed to amber. She slipped the clutch in and drove on, angry and ashamed.

An hour later, she drove under the arch and into the cobbled yard of Southwark Fire Station.

"Take them to the stores," said a station officer, nodding at the parcels.

The stores man drew them over the counter.

"You're Dicky Finch from substation 69Y aren't you? Have you seen today's Brigade order?"

"No."

"Well there's something'll interest you. Your china Brusher White's been made sub-officer. Only three years out of the drill class and sub-officer already. This old war's doin' some of 'em good."

There was a telephone kiosk in Rampton Road. She pulled up and phoned station 69, waiting impatiently while they sent for him.

"White here."

"Congratulations, Sub."

"Thanks Janet. When did you hear?"

She rejoiced in the pleasure that showed in his voice.

"At 60 station five minutes ago. Oh, I'm so glad, darling. I expect you're speaking from the watch-room and can't say what you want to say. Tell me all about it tomorrow. We've got all day except the evening. I'm sorry I accepted to go to dinner at the Cartwrights' but we can celebrate at midday."

She parked the taxi in the yard, and she tripped light-footed to the watch-room to be booked back.

Cissie Spence and Mollie Breaks sat at the table.

"You 'eard about Brusher White," said Cissie. "Bit of all right for you both isn't it? Mollie 'ad a bit of good news too. Go on tell 'er, Mollie."

"Tom's been made sergeant major."

"She's on a nice wicket, isn't she?" said Cissie. "What with 'er pay and a sergeant major's marriage allowance."

"I am glad," said Janet. "Please send him my congratulations."

"Thanks Dicky, I will. It's not substantive of course, only wartime rank but it'll be nice if he can keep it when the war's over. Warrant officer's quarters and warrant officer's pay; we could raise a family and bring them up decent. That's what I want; and this bloody war to be over so that we can be together again. Still the fucker hasn't started yet. Wonder whether it ever will start?"

In the mess room the men sat over cups of tea, listening to Alf Newton.

"I said to bloody Brewster, why haven't I been made a red rider? 'Because I didn't recommend you, 'e says'. I'm taking this further, I said. 'Put in a written submission and you can see the superintendent'. A lot of fuckin' good that did, nothing but fuckin' rudeness from a man old enough to know fuckin' better. I demanded an interview with the divisional officer and I fuckin' got it, even if it did mean waiting fuckin' four weeks.

"Well, what a load of fuckin' bollocks. Up to HQ. Marched in left, right, left, right. The fucker sits there in a bloody great fuckin' office, behind a fuckin' great desk and picks up my submission and fuckin' reads it out. 'Anything to add to this Newton?' 'e says in 'is lah di fuckin' dah voice. I'd got my bit all re'earsed and gave 'im the fuckin' lot; in since Munich, good knowledge of drills, position of responsibility before I joined et. fuckin' cetera. 'E just sat and listened and then said, 'I'm sorry but no man can accurately judge his own fitness for promotion, and this is promotion, you know'.

"Soon as 'e'd said it, it was about fuckin' turn and I was out of the room. What a way to run a service, and look at today's Brigade order. Seven new sub-officers made including young Brusher White at station 69. Nothing but a kid and not been in much longer than I 'ave. Now I've got to take fuckin' orders from 'im if 'e comes my way."

Janet felt her face going red as Ernest Cliff glanced across the table at her. He turned to Alf Newton.

"I'd rather take orders from Brusher White than I would from you. I put in for red riders as well and I got turned down but I'm going to keep trying instead of just bellyaching. If you don't like this mob, you can resign and join the army. Then you could go on moaning all through the war 'cos you can't resign from that mob."

"Ernie's fuckin' right. We all get effing tired of your bellyaching," said Charlie Pierce.

Newton got up from the table.

"You're just a lot of fuckin' sheep. You'll fuckin' put up with fuckin' anything. That's why they fuckin' know they can fuckin' fuck you about as they fuckin' like. I'm not putting in my week's fuckin' notice. I'm just going to walk out."

He left the table and strode from the room. Through the window they saw him walk across the yard. He stopped and stood talking to the gateman for a few minutes then he turned and walked back to the station.

"Ah, that's a pity," said Bert Foster. "I thought for a minute the bugger really meant it."

Bill White took Janet to the Cartwright's' house the next evening.

"I do feel awful about this," she said as they walked from the bus stop. "I would never have accepted if I had known that it would be our first leave day since your promotion."

"That's all right. We've had a lovely day and I don't want you to feel that you're tied to me every spare minute. See you in two days' time?"

"Yes! Two days' time. Goodnight, Sub."

He smiled and he bent to kiss her. Janet put her arms around his neck, and she put her tongue into his mouth and again her whole body trembled with desire.

"Goodnight Firewoman," he said, as he pulled away.

Jim Cartwright opened the door to her ring.

"I see he's got a peaked cap now."

"Oh Jim, you were watching from a window? You're as nosey as Aunt Kitty."

"Just looking out for you, my dear, to save you waiting on the doorstep. Couldn't help seeing everything. You're getting very familiar."

"Jim, congratulate me, I'm going to marry him."

His face fell.

"I don't know about congratulations. I'll congratulate Brusher White and wish you the best of luck, my dear. Is it public yet? Are you going to tell my parents?"

"No, not yet. I've got to get one or two things sorted out. I'm afraid that my mother may be rather silly about it. I want her to meet Bill before she knows. When she sees what a wonderful man he is, I know that she will welcome it."

"I think you're going to find it all rather troublesome. I'll help if I can. Perhaps she could meet him here. Come in. We'd better go and meet the family."

Mr Cartwright welcomed her by the drawing room door.

"Come in and have a glass of sherry. Well, how are you getting on? Nice to see the evenings drawing out. Makes the dammed blackout a bit shorter. I suppose you've heard of Jim's disappointment."

Janet started and said she had not.

"He was accepted for this party of firemen that's off to help the Finns by manning a pump or whatever they call it in Helsinki. You know that the Russian bombing has started a lot of fires there. Anyway, he's just heard that they had to cut the number down and he's one of the ones to be left out. Bad luck isn't it? It would have been a good experience. The Finns have certainly shown the Russians up. The Germans are welcome to them as allies. Still it's a pity that Jim didn't get in on the trip. I've advised him to leave the fire service and join one of the armed forces, doesn't matter which. Much more prestige you know. Tell Janet what happened to you yesterday, Jim."

"Well, I was sent from number two to stand by at one of the substations because they were short and they couldn't man all their pumps. First thing that happens to anyone sent on standby is to be put on gate duty and that was the fate of yours truly. I'd stood there all rigged and correctly dressed for about an hour when a little girl of about seven with a runny nose came and stood opposite me and she looked me up and down very severely for at least two minutes.

"I tried to be civil and pass the time of day with her. I asked her name. Not a word did she say until finally she broke her silence with; 'My Dad says you're a waste of money'. Then she turned on her little heel and she walked away."

Janet laughed and told them of her experience while driving the taxi in Bayswater Road.

"That's just it," said Mr Cartwright, "if there hasn't been an air raid in nearly seven months, I don't see how they're going to start at any time. If the Germans thought, they could do it successfully they'd have done it by now. You can understand the public getting restless, what with rationing starting and the blackout. There was a headline in one of the papers the other day; 'Turn out the ARP workers and turn up the lights'."

The ringing of the telephone interrupted him. Mrs Cartwright answered it and she turned to Janet.

"It's for you. It's Mrs Farrow."

"Ah, Janet, I knew that I would find you there. Such wonderful news. Claude has got his commission and he's got seven days leave. He's coming to London straight away to get his new uniform. He's taking me out for a little celebration as soon as he's been fitted out and then he would like to take you out to dinner with him. I know that you will say 'yes'."

Janet did so reluctantly, making the arrangement for the last evening of Claude's leave.

"My word, you do look smart," she said, as he walked into his mother's drawing room. "I thought that it would only be battle dress."

"That's all we get an allowance for now, but you can still buy the proper outfit if you pay the extra yourself."

"And you thought that it was worth it?"

"Yes, of course."

He looked at himself in the long mirror on the wall; the short figure dressed in khaki tunic with Sam Browne belt, the single gilt pips shining brightly on each shoulder strap, his cap in one hand and a leather covered swagger stick and gloves in the other.

Janet looked down at her own well-cut dark suit.

"Well, it's a good thing that I'm not wearing my uniform. I'm afraid my blue gabardine is getting a bit shiny."

"Shall we go? I'll try and get a taxi. I've booked a table at the Criterion."

"Please buy me a drink first."

"I thought that you didn't drink?"

"I didn't but the second bore war does things to you."

The taxi turned down St James. Janet was already bored.

"Stop there," she said. "That's a good pub."

"Good heavens! You can't go into a place like that."

"Why not?"

"Well it's simply not done. I couldn't go in there in

uniform. I'll take you to a club if you like. We could go into the RAC."

"I didn't know that you were a member."

"Officers visiting London can become members of practically any club for a nominal subscription."

"Well I don't want to go to the RAC or any other club. I want a pint of bitter."

She felt irritated and she thought that if circumstances hadn't forced her to accept this invitation, she could have been drinking bitter in a cosy bar parlour and be talking of the future with Bill.

Claude said that they could get a drink at the Criterion bar. It was crowded and he was handicapped by his lack of inches. He found it difficult to get served, standing behind four tall figures in double-breasted navy-blue suits, with stiff white collars and black ties.

Janet recognised the divisional officer standing with three colleagues. Claude put his shoulder between two of them and edged in, as the barman walked away to the other end of the counter.

Looking back at Janet, he said loudly, "You can't get served in this bar for bloody civilians."

She turned in fury, walked to a table, and sat down. She looked back to see that they had made way for him.

The divisional officer walked up to her and smiled.

"Forgive me, it's not the old try-on but we really have met, haven't we?"

She stood up.

"Yes, sir. I was at substation 69Y when you visited last September."

"Yes, of course. Please sit down. You're not on duty now. Are you still with us?"

"Yes."

"Well done. The first flush of enthusiasm didn't last long with a few thousand of your colleagues. As soon as I saw you, I knew that we had met before."

"You should have done. Last time you winked at me."

"Did I? How very remiss of me and prejudicial to good discipline. Well here's your escort returning. Do be on guard against the brutal and licentious soldiery, who seem to be in rather an aggressive mood this evening."

Claude brought two glasses of sherry, which he had difficulty in carrying along with a cap, stick and gloves.

"Rotten service," he said, as he carefully placed them on the table. "They used to have floor waiters here."

She glowered at him and said, "If you dress up like an officer, can't you try and behave like one."

"Here, I say old girl, what's the matter?"

"Is it necessary to refer to four principal officers of the London Fire Brigade as bloody civilians? Well they are civilians, but they run a smarter and better disciplined service than the ack-ack and without King's Regulations and the threat of Junkers behind them."

He looked back at the bar.

"Are they fire officers? Well I should have thought that they'd have worn uniforms. I thought that they were undertakers in those dark suits and black ties."

"Did you really? I think that we had better change the subject. Isn't it rather dangerous becoming an officer? They might send you to France. I gather from your mother that you wouldn't like that."

"No, they're not sending me. I've applied to specialise on training. It will probably be in Scotland."

"Well that's a nice long way away from the danger area. Your mother said that you wanted to stay near me. Scotland is further away than France."

"Yes, but there's a good train service and we get quite decent leave."

"But what'll you do if London gets raided?"

"That doesn't seem very likely does it?"

"I don't know. The war isn't over yet. It hasn't even really started yet. Is our table ready?"

Her thoughts were elsewhere, and the conversation and her escort bored her. The dinner was not a success.

***

The light April evening with the slanting sun shining onto the south wall brought substation 69Y's White and Blue watches away from the stove to seats in the yard. The old wireless set brought from Augur Street stood on the windowsill.

"Well, we've mined the Norwegian coast and we've made the Norwegians very cross, but at least we've done something," said Charlie Pierce.

Bert Foster sat in one of the easy chairs brought outside from the mess room and he worked at an elaborate arrangement of wire and lamp sockets arranged on a piece of board on his lap.

"What are you up to now, Bert?"

"I'm making an indicator board. These 'ere will 'ave different colour lamps in 'em. We'll 'ave a yellow lamp for an escape carrier, a red one for the self-propelled, and different colours for each of the trailer pumps. When we get a call, the girl in the watch-room can press a button and light up the lamps for whatever machines are ordered; just like the regular stations 'ave got."

"Ah, when we gets a call, if we ever gets a bleeding call."

"One of Deptford's substations got a call last week. Running call from a ware'ouse just across the road and they got there and 'ad two fuckin' jets to work before the regulars arrived. Still they was fuckin' lucky. Per'aps this load of fuckers 'ere never will be fuckin' needed. Not after what little old chambermaid said last week. 'Itler 'as missed the bus. Well, if 'Itler's missed the bus, we might as fuckin' well get the 'ell out of this lark and back to our old jobs or join the army like everyone's fuckin' telling us to do."

"There was a chap 'ere from the LCC education department this afternoon," said Cissie Spence. "'E came in the watch-room with the district officer who said 'e didn't want Taff Davies sent for. They stood outside the door and I could hear most of what was said.

"'The children are nearly all back and we've got to arrange their education', says the bloke. 'You'll have to hand it back to us'.

"'We can't do that', says the District Officer. 'We've nowhere else to go'.

"'You must remember,' says the bloke. 'This is the

education committee's property and it is urgently needed again for their commitments'.

"Then they walked away down the mess room and I couldn't hear anymore."

"Cor, if that means that we're going back to Augur Street, I'm not going."

"They wouldn't fuckin' stick us back in there. It's not fuckin' fit for 'uman 'abitation."

"Wouldn't they? Fuck. If they fuckin' felt like it, they'd fuckin' stick us anywhere. Probably under some fuckin' railway arches like 61Z. What do you reckon to sleeping underneath the arches, Dicky?"

"I wouldn't like it a bit."

"Dicky's all right. She's got 'er love to keep 'er warm 'aven't you, my old duck? You told yer mum yet?"

"Don't you take any notice of 'im, Dicky. Tell 'im to mind 'is own business. 'Ere it's six o'clock. Just reach up and switch the news on."

They listened in silence to the news of the invasion of Norway. Oslo, Kristiansand, Stavanger, Bergen and Trondheim were already in German hands. The bulletin ended.

"There you are. That's what fuckin' comes of mining Norwegian waters," said Alf Newton.

"Don't talk so daft. An invasion like that would take weeks to prepare."

"Well, 'ere's the little old Norwegians crying their eyes out this morning because we infringed their neutrality and tried to stop the Germans collecting their iron ore and 'ere they are this evening calling on us for 'elp."

"Ah and it's on the way. Things is 'otting up at last. I knew that the Jerries would never dare attack the Maginot line. They 'ad to take on something easier. Well they've made a right Charlie of it. You see we can land in Norway and Denmark and drive right down into Germany. We shan't 'ave to 'ang our washing on no Siegfried Line."

"Well the Norwegians are getting bombed. I wonder if they will ever start on us," said Bert Foster.

"Per'aps they'll call for volunteers to go to Norway like they did for Finland. I put my name down for that but only the West End boys got accepted."

"Just as fuckin' well you didn't go Bert, seeing as how they didn't get there until the Finns had fuckin' packed it in and now, they can't fuckin' get back."

The wireless was switched on for every news bulletin, as it had been the previous September. The papers with their optimistic headlines, belied by the paragraphs below, were eagerly scanned each day. Mollie Breaks was given two days compassionate leave to see her husband on embarkation leave.

As April passed, they slowly realised that things in Norway were not going according to plan. At the end of the month an infantry sergeant major lay dead in bloodstained snow near Namsos and Mollie Breaks reported for duty red-eyed and pale faced. They plied her with little kindnesses that made the tears flow again. The war was coming closer.

Janet went to see Colonel Boyd at the beginning of May.

"Hello, my dear," he said, "and what have you been

doing since I saw you last? Christmas Eve – wasn't it at Kitty's?"

"I've been driving taxis and cleaning taxis and studying topography and falling in love, but it's only the last part I've come to see you about."

"Well, you're nearly twenty, so the last part was to be expected. Is it Claude Farrow? Kitty seemed to infer that you were getting pretty well-acquainted the last time I saw her."

"No. It isn't Claude Farrow."

"Can't say I'm surprised. Doesn't seem quite your type. Well, who is it?"

"Uncle Neville, I want you to help me. It's the fireman in the round cap I told you about in September; only he hasn't got a round cap anymore. He's been made a sub-officer after less than four years' service and I love him very dearly and we want to get married."

"Do you, by Jove! And I expect that your mother is very cross about it, and you've come to see me to put a word in with her."

"Mother doesn't know yet. Oh, it all sounds very silly, but I know that she'll oppose everything and make things that have become so wonderful difficult, and because of that, I just haven't been able to bring myself to tell her. I keep putting it off until she comes to London and she keeps putting off coming to London because she's so busy with the evacuees and her other war work.

"She thinks that I am going out with an AFS man from Manchester Square who went to Marlborough and has rich parents, because that's what Aunt Kitty, who thinks that, keeps telling her. I know that I must tell her soon, but I am worried that she won't understand. I want you to meet him so that you can tell her what a wonderful man he is. There'll never be anyone else as far as I'm concerned."

"Ah, that's what they all say my child. They said that in the last war. Lot of very unsuitable marriages then. Seems to be the same again this time. Want my advice? Just stay friends until the war's over, then look around and see if you still feel the same."

"No. I can't do that Uncle Neville. I love him very dearly and we want to get married."

"Want to get married. You can't do that without your mother's consent you know. Not till you're twenty-one. Why not wait until then? Things might be different."

"They will never be different. I know that they will never be different."

"Dear me. Don't look so intense child. What do you want me to do?"

"I want you to meet Bill. When you see him, you'll know that he's a man and a gentleman and you'll tell mother so and make it easier for her."

"Why yes. I'll meet Bill but I warn you, that what I tell your mother about him will depend entirely on my own judgement, which may not tally with yours."

"You're a dear, Uncle Neville." She put her hands on his shoulders and kissed him.

"Am I, my child?" He looked pleased. "Well, when do we meet?"

"Now, if you don't mind. He's waiting outside."

"I say you don't let the grass grow under your feet, do

you? Well you'd better fetch him in."

He was wearing his uniform, his cap under one arm.

"Bill, I want you to meet Colonel Boyd. He is a very old friend of my family and of my mother."

He stood to attention and said, "How do you do, sir?" as he took the proffered hand.

"How do you do, Bill? Janet's been telling me about you. Says she wants to marry you. Do you want to marry her?"

"Yes of course, sir. Who wouldn't?"

"Well, I would if I was your age. Would you like a drink? Whisky and soda?"

"Have you a beer, sir?"

"I think so. Yes, Whitbread's light ale. What about you Janet? There's some sherry here but you're a teetotaller, aren't you?"

"I'd like a light ale too, please."

"Would you, by Jove? You know when I was young it was considered rather indelicate for a young lady to drink beer. Did Bill teach you?"

"No. They taught me at the substation. Bill tried to stop me at first."

"Good for him. I suppose you two are both on leave today."

"Yes. Bill's taking me out to lunch."

"Let me stand the honours for you both. There's a ladies' annexe at my club now. I'll get a taxi if you people have left any on the street."

"I'll go, sir."

"Thank you, Bill."

"Well he's got good looks Janet. I must say you make a handsome pair. Clean too and nice manners. Where did he go to school?"

"Why, the local Board School of course, somewhere near New Cross."

"Funny thing. On first acquaintance you'd think that he was a Wykehamist."

"Then you like him?"

"Of course, I like him but that's a very different matter to urging your mother to let you marry him. Anyway, let me get further acquainted."

He walked to the window and looked out.

"Well he's got initiative. He's managed to grab a taxi and it's raining. We'll walk down to save him coming up."

They lunched at the Army and Navy club and the talk turned inevitably to the war.

"It's serious," said Colonel Boyd. "I hear that we've decided to pull out of Namsos and Ändalsnes and to leave the Jerry in possession. Hope that the Navy can get them off safely. I think that we're going to try and hang on around Narvik and try to capture the port, to deny Jerry the iron ore. We've been defeated, you know, and I don't like it. We haven't been taking the war seriously. Only the other day, a chap here told me that his troops had a lecture from a general who'd told them that the Germans were not nearly such a tough proposition as they were in 1914. I don't believe him. This Norway business is only the beginning. I think that things will hot up soon on the Western front."

"Do you think that London will be bombed, sir?"

"I don't know Bill. They bombed Warsaw, didn't they, and they've bombed the Norwegians. Some people say they'll use their aeroplanes only to support their troops because that's the most efficient way to use them. I think that it depends on how the battle goes when it starts, because it will start, you know. If we hold them and start to maul them as I think we will, they'll be up to any nastiness. How'll you chaps stand up to bombing? You'll have a pretty horrible job to do."

"I don't know sir. We'll be all right, I think. You know, the AFS are really very good. There've been thousands of resignations since last September, but somehow most of the best ones are staying."

"Yes, the rescue people have been resigning too. I'm light rescue, part-time unpaid, you know. I walk around in the evening in the old blue battle dress and do a bit of practise and listen to a few lectures."

"Some of the AFS part-timers are very good. They come around to evening drills after a really hard day's work in a factory or on the docks."

"I'm afraid I don't go around after a hard day's work. Nobody will employ me at my age. Did you ever think of joining the army? You'd do well you know. You'd soon be posted to an OCTU and come out of it with a commission. Might solve one particular problem for you in a way."

"No. I haven't sir. You see the fire brigade is my career. I was very lucky to get in and although they've called up all the firemen who were reservists and their jobs are preserved for them when they come back, I'd just have to resign and I wouldn't be reinstated."

"Yes, I see; silly suggestion of mine, eh Janet." He looked at his watch. "Well, it's past two o'clock. I'll be getting back home now. Be a good chap Bill and see if you can work the oracle for a taxi again. The porter will probably fix it."

He sat with Janet at the table.

"He's a nice boy. I can see why you want to marry him, but you know you'd have an awful lot of things to iron out. Anyway, you ought to tell your mother if you're so serious, being the only child and all that."

"Yes, I know I must tell her. I should have done so before. I just wanted a bit of support, that's all. Will you support me, Uncle Neville?"

"I'll tell her he's a very nice, well-spoken young fellow. When do you want me to do so?"

"I'll write to her this afternoon. If she got a letter from you by the same post, it might help."

"All right, we'll do that."

Betty Carew-Finch put the two opened letters down on the breakfast table and said to her maid, "Mary, please ring up Mrs Carson and ask her if she'll take the chair at the WVS meeting this afternoon. I'm catching the ten o'clock train to London. I hope to be back this evening. You'd better get Miss Janet's bedroom ready. She'll probably be returning with me."

Chapter 6

Colonel Boyd stood by the fireplace looking uncomfortable.

"It's no good being cross with me Betty. I knew nothing about it until yesterday and I wrote to you then. All I can say again is; he's a clean, good-looking, well-spoken lad and if I can read the symptoms, they're head over heels in love."

"He doesn't drop his aitches then?"

"No, he doesn't. He speaks damn well, as a matter of fact."

"I expect that is because his mother was in service."

"Maybe it is, but Janet's nearly twenty, you know. It's absurd to talk about dragging her off to Brandon. What'll you do if she refuses? It's not a crime for a young woman to fall in love, you can't call the police in."

"I shall write to the chief officer."

"You can if you like, but with several thousand women in the service he's probably had such letters before and passes them down through a chain of women officers to some junior who will write back and say it isn't her business. You'd only make a fool of yourself and Janet too."

"Well what do I do about seeing her?"

"I told you that she was on leave yesterday so she isn't

on leave again until the day after tomorrow. You don't want to go calling at her substation. Leave it to me. I'll see what I can do."

He went to the telephone in the hall and returned a few minutes later.

"Rung their HQ. Spoke to some woman officer; had a very civil reception. They're giving her short leave for what I referred to as urgent family business. She'll be here within the hour. When she arrives, I'll slope off and leave the two of you together."

Janet sat in the mess room drinking tea when Sub-officer Davies walked in and said, "Firewoman Finch, message from Mrs Bridger, you're to be given four hours short leave to see your mother on urgent family business. See you're properly booked out. She's at this address."

He handed her a message slip with the pencilled address of Colonel Boyd's flat, as fourteen pairs of eyes turned in her direction.

"What oh, Dicky 'as your mum found out about you and Brusher?"

"I wrote and I told her yesterday."

"Crikey, she's quick on the draw if she's come all the way from Norfolk."

"Do you want to borrow a cushion to stick down your knickers in case she takes the stick to you?"

"Don't be so daft, she's a grown-up girl. She can make 'er own mind up and 'er mum nor nobody else can stop 'er."

"Ta, Ta, my old duck. Give your mum our best respects and roll on Christmas and let's 'ave some more turkeys."

In the watch-room Mollie Breaks was writing in the occurrence book.

"Off you go. I'm just booking you out and the best of British luck to you."

She was still there when Janet returned four hours later.

"Well how did you get on?"

"Very well. It was so nice to see her again. We had dinner together. She had to catch the midnight train back, but when we get our week's leave, she's going to ask Bill to Brandon with me to stay."

"You won her round then."

"Well no, not really, not yet. She wants to meet him of course and then I'm sure it will be all right. I've promised her not to do anything rash or silly and well, you know what, she got frightfully embarrassed and she started telling me about what she called the facts of life. I said that I already knew and then she got cross, because she thought that Bill had told me. I said he hadn't; it was you and she seemed relieved. Oh, Mollie it's such a relief to have told her. I'm sure that everything's going to be all right and we'll be able to marry before I'm twenty-one."

"Yes, you'll be all right kid. You both deserve the best. Better get to bed or you won't be in time with your lamps in the morning."

"Goodnight, Mollie."

"Goodnight, Dicky."

Molly sat with her elbows on the watch-room table and tears pricked her eyes.

"She'll get her man," she murmured, "I've lost mine. Did you die quickly, Johnnie boy, when you lay there in the snow? Did you call for me?"

Her tears fell on the open logbook. She picked up the blotting paper and soaked them up. The substation was quiet around her except for the heavy breathing of Cissie Spence who lay asleep on a trestle bed against the wall.

She felt in her pocket and brought out a cigarette packet. It was empty. She swore softly, got up and tiptoed out into the yard. She would be able to hear the telephone from the gate where Charlie Pierce was on duty.

"You got a cigarette, Charlie?"

"Of course, I 'ave, anything for you, my old duck."

He produced a packet of Woodbines and a box of matches.

"Has Taff Davies gone to bed? I could do with a fag myself."

"Yes, I think so. We'd better stand around the corner to light up. If we're caught, I'd be in just as much trouble for leaving the watch-room as you would be for smoking on gate duty."

"Ah, that's right girl. Look at that old moon up there. They can't black that out, now can they? In the last war the Zeppelins used to come over on the moonlit nights. It was the only way that they could find their way around."

"Yes, it's nice to see the moon. Johnnie's last letter told me to look at the moon at ten o'clock one night and he'd be looking at it at the same time. It would make us closer, he said, looking at the same moon. I came out here in the yard and it was all clouds. I wish it had been clear that night."

His hand went to her shoulder.

"You're doing well, my old duck. You're fighting 'ard. Time'll 'elp you."

"They all say that, but I can't believe it."

"It's true enough. You'll see."

"Did you see 'er little ladyship tripping in 'arf an hour ago. She came walking down Rampton Road in the moonlight as if 'er feet was 'ardly touchin' the ground," she said.

"What's 'appened?"

"Her mum's agreed to Brusher White going home with her for their annual. I suppose so that she can give him the once over."

"Well that's nice, better than flying off the 'andle. You know, if she's anything like her daughter she must be a very nice lady, very nice. Nowt wrong with it, you know. She's top people and Brusher's going to the top one day, you mark my words!"

"Yes, Brusher'll go to the top in this old lark but it's not her family's sort of top you know. I wonder whether they'll make it and if they do whether it'll work?" she looked at her watch.

"Time, I gave Cissie a shake and told her to take over the telephone. What time's your relief, Charlie?"

"Only another 'arf hour. You go and get some sleep, my old china. The old Dutch is expecting you to tea tomorrow."

"I won't forget Charlie. Good night. See you tomorrow."

"Goodnight Mollie."

He contemplated the glowing stub end of his cigarette as she walked away.

He softly said, "War widows. To think you'd be seeing them again at your time of life, Charlie Pierce. God bless 'er and God bless little Dicky Finch and the best of British luck to 'er and 'er Brusher."

Ernest Cliff was made a red rider the next day and was posted to station 69. Janet was detailed to drive him in the spare taxi to hand in his AFS uniform and to collect his LFB kit. He came out wearing his round cap and brass buttoned undress tunic, carrying a bulging kit bag and a large parcel, which he sat beside the taxi's driving seat.

"Cor! Two of everything, leather fire boots and all. It ain't right you know, like a privileged class, ain't we? All this and the extra money. I'll pay you off the rest of the little bit I owe you now, Dicky."

"All right Ernie, no hurry you know. How's things going with Edie these days?"

"Oh, that's all over. She's a bit daft you know. She wouldn't have copped out like she did if she 'adn't been. It wasn't all my fault. She thought that she knew it all but of course she didn't. I'm going to be in Brusher White's watch. Tell 'im 'e's not to be too strict with me. 'E ought to be all right eh, with this new unification scheme coming along. Fancy going to make up all those ranks to bring the officer establishment up to the number of regulars and AFS what's serving. Some of 'em are going to be AFS blokes they say. What'll some of the regulars say when they have to take orders from an AFS bloke? What'll

Brusher say?"

"He'll do what he's told as usual and do it well."

"Ah, that's the right way. That's me. Do you think they might make me a sub one day? They're talking about some of the AFS blokes at HQ being made up as high as district officers. That'll cause a stir. I'm sorry to be leaving substation 69Y. I've got some good chinas there. You coming to my farewell party, Dicky?"

"Yes, I'll be there. Blue watch is on duty anyway."

Chamberlain had resigned and the party was interrupted to listen to Winston Churchill's first broadcast as Prime Minister. The German attack on Holland and Belgium had started and there was an air of tension in the hitherto calm May evening. They stood and sat around the old wireless set, forgotten glasses held in their hands. The decisive confident voice finally stopped speaking and for a moment nobody said a word.

"Well, that's that."

"Cor! You 'eard what 'e offered us: blood, sweat, toil and tears. We've 'ad the sweat and toil when old Brewster come down to take the drill. 'E and poor old Mollie 'ave 'ad the tears. When does the blood start?"

"Started already, I should think for the poor fuckers in France. Come on, this is a party! Start the old piano going again, Harry."

"What'd you like: Land of Hope and fuckin' Glory?"

"No, play us Underneath the Arches."

At the end of the evening Station Officer Brewster called in. He stood with Sub-Officer Davies and slowly sipped a glass of beer watching the dancing.

At midnight, Davies rapped on the table and said, "Station Officer Brewster would like a few words with you."

He spoke quietly and directly. He hoped that they had heard Mr Churchill's broadcast, he thanked them for their eight months loyal service, he told them that their efficiency had increased throughout their time and he gave his opinion that it would soon be tested.

"'E ain't a bad old codger really," whispered Arthur Clayton to Janet and she nodded.

Davies rapped on the table again and said, "I 'ave just introduced Station Officer Brewster, the guvnor from station 69. Now, I just got some good news. In orders this evening 'is name appears among the list of newly promoted district officers and from tomorrow, though 'e will still be in direct command 'ere, we shall be calling 'im Mr Brewster."

They crowded round to congratulate him. The grim pale face was relaxed and smiling.

He walked to his car and got in.

"Goodnight, sir and congratulations again," said Taff Davies.

He drove back to station 69 and walked up the stairs to his quarters.

"Where've you been?" his wife demanded.

"You know where I've been dear, at a meeting at Southwark and a drill in the docks."

"That drill finished at eleven thirty. I heard the pump sent from here come in," came the reply.

"I called at a party at Y substation, I've ..."

"That's right, a party. You go out enjoying yourself and I'm left stuck here alone in quarters."

"I've got some news for you. I rang at seven. You weren't in."

"What news?"

"I've been made a district officer."

"You've been made a district officer. I got that from downstairs two hours ago. Call that promotion; being made district officer? Thirty names in the list under the unification scheme, three of them ex AFS. You only just escaped being commanded by an ex AFS man. That's all you did. If you had any go in you, you'd have been a substantive district officer years ago then you'd have been a superintendent under unification.

"Now here I got to kowtow to the new superintendent's wives when I meet them at a social; and another thing, you took two hours short leave yesterday afternoon. Did you ask me if I'd like to go to the pictures? No. You puts your civvy hat on downstairs and go sloping off with the AFS messenger kid in the park. What's the idea? Do you want your men to think you're queer or something?"

"I'm sorry, Doris. He's a nice kid, big family, doesn't get much attention at home, I should think, and well, somehow he reminds me of somebody."

"He reminds you of somebody does he? You got our boy killed by pushing him into the navy when he didn't want to go and then you start making a fuss of a snotty nosed little urchin from a back-street home and ask him up here to tea to eat our rations. Where do I come in?"

His hand went to his pocket and the bottle of bismuth tablets there and his eyes blazed with anger. He turned on his heel and went through the door and down the stairs. Stopwatch in hand he pulled the brass knob on the front of the station and the alarm bells sounded.

"Where to?" said the duty man opening the wicket gate.

"Turn out for drill."

He inspected the crews with caustic comments on dress and turnout; wrote the time in the occurrence book and then he got into his car and made the tour of his five substations.

Bert Foster's homemade fire alarm system sounded at substation 69Y and the men rolled out of bed and into boots, leggings and tunics. He used two stopwatches and timed each machine through the gate.

"Not over an hour ago, Sub-Officer Davies, I think that I complimented you and your substation on increasing efficiency. A turnout time of over thirty seconds for some of your crews seems to indicate that I was mistaken. See me at nine o'clock."

"Cor, the rotten old bastard. Comes 'ere all social like and drinks our beer an' we says 'goodnight, sir' and 'congratulations sir' and e' says 'goodnight all' with the nearest 'e gets to a smile on 'is ugly mug. Then 'e comes sneaking back with this bloody caper. There's no fuckin' accounting for some fuckin' people."

The news from France grew worse and the cautiously worded BBC bulletins and over optimistic newspaper headlines no longer disguised the fact that the British army was retreating to the Channel and that the French army was disintegrating.

"We was getting on all right till that little old King Leopard packed it in," said Bert Foster. "Any 'ow, what happened to that Maginot line they was always talking about?"

"There wasn't no Maginot line where the Jerries came through."

"Well, I call that plain daft."

The evening paper lay in Bert's lap.

"You see these pictures of great big oil fires at Dunkirk? Now that would be a nice little blaze to be called to. I wouldn't mind that at all."

"You'd better 'urry up and send your name in then. Cissie Spence 'as just 'eard over the blower from station 69 they're calling for volunteers to take the big fireboat that lies at Blackfriars pier over. What's 'er name?"

"The *Massey Shaw*"

"Ah, that's it."

"Well they can't be expecting no raids 'ere if they're sending that over."

"Where do you send your name in?"

"Sit down Bert. Don't get so fuckin' excited. It's river service only and it's over fuckin' subscribed. They got two hundred names in and asked for twenty. That's what the Sub in station 69s watch-room said. They're loading 'er up with fuckin' foam and going over this evening."

It was three days before they learned the reason why the *Massey Shaw* had gone to Dunkirk, not to fight fires but to help in the evacuation of the British army. A mixed air of tension and depression hung over the station in the fine midsummer weather as the news grew worse each day.

"So, the fuckin' French 'ave packed it in and we're all on our own now. Well, the fuckers never was much fuckin' good. My lot was alongside 'em in 1918. Blimey, they was dirty fuckers in the trenches and the buggers only shaved about once a fuckin' week."

"Do you reckon it's possible to take the Germans on all alone?"

"Of fuckin' course it's possible. If it isn't, you're going to 'ave little old Nazis in top fuckin' boots fuckin' bossing you about. You wouldn't like that, now would you?"

"I wouldn't mind that so much as those bleeding Italians bossing me about."

"Well neither of 'ems going to. You 'eard what Winnie said. We'll fight 'em on the beaches; we'll fight 'em in the streets; where else did 'e say we'll fight 'em? Every fuckin' where I reckon."

"Well if we're going to fuckin' fight 'em we might as well get out of this lark and go for sogers."

"You can forget all about that," said Taff Davies, entering the mess room with a piece of paper in his hand. "I'm just going to pin this up on the notice board, but for the benefit of those who can't bloody read, I'll tell you what it says: 'Police and Fireman Employment Order 1939 SRKO No. 1041' is its 'eading and it goes on to say in a great many words that you can't no longer give a week's notice and scarper off out of it. You're frozen in this 'ere service for the duration and if anyone goes absent without leave, 'e'll be taken before a magistrate and be fined or put in chokey. So now you know and I've another nice little surprise for you. All pumps on this station are ordered to a night exercise in Surrey Commercial Docks at twenty-three hundred hours. The super and the DO will be there, so let's 'ave everybody properly dressed and on their toes."

The drills and the exercises took on a new meaning with the realisation that the German air force was now ensconcing itself on Dutch, Belgian, and French airfields less than a hundred miles away. Orders came to clear away the rotting sandbags from the watch-room window and contractors came to replace them with a neat blast wall of reinforced concrete and brickwork.

"That's better," said Edith Brown. "Those old sandbags were beginning to pen and ink. I reckon that the gateman wasn't too particular when 'e got taken short during the night. It lets a bit of light in too. You could almost do without the electric when the sun's shining. And now the post office men 'ave been and stuck a couple of extra phones in. Somebody must be expecting something to 'appen. Looks like we'll be using your old calling-out apparatus Bert."

"Well, it'll work when it's wanted. 'Ere, you 'eard? German planes 'ave raided Falmouth and dropped bombs. What if they don't never come to London 'cause the barrage balloons is too thick? That'll be a sell won't it?"

"I don't know. I don't fuckin' reckon I want to be bombed. I don't know if I shouldn't get the wind up."

"You'd be all right, Edie, sitting in there be'ind your little old blast wall answering the dog and sending us out to fight the fires. You got on the rota for your week's annual yet?"

"Yes, 25 July. Don't know where to go though. Nearly all the seaside's restricted area."

"'Ow about you, Dicky? 'Aving a bit of trouble fitting it in at the same time as Brusher aren't you?"

"No. It's fixed now, 18 August."

"Cor! That'll be the day when young Brusher gets 'is legs under your mum's ma'ogany. 'Ow'll 'is table manners stand up to it do you reckon?"

"Perfectly well, I'm sure."

"You got to be right; 'es a good old boy. Best of luck to you both come 18 August."

The day came bright, warm and clear with the Battle of Britain still at its height. The Alvis was filled up from hoarded petrol coupons and they met at the Bermondsey garage where it had been kept since September.

"Do you think I ought to go, Janet? Things are really hotting up. A hundred and twenty German planes shot down yesterday. They must start on London soon. It would be awful if I was to miss it."

"Do you really mean it, Bill? Or is it cold feet because you're going to meet my mother. She's not a dragon you know."

"A bit of both per'aps. It's a lovely day to see a bit of the country. Come on. Let's go."

"Do you want to drive?"

"If you like and we'll swap over when I get lost in the

wilds of Norfolk."

They arrived early in the afternoon. Mrs Carew-Finch heard the car on the gravelled drive and went to the front door.

"Mummy darling, it's so nice to be home again." They hugged and kissed. "And this is Bill."

He put his own and Janet's suitcase down on the steps.

"How do you do, Mrs Carew-Finch? It is very kind of you to invite me."

They left a week later, and she stood by the front door again, watching the blue Alvis turn out of the gate in the evening light. The phone was ringing, and she went indoors to answer it.

"Brandon 330."

"That you, Betty? Neville here. I suppose they've left you. Don't think me inquisitive but I couldn't help ringing to find out what you make of the situation now."

"No, I don't think that you're inquisitive. In fact, it's nice of you to ring. They left half an hour ago and they are now officially engaged. I suppose that I should send the announcement to *The Times*."

"Engaged with your blessing?"

"Oh Neville, what can I say? I suppose so. They're so hopelessly in love and oh my goodness, he's so handsome and so kind to her and he's been so helpful to me. You know Hart has been called up and the garden was getting in an awful state. I just had to order him to stop working and relax.

"You never saw lawn edges so beautifully cut, as though they had been done with a ruler and I've been waiting for the plumber for six weeks, half his men have been called up too. Well, I don't need one now. It's all been done with the real professional touch. And he didn't eat peas with a knife or any of the other awful things I was afraid he might do.

"There were lots of rough edges of course but I feel sure that they can be smoothed off. I know it's an awfully snobbish term, but he is definitely one of nature's gentlemen and I'm very fond of him already. Well what could I do? At least, if this war turns the whole world upside down, she'll have a man who can turn his hand to anything apparently."

"She may get over it and break it off."

"If she does do, you know I would feel some regrets though I always thought of a big wedding into one of the county families, with the bride's mother a gracious hostess and dear Uncle Neville giving her away. Now I suppose, if it happens, it will be one of those hurried little war weddings like we both had: all khaki and courage. Only it won't be khaki."

"No, it won't, my dear, it'll be dark blue. You know she's been to see me several times lately. I've got a feeling that she's not only in love with young Bill but with this extraordinary service of his with its tradition and discipline like the guards, and all run by a Labour controlled LCC. It seems to have got right into her bones. I told her that I've got friends who could fix her up with a commission in the ATS, in a matter of weeks and she laughed me to scorn. Well, what's the form now? When are they going to get married?"

"They promised that it will be at least a six months engagement but it's official. They went off into Norwich and he bought her a ring. Quite good taste. I don't know how he could have afforded it on less than five pounds a week. I don't know how they're going to live. He's as proud as a peacock and I can't see him accepting any sort of allowance. I'm sure he'll get promotion but he's been perfectly frank. He could never get higher than superintendent at the best. All the top officers are direct entries from the services."

"That might not be for so long. By the time this war's over lots of things will change."

"Do you think so? Oh God! Aren't these anxious times? Is it true they're flattening our fighter aerodromes one after another and don't mind how big their losses are while they do it? And when we've got no fighters left, they're going to invade."

"That's careless talk, I should say. Look, old girl, I've got to walk down to the rescue depot now. A Spanish chap who was in Guernica when it was bombed is going to give us a talk on how to pick up a bombed house brick by brick to get the people out from underneath, Don't want to be late. Tell Janet to come and see me anytime if she's at a loose end or wants anything."

"Yes, I will, Neville. I'm very anxious about her. If raids do start, I suppose the fire brigade is well equipped with shelters for women staff."

"Oh, sure to be. Must go now. Goodnight, Betty."

"Goodnight, Neville and thank you for ringing."

"So, your mum's agreed and you're going to be

married in the spring. Well, that's very nice," said Charlie Pierce. "Are you going to ask us all to the wedding?"

"Oh yes! And I hope that you'll all come."

"'Ere can you 'ear what I think I can 'ear?"

A distant siren was wailing the red warning note. It was taken up by a nearer one and seconds later, the warm late August night vibrated with the sound as the siren in Rampton Road howled out its message.

They sat listening until the last ululation died away.

"Well that's the first fuckin' time we've 'eard that fuckin' din since last September," said Arthur Clayton.

Sub-Officer Davies hurried in.

"Come on, get rigged all of you. Drivers get outside and check pumps and towing vehicles and then return to the mess room. Orders are to keep under cover until turned out for a fire."

"'Is exact words 'e used last September fourth. I wonder whether it's a fuckin' false alarm this time."

The telephone rang in the watch-room and they heard Section Officer Casey answer.

"One self-propelled, one escape carrier, four trailer pumps fully manned. Sub-Officer Davies in charge."

"'Oo, was that?" said Davies going to the watch-room door.

"Station 69 asking for our availability."

"Blimey! That's been sent up to the fuckers every fuckin' day for the past eleven and an 'alf fuckin' months."

They stood in the mess room, the men fully rigged in boots, leggings and fire tunics, gas masks on their chests, steel helmets on their heads. Outside, the night was very quiet. Janet had put on her steel helmet and she stood next to Fred Mason.

"You all right, Dicky?" said the old man.

"Yes, of course I'm all right."

"Don't know what we do if it's the real thing this time. We're both spare drivers. Nothing for us to drive bar the spare taxi. Per'aps they'll send us round in them, taking messages. Ought to be a shelter 'ere for you young ladies. Still they reinforced the watch-room. You ought to go in there."

"No. I'm all right here, Fred."

The men were edging closer to the door into the yard and they were soon spilling out around the porch.

"Listen everybody!"

For the first time they heard the peculiar irregular beat of the unsynchronised engines of the German bombers.

"There's planes up there."

"Probably ours, patrolling."

"No, we're firing at them. Look. There's a tracer."

In the distance, red blobs were chasing one another from the ground and disappearing into the sky.

"Where's old Taff?"

"'E's gone in the watch-room."

"Let's get up on the roof. We'll get a better butcher's from there."

Eight men with Janet and Mabel Smith were soon on the flat roof between the gables.

"Nothing else to see from 'ere," said Bert Foster as a low loud whistling rent the air.

They threw themselves flat on the narrow leads. Piled

one on top of the other. Four loud thuds followed.

"Fuckin' 'ell. That was bombs. I saw 'em fuckin' burst," said Bert, "right over there. Cor! I thought they was coming on top of us."

"Over where?"

"Over there! Look, there's a fire starting."

"Crikey that's a long way away. That could be the ones we 'eard whistling down."

"Yes, it was. I saw the fuckers burst. Fuckin' great red flashes."

"Where the fuck is it, do you think?"

"Dunno. Let's ask Taff."

They went to the watch-room.

"Ask station 69 where it is," said Sub-Officer Davies.

Section Officer Davies picked up the telephone.

"They say it's in Fore Street in the City and they've asked for forty pumps. There's another one not so big in the East End."

"Forty pumps," said Bert. "They'll be calling us to that."

"No, they won't. You just hold on, old cock, until another one on our side of the friggin' river turns up."

A little later the sirens sounded the all clear.

Half relieved and half disappointed, the crews put away their gear and went to bed.

"Well, if an air raid's no worse than that we 'aven't much to worry about," said Jack Adams.

Three days later Mrs Bridger sent for Janet.

"I suppose you've never driven a lorry, Finch. It's quite easy really. Just like a car only bigger. The trailer pumps have rather small petrol tanks and there was some trouble in refuelling them at Fore Street the other night.

"The brigade is going to put some petrol lorries on the run. They will be loaded up from can stock and driven round to any really big fires that happen in the future. It's really a job for the C class men but there are not enough of them who are drivers.

"I think that it's a job you could do, and substation 69Y has enough room in its yard for two lorries. I want you to take one of them over. Remember it is all can stock and therefore portable. You will be in charge of about three hundred and fifty two-gallon cans, which in these days of rationing is a heavy responsibility.

"Go to station 60, Southwark and see Station Officer Price. He is expecting you and he has arranged a driving lesson for you, and he will then hand over the lorry and its load for you to take to substation 69Y."

Station Officer Price was a small dark fellow who looked Janet up and down with an appraising eye.

"So, you've been posted as a lorry driver. What've you driven so far?"

"Only cars and taxis."

"Well it's just the same; only bigger and harder on the steering. Remember your width when cornering and use your gears on hills when loaded. You'll sail up in top when you're empty. They're all old 'uns that have been requisitioned. You'd better take this one. It's loaded and sheeted down. Have a look at the knots and sheets once or twice a day and if you see any of 'em undone or tied differently you'll know someone's been at it. Can't be too careful. All these AFS skulking around and petrol is a bit of a touchy subject with all the tankers being sunk in the Channel."

"Are the AFS so much worse than the LFB?"

"Sorry, perhaps I shouldn't have said that with you being in the AFS yourself, but they haven't got their whole career to think of, you know, and they didn't have to give references before they joined."

The lesson was completed within an hour.

"You'll do," said Station Officer Price. "Take her to substation 69Y and don't forget to use your mirror in traffic."

Janet drove into the yard at substation 69Y to find Sub-Officer Davies waiting for her.

"Stick it over there next to the other one and get it washed down and smartened up; all bright parts polished. Blimey 'ere's a responsibility for a mere sub-officer — seven 'undred tins of petrol on my substation."

Fred Mason was already busy hosing down the other lorry.

"Got a nice little number 'aven't we, Dicky, driving these around? I reckon we'll be popular with the ones that 'ave got motorbikes and a bit short of petrol coupons. I wonder what will 'appen if a load of incendiaries falls on the back of one of these when we're driving it. Make a nice little blaze I should think."

The telephone rang in the watch-room and Section Officer Casey came to the door that led onto the yard.

"Air raid warning yellow, Sub-Officer."

It was the preliminary warning that enemy aircraft

were in the vicinity but not close enough to warrant the red warning and the sounding of sirens.

"Get rigged," said Davies.

The men stood about in their fire kit for an hour. Then the message 'Air raid warning white' was received and they took off their gear and relaxed again.

The last few days of August and the first few of September passed with yellow warnings becoming more frequent and there were a few minor scattered raids causing some fires to which substation 69Y was not called.

Bert Foster chafed with impatience.

"This bloody war'll end without us ever getting to a bleedin' fire," he said. "There ain't even been a fuckin' red warning today."

The watch-room telephone rang and seconds later Bert's alarm system was ringing with green, red, yellow and blue lights flashing.

"Self-propelled and three trailer pumps that includes me," he shouted as he joined in the scramble for fire tunics and leggings which hung on hooks against the wall.

"Must be a peace time one. The little old sirens 'aven't gone."

Sub-Officer Davies ran to the watch-room. "Where to?"

Cissie Spence handed him a written message.

'Take your self-propelled and three trailer pumps to Thames Haven. Report to divisional officer in charge'.

"Thames Haven. Blimey! That's twenty miles beyond the LCC area."

Outside, the self-propelled and three taxis burst into

life with much revving of engines.

Davies ran to each of the three taxi drivers and said, "Thames Haven, oil fire, follow the self-propelled, keep close and don't miss the way."

The four vehicles, with dimmed sidelights and single hooded headlights, pulled out of the yard, turned right into Rampton Road and were away. Janet and Fred Mason watched them go.

"'Ear what 'e said. Keep close and don't lose the frigging way. Blimey! Those bleeding taxicabs are going to 'ave a job. That self-propelled fucker's got a Ford eight engine under 'er bonnet and them taxis was built for two passengers and a bit of luggage. Think of 'em trying to keep up carrying a crew of five and all that fuckin' 'ose on top and towing a trailer pump an' all. They was never made for that job and they aren't up to it."

Bert Foster sat next to Sub-Officer Davies in the front of the self-propelled pump.

"Aren't you going to ring the bell, Sub?"

"What's the good of ringing the bell? There's no fuckin' traffic and we've got three bleedin' trailer-pumps tagging along behind, and I've got to get them to their destination."

"Go on, Sub, just a bit of a ring. I ain't never been to a fire on a fire engine before and I always thought of weaving through the traffic with the bell ringing. This don't seem right."

They came to a crossroads and Davies humoured him with a loud jangling of the bell. The dark deserted East End streets gave way to scattered factories and then to open country.

Jack Adams bent over the wheel, peering through the windscreen and trying to see the road, with the inadequate hooded headlights. All signposts had been removed lest they should assist invading troops or parachutists.

"Fuckin' 'ell, I 'ope we're on the right fuckin' road," said Davies. "Are the others there still be'ind us?"

"Yes, I can see 'em, Sub. 'Ere what's that in front?"

The Eastern sky was suffused with a red glow.

"That'll be it," said Davies. "We shan't miss the way now, oil tanks well alight. If it's one of the big tank farms they'll be about forty foot 'igh and 'old about twelve thousand tons of oil or petrol each. You're going to 'ave a nice little bit of practice on your 'ands me 'earties."

The glow grew larger and brighter and soon they could discern the shape of the huge cylindrical tanks, topped by red flames and a great cloud of smoke, which stood out as a jet-black smudge against the dark blue sky.

"Cor! 'ow's any number of 'uman beings going to put that lot out. Do we use foam, Sub?"

"Doubt it. Doubt if you could get near enough because of the 'eat to get foam onto those. I never seen anything like that in all my service. But I ain't in charge, thank Gawd. When we gets there, I takes orders and carries 'em out. An' just all of you do likewise."

They could see the road and hedges plainly now in the lurid red light and they soon passed through the gates into the tank farm, a chequered flag by a telephone kiosk marking the control point. Davies jumped down and ran to it and saluted.

"Self-propelled and three trailer pumps from substation 69Y, sir. Sub-Officer Davies in charge."

They strained their ears to hear the answer of the control point officer, but it was drowned by the roar of flames and pump engines. He ran back to his crews.

"We're to get to work from the bund, two jets from each pump. Follow the self-propelled."

They bumped over lines of hose; iron hard from the pressure of water pumped from the fireboats moored along the riverbank and jetty. The bund was a rectangular ramp that enclosed each tank farm, sloping up from the outer side and with a perpendicular face about five feet high, facing inwards. Its purpose was to contain the contents of the tanks if they were accidentally ruptured.

About forty pumps, mostly the big red regular machines, were parked around the bund wall on which two hundred firemen stood directing jets onto twelve furiously blazing tanks and providing a water curtain between them and eight others, which were so far undamaged.

As they got closer, the heat hit them as though from a furnace door. The tanks towered above their heads like huge squat chimneys belching flame and dense black smoke, through which red tongues flickered.

Some of the tanks had holes in their sides caused by bomb splinters and from these, oil or petrol spurted into the bund below, across which great gouts of flame occasionally ran. They were doused by the spray falling from more than eighty powerful jets or, if they persisted, by a pair of firemen lowering their branch and hitting the flame with a solid jet.

The men from substation 69Y uncoupled the trailer pumps, pushed them up the slopes and backed the self-propelled up.

"'E can't mean to pump out of that" said Harry Booth. "It's all oil and petrol. Look, it keeps catching fire."

"Do what you're fuckin' told and don't be a twerp. It's only oil on top. It's the water from all those 'oses underneath," shouted Davies. "Get all eight of our jets concentrated around the top of that tank. Its aviation spirit and they're anxious to save it."

The suctions dropped in and the engines roared as the primers were depressed to fill the pump casings. The valves were opened and the flat hose behind the branch hardened and straightened and water shot from the branches, crackling loudly at first with expelled air that had been trapped. The needles on the pump gauges rose slowly to pounds pressure. The eight jets hit the top of the distant tank and broke into spray that was tossed into the air as steam. It showed as a grey smudge against the black smoke. The tank still roared and flamed.

Bert Foster held the branch with Harry Booth backing him up, lying against his back and holding on. For two hours they held the heavy back pressure and watched the solid column of water break up against the tank.

"Cor! My arms don't 'arf ache."

"Well, for Gawd's fuckin' sake don't fuckin' let go, Bert. If this fucker were to take fuckin' charge it would be like a dancing fuckin' dervish."

"Couldn't we ask Jack to ease the pressure off a bit so that we can change places?"

"I'd ask 'im mate but 'e can't fuckin' 'ear from 'ere and if I was to leave you, this fucker'd lift you right off your fuckin' feet."

"Taff Davies ought to be around seeing to that. Eh, look to your left there's 'is fuckin' nibs."

Fifty yards away the divisional officer was standing on the bund wall. They saw the solid jets around him fall away in a graceful arc and disappear.

"'Ullo! They've knocked off. What are they doing?"

"Sticking another length of 'ose in by the look of it."

"What for? They can't get any closer. Blimey look! 'E's taking them into the bund. That can't be safe. It keeps catching fire."

The divisional officer had clambered down the bund wall and he stood waist deep in the water on which floated several inches of oil and petrol. He waded slowly towards the tank, shielding his face from the heat with his arms. Behind him the branch men were following dragging their uncharged hoses behind them. They saw the jets start up and hit the tops of the burning tanks again in a great spurt of spray and steam.

"Fuckin' Christ, I wouldn't like to be one of that lot," said Harry Booth.

They heard a voice shouting, "Knock off!" and suddenly the intolerable pressure eased.

"Cor! What a fuckin' relief," said Bert Forster.

"Come on, 'Arry. Swop places quickly before they boost 'er up again."

A district officer who was unknown to them, shouted, "Get another length into those eight lines."

Behind them the couplings were broken and another seventy-five-foot length of hose was inserted between them and the pump. With the pumps ticking over instead of roaring at full throttle, they heard the officer say to Davies.

"This is bloody madness. Let's hope there isn't a boil over."

He walked to the bund and dropped in.

"Come on follow me. It's nice and warm."

They followed and the warm water flowed over the top of their boots and soaked their tunics to their skin.

"What's a boil over, sir?" asked Bert Foster.

"The water going into those tanks sinks to the bottom. If too much goes in it gets up to the hot oil level and turns to steam. That mixes with the oil and about two hundred tons of it will be slung over the top of the tank well alight. Now there are six branches covering us from the bund wall so don't panic if this lot catches fire around you. They'll knock it out."

He waded forward and they dragged their hose behind him. Suddenly he disappeared. One of the bombs that had done the damage had left a crater in the floor of the bund.

"Where's 'e gone?" said Harry Booth.

The oily surface was disturbed, and a steel helmet appeared as the district officer, spluttering and swearing clambered out.

"Bloody bomb hole there. Work around to the right of it."

The heat was intolerable, and they were glad when he halted them at last and gave the order for water on.

High above their heads, the fire from the roof ruptured tank roared as it flamed and belched black smoke. Their solid jet hit it from forty feet away and the warm water splashed back into their scorched faces. Huge clouds of steam whitened the smoke. To their right, a great gout of flame shot across the bund and seemed to envelope a crew. Immediately, five heavy jets from the bund wall were diverted onto them and the flame flickered and went out.

There was another officer behind them.

"Come on. You're winning. You're winning. Move in."

Harry and Bert tugged on the heavy bucking branch and staggered a few steps forward into another bomb crater. The oil closed over their heads and they dropped the branch, but the water damped its back pressure and it only swayed slowly like some long sea serpent. The sides of the crater had an easy slope and they scrambled out and retrieved the branch. The water was getting deeper and colder as the fireboats pumped it from the river to the pumps that sent it into the fire. It grew darker as the great flames from the tanks diminished.

"You're winning. Move in. Keep moving in."

There was a faint red glow in the East. It was getting lighter. Their tank only smoked and steamed, and the sun came up to reveal the eight undamaged tanks still intact and only two of the others both twisted and distorted to half their original forty feet of height still burning.

"Knock off. Get out of the bund. We can get close enough with foam on those."

Sodden and weary they climbed out of the bund

dragging the hose behind them. Fresh crews with foam branches led by an officer, waded out towards the two crumpled tanks among the ruins of which pockets of flame still showed.

"They're going our way, Bert. This'll be worth watching."

The officer disappeared into the bomb crater.

"We ought to have shouted to warn 'im."

"He wouldn't have taken any notice of an AFS man."

***

Charlie Pierce arrived at substation 69Y with the oncoming Red watch.

"Where is everybody?"

"They've gone to a fire. That's everybody except the escape carrier crew, Fred Mason and us girls," said Edith Brown. "It was down at Thames Haven out of our area. Oil tanks set alight."

"Did Bert Foster go?"

"Yes 'e went."

"Cor, that'll please 'im. When are they coming back?"

"Gawd knows."

They arrived back at ten thirty that morning. They were stiff with cold, despite the warm September sun with scorched and blackened hands and faces, their sodden uniforms smelling of oil and petrol. Davies climbed down stiffly from the self-propelled.

"All right, no drill this morning, get that hose off and start scrubbing it."

White watch got fell in for dismissal.

"You can all go home for a change and a bath, you lucky people."

"Fuck me. I don't know what my missis will say when she sees me under clothes," said Bert Foster. "She won't let me in the 'ouse like this."

"Never mind, Bert you've been to a fire. Did you enjoy it?"

"Can't say I did. Can't say I didn't. There weren't no crowds being held back by the rozzer's like I always imagined. Not a soul there but firemen. I don't think I want another fire of that particular sort some'ow."

"Did you get bombed?"

"So, they told us this morning, when we was leaving. I 'eard some ack, ack guns cracking off from over the marshes once, but, honest to Gawd, I never noticed fuck all else."

They rigged up a line hung with blankets across the recreation room to screen it: from the watch-room and the entrance to the women's dormitory and they stripped off their wet clothing. The oil clung to the cloth and to their skins and they scrubbed one another with nailbrushes and soap and then they bent low over the infants' washbasins trying to wash the stains from their shirts, socks and underwear. Another line was hung across the yard and the washing including fifteen sets of uniforms hung out in the sun. Davies changed into his spare uniform and he rang station 69 for instructions.

"All right, since you been up all night you can go to bed. White watch will see to the 'ose."

Draped in blankets, they retired gratefully to the dormitory. It was the best of early September weather with a warm sun shining in a cloudless sky. Janet was sent to the stores with the spare taxi and she returned to find Agnes Jenkins making corned beef sandwiches to send to the men's dormitory.

"It'd be a pity to make them get up for dinner after they'd worked so 'ard all night," she mumbled.

"Besides, it wouldn't be right for 'em all to be sat down at table starkey bollocky and me waiting on 'em. Cor! I don't know what my late 'usband would say to that."

Janet walked past the men's dormitory at four o'clock and Harry Booth, a towel round his middle looked out.

"Eh Dicky, I've had a lovely zizz but I'm getting a bit restless now. Just go and feel my shirt and underpants and see if they're dry. They're on the right of the line."

She went out and felt the darned clothing and brought it back.

"It's not too bad Harry. It's been a lovely day."

"Bring mine too, Dicky!"

"And mine!" shouted the others.

"Oh, go and get 'em yourself," shouted Edith Brown. "We won't look at you."

By five o'clock most of the Blue watch were sitting about in their under clothes. The heavy uniform trousers and jackets were still damp, oil soaked and odorous. The sirens went at a quarter past five.

"Get rigged!" shouted Davies.

"We know, you silly old bastard. We can hear," said

Alf Newton under his breath. "It's a disgrace. We ought to have two sets of fuckin' gear like you've got."

They stood in the recreation room and listened to a series of distant explosions. Arthur Clayton was near the door.

"'Ere take a butchers' at what's going on up there."

They spilled out into the yard. High in the blue sky, the German planes in V formation were plainly visible, the sun shining on their fuselages making them glint like silver. Black puffs of anti-aircraft shells burst behind them.

"We're firing at them. Crikey! We ain't getting very close though."

"Cor! Take a butchers' over there."

To the east, great flames could be seen leaping high over the rooftops.

"That's Surrey Docks."

"No, it ain't. It's too far away."

"Bet you it's the docks.

"'Ere, Sub, shouldn't we be turning out to that lot?"

Davies went to the watch-room.

"Ring station 69 and say there's a very big fire to the south east of us, visible from the station yard, ask them — shall we turn out?"

Section Officer Casey put the phone down.

"They say it's out of the LCC area at West Ham. They've asked for a hundred pumps from London for reinforcements and sixty-nine have turned out to fires in Spa Road. You're to stay put until ordered on. All gatemen are to be withdrawn and used to make up crews."

"Blimey! All gatemen to be withdrawn after standing

out on the pavement there for over a year."

Davies went to the door and shouted.

"Auxiliary Fireman Clayton, you can come in and make up the spare man on number three's trailer pump!"

The crews stood in the yard and the recreation room listening to the thump of distant explosions and the occasional faint whistle of falling bombs.

The telephone rang and seconds later Bert Foster's apparatus showed every light.

"Where to?"

"Self-propelled and three trailer pumps to Surrey Commercial Docks. Report to control point at Canada Dock gate. Escape carrier to Spa Road. Report to officer in charge."

"I knew all along it was Surrey Docks," said Jack Adams as he climbed into the self-propelled. "'Aven't lived round 'ere all my life without knowing fuck something. West 'Am my arse!"

Only the women and Fred Mason were left at the station. He and Janet joined Section Officer Casey, Edith Brown and Mabel Smith in the watch-room.

"Any news?" asked Janet.

Miss Casey shook her head.

"They've told us not to ring them unless we've got something to ring about. They seem a bit harassed. I expect that you want to know where Sub-Officer White is. All I can tell you is that both station 69's red machines are out to Spa Road, so I expect that he's there."

They sat drinking tea while the section officer made up her occurrence book from the pencilled message sheets on the table. An hour later, the telephone rang.

"Air raid message White," she said putting down the receiver. "Well that was soon over. You can go and lie down, Smith and take over from Firewoman Brown at twenty-two hundred hours."

The siren sounded the all-clear sound and Janet followed Mabel Smith out of the watch-room.

"Let's go up on to the roof and see if we can see anything."

In the streets below, people were returning from the shelters carrying children and bedding. To the south-east the evening sky was suffused with a red glow and flames could be seen flickering above the rooftops. Grey smoke hung over Spa Road.

"Well that wasn't too bad," said Janet. "We didn't even really hear any bombs come down. The way we all fell in a heap up here when those dropped on Fore Street, I felt so silly afterwards."

"I didn't feel silly. I felt bloody frightened," said Mabel. "Give me the watch-room with the strengthened ceiling and the blast walls any time. I won't envy you, Dicky, with that old petrol lorry if you ever get sent out with it while a raid's on."

They sat at their vantage point, watching the fires and as dusk fell, the red glows seemed to increase.

"They don't seem to be putting them out very fast,." said Mabel.

It was dark when the wailing of the sirens startled them. By the time they reached the watch-room they could hear the whistle and thump of bombs. They hunched their shoulders as a louder whistle rent the air and the explosion rattled the windows and made the electric lamp and shade swing on their hanging flex.

"While I was doing the lamps, I saw six 'ouses 'ad been knocked down in Spa Road," said Fred Mason.

"Did you see the fire there?"

"Yes, Dicky, I saw it. There were ten pumps and the guvnor 'ad gone somewhere else and 'oo do you think was in charge? A sub-officer in charge of a ten-pump fire and doing it real proper by the look of things. Sub-Officer White I reckon 'is name was."

The old man grinned and winked.

"I'll go and get Aggie to make a cup of tea for you girls. She'll be getting windy all by 'erself in the kitchen."

A short loud whistle and a resounding crash shook the building and made the light swing violently. Agnes Jenkins appeared at the watch-room door, pale and shaken.

"Miss Casey, could I come and sit in the watch-room? I won't be in the way."

"Yes. Sit over there Jenkins, but Fireman Mason did say something about a cup of tea."

"I'll go and make it," said Fred.

"Ah thanks, Fred. The kettle's on and the mugs are out on the tray. There's a plate of rock buns there. Bring them and, I say, Fred, bring my teeth, will you? They're on the stove."

Aggie sat blinking in the strong light and then she got up.

"'E's no good at making tea. I'll go."

"Good," said Miss Casey, as Agnes left the room.

"She'll be much happier if she's kept busy."

They sat and drank tea as the raid went on around them. A cycle bell sounded outside, and they heard the door into the yard open.

"Who's that, I wonder?"

Edith Brown opened the watch-room door.

"'Ullo Bert what are you doing 'ere? White watch is on leave."

"Ah I know it is," said Bert Foster, "but crikey you want to see what's going on out there. There's fires everywhere. There's a bloody great 'ole in Rampton Road just near the police station and some of the glass is broken in the windows. I bet that shook the slops up in their little ol' basement shelter."

"It shook us up," said Miss Casey, "but you still haven't said why you're here?"

He looked embarrassed.

"Well you know what it is. There's a war on ain't there? They say we got more pumps than we can man. I thought if some of the off-duty watch reported; we could man one of the spare pumps."

"Blimey you're a glutton for punishment," said Edith Brown. "Thames Haven all last night and 'alf the morning and now you want to get mixed up in that lot outside."

Miss Casey picked up the telephone.

"I'll see what station 69 says."

She reported the presence of Auxiliary Fireman Foster, White watch, listened and then she turned to Bert.

"Members of the off-duty watch reporting at substations are to go to station 69. They've already made up one crew and have three waiting to form another. Off you go, Bert."

He left ringing his bell as he cycled across the yard.

"They told me they'd asked for two hundred pumps in Surrey Docks. All the timber's well alight, besides six ships and nine warehouses."

It was past midnight when the telephone rang.

The section officer wrote on a message slip with the receiver at her ear and then putting it down, she looked towards Janet.

"Number three petrol lorry to Woolwich Arsenal. Report at control point at main gate. Number four petrol lorry to Surrey Commercial docks. Report at Pageants Wharf fire station."

"Come on, Dicky. That's us," said Fred.

They went out into the yard to find the sky all around suffused with red light. They started up the lorries. Fred got down from his cab and lent into the window of Janet's.

"You know the way to Surrey Docks?"

Yes, I know it."

"All right, my old duck. You can follow me the first bit of the way."

He drove out of the yard and turned right down Rampton Road. The streets were completely deserted until they came to a fire where two pumps and an escape were at work, their hose lying across the road. Janet saw Fred's lorry bump over it and was about to follow but she was waved down by a sub-officer.

"Do you want to burst my bloody hose? Wait till I get a ramp round it."

The wooden hose ramps were thrown down and she drove carefully over them and accelerated to catch up with the dim rear lamp of the lorry in front. She hunched her shoulders as a tearing rushing sound rent the air and she saw a great orange flash where the tail lamp had been and, seconds later, she heard the roar of an explosion, which swept through the open window of the cab and rocked her in her driving seat. She had braked automatically and sat for a minute, watching a cloud of dust settling in the road ahead of her and lit by a house roof that was on fire. She slipped in the clutch and drove on. There was a crater in the road, and beside it, stood the tailboard of the lorry, nothing else.

Footsteps were running down the street and the sub-officer caught her arm.

"You all right, Miss?"

"Yes, I'm all right. But where's Fred Mason? Where's his lorry? Has it been blown to pieces?"

"He pointed to the burning roof. It's up there."

"It's got petrol aboard, cans. Is Fred all right? Is he still in it?"

"He's still in it but I doubt if he's all right. The cab's alight. We're dealing with it."

One of the pumps from the fire up the road drew alongside and the men at a smart trot, were running the escape by hand. It crashed against the side of the house and the sub-officer climbed it while a jet from the pump sprayed him and the burning lorry and roof.

She could see him tugging at the cab door surrounded by steam and smoke. Then he was coming down the escape with a smouldering bundle on his shoulders. He laid it in the road in the beam of the lorry's headlight. The steel helmet was canted over one side of the face and he took it off. Janet had turned her face away, but an irresistible urge made her look over the sub-officer's shoulder. The steel helmet had preserved one side of the lined old face. The other side from which charred flesh hung in an ugly fold, showed a blackened cheek and jawbone and an empty eye socket. The singed grey hair stirred in a gust of wind giving a hideous impression of life and movement.

She swayed and clutched the fireman next to her as she heard the sub-officer say, "He's a goner. Put him on the pavement and stick a salvage sheet over him. Put the branch on him first though. His tunic's still smouldering. You all right, Miss? You shouldn't have looked you know. Where you bound for?"

With a deep breath she pulled herself together.

"Yes, I'm all right. I'm bound for Surrey Docks."

"All right, get on your way. If you drive onto the pavement, you'll get past the crater. I'll send the message to control. Who was he and where was he ordered to?"

"He was Auxiliary Fireman Mason from substation 69Y ordered to Woolwich Arsenal," she said.

Janet drove over the curb and around the crater into Jamaica Road. It was a straight wide run now with the glow of fires ahead. She put her foot down, pressing the accelerator to the boards to shake off her horror. The lorry swayed as it overtook a row of trailer pumps drawn by overloaded taxis. She reached the corner of Lower Road, which was suffused by an angry red light that made the street almost as bright as day. An elderly air raid warden had taken up traffic direction at the junction and he waved her on as he held up more trailer pumps coming from the north.

An officer stopped her at the dock gate.

"Where are you ordered to?"

"Pageants Wharf."

"You'll have a job. Even the pavement blocks have been alight down Rotherhithe Road and that's the only way. You'd better hurry. Some of these pumps have been at work on full throttle since a quarter past five. They'll be running dry."

She swung round into Rotherhithe Street between the Thames on her left and on her right, great stacks of timber that blazed and crackled, sending flames and sparks a hundred feet into the air. Her right cheek began to scorch, and she tilted her steel helmet and her head towards the flames.

Hose lay across the road. Some was ramped, some not, and she bumped over it, praying that she had not caused a burst. She could see that in places the blocks of the wooden road had been on fire. The fire station came in sight, its yard facing the riverbank. Its doors, which stood open, showing empty appliance bays, faced Rotherhithe Road.

She pulled up and, looking through the appliance room, saw splintered baulks of timber lying in the yard. The small dry dock onto which fireboats were floated at high tide for repair had received a direct hit. The station itself had little glass intact and seemed deserted. She got down, found the watch-room and opened the door.

A section officer sat at a table with three firewomen and an AFS messenger.

Janet saluted and said, "Petrol lorry with three hundred and fifty cans from substation 69Y, Auxiliary Firewoman Finch in charge."

"You were sent for half an hour ago. You've taken your time. The divisional officer himself has been around here twice to enquire. It's been rough here. What's it like your way?"

"A bit rough. The driver of the other lorry's been killed."

"Well we only sent for one. Jimmy, scamper off and find the DO and tell him the petrol lorry's arrived. Know where he is? Down by Lavender Dock."

The boy put on his steel helmet and left the watch-room. Janet followed him to the station doors.

It was an awe-inspiring sight. Britain's main timber importing dock was a great sea of flame that stretched from the riverbank as far as the eye could see. The timber was stacked partly in the open up to forty feet high and partly in open shedding.

She could see two ships on fire in a minor dock and firemen with branches were scrambling over their superstructures. Flames were leaping a hundred feet in the air, and the fire roared and crackled, casting a red light as bright as day and making the place where Janet stood by the open appliance room door uncomfortably hot.

Above the noise of the fire, the whistle and the thump of bombs could be heard and each time the rows of firemen holding the branches down Rotherhithe Road lowered their heads and stooped slightly, so that they looked like a church congregation genuflecting.

A louder whistle made Janet step inside the appliance room as an officer came up to her.

"You brought the petrol lorry. Well, come on. Don't stand about. Get that tarpaulin off. Some of the pumps are running dry."

He was undoing the knots as he spoke, and she helped him.

"Right, get moving down the road that way. First lot of trailer pumps you come to, fill them up, then move on to the next lot. You needn't bother with the red appliances. They've got twenty-gallon tanks."

She slipped in the clutch and she drove twenty yards to a group of five trailers.

A sub-officer shouted, "Petrol up," above the noise of the roaring engines.

She dropped the tailboard and started handing out cans. She carried one to a pump and the operator lifted the bonnet and she began to pour the can's contents into the tank. The petrol slopped over the red-hot manifolds and she wondered why it did not catch fire.

The heat was scorching her face and when she lifted a hand to protect it the discomfort to her palm was just as bad. One of the nearby men beckoned to her and he put his hand to the solid jet that issued from his branch so that the cold river water sprayed over her face, hands and tunic.

"That'll damp you down for a bit, my duck. Won't last long though if you stick around 'ere."

Her tunic steamed and her hands and face were dry in

a minute, as she fetched more cans and put the empties back in the lorry. The officer appeared again.

"Christ! What do you think you're doing? Drop the cans by the pumps and drive on to the next lot. You can collect the empties tomorrow. How do you think you're going to get at the full cans if you've got a whole lot of empties on top? Stuff me! Some of you AFS are almost sub-human in intelligence."

She drove on and the men came to the tailboard and pulled off the cans. It took three hours to make a circuit of the dock and she arrived back at Pageants Wharf with an empty lorry.

"You'd better get back to your station and book in there," said the section officer. "Then, control'll tell you what to do."

She parked the lorry in substation 69Y's yard and went into the watch-room.

"Blimey! You seen your face?" said Mabel Smith. "It's all smuts."

"No, I haven't seen it. Fred Mason's been killed."

"Oh no! Poor old Fred."

"Where did it happen?" said Miss Casey sharply.

"In Acre Road. A bomb burst just behind his lorry and blew it right onto a house roof. It caught fire."

"What, you mean the petrol did? You sure he's dead?"

"Yes, horribly dead. I saw him. It was awful."

"Well, you shouldn't have looked. I'd better send up to control and book you returned. Go and have a wash and get a cup of tea. Aggie's got the kettle on."

The all clear sounded as dawn broke.

"Cor, what a relief!" said Mabel.

Janet looked at her watch. She was off duty at nine o'clock. The time went slowly, and the White watch reported for duty.

Miss Casey put their names in the occurrence book and said, "Well there's no officer to take the parade so you'd better just go."

She hurried out of the substation. Bill White normally met her halfway between it and station 69. There was no sign of him. She walked on to Piper Place and looked into the watch-room.

"Is Sub-Officer White back yet?"

"No. None of them are back. They're all still out at fires."

Disappointed she took the bus on her way to Kensington and Kitty Farrow's house.

Chapter 7

Each night, the sirens sounded at dusk and the all-clear came with the dawn. Sometimes there were minor daylight raids, which caused scattered fires. The substation fell into a new routine. The two-night duty watches would return wet and tired; one for dismissal, the other for a further twenty-four hours duty. The incoming watch would take over the cleaning, the servicing of vehicles and the drying and re-stowing of hose. There was no drill and the men were allowed to rest on their beds in the afternoon. Janet was kept busy throughout her forty-eight hours of duty periods,

Fred Mason had not been replaced, but a new lorry had arrived without petrol stock and it was used by her to collect hose from the streets and take it to the regular fire stations for drying in the hose towers. She also fetched stores and continued her morning and evening rounds of the red lamps on the street water tanks. And on the nights of heavy raids she would be sent out with the petrol lorry.

On a late September evening, she set out on her round of the lamps. A knot of men stood by the gate and Jack Adams lifted his hand to stop her.

"Aggie says it's what she calls luncheon meat for supper. I can't stand the stuff. Slip into Old Ma Judge's for me when you've finished your round, Dicky and get me a two and one."

He handed her the coppers.

"Do the same for me, Dicky."

"And for me. If we're going to be out all night again, I'd like a bit of 'ot supper inside me."

She made her round in the failing light, noting the new gaps in the buildings, caused by last night's raid. Finally, she pulled up at the fish and chip shop in Augur Street.

A line of people were waiting to be served.

Ma Judge looked up and said, "Hello, dearie, so, it's one of you is it?" And to her other customers she shouted. "Make way for the Fire Brigade."

"These people were before me," said Janet.

"That's all right. They won't mind, do you my dears?"

There was a general murmur of assent.

"Now, what can I do for you?"

"Four two and ones please."

"Four two and ones is it?"

She leaned confidentially over the counter.

"I've had to cut down on portions. Fish has gone up, so's fat and spuds. I didn't like to put my prices up like most people, so I'm selling smaller portions at the old price. There it is see, written up along with a little joke. You've got to keep your pecker up in times like these 'aven't you?"

She jerked her head towards a notice scrawled on the flyblown mirror.

'Owing to Hitler the fish will be littler. Owing to Hess the chips will be less'.

"There you are," she said, her voice dropping to a

whisper, "for you and your boys, the same price and the same size portions as before."

Janet drove into the yard, got down and joined the knot of men by the gate.

"It's in the taxi. Shall I put it in the oven to keep warm?"

"I'll eat it straight away," said Jack. "Old wailing Willie'll be sounding in a few fuckin' minutes I expect."

The sirens began on his cue. There was no longer a rush to don tunic, boots and leggings. The lag between the start of a raid and the first call to a fire was rarely less than a quarter of an hour.

They stood at the gate for a few moments, watching the sky and the people hurrying to shelters. Two policemen went by at a smart trot towards the police station and its shored-up basement.

"Run, rabbit, run!" shouted Jack Adams.

One turned his head, but he did not slacken his pace.

"You want to be careful," said Charlie. "It's best to keep on the right fuckin' side of those fuckers."

Davies stood at the schoolroom door and shouted across the yard.

"What do you think you're doing hanging about by the gate. You know the orders. Stay under cover when the siren goes until ordered out, and get rigged — and get your supper unless you want to be ordered out without it."

They sat around the table, drinking tea while Agnes Jenkins cleared the empty plates.

"Not much activity yet. It's over twenty minutes since the sirens went. I 'aven't 'eard anything drop. Per'aps it will be a nice light raid like last Thursday."

"Let's 'ope so. Thanks for getting the fish and chips, Dicky."

She told them of her reception at the shop.

"Ah, it's fuckin' lovely isn't it?" said Bert Foster. "Last week when we was sent up to the city we got relieved about nine o' fuckin' clock. The city fuckin' gents and the fuckin' typists were just fuckin' rolling into fuckin' work, lookin' at the fuckin' mess as they walked to their fuckin' offices.

"I didn't get in the fuckin' cab nor did Arthur Clayton. We stood on the suctions and fuckin' held on the outside as we fuckin' drove along. Suddenly some old fucker in the crowd gave us a cheer and then they all started to fuckin' cheer and to wave their tit for tats and to clap. Fuck me! It didn't 'alf fuckin' make you feel good."

"I went into a pub last leave-day," said Harry Booth, "and they all started standing me pints. Blimey I 'ad a skin full and never spent a penny. It didn't make me feel so good afterwards."

"Well we're all bloody 'eroes now. Bit different to what it was a month ago."

"'Ow many us been killed to date?"

"Well, according to the number of whip rounds there's been for widows and orphans it's well over fifty. I've paid twenty-six bob in just over three weeks. It ain't fuckin' right you know. Shouldn't be necessary."

"It's the poor fuckers that's got badly 'urt that worries me and there's over five hundred of 'em. A fortnight's pay and then out on your neck and you lie in fuckin' 'ospital and the missus goes around to the assistance board and 'as the fuckin' means-test man poking round the 'ouse."

"There won't be any more tanner whip rounds. They've started a benevolent fund up at HQ and got some very 'an'some contributions from the public."

"Well, it fuckin' still isn't right. If some poor fucker gets hurt or killed at this fuckin' lark his family should be properly looked after by the government, especially now we're fuckin' tied up and can't resign anymore."

"Well I know one thing," said Bert Foster. "I'd as soon be out fighting fuckin' fires with my chinas around me, as sitting in a shelter with fuck-nothing to do. The missus dragged me off to a public shelter in a big fuckin' basement, on my second leave day since it started. An 'orrible, fuggy, smelly crowded fuckin' place, but you some'ow felt safe there until you'd seen what we've seen and 'eard about since, like Morley fuckin' College in Lambeth Road.

"I was relieved for a cup of tea at the canteen van, and I saw the breakdown lorry and crane from HQ helping the rescue parties there. I just went over and 'ad a butchers'. It was fuckin' 'orrible."

"The 'ole building 'ad come down and buried all the women and kids and blokes. Buried 'em alive in dust and rubble and smashed beams. You could 'ear some of 'em moaning and crying. If they'd been out in the road, they'd 'ave died quick and clean like."

"'Ow about that crew from fifty-one that the wall fell on. That's just as bad as 'avin a big building fall in on you. All them 'ot bricks."

"No, it fuckin' ain't. There was all their mates around them saw it fall. They 'ad 'em all out in 'alf an hour and two of 'em still alive. Some of the poor fuckers you read about 'ave been got out alive after over twenty-four hours and then died in 'ospital. Fancy fuckin' lying there not able to move 'and or foot, packed in the rubble with a fuckin' great beam across your chest for twenty-four hours and then dying. Give me the open air every time and I'll risk the bombs and the bomb splinters."

"It's those little kids that get buried alive that worry me. They all ought to be evacuated."

"Talking of kids and bleeding fuckin' shelters 'ave you 'eard about the AFS messenger boy at station 69? The little fair 'aired Charlie Gregory. 'Is mum, 'is dad, 'is four sisters and 'is two brothers all killed in a shelter last night."

"Yes, I 'eard. Poor little fucker. What must it be like to lose your 'ole fuckin' family in one go? 'Ow did they break it to 'im?"

"A woman came around from the welfare. She 'ad a cup of tea made, and she stuck it on a mess room table in the corner and then she broke it to 'im. 'E just sat all pale and still and wouldn't drink 'is tea. She put 'er 'and on 'is shoulder and 'e sort of shook it off and then old Brewster walks in. 'E sort of 'alf opened 'is arms and the kid got up and walked into them. And 'e just talks to 'im in a gentle low voice and then takes 'im upstairs to 'is quarters."

"Ah, e's a funny old stick is Brewster. Kid's living on the station now I 'ear. Sort of continuous duty. Got nowhere else to go. It's fuckin' bad enough two days on, one day off. What can it be like every night and never a rest? Take the old super. 'E's grey 'aired and knocking on sixty. It must be tough at that age."

"You can fuckin' take 'im and stick 'im and 'is grey fuckin' 'airs!"

"Ah, but you've got to give 'im 'is due. Do you remember Alf a year ago telling us that when it started, they'd get into the underground control rooms and send the AFS out to the fuckin' fires?"

A loud whistling followed by four thumps that made the windows rattle interrupted them.

"That was quite near. It's 'otting up a bit."

Jack Adams walked to the door and looked out.

"They're dropping flares. It's usually going to be a bad one when they do that. There's quite a big fire north of the river. Any news from station 69 Mollie?"

"They say both their red pumps are out and four of the AFS ones. U and Z 'ave got all theirs out. The other two subs 'aven't been called yet, same as us."

"I 'ate this fuckin' waiting about. Give us a tune, 'Arry."

He walked to the piano.

"Are you going to sing?"

"No, I can't fuckin' sing without a drop of beer inside me."

"No sing, no play."

"All right. Give us the moonlight."

They gathered around the piano and they began to sing only to be interrupted by the bell ringing and the indicator showing lights for the escape carrier and the self-propelled. The two crews hurried away, dressing as they went.

"You not on the SP tonight, 'Arry?" said Charlie Pierce.

"No, number three trailer pump."

"All right, might as well carry on where we left off."

They went on singing. The bells rang again for number one and number two trailer pumps and a little later for number three. Harry Booth crashed his fingers down in a final chord, got up and reached for his belt and tin hat. Janet and Agnes stood together by the piano.

"Do you think it's going to be a big raid tonight? I don't like it when they're all gone out and just us women left in the station."

"I don't know," said Janet. "Let's go and sit in the watch-room. They may have some news."

"'Alf a mo' while I put the kettle on."

The escape carrier and the self-propelled had been ordered to Paget Street near the river. The street was faced on each side by grain warehouses.

"Looks like they're going well," said Davies "but I can't see any jets at work There's the control point. Pull up alongside."

They waited by the machines while he ran forward.

Returning he said, "Shortage of water; the mains have been broken by HE and they've already emptied all the street tanks around. We're to go to the river with the SP as part of a water relay. Escape to be pitched against the warehouse third floor. Crew wait with it for instructions."

A hose lorry was laying hose, the lengths flaking out behind it, as it drove down the street. Sparks and burning brands fell on the dry flat hose as it lay in the road and burned holes in it. They took a side turning and drove down to the river. Silhouetted against fire on the other bank, they could see a fireboat lying in midstream.

"Fuck me! It's dead low tide," said Davies.

Between the quay, to which they had driven, and the water, stretched thirty yards of deep black mud an officer was waiting for them.

"You're to receive water from the fireboat as soon as they can get their hose ashore. Pump it on in four lines to the SP I've got up Bushel Street. They'll boost it up to Paget Street."

A flare lit the scene with a brilliant white light. They could see that the fireboat had put off a dinghy full of hose attached to its pumps and had reached the far side of the mud flats. The crew were floundering up to their waists trying to drag themselves and the hose towards the shore.

"They'll be all night at that rate," said the officer. "It'll be harder and less sticky on the shore side. Take your hose down and get out to meet them."

He walked away towards Paget Street.

"Christ!" said Davies. "Drunks have fallen off the quays into that lot and never been seen again. Unship the ladder and drop it down."

The flare had died out but by the light of Davies' torch they saw the heel of the ladder and three rounds disappear into the mud. He climbed down.

"Come on all of you. Bring a length of hose each. It's only knee deep here."

They dropped into the mud beside him and started to

inch their way forward. The mud squelched as they laboriously withdrew one foot after the other.

"Crikey! It's getting deeper and wetter."

"Come on. Keep moving. Where's that fuckin' fireboat crew? I can't see 'em now."

He stopped and shouted across the mud and received an answering call. They were three quarters of the way across and thigh deep when they met the exhausted river firemen and the couplings of the two lines of hose were screwed together.

"Is it still slack water?" asked Davies.

"No, the tide's turned. It's just beginning to flow again. Don't hang about."

"We're not going to."

"Give us the signal when you want water on."

The fireboat crew turned around and they started floundering back towards their dinghy. The mud that they stirred up in their progress smelled strongly of sewage.

"Come on back to the shore," said Davies to his men. "The sooner the better."

They turned slowly in the sticky mud and began the laborious journey.

"Oi, Sub!"

There was a note of panic in Bert Foster's voice.

"Now what's the matter."

"I'm fuckin' stuck."

"Give us yer 'and. Come on now while I pull."

"I can't. I can't move either foot."

Davies shone his torch. Bert Foster was waist deep.

"You, silly twerp. Why didn't you keep in line with

the rest of us instead of wandering off into a soft spot?"

A bomb whistled loudly and crashed with a great spurt of orange flame and smoke against the quay wall. They heard its steel splinters whine above their heads but they didn't dare duck.

"Blimey! That was close. Come on Bert try. Fuck! I'm sinking myself. Keep away you there! Keep by the 'ose. Keep by it and make for the shore."

He took a bight of hose and he wrapped it under Bert's armpits and shone his torch towards the river. He could see that the line of hose was kinked and winding as it made its way to the river and the fireboat.

He shouted to the other men.

"When you get to the ladder, nip up sharp and start the SP. Drive her very slowly forward in bottom gear. 'E should come out as you drag the 'ose. Let's 'ope the couplings will 'old. I'll stay 'ere with 'im."

They struggled ashore and carried out their instructions. As the pump moved forward, the hose attached to it, lifted out of the mud and stretched taut.

"I can't fuckin' breathe," gasped Bert as it tightened around his chest.

Suddenly with a great farting squelch he was pulled clear like a salmon on a line and he staggered to his feet.

"Now you're all right," said Davies. "Keep 'old of the 'ose and drag yourself along by it."

"All right but I'm buggered if I haven't left m'boots and leggings be'ind in there."

"That don't matter. You can stay with the pump. We shan't need any branch men tonight. We'll just take our 'ose along to the next pump up the road and couple it into that and they can pump the water on up towards the fire."

The fire in Paget Street now showed a great red glow that penetrated to the side streets and lanes near the river and yellow tongues of flame flickered over the warehouses. The relay was finished at last and the hose snaked from pump to pump and out into the river to the fireboat, to which a signal was flashed by lamp for it to start its powerful pumps. Soon, the hose hardened and straightened as the water rushed through it.

"That'll please Mr District Officer up at the fire," said Davies. "'E's been pulling 'is 'air out watchin' it spread for 'alf an hour."

A rushing tearing sound rent the air and the explosion rocked them as they crouched. Brick dust in a choking cloud came drifting onto the quay from Bushel Street. The pump roared as its load was suddenly released and Jack Adams reached for the throttle to cut down the revolutions.

A crater had appeared in the road into which the jagged ends of the severed hose spurted the river water. An officer ran up.

"Everybody all right? Good. Then get cracking and put some spare lengths into the gap. Come on! Move now. They're waiting for water again up there."

The tide moved in and the fireboat moved closer to the quay. Another boat arrived and put more hose ashore to other pumps. A red glow in the east that at first looked like another fire spread into dawn and the sirens sounded the all clear. Soon, the water was lapping the quayside and more pumps arrived and dropped their suctions straight into the river.

"You can knock the pump off now," said the officer.

Jack Adams closed the throttle. The sudden silence brought relief.

"There's a canteen van in Paget Street. Take your crew over there, Sub-Officer, for a cup of tea and fifteen minutes stand easy."

"'Ow am I going to get the fuck up there without my bloody boots?" said Bert Foster.

"All right we'll fetch you a Rosy Lea down 'ere."

"It'll be cold by the time it gets 'ere."

"Maybe but your feet'll be bloody fuckin' warm by the time you get to the canteen van. The road's all covered in 'ot fuckin' brick rubble."

They left the disconsolate Bert sitting on the pump scraping black mud from his tunic and they picked their way over the smoking rubble to the canteen.

Both sides of Paget Street were jagged steaming ruins in which pockets of fire still flared.

"That wasn't such a big fire when we arrived," said Davies. "That what comes from trying to rely on street water mains with all this HE being dropped. They oughta 'ave put a 'undred water tanks in the streets where they put one."

The nights grew longer and colder and the raids went on throughout October. To the growing list of casualties were added the sickness cases of men who wore sodden uniforms all night and had no change of clothing for the next day. As a result, some pumps stood unmanned in station yards.

November came and on its third night the Blue and White watches sat around the mess table.

"It's two hours since dark and no siren yet."

"You wait, my old china. What are you in such a fuckin' 'urry for? It'll blow."

"You 'ad enough fire-fighting yet Bert?"

"Yes, I've had a fuckin' bellyful. I wouldn't fuckin' mind if I never saw a fuckin' fire again."

"I've 'ad enough," said Charlie Pierce. "I reckon this lot's worse than the Western Front. I'd rather be shelled than bombed anytime. You always knew what direction a shell was coming from. What do you think, 'Arry?"

"Well, it was a long time ago, over twenty years now, but if you kept your 'ead down you seemed to be all right. We was younger then, Charlie. It's funny isn't it 'ow the young 'uns don't seem to mind the risk of getting blown to fuckin' pieces and us old 'uns get jittery. After all, we've 'ad most of our lives. Look at little Dicky there driving round all on 'er lonesome with four hundred gallons of petrol on 'er tail and not turning an 'air."

"Well, I do get the heebie jeebies. In fact, I get fuckin' frightened, especially in the dark streets between fires where there's nobody about. I drive very fast then. When you get to the fire though it's all right. With everybody around, you just get on with the job."

"I think you're a little 'ero, Dicky. Still I don't think Bert Foster should be complaining. 'E's the only one 'ere what's been issued with new boots and leggings."

"Ah, but they didn't issue no socks," said Bert. "Cor! Rubber boots all bloody night is 'ard on socks. My missus can't darn mine no more."

Davies came in carrying a large cardboard box.

"'Oos grumbling now? Look what I've brought you lucky people."

He placed the box on the table.

"Books donated by grateful Londoners to form station libraries. This lot's our share. Come down from station 69 this afternoon. Very useful for those of you what can read."

"Cor! That's 'an'some of them treating us just like frigging soldiers."

The contents of the box were tipped out onto the table. It was a sorry collection of dog-eared classics with dirty covers. Dickens and Walter Scott predominated. They picked them over.

"Not much 'ere. I bet that station 69 fuckin' sorted 'em out well before sending 'em to fuckin' substations."

"Ah, and I expect HQ and Southwark 'ad first and second pick before anything arrived at station 69. Stick 'em over there on the shelf."

"Wait a minute," said Janet. "Let me have a look."

She picked out Tess of the D'Urbervilles and opened the cover. Inside was pasted the label of the Bermondsey Borough Library with the notice: 'This book must be returned on or before June 8th, 1907 after which a fine of one penny per day will be payable'.

"Someone owes the Borough Library quite a lot of money," she said. "Anyhow, I'll take this one."

"Ah well, there you are. You're a scholar Dicky. Come on, get the cards out and let's 'ave a game of solo.

It's nearly three frigging months since we last played."

The clock in the watch-room ticked on to midnight.

"Ask station 69 if anything's doing anywhere," said Davies.

Edith Brown made the enquiry and shook her head.

"They say there hasn't even been a yellow warning in."

"Well there's a thing after fifty-eight bloody nights of blitz. I'll tell the crews to go to bed. I wonder what old Jerry's up to."

There was no raid that night and on the following nights only minor ones, during which substation 69Y was not called.

Late on the night of November the 14th, Janet was walking to the women's dormitory when Edith Brown called her to the watch-room.

"You're wanted on the blower, Dicky."

She took the receiver.

"This is Sub-Officer Evans speaking. I've got a message for you from Sub-Officer White. He's sorry he won't be able to see you tomorrow. They've sent him to Coventry."

"What do you mean? Won't anyone speak to him?"

Evans laughed.

"No, don't sound so worried. Coventry is having a bad raid. Three hundred bombers they say. They're collecting two hundred and fifty London firemen and putting them in buses and sending them up there to lend a hand. Brusher's gone with the whole of his watch. They've no idea when they'll be back. Bit hard, they were all due for leave tomorrow. Promised him I'd let you know. Goodnight."

She went back to the card players.

"Just heard from station 69 there's a bad raid on Coventry. Three hundred bombers and two hundred and fifty of our chaps have gone up there in buses to help."

They laid down their hands.

"Well that's a relief. If it's Coventry it can't be us. I expect they're after the munitions works."

"It's not right. It's only a small place. If they get three hundred bombers over 'em it won't 'alf be concentrated. Besides they're not fuckin' used to it, poor fuckers."

"Well that's their pigeon. They'll 'ave to fuckin' get used to it like we did."

"No, London's a big place. It can take it. Everybody keeps saying that. It's a bit hard on a little place, three hundred fuckin' bombers. Let's 'ope they'll be all right."

"Well they can't be all fuckin' right. Some fucker's bound to get hurt in these rough games. Come on, I'm fuckin' going solo."

Janet met Bill White on their leave day two days later. He stood on the corner waiting for her, his bloodshot eyes blinking in the pale November sunlight. The conjunctivitis that was the bane of the firemen from long exposure of their eyes to smoke and sparks had not spared him.

"Oh darling, I did miss you. What was it like in Coventry?"

"The raid was over when we got there. Nothing dropping any longer but the whole of the centre of the city was on fire. They missed all the factories outside. The DO met us on the outskirts and gave us a pep talk — about us all being veterans and to show a good example, especially as they expected another raid the next night, and then in we went but there wasn't much we could do.

"All the water mains were burst and there were no relays set up. Most of their chaps were part-timers due for work in munitions factories at eight o'clock. They just packed it in and went back to their jobs. Can't blame them. They probably did more good there, than in that chaos. We could have done with you and your petrol lorry. Lots of pumps had run out of petrol.

"There were reinforcements from other towns too. Some just single pumps with AFS only. Everybody was skulking around looking for somebody to give orders to or take orders from. We got a pump to work from a canal in the end, but I think most of the fires just burned out.

"Lovely old cathedral there with a tall spire. That's burned out. There were no canteen vans and the feeding arrangements weren't so hot, only spam sandwiches. We were glad to get back into the buses the next day and on the way back to London. Still it was an experience. I don't know why Jerry didn't come over again the next night instead of to London."

"Yes, darling. You're getting lots of experience. Heard any more about the new station officers' posts under the unification scheme?"

"No. They're a bit slow coming through. I mustn't complain you know, sub-officer already with my short service. The biggest jump from there is from sub-officer to station officer."

"Oh, but you would make such a wonderful station

officer. I want to see you in your blue suit. Make it soon. I'm tired of those brass buttons."

She fingered the second button on his tunic.

"Well we're lunching with Colonel Boyd. I'm going to Aunt Kitty's to change. This uniform's getting in an awful state. I was thinking of buying a new one, but I thought better of it. All the other women on the station have had theirs longer and I thought that it might make them jealous."

"You're going to St Elphin's Hospital to see Tom Blake, aren't you? How is he?"

"Oh, not too bad when I saw him last. It was a bomb splinter. Went into his chest and came out of his back. Funny thing there's a much bigger hole in his back than in his chest. He's got a lovely nurse. She's a sweetie. There are some sick soldiers in the hospital, and she says he needs building up, so she keeps working him a soldier's meat ration for his lunch instead of a civilian one."

"Now Bill, don't start falling for nurses and calling them sweeties, or I shall start getting jealous."

"You're the only sweetie in the world for me, darling."

"Good, then I'll see you at a quarter to one."

They arrived at Colonel Boyd's flat together.

"Hello," he said. "How are you Janet? How are you Bill? You both drinking light ale? Not too bad last night was it? How's Kitty bearing up? I suppose you know that she wrote to your mother and told her that she only stayed in London to provide you with a home on your leave days and to keep an eye on you."

"She told me the same thing. I said. 'What about the first aid post' and she answered, 'well, I'm only part-time unpaid there and most of the time people seem to resent us anyway'."

"Poor old Kitty, she's the biggest bomb snob in London. I think that's really why she stays."

"What's a bomb snob, sir?"

"Didn't you know, Bill? It's a sort of game now. You have to tell the assembled company how much nearer a bomb has burst to you than one ever burst near them with a full description of the occasion. Don't suppose it means much to you people who serve down in the East End and around the docks. Up here, we only get the wides and the overthrows. Still it can be damned unpleasant.

"I never thought that London would stand up to it so well. You people are doing a wonderful job. The way those damn fires are all in hand the next morning amazes me and a lot of other people too. I hear you've had more casualties than all other departments of civil defence put together.

"Still, you don't have to worry about feeling your way around in the blackout. I went in the light rescue van past Lewis's in Oxford Street when it was on fire. You could read a newspaper quite easily. You know I think that this blackout is the worst thing for morale in the whole war. I wonder if it's essential when the Germans are flying two miles high. I carry a little pocket torch when I go on duty and if I shine it on the job, it causes a real panic. 'Put that light out. They're right overhead' is the crazed reaction.

"A chap said it the other night and I said, 'Yes all right, but you're standing on a little girl's face'. He was too. She was buried right up to her ears with her head thrown back and when we knelt down and I shone the light again, the marks of his rubber boots were right across her face. She was trapped around the waist and buried in rubble with only her face showing. It took us five hours to get her out, but she was a brave little thing and never cried once.

"Now I've managed to get a chicken for lunch. A living alone widower's meat ration won't run to entertaining."

"Well, I think that's very clever of you and very kind," said Janet, "and thanks for what you said about the Fire Service. We've got great admiration too for elderly retired colonels who go out in the blitz with the light rescue squads, haven't we Bill?"

Colonel Boyd laughed and shrugged his shoulders.

"Elderly that's it, my dear, and unskilled. Only a bit of shovelling and that's about all I'm fit for. Soon makes my back ache. But some of these builders' labourers we've got are wonderful fellows. The way they tunnel under a half-wrecked building that trembles every time a lorry goes past, using bits of furniture and what you will for props, is a sight to see and they always seem to size the job up and go the right way in. It's a wonderful experience to be with them, on an equal footing."

"Well, what are you, young people, going to do with yourselves this afternoon?"

"We're going to the pictures."

"Ah yes, I see, and soon after that I suppose you must part. Where do you go at nights Bill on your off-duty day?"

"I generally go to mother's house down at New Cross. She's evacuated at present with my sister's children. I sort of keep an eye on the house for her and keep it aired."

"Well, look here, any time you both want a cup of tea or somewhere to sit, just come here. If I'm out, my man will let you in. I'll tell him about it. Just come in and make yourself at home."

"That's very kind of you, Uncle Neville. We'll do that. It will be very nice to have somewhere private to sit, won't it, Bill?"

November passed with minor raids on most nights. The veterans of substation 69Y took it in their stride. They sat around the mess room table on a December evening.

"Do you remember last September 'ow we used to duck every time a fuckin' bomb whistled," said Jack Adams.

"All fuckin' right for you. You're a fuckin' driver and pump operator. You could fuckin' duck. You fuckin' couldn't when you'd got a charged branch in 'and, a silly fucker like someone we know of; a pump operator boosting the pressure to about one hundred and fifty fuckin' pounds."

"Yes, but you never see nobody ducking now. Not for a fuckin' whistle."

"Well, what's the good of ducking for a whistle? If you 'ear that you know it's 'alf a fuckin' mile away. If you 'ear a noise sharp and sudden like an express train, that's the time to fuckin' duck."

"Ah, I reckon most of them what's been killed didn't fuckin' 'ear the bomb when it was coming. I didn't 'ear the one that knocked me arse over tip. Not till it fuckin' went off any'ow."

"You fuckin' sure it was the fuckin' blast what knocked you over, or your own fuckin' wind up?"

"Course it was the blast. I was all covered in dust."

"Well, I bet Dicky's the one on the station what's 'ad a bomb drop as near to 'er as anybody, the night poor old Fred Mason was killed. That was pretty damn near you wasn't it, Dicky?"

"Don't let's talk about it. Poor Fred. I still see his face sometimes at night."

"No, all right then. Roll on Christmas; only another seventeen days. Your mum going to turn up trumps with a couple of turkeys again?"

"Yes, I'm sure that she will."

"I'll be on leave Christmas day but I'm coming in for dinner. Might as well. The missis couldn't stand it anymore and 'as evacuated 'erself alongside the grandchildren. 'Ullo there she goes."

As the siren wailed, the men got rigged and walked out into the yard. The night was very quiet.

"Only a little 'un, I should think."

The anti-aircraft guns started up and their noise was soon interspersed with the whistle and thump of bombs.

"Dunno about that. Look over there. Look at them fuckin' flares. Let's go inside before we get into trouble. Going to give us a tune, 'Arry?"

Half an hour later, all the crews had been ordered out.

Janet sat in the watch-room until the telephone rang.

Miss Casey answered it, looked at her and said,

"Petrol lorry to Deptford High Street. Look after the phones a minute, Brown."

She walked with Janet out into the yard. Incendiary bombs were burning on the road and pavement outside, casting a white flickering glare onto the school walls.

"I just wanted a breath of fresh air. Oh dear, it's a heavy one tonight, the worst for weeks. When there've been gaps between the raids it makes you jumpy again when they return. Good luck, Finch. I just wanted to say you've turned out one of my best firewomen. I never thought that you would a year ago. We'll have the kettle on for you when you're back."

Janet leaned out of the cab.

"Why, thank you, Miss Casey."

She let in the clutch, turned into Rampton Road and headed east for the great red glow that marked her destination.

Two hours later she had completed her task and was ordered to return to her substation, report to control and ask for instructions.

She was a hundred yards from substation 69Y when a loud, short, whistle made her hunch her shoulders and lean over the steering wheel. She saw the flash of the bomb and the gables of the substation lit up by momentary glare. In sudden panic she accelerated and swung into the yard. The faint headlight picked up broken windows and a cloud of dust. She dropped from the cab and ran to the station door. It was hanging open and splintered as she hurried through. Inside, it was pitch dark and she groped towards the watch-room door.

"Oh lawks, 'oos that?"

Agnes Jenkins' voice trembled as Janet's searching hands touched her arm.

"It's Dicky. Where did it drop Aggie?"

"I dunno. I was in the kitchen. The ceiling came down and the lights went out. The gas went out an' all, but I'm sure it must 'ave been on the watch-room and Miss Casey and Edith are in there."

"Have you a match?"

"They're on the gas stove."

"That you, Dicky?"

Relief suffused them as they heard Edith Brown's voice.

"The door's 'ere. I'm trying to find the bleeding matches for the emergency lamp. Ah got 'em."

A match scraped and it shook in Edith's hand as she held it to the oil lamp. Everything in the room had a thick coating of grey plaster dust; the table lay on its side, its telephones on the floor; a hole gaped in the wall from floor to ceiling, through which the cold night air blew. Section Officer Casey, lay face downwards, partly buried in bricks and broken plaster a patch of which was red.

Janet knelt beside her and Edith held the lamp over them.

"Miss Casey, are you all right?"

One hand and arm was buried in the rubble. She seized the other hand, which felt icy cold. To her relief, the recumbent body stirred.

"Where's the occurrence book? Is it there?"

"Yes, it's on the floor, Miss. Are you all right?" said

Edith

"I can't move my right arm. Get on the phone to station 69. Tell them what's happened."

"The phones are dead."

"Go to the telephone kiosk up the road. Take the occurrence book with you. Dial station 69 and say from Section Officer Casey.

"Substation 69Y hit by an HE bomb. All phones are out of order. Temporary watch-room set up at telephone kiosk, Rampton Road. Give them its number."

"Yes, I will. Might as well go this way," said Edith and she went through the hole in the wall.

Janet ran after her.

"Tell them Miss Casey's badly hurt and ask for an ambulance."

"All right, I'm not daft. I was going to tell them that first."

"Come on, Aggie. Give me a hand and move these bricks. They're all lying on her."

They threw bricks and rubble out into the yard until they came to a piece of wall with bricks still mortared together, that was too heavy for them. They heaved them on end away from the prostrate body.

"Ooh look at 'er poor 'and," said Agnes.

The bones were broken and stuck out white from the pulpy mess of blood and flesh.

"Lift her up," said Janet.

"I can get up myself. Please get me a drink of water."

Janet picked up an overturned chair and Miss Casey sat on it.

An ambulance drew up in the yard. The two young women in charge of it led their patient to it.

A few minutes later Brewster walked in.

"Anybody hurt?"

"Yes, Section Officer Casey. Her hand looked very bad."

"Where is she?"

"An ambulance has just taken her away."

"Where to? First aid post or hospital?"

"I don't know, hospital, I should think. They didn't say."

"You should have asked. Where's the other watch-room woman?"

"Up at the phone box."

"All right. What are you doing here? There are instructions for you to go to Southwark, fill up the petrol lorry and take it to Woolwich. Don't hang about, get moving."

The first aid repair squads arrived with their lorries soon after dawn. Damaged fire stations got priority. By evening, the watch-room was reinstated, and the telephone repaired. Substation 69Y was a working station again. Mollie Breaks sat in the watch-room with a red stripe on each shoulder.

"It's only acting rank," she said. "Casey'll be back."

A fortnight passed. Mollie sat at the mess room table.

"I went to see Celia Casey in hospital today. She's quite cheerful. She's got her hand in a sort of wire contraption with all the broken fingers spread out. All she could talk about was when she would be back on duty."

"Ah, poor old Casey. I expect that is all she can talk about and all she can think about an' all. You know 'ers was the only money coming into that 'ouse. 'Er old dad's just about getting to the DT's stage. 'E reckons the blitz don't suit 'is nervous temperament."

"Well, they've put the period of sickness pay up from two weeks to thirteen weeks."

"And they've promised us a second uniform," said Bert Foster. "What with the Thames Haven oil and the Thames mud and a burn down the back of my old tunic which makes me look more like a tramp than a fireman."

"They promised us a second uniform at the end of last month."

"They've started issuing 'em. All the substations on 60s ground 'ave got theirs already."

"And second 'and fuckers too, off blokes what fuckin' resigned before June or 'ave been invalided out since!"

"Never mind. It'll soon be Christmas; only another three fuckin' days. What-oh for a bit of Norfolk turkey!"

"That's all you fuckin' think about, your fuckin' guts."

Davies walked over from the watch-room door.

"I don't know if you'll be getting any turkey this year. Self-propelled and escape carriers just been ordered to Manchester. 'Aversack rations will be dished out there. It's a nice night for a drive and mind you be'ave yourselves."

"Oy, I'm on leave tomorrow."

"Well isn't that too bad. I'll 'ave to send a message round to your missus. Come on get moving. There's a war on."

"Aren't you coming with us, Sub?"

"No, much as I'd like to, but someone's got to be in charge of the substation. Now if you 'urry up and put them fires out, which by all accounts are pretty extensive. You'll be back in time for Mrs Finch's turkeys."

The Manchester party arrived back on the evening of Boxing Day.

"Well, what was it like up there?"

"Cor, it was fuckin' chaos. Never seen such a fuck-up. Do you know they 'adn't enough fuckin' towing vehicles for their trailer pumps and they was pushing them to the fires with the fuckin' 'ose piled on top of the bonnets and falling off all along the fuckin' road. And they didn't seem to 'ave any canteen vans, leastwise I didn't see none."

"Ah, it was a bugger," said Bert Foster. "Come Christmas fuckin' Day we 'adn't 'ad a bite to fuckin' eat since our 'aversack ration. Blimey, I was that 'ungry I could have eaten a bread poultice off a gammy foot. The DO, 'e says, 'That's all right I've seen the Lord Mayor. 'E's promised the corporation will fix you with a Christmas dinner. We was relieved and taken to an 'alf bombed school and each got 'anded a plate with two sausages and a spoonful of boiled spuds. That was our fuckin' lot."

"Never mind, Bert. We've got a little surprise for you," said Agnes. "We didn't 'ave no Christmas dinner 'ere either. It was Dicky's idea. The turkeys are still in the kitchen. I'm cooking 'em tomorrow."

"Well isn't that nice. Dicky Finch, you're a real little duck."

"A 'appy New Year to you one and all and may 1941 bring us all to victory."

Charlie Pierce gave the toast at midnight.

"Don't know why we waited up for that," said Alf Newton. "We might as well 'ave gone to bed an hour ago."

"Oh, I don't think so," said Agnes. "It's nice to see the New Year in. I always did when my 'usband was alive."

"Well, I don't know about victory in 1941. I think we've got a long way to go yet. If little old 'Itler does the same for the rest of London as 'e did to the City two nights ago, I think this war's going to take some winning."

"And what did 'e do to the city two nights ago? Set 'alf the bleedin' lot on fire and then packed it up at ten o'clock. Cor wasn't it a relief to 'ear the all clear sounding that early. I don't mind fire-fighting when there's no bombs dropping."

"Well, I don't like fuckin' fire-fighting when there's no friggin' water in any of the mains. It's fuckin' dis'eartening. Sixteen of our blokes killed, more by falling walls and getting cut off by the fire than there was by bombs."

"You still stink, Arthur, from getting your branch to work from that bombed sewer. Fuckin' lucky the pump got clogged up with fuckin' paper before you 'ad much more of it. Can't you fuckin' get it out of your fuckin' 'air. That's what still pongs, I reckon."

"No, I fuckin' can't and I can't get it out of my fuckin' tunic neither. I 'ate to put the bloody thing on."

"Never mind. The second uniforms 'ave arrived at station 69. They're dishing 'em out tomorrow."

"About fuckin' time too."

Janet was sent to Piper Place in the spare taxi the next morning, to pick up the uniform. It was in depressing bundles tied with thick string. The tunics and trousers were separate; each garment tagged with a man's name and allocated according to previously filled in self-measurement forms.

Sub-Officer Davies handed each man his tunic and trousers in the mess room. Charlie Pierce held the trousers against his ample stomach.

"Well, they maybe second 'and but they seem about right for length and they're better than the ones I'm wearing."

He opened up the top of the garment and looked inside. The small gusset of lining material was stained a dirty brown.

"'Ere Sub this isn't good enough. I'm not wearing these."

"What's the matter with 'em."

"Some fucker has fuckin' shat himself in 'em when 'e wasn't wearing no fuckin' underpants."

"Well don't 'old 'em under my nose. Per'aps a bomb burst a bit near 'im. If you don't want them, you can do without."

"No Sub, that ain't right. We was promised a second uniform. If you won't get 'em changed for me I'm putting in a submit to see Mr Brewster."

"Give 'em back to me. I'll send 'em back to station

69, if you're so particular."

Ten days later Charlie Pierce was issued with a pair of brand-new trousers.

"There you are," he said. "It pays to stick up for your rights."

"That's what I keep fuckin' telling you," said Alf Newton.

"Well I can tell you something," said Janet. "I was sent to HQ the other day and heard it. They were sent back to station 69 with Charlie's submit endorsed by Taff Davies. Brewster wrote his bit and sent them off to Southwark where the superintendent added his two penny's worth and sent them on to HQ. There they ended up in the divisional officer's in tray. He picked them out and looked at them and said, 'Who put these disgusting things in my basket!' Then he read the submits and said, 'go and burn these and issue a new pair'."

"Well, if it takes the fuckin' DO to condemn a fuckin' pair of second 'and trousers that were in that shit state it's a poor old do. I should 'ave thought Taff Davies could 'ave put those in the dustbin and at least if he couldn't, Brewster could 'ave."

"Poor old fucker. There was 'alf a fuckin' bull and cow between 'im and 'is missus this morning all on account of little Charlie Gregory. The door of 'is quarters was open part of the time and you could 'ear it all over the station. 'I'm not 'aving that boy in this flat over the weekend', she shouts. Of course, they couldn't 'ear 'is reply 'e always speaks quiet even when 'e's giving you a fuckin' bollocking but then before the door closed there was such a 'ullaballoo from 'er. You want to ask Ernie Cliff about it. Anyway, down the stairs 'e comes chewing 'is indigestion tablet straight to the alarm bell and turns 'em out for drill. They was waiting for it of course. Out in ten seconds but 'e still fuckin' didn't think it was good enough."

Mr Brewster stood in a corner of substation 69's yard.

"Well, there you are Charlie. I'm sorry, boy, but it just isn't convenient to my wife this weekend. Another time and I'll arrange it."

"That's all right, Mr Brewster, but do you think I could ride the SP tonight. They're one short on the crew you know."

"Now Charlie, I've told you before, messengers aren't firemen and they're not allowed to ride pumps. You wouldn't like to get me into trouble, would you? You've just got to be a messenger until you're old enough to be called up for the army and make yourself generally useful as you always have done."

"They're one short in the SP's crew, Mr Brewster. I couldn't be more useful than that if we get a raid tonight. I'm stronger than some of those old men and I've learned pump drill. I've got boots and I could borrow a tunic and leggings."

The fire officer looked down at the eager young face.

"All right, Charlie, you can make up the number in the SP's crew if there's a raid tonight."

The sirens sounded soon after dusk and Brewster went to the watch-room where four AFS women sat at the telephones under the supervision of Mrs Bridger. She stood up and reported to him.

"Southwark have just been through and say that the beam is on London."

The radar beam laid by the Germans on the route, which their aircraft were to follow, was easily detected. At first its direction and even its existence had been kept secret but now, the information was passed to fire stations and indicated that a large force of planes was on its way along the beam route.

"All right, I'll go and get rigged."

He left the watch-room and returned a few minutes later to the sound of gunfire and bombs falling. A telephone rang and a woman answered it.

"One trailer pump from Y substation out to Rampton Road, a running call by warden."

Mrs Bridger removed a coloured disk from the mobilising board. The phones of other substations rang, reporting their machines out to fires. A woman looked up from her instrument.

"W substation report all appliances out and a running call received by warden to a fire in Cory Street."

"One trailer pump from here?" queried Mrs Bridger.

"Of course. Get on with it. You're doing the mobilising. I'm just watching," said Brewster.

She touched the bell four times and the trailer pump's crew reported to the watch-room door. They were handed the message and departed.

The phone on a direct line from Southwark rang and the girl wrote out a slip as she listened.

'Ten pump fire at Foundry Road. Pump escape and SP

required. District Officer Brewster to go and take charge.'

The bell switch was left on for a loud continuous ringing and the crews ran to their machines. Sub-Officer White came to the watch-room door to take the address slip. Brewster went to the yard where an AFS woman driver stood by his car.

"Foundry Road. Follow the pumps. Overtake them if you can. It looks like being a rough night."

They drew up at the fire. A range of three-storey factory buildings burned fiercely. Brewster went up to the sub-officer in charge.

"I'm taking over. When did you make it ten pumps?"

"Six or seven minutes ago."

"How many have you got so far?"

"Four trailer pumps and one self-propelled."

"Well here come three from station 69. What have you got around the back?"

"Two trailer pumps. They're only off a four-inch main. Not much water in it."

"Right, get around the back and take charge there. I'll send you another pump as soon as I can. Get your jets right inside."

Sub-Officer White reported to him.

"Get the pump escape and the SP to work here. Send the pump up to the canal and tell them to start laying hose up to the fire. These mains won't supply ten pumps. We'll need a relay."

He followed the hose into the building and spoke to the branch men.

"There's a small cellar to your right, sir. Got some sort

of stock in it, in cardboard boxes. It's well alight. Shall I take the jet into it?"

"No, keep moving into the main fire. I'll get another branch from another pump taken down there in a minute."

He came out into the road where he told a sub-officer to get a branch to work in the cellar and went at a brisk trot round to the back and spoke to the crews there. He had reached the corner on his return when the bomb fell. He saw the crews in the road scatter and crouch, and noticed their jets fall away.

"Damn! That hit the main," he said as he ran up. "Anybody hurt?"

"We're all right sir. I don't know about those inside."

The crater lay in the pavement against the side of the building and it was rapidly filling up with water from the shattered main. Part of the brickwork of the building lay in the road.

"Get a suction on to that crater and pump that lot onto the fire."

He went to the door and met two branch men and Sub-Officer White coming out.

"Our water's been cut off."

"I know. The main's gone. Get everybody out of the building. Are there any others?"

"There's a line of hose from the SP into a small cellar over on the right."

"Who was manning it?"

"Richards and young Gregory."

He hurried to the place, down six steps and into darkness. Water ran up to his knees. He fumbled for his

233

lamp and switched it on.

"Thank God, you've come, sir," said Richards. "We put the fire out but I'm stuck. We're both stuck."

"Where's Gregory?"

"Behind me sir. I think he's hurt. He's breathing funny."

The wooden roof of the cellar had collapsed in a V-shape with splintered beams stinking out at angles. Richards was sitting in the water, a heavy baulk of timber across his lap.

"Give me a hand, White."

They knelt down in the cold water and they put their shoulders under the splintered end of the baulk.

"All right, straighten up. Heave!"

The timber creaked and gave. Richards scrambled out.

"Are you all right?"

"Legs are a bit wonky, sir."

"See him out, White."

They splashed their way to the steps.

Brewster shone his lamp beyond the point where the trapped fireman had been sitting. Its light fell on Charlie Gregory's pale face. He turned his head towards the lamp. There was frothy blood around his lips. He was in a half-sitting, half-recumbent position. Around him was a jumble of broken wood and shattered brickwork. The water lapped around his chest. Brewster stumbled over the rubble towards him. A thick timber beam lay across his chest, another under his back pinning him closely.

"Hello, Charlie boy. How do you feel?"

"Better now you've come, Mr Brewster, but I'm

terribly cold. Is Richards all right?"

"Yes, he's all right and you will soon be, old son"

Under the water he ran his fingers over the fire tunic where the wooden beam pressed into it. They contacted broken ribs sticking through the cloth. He pressed his hand against the imprisoning beam and pushed with all his strength. It was as solid as a rock. He bent down gasping as the cold water covered his chest and he felt the boy's legs entangled in wreckage. His hand came up and grasped the cold limp hand below the water.

"Well, you have got in a rum old position, son. This'll take a bit of time but don't you worry, we're all here with you."

"Don't let me drown, Mr Brewster."

The hand beneath the water was gripping his own tightly.

"Of course, we won't let you drown. You'll be out of here soon and in a nice warm bed."

He was standing on rubble. With a sudden access of horror, he realised that the cellar was filling up from the discharge from the broken water main.

"I'll be back in a minute. I'm leaving my lamp with you."

He plunged towards the steps through water that was now nearly waist deep and he collided with White who was coming down.

"Richards is all right sir, only bruised."

"You've taken your time. Stay with him." Then in a fierce whisper. "The basement's filling up."

He ran through the door and, by the light of the

increasing fire, he saw the trailer pump he had ordered to work from the flooded bomb hole standing silent with two men leaning over its bonnet.

"What the hell are you doing? I told you to get that pump to work from the crater five minutes ago."

"She won't start sir. She packed in when the bomb dropped. We can't get her going."

He seized one of the men by the arm.

"You! Get into that taxi. Drive like hell to station 69. Ring the water board and tell them to get a turn cock down here as quick as they can to cut this main out. There's one of us trapped in the basement and it's flooding. You! Get into another taxi. Get up to the rescue depot in Blair Road. Tell them the same. You! Find the nearest telephone and advise them. Turn cocks first. Where's the local sub-officer?"

"Round the back, sir."

"Double round and tell him to knock his jets off and come here."

One of substation 69Y's trailer pumps drew up and reported.

"Drop your suction in there and pump that crater out and hurry. Don't pump it on the fire. Take the branch away down the road."

"'E's gone fuckin' nuts," said Alf Newton, as he unshipped the suction.

The local sub-officer ran up and Brewster told him the position.

"There are hydraulic lifts next door, sir. The hydraulic main that works them runs through here and through the building. It's probably burst and that's what's filling her up."

"Where are the valves?"

"In the building, I should think, and it's well alight."

"Get me the hearth kit off station 69's pump."

It was a set of tools used for dealing with hearth fires and consisted of chisels, a heavy iron short handled mallet for breaking and taking out hearth stones and a special saw with a rounded blade for cutting through floorboards and joists. He took the box and hurried back to the cellar.

The boy's head lay in White's crooked arm. The sub-officer shook his head and pointed to the water surface, which had nearly reached the boy's chin. The pump above their heads roared into life and accelerated as the primer was depressed.

"That'll deal with it," said Brewster, "and there's a heavy rescue team on the way. They'll have special equipment."

He took the saw from the box and began to cut the beam. The wood was hard and the space to work the saw restricted. The cut lengthened slowly, and the saw blade kept jamming. Sweat broke out on his face despite the cold water below.

"Here you are, White. You take over."

He handed the saw over and shone his lamp on the boy. The water was lapping his chin.

"Don't let me drown, Mr Brewster."

"We won't let you drown, son. Sub-officer White's sawing away. He'll soon be through and you'll be out."

The saw jammed tight.

"She won't budge, sir. This timber's taking a lot of weight and it's nipped the blade."

Above their heads the note of the pump changed.

"Go and see what's happened."

White quickly returned and whispered in Brewster's ear.

"They've pumped the crater dry sir and the turn cock's main valve has cut out the system. It's filling up from somewhere else. Must be the high pressure hydraulic main."

"Get up there and see if you can get enough lengths of suction coupled together to reach down here. Find some buckets and get some men baling with them up the steps."

The water was around the boy's mouth and his stentorious breathing blew bubbles of blood and froth into it. Brewster got behind him and pushed his head forward and up.

"Don't let me drown, sir."

The voice was very faint now.

"I'll not let you drown, son."

His hand went up to the hearth kit on a ledge above his head. The short handle of the iron mallet met his groping fingers. He crushed it down into the back of the skull.

His hands quivered as he stood up. He put the mallet down on the ledge and shone his lamp downwards. The boy's head had fallen back below the water, which was faintly tinged with blood around the mouth and scalp.

He stood waist deep for a few minutes, breathing heavily and then he made his way up the steps and out into the street.

"Get the hearth kit, White, and put it back in the pump."

"Has he gone, sir?"

"Yes. Now get that relay going from the canal. I want at least ten jets to work on this building in half as many minutes. Sub-Officer, return to your crews at the back and get to work from the main there."

A heavy rescue van arrived.

"You mean he's in there?" said the leader. "Under all that water?"

"Yes, but he wasn't under the water when we sent for you."

"Well, he's dead. You must have known it. We've got plenty of live ones to think about tonight. We'll be on our way."

The hydraulic main was shut off after dawn. They cut through a wall and dropped suction into the cellar and pumped it out. The trailer pump from substation 69Y was the last to leave the scene. They looked at the crumpled sodden body in the wreckage.

"Well, that's the last of the Mohicans gone as far as young Gregory's family's concerned," said Alf Newton.

"That you?" said Mrs Brewster, as she heard the door of the flat open.

"You're late. It's nearly midday. What a night! You'd better have breakfast and lunch together. Would you like your egg ration?"

"I don't want anything to eat."

"What's happened? You look as if you'd seen a

ghost."

"I'm cold. I'll go and run a bath."

"That all you've got to say to me after being out all night."

"Charlie Gregory's been killed."

"Oh, I'm sorry. That's the first time a messenger boy's been killed isn't it? Well it's no good worrying, he's not the only one, and at least there's no family to mourn him. You'd better have your bath and a lie down. You're not going to the office this afternoon surely."

"Yes, I must for a bit."

"That's right. Stay out all night and then go down to the office when you're entitled to the time off. You don't think I might like a bit of company after an air raid like last night!"

"I shan't be there long."

He walked into his office at four o'clock, sat down and picked up the papers from the in tray.

"There's a submit from Auxiliary Fireman Newton for a personal interview, sir," said the duty sub-officer.

"What does he want?"

"Says it's personal, sir."

"All right, send for him. He can walk up from Y substation."

He sorted the papers out and began to read.

"Newton's here, sir."

"Show him in. Personal matter is it Newton?"

"In a way personal, sir."

"Well, what is it?"

"When the hearth kit was collected this morning, the

hammer wasn't in it. I went down into that basement and saw Gregory's body. There was a dent in the back of the skull. I found the hammer on a ledge above his head. I've put it in a safe place. It's got a little patch of blood on it and some fair hairs sticking to it."

"Well hand it over to the sub-officer here."

"I don't think you've quite got my meaning, Mr Brewster. Gregory was badly injured, and his body had been under water, but I don't think he died of chest injuries and I don't think he drowned. You were the only one with him most of the time."

"What are you after, Newton?"

"Mr Brewster, I want to be made a red rider. I think it would pay you to alter your recommendation on my application."

"Get out of my office."

"If you want it that way, sir."

He saluted and walked out closing the door behind him.

Brewster sat at his desk staring with unseeing eyes at the papers on it. His hand went to a drawer and he took out a packet of indigestion tablets.

"God help me. I couldn't have done anything else," he murmured.

The continuous clamour of the station bells made him start and jump up. In a few steps he was at the watch-room door.

"What have you got in?"

"Verney Street sir. Albrights. Repeat a call by telephone and a call by fire alarm."

"All right, I'll ride the pump."

The escape and pump turned out, the crews dressing as the vehicles threaded through the mean streets that were gapped and partly derelict from fire and high explosives.

"Ought to be a law against ordinary fires at a time like this. I was having such a lovely zizz."

"Hope it's not going to be a long job, especially if we're going to be out all night again. What's Albrights?"

"Mattress makers and flock warehouse. Let's hope it isn't the basement."

They smelt the smoke some distance away. A small crowd stood in Verney Street watching it pour from pavement lights and ground floor windows. Brewster jumped from the pump, ran to the door and opened it. Thick acrid smoke enveloped him and made the crowd retreat.

"All right," he said. "BA job. Get your sets on. Set into the hydrant over there two lines of hose down the basement steps. Sub-Officer, take the pump escape to the corner, set it into the hydrant there and lay two lines out to the back of the building."

He made a quick reconnaissance. No flame showed, only thick smoke. He returned to the front of the building and he saw the two hose lines leading from the pump across the street and into the smoke-obscured entrance to the building.

He picked up his own breathing apparatus; pulled the webbing straps over his shoulders and he went through the routine. Rubber mouthpiece in; grip between the teeth; open main valve from the oxygen cylinder on his back;

check bypass valve; two deep breaths out of the breathing bag exhaled through his nose; nose clips on; check passage gauge. The performance was followed automatically without conscious thought.

He counted twenty steps to the bottom and he felt the hose running ahead on a level cement floor between walls four feet apart. The smoke was opaque, and he held the lamp up close to his goggles, but he saw only a faint yellow glow. Without the line of hose to guide him a man would be lost in this atmosphere in seconds and would die in the same time without breathing apparatus. He felt his way along the wall and found a doorway on his left. The hose went straight on. He followed it into an open area and touched the shoulder of one of the men holding the branch.

"Have you found it?"

The mouthpiece between his clenched teeth blurred the words.

"Yes, straight on, guvnor."

Ahead of them the smoke glowed red and a faint crackling could be heard.

"Right. Turn On."

The hand control branch was opened, and the jets shot out towards the fire. There was a hissing noise and hot steam wetted their hands and faces.

"Move in. I'll lighten the hose up for you."

He crawled back with his hand on the hose and when it reached the passage he stood up and walked slowly along the hose between his feet. His right hand found the doorway. He turned into it and walked on. His groping hands found a wooden packing case and he leaned his back against it.

He stood thinking of the cold waters of Scapa Flow that had closed over his son's head. Then his hands went up and he gripped the tubes that led from the breathing bag to the mouthpiece. With a quick movement he snatched it from between his teeth. Choking hot smoke seared his lungs and twenty-five years of training took control of his reactions. He dropped on his hands and knees and pressed his mouth against the concrete floor sucking the cooler air that lay there.

The chief superintendent sat at his office desk, the superintendent opposite him.

"I can't make it out; an officer of Brewster's experience. One of the best BA instructors in the Brigade."

"Do you think his breathing tubes could have caught up in some projection and pulled his mouthpiece out as he walked along?"

"Do you think so? What projections were there? You saw where his body lay. He had good teeth. It would take a hell of a pull to snatch a mouthpiece out. Besides what was he doing all alone, twenty yards from the hose lines and the crews in smoke like that. It's a mystery. Come on. Let's go and get it over with."

"Piper Place," he said to his driver.

They pulled up at station 69.

"You can wait in the car or in the station."

A quarter of an hour later the chief superintendent came down from the station quarters.

"You weren't very long," said his colleague.

"No. It was the easiest sort of job I've ever had. The

first thing she wanted to know was what pension a district officer's widow got when her husband had been killed due to service. I had it already worked out."

"You know, I always wondered why Brewster didn't get further. He was a good officer."

"It was Doris. She'd never have made a senior officer's wife and everybody knew it."

Chapter 8

Blue watch was dismissed. Janet hurried through the gates and made her way towards Piper Place and Bill White, who met her halfway between the station and its satellite.

They kissed in the half-ruined street that smelled with the sour stench of wet ashes and bombed buildings.

"Are you all right, darling? Wasn't it a beastly one the night before last? They seem to be getting heavier, even if they don't come so often."

"Yes, I'm all right. Yesterday afternoon shook me up more than the raid the night before, though that wasn't very pleasant with poor little Charlie Gregory going like that."

"Poor Mr Brewster. Whatever happened?"

"It's a mystery. When we got the fire out and the building vented, we found him lying face down with his mouthpiece out. His set was in perfect order."

"They can't blame you in any way."

"No. They can't blame me. Sub-Officer Evans was there anyhow and he's my senior."

"Well I'm going home to change. Meet you for lunch, same time, same place."

"Yes. Same time, same place, my darling."

She caught a bus to the West End and from its upper

deck she saw new gaps in the buildings that lined the streets and the curious opened dolls house effect of those that had had their front facade torn out, leaving rooms and furniture exposed.

The damage seemed widespread. She put her key in the door as Alice opened it.

"Oh, Miss Janet, I've been waiting for you. It was terrible here the night before last, and Mrs Farrow decided she just couldn't stand it anymore. Just after the siren, while she was still in the drawing room, a bomb came down only four doors away. You can't imagine how the house shook and all the soot came down the chimney and nearly smothered her. Some of the windows are broken at the back. She's gone up to Inverness. She wanted to see Master Claude anyhow. He wouldn't come down to London for his leave. I think he's rather a nervous young gentleman.

"She's given me a holiday with board wages and I'm off to see my sister in Wiltshire. I'm not sorry to be out of it. She told me to wait until you came and to see you all fixed up. You've got your key and here's a list of the tradesmen where your ration books are. Will you be all right, Miss?

"I'm afraid you'll have to make your own bed. Oh, and Mrs Farrow said to please her, would you sleep on the ground floor."

"Yes, I'll be all right. So, Mrs Farrow got all covered in soot, did she?"

"Oh, you shouldn't laugh Miss Janet. She was very upset and the drawing room's in a terrible state. I can't do anything with it. I'd like to catch the twelve ten from Paddington if you don't mind. I know you're never in for lunch but I've left you cold supper laid out."

Janet and Bill met for lunch in a small café in a side street off Oxford Street. The proprietor greeted them as he had done for over a year.

"Doesn't get much better does it? What a night the day before yesterday. It's bad for trade. It was just beginning to pick up again with some of the old pre-Blitz regulars coming back. I don't know how we carry on what with the rationing and the Blitz. I've got some steak and kidney pie or you can have fried plaice."

They ate their lunch and over the empty coffee cups, Janet said, "I've got some news for you, Bill. I'm all-alone in London. Aunt Kitty's evacuated herself and her maid too."

"Are you going to sleep all alone in that big house then?"

"Do you think I should?" she smiled at him and squeezed his hand under the table.

"No, you'd be very lonely and I'd be worrying about you."

"Well, you wouldn't worry about me if we were together."

"What about the promise to your mother?"

"I have forgotten it. We must be very good. Oh, Bill, we have been good so far haven't we and it's still a long time before spring. I hate parting with you on the evening of every leave day."

They caught the underground to New Cross that

evening; changed at Whitechapel and passed through Shadwell, Wapping and Rotherhithe stations.

The platforms were crowded with people sitting or lying on their mattresses. There were family groups with children playing, old people sitting over their knitting or their books, and babies in portable cots.

"What a place to spend the night," said Janet. "Do you think they're really safe here?"

"They weren't at Clapham. It was a nasty night; so many people close together and the main broke and washed tons of sandy soil on top of them. They said that the bomb went down a ventilator shaft or something."

"Where we're going there'll only be the two of us and not very much to fall on top of us. It's not much of a place but it's cosy."

They walked from the station through dark deserted streets. He carried her suitcase with one hand and held her arm with the other. His mother's house was one of a row of cottages each with a little garden fronting the street, a relic of a forgotten village engulfed by London one hundred years ago.

He pushed a key into the door, opened it and led her through.

"Wait here a minute while I draw the curtains then I'll switch the lights on."

She found herself in a narrow hall from which a steep staircase rose opposite the front door.

"In here," he said. "It's cosier than the front room. I left the fire laid and I've just lit it."

She followed him into the kitchen. A dresser with

shelves lined with china took up one wall. From the other the long dead, heavily moustached sergeant looked out benignly from a large picture frame. China dogs flanked the mantelpiece with a large ticking clock between them. A rug mat lay in front of the fender with basket chairs at each side. A scrubbed deal table took up the centre of the room.

"What do you think of it? Not up to Brandon standards, I'm afraid."

"Why, it's a darling little room, Bill. We can be so cosy here. I've brought some eggs in my suitcase and I'm going to cook your supper."

"There's some of my bacon ration left. Let's have bacon and eggs and fried bread and I'll go around the corner for some beer."

They ate their supper and listened to the comedy show 'It's That Man Again' (ITMA) on the wireless and talked of the future and the past.

"Tell me something. Just before the call came in yesterday, Brewster saw Newton on a personal matter. The interview only lasted about a minute, but Newton came out looking sort of pleased with himself. He's at your substation. Do you know what it was about?"

"No. Nobody does. You know better than any of us that any interview on a personal matter is private. But Newton came back saying he'd left Mr bloody Brewster with something on his mind. He wouldn't say what it was when he was pressed."

"It's a queer business. I liked old Brewster. He always stuck to the rules but yesterday afternoon he broke the most important rules of BA procedure."

"Don't talk about it anymore, Bill. I hate the idea of you going into those smoke-logged buildings. I keep thinking it might have been you. Whatever should I have done then? I think I should have gone mad."

"No, it couldn't have been me. A BA man is safe if he sticks to the rules. Keep by the hose to find your way out. Keep by your mates so that they can help you if your set goes wrong. They are the two most important ones. Why did Brewster break them? All right, my darling, let's talk about the spring again."

At eleven o'clock Janet yawned.

"I don't know about you, but I'm ready for bed."

"All right, darling. You're in mother's bed. I hope it's comfy. I'm in my own room next door to you."

The bed was a double-one that sagged in the middle. The bedstead had brass ends with round knobs that were loose, and they rattled as Janet sat down on the mattress and bounced to try its spring. She undressed, put on her nightdress and got into bed.

"You can come and say goodnight. I'm quite decent."

The sirens sounded as she finished speaking. He walked in dressed in pyjamas.

"They're late. I expect it will only be a small raid. Nice to think we're on leave and only Red and White watches will get wet shirts tonight."

They heard the sound of gunfire and the whistle and thump of distant bombs.

"Turn the light off, Bill and draw the curtains. See if there are any flares dropping."

He did as he was asked. The sky had cleared and there was moonlight outside. She was sitting up in bed and he could see the white night dress and her head very faintly.

"Not a sign of anything."

"Come and sit beside me on the bed."

He sat down and her hand clasped his.

"This is a nicer way to spend an air raid than driving that old lorry round the streets."

"I wish you'd put in for watch-room duties. I hate to think of you driving round alone in the Blitz. It worries me stiff."

"Now that's silly, darling. Seven women have been killed in watch-rooms, but we haven't lost a woman driver yet. I'm much more worried about you sometimes, but we mustn't think about such things. It can't happen to us. We're so happy. You're cold, darling, sitting there. Come in and talk to me."

She lifted the bedclothes and he slipped beneath them and into her arms. Her mouth met his and as their tongues entwined, her whole body melted into his and they shuddered with desire.

A loud whistling and the rush of disturbed air filled the room and made the curtains by the partly opened window billow inwards. Four almost simultaneous explosions followed, and they heard the tinkling of falling glass. The house shook and the brass knobs on the bedposts rattled.

"A stick of four HE. That was close," he said.

"I wasn't the tiniest bit frightened, not with you here. I wouldn't mind dying if I died in your arms. Oh, dear though, what would they say when they found us?"

"We wouldn't be worrying."

"No, I suppose we wouldn't. I can hear fire bells. Look there's a glow in the sky over the houses opposite."

"Yes, there is but it's none of our business tonight. We're on leave. Let the on-duty watch from New Cross deal with it. I've got you and I've lost all interest in fires for tonight."

"Yes, and I've got you and I'm going to enjoy every minute of it."

She sat up in bed; pulled her nightdress over her head and dropped it on the floor. Moments later his pyjamas fell on top of it.

His penis immediately jumped to attention as his eyes feasted on her breasts with bright pink aureoles, but he wrapped his body around hers and his mouth became glued to her mouth as both tongues darted with pleasure. He then in turn kissed her neck, her ears and her sweet rose bud nipples, which hardened with desire for him.

Janet grasped his penis. It felt so strange to her, yet so exciting, throbbing under the touch of her fingers. She gently stroked it and it pulsated as if it had a mind of its own. He in turn put his fingers into her vagina and she experienced a wave of such pleasure she cried out.

"Please take me now!"

It was hard at first and quite painful as he gently pushed his penis into her. But she kissed him fiercely as he continued to push and suddenly it was in. She pulled her legs up around his back and allowed herself to be swept along by the rhythm of his sweet thrusts. Oh God, if there is a god, how she loved him.

"Oh Bill, I love you and I'll love you till the day I die."

His lips met hers again and the passion of their kiss, combined with the delicious fucking sent further waves of desire right through her body from a tingling in all her extremities to every other part, but above all the inexplicable response of her sex to his.

After what seemed a helpless eternity she came as waves of desire swept over and he spent his seed inside her

They were oblivious to the noise of guns, bombs and fire bells. The all clear sounded. The brass knobs on the bedposts still rattled.

She woke up to hear him moving softly around the room.

"It's seven o'clock, darling. I'll just draw the curtains and put the light on. Mustn't be late for duty."

He sat on the edge of the bed. She put out a hand and found him putting on his pyjamas.

"Are you shy, darling?"

"No, not really. Not of you."

He switched the light on. She got out of bed and went to the bathroom.

"Ooh, it's cold out there. Can I have a bath?"

"Yes, of course. I'll go and get the geyser going if the gas mains haven't been broken. I'll shave in the kitchen."

The little bathroom was full of steam and the old-fashioned copper geyser roared. She ran some cold water and got into the bath. Its surface was rough where the enamel was chipped away, leaving black speckles on the surface. The water from the geyser was scalding hot and she wallowed in comfort and shouted.

"Bill, how do you turn this thing off? It's reaching the overflow."

He came in, shaving soap on his face.

"Like this, see."

"Now you can stay and talk to me. Do you think I'm very abandoned? It's nice being abandoned, isn't it. The bottom of this bath is all rough."

"I'll get it re-enamelled for you."

"No, don't be silly. I can scratch my bottom on it. It's rather a nice sensation. I'm so full of nice sensations. Have you ever seen a girl in a bath before?"

"Only on the films and they always have soapy bubbly water round them. Rather frustrating."

"I'm not frustrating, am I?"

"No, darling. You're not frustrating. You're beautiful and loveable and satisfying but if you don't hurry you won't get any breakfast. Here's the towel."

He was drying her back in the bedroom. She stood facing him, her hands on his shoulders. He moved closer and the slight pressure tipped her backwards onto the bed.

"Oh Bill, if you don't hurry you won't get any breakfast."

They parted at the tube station. Janet hurried into substation 69Y as the Blue watch fell in to answer roll call. She went to the watch-room where Mollie Breaks sat at the table.

"Any jobs for me?"

"Yes, two."

She looked up from the message pads.

"You look very gay and blooming this morning. In fact, you look like a satisfied cat that's been pinching the top off the milk."

"That's rather how I feel."

"Well you mind the milk doesn't turn sour on you. 'Ere you are: general-purpose lorry to Southwark to pick up hose. Take it to station 69 and then to all substations. Make this the last call and I'll give you the other job."

The days grew longer, and the night raids were interspersed with periods when no enemy planes reached London. Sometimes when the weather was overcast the sirens sounded by day, but few bombs were dropped on these occasions. The little house in New Cross became Janet's leave day home.

It was early in March when she heard of Bill White's promotion to station officer. The news came to her when District Officer Sutton who had succeeded Brewster called at substation 69Y on a routine visit, bringing the day's Brigade order with him for posting on the notice board. He stepped out of his car in the yard when Janet was cleaning her lorries.

"Something to interest you here, Miss. Here, you can have a spare copy."

He walked on to the watch-room, leaving the paper in her hand. The promotions were at the bottom. There were five new station officers listed in alphabetical order. The last name was Sub-Officer W.B. White. She finished cleaning the lorry, her heart beating with excitement.

The district officer walked out to his car accompanied by Sub-Officer Davies. Janet hurried to the watch-room.

"What 'o Dicky! You've seen it already. I can tell by your face," said Mollie. "Pity you were on leave yesterday. You'll 'ave to put off your little celebration 'til the day after tomorrow. I'll get 'im on the phone." She lifted the receiver.

"Can you get Station Officer White? Someone 'ere wants a word with 'im. Edith you can go and get yourself a cup of tea. That you, Brusher? Dicky Finch for you. Now I'll break the rules and leave you alone in the watch-room for a couple of minutes."

She went out, closing the door behind her.

"Hello guvnor."

"Hello, darling. When did you hear?"

"About five minutes ago. When did you?"

"Sent for by the superintendent for an interview at Southwark this afternoon. Just got back."

"Where are you?"

"In Sutton's office."

"Good then, you can tell me how much you love me."

"The watch-room's probably listening in."

"I don't mind."

"Well, I can't tell you because it would take too long. Darling, it's March. It's nearly spring. Would your mother agree to us getting married now?"

"I think so. I'll write and tell her the wonderful news. You are a clever boy and I'm proud of you. I won't meet you at five past nine on Thursday. I'm going straight up to the West End and I'm going to buy the food for a marvellous meal, something off ration and we're going to have a wonderful celebration all to ourselves."

257

"Very extravagant of you."

"No, it isn't. You aren't made a station officer every day. When do you get your new uniform?"

"I'm going up to stores now for the tunic. Shan't get the blue suit for a day or two."

"All right, darling, you'd better go and I'll count the hours 'til I see you."

"I'll be all right for next leave day, but after that it's continuous duty. Short leave in the afternoons, subject to the exigencies of the service."

"Oh, how awful. I'd forgotten that. What shall we do without our leave days together?"

"Part of the price of promotion, I'm afraid, but we'll work something out. Goodbye, darling."

The supper things were cleared away and she sat silent and happy, in the mess room, listening to the conversation.

"You seen station 69,s new pump?"

"Yes, she's a beauty. Real up to date peacetime model, all enclosed and she's chromium plated, no brass to polish."

"Why the fuck don't they fuckin' dish out pumps like that to the AFS instead of these rotten old trailers with fuckin' taxis to pull 'em?"

"Well, she was ordered before the war and only just been delivered. Got held up for parts or something."

"You 'eard about the bloody inventory on 'er. There isn't 'alf a fuckin' row going on. They checked the inventory within an hour of it getting to station 69 and 'alf the fuckin' tool kit's missing. Screwdrivers, pliers, four spanners and a couple of fuckin' branches as well."

"Ooh the fuckin' 'ell would want to pinch branches?"

"Scrap brass is fetching a fuckin' fortune. Anyway, Sutton starts tearing 'is 'air out and shouting blue fuckin' murder and blaming the AFS. Always fuckin' blames the AFS when something gets 'alf inched. Couldn't 'ave been a regular fuckin' fireman could it?"

"Well, a bloke what would pinch gear off a pump at a time like this deserves all 'e fuckin' gets. 'Ullo there's moaning Minnie. I fuckin' 'ate the sound of those bloody sirens."

The raid built up rapidly. Harry Booth played the piano until his trailer pump was called. Janet was sent out with the petrol lorry before midnight.

District Officer Sutton stood at his control point near the docks and saluted as the superintendent's car drew up.

"I've asked for fifty pumps, sir. Got twenty-four, so far. There isn't a main with water in it for a mile. They've all been smashed. I've got a relay working from the dock basin. I haven't sent anything to Link Road baths yet. There's a hundred thousand gallons there."

"All right I'll take over. First big machine up to the baths. Here you are: station 69's new Merriweather and its new station officer."

White jumped down as the pump drew up at the control point.

"Station 69s pump with crew of five. Station Officer White in charge, sir."

"Right, Station Officer. Get up to Link Road baths. Set in there two lines of hose down to here. Quick as you can."

White saluted, remounted and the vehicle drove away. It had gone thirty yards when the bomb fell. A rush of air that sent the superintendent and the district officer crouching into a warehouse doorway, a red flash, a deafening roar and the pump disappeared in a cloud of smoke, dust and disintegrating metal.

The two men crouching together saw it happen. They looked at one another.

"That's sorted out the bloody inventory," said Sutton.

They straightened up and ran towards the smoking crater. In it lay the twisted chassis; the contents of the petrol tank flared up and by the lurid light they saw the shattered bodies that lay among the wreckage.

"Get those branches over here and get this fire out."

The men dragged the charged hoses from the building they were working on and directed the jets on the remains of the pump. The two officers dragged the bodies out and laid them down on the pavement.

"Check the identities."

They opened the tunics and read the discs tied on string round each neck.

"No. 237154 Station Officer W.B. White. He was only made up at midday. Got a new disc already. He was a keen type."

Janet had been sent out three times with the petrol lorry. It was after ten o'clock the next morning when she drove the empty vehicle back into substation 69Y's yard. She got down from the cab, tired and dirty, and walked to the station door. Two of the trailer pumps had just come in, their crews wet through and with smoke blackened faces. They stood aside to let her pass.

Charlie Pierce said, "Hello, Dicky" and then he looked down at his feet. "Have a word with Mollie Breaks will you, my old duck. She's in the watch-room."

"Come into the dormitory, Dicky."

She followed the section officer who was preceded by Agnes Jenkins carrying a cup of tea. She put it down on a locker and shuffled out closing the door.

"Sit down, Dicky. You've got to be very brave. I want you to prepare yourself for a shock."

"Is it Bill?"

"Yes."

"Is he dead?"

"Yes, I'm afraid so."

The older woman looked down with compassion at the set pale face in which the lips moved silently.

'Pray God let me wake up from this horrible dream'.

"Four hours compassionate leave granted to Auxiliary Firewoman Finch to attend a funeral."

Mabel Smith wrote the message down and put the slip in the tray for the sub-officer.

"See that," she said to Cissie Spence.

"Yes. Service funeral isn't it or sort of?"

"Sort of. There's nine of them together. All from last week's raid. There's more in the North Division at a different cemetery. It was a nasty old night."

"Yes, they get worse don't they, but they don't come so often."

Janet went to the funeral alone, refusing Colonel Boyd's offer to accompany her. It was at two thirty on a cold overcast day with drizzling rain. The sirens sounded as she reached the cemetery gates having walked from the bus stop. She looked over the desolate landscape made hideous with tasteless stone and marble, pocked with the craters of bombs that had left shattered memorials lying broken in the half-filled saucer-shaped holes.

A canopied lorry overtook her on the gravelled drive. She saw three trumpeters from the brigade band sitting in the back, nursing their bugles. The lorry drove at walking pace between the gravestones and she followed it to a corner where the wet earth was piled around a large hole in the ground across which planks were laid.

A small party from station 69 and other stations, wearing fire tunics, caps and belts with axes stood at ease in two rows opposite one another. A group of relatives, mostly women slowly formed the third side of a square between them. She saw Bill's mother and sister among them, but she did not approach. She did not want to talk to people, but to nurse her overbearing sorrow in solitude. The rain grew heavier and a battery of anti-aircraft guns opened fire against planes flying above the low clouds.

The divisional officer's car drew up behind the lorry and the DO got out and spoke to the station officer in charge of the men. They were called to attention as a procession of nine coffins, each covered with a Union Jack came slowly down the gravelled path, a surpliced clergyman leading. She could not tell which was Bill's coffin as the firemen bearers lowered them to the ground and fell in beside the others.

The clergyman stood at the edge of the grave and

opened his prayer book.

"I am the resurrection and the life, sayeth the Lord; he that believeth in Me, though he were dead, yet shall he live."

A salvo from the guns drowned the next words. They said the ninetieth psalm, reading from copies spotted and blurred by rain and the flags were removed from the coffins. The firemen began to lower them one by one into the grave.

"Forasmuch as it hath pleased Almighty God of his great mercy to take unto Himself the souls of our dear brothers here departed, we therefore commit their bodies to the ground," said the clergyman.

Bang, bang, interrupted the guns. A woman was sobbing loudly. Janet was standing behind her, a rolled-up handkerchief clasped firmly in her hand.

"I mustn't break down here. It's not done."

Colonel Boyd's words came back to her.

"I went to the funeral you know. Your mother was a very brave woman. I can see her now standing in the rain eight months gone, with you on the way."

She was three weeks overdue.

The Anglican priest read the collect and gave the blessing. The trumpeters stepped to the graveside and the long sad notes of the Last Post filled the air. The firemen fell out and walked to the lorries. Bill's mother with a handkerchief to her eyes, walked on her daughter's arm towards a hired car. She looked over her shoulder as if seeking Janet out. They had only met once at the time of the engagement.

Janet stood irresolute for a moment.

"I must be alone. I can't bear to talk about it," she said.

She turned and walked in the opposite direction, hoping to find a different way out of the cemetery. A devious route among the gravestones brought her to an exit on the main road, and she began to walk along the pavement to the bus stop. A big black car with a silver bell on the side drew up alongside her. The divisional officer opened the rear door and leaned out.

"You'd better have a lift. You look wet through."

She got in, reluctantly.

"It was kind of you to go to the funeral; it looked right to see one or two of the women there in uniform."

"I wanted to go."

"Well anyway, it was a nice gesture; rather an austere affair wasn't it? Couldn't have taken more than twenty minutes."

He looked at his watch.

"Do you go to many of them, sir?"

"Too many I'm afraid. Where do you want dropping?"

"I'm going to substation 69Y. It's in Rampton Road."

"Yes, I know it is," he replied, and then he said "Rampton Road" to the driver.

"Please don't go out of your way sir. If you drop me off in Old Kent Road, I can get a bus."

There was a sort of insistence in her voice.

"As you wish," he said and redirected the driver. "You ought to have been wearing your Mac."

"It wasn't raining when I set out."

"Still, it looked as if it was going to. Too much sickness in the service already, after the winter and we're short of drivers. You've been looking after one of F districts petrol lorries, haven't you?"

"Yes sir."

He asked her about her experiences, and she answered in monosyllables. The car drew up at the corner of Old Kent Road and Ilderton Road. She got out, saluted and watched it draw away. He picked up a file from the seat beside him and turned the pages, but he could not concentrate. 'She's a pretty little thing,' he mused, 'but a bit dumb. Almost surly. Funny, I thought she was quite a gay little spark when I bumped into her in the Criterion bar last year'.

She walked into the watch-room.

"Book-me back from short leave, Mabel. I've gone up to the dormitory if anybody wants me."

She threw herself on her bed and her pent-up emotions burst out at last, as she sobbed and cried and beat the bedding with clenched fists. The door opened quietly as Mollie Breaks looked in then closed it again. She was back in a few minutes with two cups of tea on a tray.

"It's good to see you having a good cry, Dicky. It'll do you good. We were all getting properly worried about you. Now sit up and drink this and tell your old Mollie all about it. Have a cigarette."

"I don't smoke."

"Try one. It'll help calm you down."

She coughed between her sobs as the smoke tickled her lungs.

"You won't believe me, Dicky but time does help. I didn't believe it when they told me that last April but it's true."

"I'm sorry; everybody here has been so kind. I'm afraid I haven't shown much appreciation."

"That's all right, they're kind people here aren't they?"

Spring came and with April, two raids bigger than any before. Colonel Boyd was bombed out and stayed at his club and then, with Kitty Farrow's permission, he moved to her Kensington house. Janet found it a relief to have his company on her leave days.

She was beginning to suffer from morning sickness. She got up hastily from her bed in the dormitory and hurried to the bathroom. She vomited and the nausea left her. Mollie Breaks stood behind her, dressed in pyjamas and dressing gown.

"I wondered where you were going when you jumped out of bed so quick."

"I think it must have been something I've eaten."

"I don't. You were sick in your bed the other morning. Don't think I didn't notice it or are you washing your sheet in one of the lav basins when you thought nobody was about. You're preggers, Dicky, aren't you? Come on. You'll need a bit of help. Let me give it to you."

"Yes, I'm 'preggers'. I'm not really sorry. It'll be something to remember Bill by for always."

Mollie sighed.

"You don't know what you are taking on. What will your mother think?"

"She'll be terribly distressed."

"You'll have to leave the service. What'll you do?"

"I don't know. That's the worst part. Go to Brandon I expect. It's very quiet there. Mother will help me."

"Go and get dressed. You're off duty at nine, aren't you? See me after that."

They met in the dormitory after the off-going watch had been dismissed.

"Now this is between Mollie Breaks and Dicky Finch, not between Section Officer Breaks, and Firewoman Finch. I'm quite fond of my stripes and little bit of authority and I don't want to lose them. I'm meant to pass a little note up to Mrs Bridger at station 69, who'll send it on to Southwark, who'll send it on to HQ. Then you'd be sent for by one of the top ladies there who'd have the welfare officer sitting with her and you'd be out, Dicky my dear, and there would be a letter on the way to your mum. If I deal with it a different way and it comes out in the end, I know nothing about it, see. Got a cigarette."

Janet produced a packet and said, "Yes, I see. I won't say anything."

"You've got two alternatives. Get rid of it or have it. It's up to you which you take and I'll have no part in persuading you, either way."

"How do I get rid of it?"

"Same way as Edith Brown did, of course. It's a pity that stupid little cow has gone off sick. She's not at home either. Gone to the country somewhere. She's got the address. She got it from Mrs Judge at the fish and chip shop. That old bag used to be quite handy with a knitting needle herself, but she was too windy; wouldn't do it for Edith. You'd better go and see her and ask the address. It was a chemist up west somewhere. When you've got it, make your mind up what you're going to do. I'll help you either way. It's rotten luck, Dicky."

Janet walked down Auger Street in the early May sunshine. It was several weeks since she had been that way, and it had suffered badly in the April raids. Many of the mean little houses were deserted, with broken windows and fallen slates. Several were demolished and lay in a ruin of rubble and gaping walls. Little Union Jacks had been fixed in the wreckage and fluttered in the breeze. And even here among the very poor, the looters had been busy.

'Hitler bombed me, another swine robbed me', was chalked on a door. The old tannery that had been substation 69Y was a burned-out shell. She walked past it to the fish and chip shop. It too lay in ruins, with the zinc topped fish bar open to the sky, the mirror behind it cracked and peeling but with Mrs Judge's jingle written across it still legible.

'Owing to Hitler the fish will be littler. Owing to Hess the chips will be less'.

Beneath it, a rude and alien hand had added another line.

'Owing to Goering, the proprietor has taken up her former occupation'.

She stood and looked at the ruins, then she clasped her hands beneath her stomach.

"You're all right, little Brusher. I'd never have murdered you anyhow."

She looked up at the blue cloud flecked sky.

"I wouldn't have killed your child, Bill. You know that, don't you?"

"Well, if that's the way you want it, that's it," said Mollie Breaks the next morning. "All I can say is you've got guts, kid. Better say nothing to anybody for the time being, but it'll begin to show in a few months' time. Then you'll have to leave us. We'll all miss you. Meanwhile, just keep your pecker up and keep working and don't let your mind dwell too much on what's happened.

"What do you think of this Liverpool lark? Raided seven night's running. That's the most any place in the provinces has had to put up with. There's about five hundred of our blokes up there. I hope they're enjoying themselves."

Chapter 9

The heaviest raid of the war came on 10th May. It started early without the slow build-up that had characterised some of its predecessors. From the start, the whistle of bombs seemed almost continuous. The great candelabra flares hung in the sky, casting white light over everything and dimmed the incendiaries as they lay burning in the streets and on the rooftops. The fires took hold rapidly, casting a red glow on the clouds, and above the beat of many aircraft engines could be heard. Janet stood at the substation door and watched the sky.

The escape carrier and every pump had left the station within half an hour of the sirens sounding. The watch-room telephones rang continuously, and she could hear Mollie Breaks' voice.

"I've told you that all our pumps are out. No, none of them-have reported back. Of course, I'll let you know as soon as one does. What do you think I'm here for? Yes, I'll send any crew that reports back on to Five Ways. You should worry. We've had six running calls here we couldn't attend to. I sent the messages up to you an hour ago and they haven't got a pump there yet. All right, keep your hair on."

She slammed the receiver down as Janet walked into the watch-room.

"That was Section Officer Banks. She seems to have got the jitters. Says the Brigade's attending to two thousand calls and they've asked for a hundred pumps at five of them."

The phone rang again and she wrote on a message pad as she answered it.

"Here you are, Dicky. Petrol lorry to Surrey Commercial Docks. Quite like old times isn't it? I didn't think there was anything left to burn there."

She handed over the message slip.

"It's a rough old night out there. Mind how you go."

Cissie Spence was on the phone, repeating messages and writing on a message slip as she spoke.

"Abbey Street blocked to traffic east of Tower Bridge Road junction; Druid Street blocked to traffic west of Sweeney Crescent; Jamaica Road blocked to traffic; Pages Walk blocked to traffic; Bevington Street blocked to traffic; Dunton Road blocked to traffic; Lynton Road blocked to traffic: Tabard Street blocked to traffic, east of Pilgrim Street; Snow's Field blocked to traffic at junction with Western Street. That the lot?"

"Blimey," said Mollie. "We won't be able to get in or out of here soon. Can you make it, Dicky?"

"Yes, I can take Grange Road and Southwark Park Road and up into Hawkstone Road. It's a bit of a detour."

"Ah, you know your way about. Pity you didn't know your way about in some other sense," she added, under her breath.

Janet went out into the yard. A flare was dropping, its small parachute visible above the swinging balls of white light.

"Thanks for the illumination, you bastards," she said, as she swung the lorry out of the playground gates and into the road.

She passed an unattended fire in a shop premises and wondered whether she should report it, but she decided that it would take too long to find a telephone. The streets were no longer as deserted as they had been in the autumn raids. Fireguards scuttled out of doorways and dropped sandbags on incendiary bombs in the streets, and she saw policemen patrolling.

Southwark Park loomed up, its trees silhouetted against the glow of fire in the docks, towards which she was headed. As she passed the belt of green, the anti-aircraft guns there loosed off a deafening salvo that made the windscreen rattle.

A station officer met her at the dock gates.

"Take it up to Pageants Wharf. Report to the district officer there. Rough old night isn't it?"

She agreed with him and drove on. The fire station had had its doors and windows repaired since she was there in September.

She walked through the empty appliance room, saluted the woman officer and said, "Petrol lorry from substation 69Y with seven hundred gallons. Auxiliary Firewoman Finch in charge."

"All right, I'll book you in. Better take it straight on down Rotherhithe Street to the warehouse there. That's where the fires are. You'll find the district officer at the control point. This is the worst raid yet. What sort of a journey did you have?"

"All right. I had to make a detour."

"Just wondered. We've had a report from Southwark that there are nine roads blocked to traffic around here. I don't know how you'll get back. You'd better call in for the list when you've unloaded."

"How much have you got aboard?" asked the district officer.

"Three hundred and fifty tins, sir."

"Shan't need half that. See the scaffolding down there with the pumps set in around it? Dump forty tins there and the same at the other dam a quarter of a mile on. That'll do us. We've nearly won. Plenty of water here. I've got two fireboats lying out there pumping eight thousand gallons a minute ashore. Makes a difference.

"See that warehouse there. It was full of margarine and well alight. We've beaten it. Took us two hours but we've saved two-thirds. Now that's where the real trouble is."

He pointed to the west where a great red glow arced into the sky.

"That's Five Ways. Look, the bastards are stoking it up. That's HE."

Pinpoints of flame topped by puffs of smoke could be seen stabbing upwards out of the glow.

"You keep away from there tonight, miss. I'm glad it's not my pigeon. All right, off you go."

They both crouched to a loud short whistle. The margarine warehouse disintegrated as the bomb hit it, bursting the walls asunder in a cascade of falling brickwork. Flames and black smoke leapt up from the ruins.

"Oh, my Gawd," said the district officer. "Two hours work by twenty pumps' crews all gone for a burton."

Janet took the lorry bumping over the rubble to the dam. It was built up by portable scaffolding, supporting a huge canvas bag. Open-ended deliveries from the fireboats were discharging water into it, the hose snaking away into the darkness and the river. Round the dam, eight trailer pumps were grouped with their suctions lying over the lip, their engines running at full throttle, making an ear-splitting roar. She found a sub-officer and shouted into his ear.

"Petrol up. Where do you want it?"

He pointed to the kerb and shouted back.

"I'll lend you a couple of men to help unload."

She undid the ropes that held the tarpaulin in place and threw it back, climbed on top of her load and she threw forty two-gallon cans down to the men below, who stacked them up on the pavement. She drove on to the next dam and repeated the operation. As she finished, the steel helmeted AFS messenger from Pageants Wharf cycled up and handed her a message slip.

It read. 'Take any unused petrol to fire at naval victualling yard, Deptford'. A list of blocked roads was attached.

Having fulfilled the order, she drove the empty lorry back to substation 69Y and to her left the glow over Five Ways seemed bigger than ever. She looked at her watch. It was two-thirty a.m. The fury of the raid was unabated. She drove into the station yard and booked in at the watch-room.

"Blimey, Dicky, where've you been?" said Mollie Breaks.

"Naval Victualling Yard, got sent on there from Surrey Docks."

"Got any rum or baccy?"

"Afraid not."

"Well, I'm glad you've turned up because station 69 have been on the phone, asking for you ten times in the last ten minutes. Get up there at once and report to Mrs Bridger. There's some sort of panic on and they can't lay their hands on a spare driver anywhere."

Mrs Bridger heard the lorry drive into station 69's yard and she hurried out.

"Thank heavens you've come, Finch. Southwark have been phoning on and off for the last twenty minutes. Every driver and every vehicle is out. There's a shortage of water at Five Ways and they're trying to relay from the river nearly two miles away.

"The dam has been destroyed, I think by a bomb. There's a spare here and it must be got there as soon as possible. There are two C class men* to help you load it. When it's on the lorry put your foot down and get it there as soon as possible. Goodness, what a night," she added, as a stick of four bombs crashed down a few streets away.

The men hauled the folded canvas into the lorry and

---

* *non- operational firemen*

threw the metal scaffold poles on top of it, one after the other. Janet got into the cab.

"It's all aboard," said one of the men and she drove out of the yard.

She accelerated and swerved around a crater, picked out just in time by the single hooded headlight. There was a fire ahead of her with pumps at work and the lorry bumped as it drove over charged hose. She drove on for a quarter of a mile of dark streets until she came across another fire. She slowed down and steered between groups of firemen, the spray from their branches blowing into the cab and wetting her face. Men and machines blocked the road.

"Where are you going?" said a sub-officer looking into the cab.

"Five Ways. I've got a portable dam aboard. It's wanted urgently. Please get that pump moved."

"Five Ways! They've made it one hundred and fifty pumps; they've had twenty-two killed and the Jerries are stoking it up. The best of British luck to you. You've got about a mile to go. I'll get it shifted for you. The bugger's got no water anyhow."

They moved the pump and chafing at the delay, she slammed through the gears and pressed the accelerator to the floorboards. She was only twenty yards from the crater when the headlamp picked it out. The tyres screamed as she braked. The lorry bounced as it hit the debris round the rim and pulled up with a jolt; the front wheels hanging over the edge. Her body jack-knifed forward and the steering wheel crashed into her midriff as her face hit the windscreen. She groaned in pain as feet came running up the road behind her.

"You all right? Blimey. You nearly drove straight into the bomb 'ole. Didn't you 'ear us shout?"

It hurt her to draw the breath to speak.

"Yes, I'm all right. Help me to get it out."

The sub-officer came up.

"Stick her in reverse and accelerate slowly while we lift and push at the front."

The men heaved and strained around the bonnet and front axle. Slowly, the lorry came backwards dragging the front wheels over the edge of the hole and the lumps of broken road metal that lay around it.

"You'll get past if you drive over the pavement."

The steering felt slack and then tight in her grasp. The lorry veered over to the pavement, mounted the kerb, came around the crater and then veered across to the other pavement. The sub-officer ran to the front, waving her down.

"You can't drive that. The track rod's all bent. She won't answer her helm."

"I've got to get this to Five Ways. Look out."

She drove on, zigzagging from side to side of the road, heaving first one way and then the other on the steering wheel to try and keep a straight course. She could smell burning rubber from the front tyres as they half rolled half rubbed over the road surface.

Shafts of pain stabbed through her body each time she wrenched on the wheel to get the lorry straight. She somehow managed to pull it through a left turn into the long straight road from Blackfriars Bridge to Five Ways.

The scene was as bright as day. Lines of hose ran down the street, some charged but most flat and dry. The relay pumps were spaced at long intervals, those in the lines of charged hose with their engines running, the others silent, with their crews sheltering in doorways or walking the lengths of dry hose, stamping on the embers that floated down from the sky and burned.

The damaged truck swayed from kerb to kerb down the road, bumping over hose and narrowly missing the pumps. A fireman leaped out of the way.

"Fuck me. Did you see that?" he said to a colleague. "That was an AFS woman driving. She must be pissed."

She could go no further. Pumps, men and rubble blocked the road. A station officer walked up to the cab door.

"What've you brought?"

"The scaffolding dam from…"

"And about time too. You'd better come with me and report its arrival to the control point. The divisional officer there isn't half in a flaming temper about it. He's got four charged lines arrived at the fire from about two miles away and nowhere to stick the water except into four pumps. He could have got eight to work if he'd had that dam."

"Get it unloaded and up to the crossroads," he shouted to the crew. "Follow me, Miss."

The fire was the biggest Janet had seen. Shops, office buildings, and warehouses burned fiercely, the flames shooting out of window openings and licking up the facades of the buildings. A roof fell in, sending showers of sparks into the sky, the up-draught of hot air flinging flaming brands whisking up like autumn leaves on a windy day.

A bomb crashed down to their left and they heard the roar of tumbling masonry. Firemen waiting for water, crouched by their pumps. Gusts of warm air swept down the street as it was dragged in from around by the hot air rising from above the fires. They stumbled over fallen masonry and into a side road that was almost undamaged and darker where the high buildings shielded the light from the fires.

A salvage sheet lay on the pavement, humped in the centre. A current of air lifted and folded back the edge so that a row of boots stuck out from the concealing canvas. She counted them as they passed. Sixteen pairs of boots. Twelve of them were the mass-produced rubber wellingtons of the AFS, four pairs the hand-sewn leather fire boots of the LFB. Old rivalries and frictions had disappeared in the fellowship of death.

They turned a corner and came into the circus where the five south London roads met, which included the former landmark pub, 'The Elephant and Castle'. The buildings blazed around the perimeter and up the streets that spread out from the centre. The control point was on the pavement, in front of the burning hotel where two of the visible jets were at work.

The divisional officer stood there with his staff. His uniform was torn at the sleeve and from the bandage on his hand blood dropped down his tunic to the pavement. A misshapen silver epaulette hung from the retaining button.

His face was black from smoke and his eyes bloodshot.

"Go on. Report," said the station officer, pushing her in the back.

She winced with pain as she raised her arm to salute.

"Scaffolding dam from station 69, sir."

He looked up at her.

"You've been a bloody long time getting it here," he said. Then to one of the officers. "Get it put up where the other one was, and then get all hose lines into it. Set as many pumps as the hose lines will supply."

Janet stood waiting for dismissal.

"Don't stand there gawping. Report back to your substation. We're short of drivers tonight."

"I told you his nibs was in a bit of a temper," said the station officer, as they made their way back to the lorry. "It's hell for a fireman to be helpless at a fire because there isn't a drop of water."

A group of men stood by the lorry, looking down at the front wheels and one lay on the ground shaking the tie rods with both hands. A stick of bombs whistled and exploded close by.

"Oh, my Gawd. Won't anyone please go and blow the all clear on that there siren?" said one of the group.

"You can't drive this anymore, Miss. The track rod's bent, and your front wheels are all out of true. I don't know how you got it 'ere. What 'appened?"

"I half drove into a crater. I was going rather fast."

A surge of pain shot through her. She swayed, clutched the station officer's arm and swung round to a sitting position on the lorry's step.

"She's hurt. Look. Her nose is swollen, and her eyes are blackening up."

"What did you do, Miss?"

"My tummy hit the steering wheel and my face hit the windscreen."

The station officer knelt down opened her tunic and lifted the shirt below. She felt rough skinned but gentle hands run over her body.

"Here get her lying down. Get up to the phone box and order an ambulance. She's got four broken ribs. They'll be through her lungs if we're not careful."

They laid her down on her back in the road. The red tinged clouds above her were broken, showing a patch of night sky in which, a bright star shone. The star swayed and made circles before her eyes. The rending pain seared through her belly again. She moaned and fainted.

The all clear sounded just before dawn.

"What a relief," said Mollie Breaks. "Perhaps those bloody phones will stop ringing for a few minutes now. Go and ask Aggie to make a pot of tea, Cissie."

She pulled a cigarette from the packet on the table and lit it.

A telephone rang and she picked it up.

"No, nothing from this substation's reported back yet. Surely you don't want any more now the all-clear's gone. What? Fires still spreading in the city. Of course, I'll let you know as soon as any of ours comes in."

The White watch reported for duty at nine o'clock and were sent up to seventy-nine to man spare pumps there, to be sent to fires. It was half past ten when the self-propelled followed by two trailer pumps drew into the yard. The men got down, their faces pale with fatigue beneath the sooty coating of grime.

"All right, get them lined up and you can fall out for a cup of tea before cleaning down. White watch'll see to the 'ose," said Davies.

His fifty years lay heavy on him as he stood by the pump, his hand resting on the suctions for support while he surveyed his crews through bloodshot red-rimmed eyes that blinked in the sunlight.

Mollie Breaks had come out into the yard when she heard the pumps drive in and her heart sank when she saw the condition of the men.

"I'm sorry, Sub, but there are instructions from station 69 for every pump reporting back to go at once to the city. Report to control point in Upper Thames Street. That includes the off-going watch."

He turned his head towards her.

"They can't do it. Tell 'em they can't do it. Some of these men have been swinging on the end of a branch for twelve hours. Where's White watch?"

"They're all out. They were sent out the moment they booked in at nine o'clock. They're manning the spare pumps."

"All right, book us back and then out to Upper Thames Street."

"I haven't booked any of you in yet or reported you back. Aggie's had two kettles on since before nine o'clock. Give them five minutes for a cup of tea and a rest."

He looked at her doubtfully.

"You wouldn't let me down, Mollie Breaks?"

"Of course, I wouldn't. Every officer is still out at fires. Nobody will know. Say I didn't pass on the message for five minutes if you like. A short time like that can't make any difference."

They trooped disconsolately into the mess room and slumped on the benches, their elbows making wet patches where they rested them on the table.

"Cor, what a night," said Harry Booth.

"Oh, for Gawd's sake stop saying that. That's about the tenth effing time. You sound like some bloody old housewife complaining about the weather."

Tempers were frayed.

"Sorry it's not very sweet," said Agnes. "The sugar ration's run out and we don't get no more till Monday."

"Someone's been 'alf pinchin' it, I shouldn't wonder."

"Nobody 'alf pinches the sugar in my kitchen. I keep it under lock and key. Come on, drink up! It's 'ot and strong."

"Ah, its jolly good Aggie. You're a good old girl. What wouldn't I 'ave done for one of those, once or twice during the last few hours. We never saw a canteen van once."

"We didn't even get relieved once."

"We got relieved for about ten minutes when our pump lost its water after the main got broke. There was a NAAFI canteen under the arches at Waterloo Station. Charlie and I went in. It was deserted except for a snooty old cow be'ind the counter."

"Could we 'ave a cup of tea please, missus," I said. "She draws 'erself up and says very 'aughty like. 'This canteen is for members of 'Is Majesty's Armed Forces only. We don't serve civil defence people 'ere'. I told her to fuckin' stuff it."

"Come on. Get moving," said Davies. "You've 'ad yer five minutes."

"Isn't there enough time to change into dry tunics and trousers?"

"What'd be the good when yer underclothes are wet through? You can thank your stars that it isn't still winter. When you get up to the city get stuck in close to the fire and no long shots. Then you'll soon dry out."

They walked to the pumps.

Mollie Breaks picked up the phone and said, "Self-propelled and two trailer pumps returned and ordered on to Upper Thames Street. What's that? Dicky Finch. Only broken ribs, Oh Good."

She saw the last pump out of the gate. Charlie Pierce was driving.

"Dicky Finch has been hurt and taken to hospital. Tell Davies."

He pulled up with a jolt.

"Is she bad?"

"No, only broken ribs. It wasn't a bomb. She drove into a crater."

"Oh Good! You gave me quite a turn. Well she deserves a little rest. We'll 'ave to go and see 'er."

She came to among clean starched sheets and she looked at the ceiling, wondering where she was. It was quiet in the ward. She remembered the crash of bombs and the roar of flames around the Five Ways, the star in the patch of clear sky and the hardness of the road surface against her back.

She could see her nose quite plainly and she wondered why. She lifted her hand from beneath the bedclothes and felt it. It was swollen. Her hand went below the sheet again. There was a large piece of sticking plaster on her left side and a tight bandage and wadding between her legs.

A nurse came to the bedside.

"How do you feel?"

"All right, thank you."

"You've got four broken ribs, a broken nose and two lovely black eyes but we'll soon have you right. Just lie still and take it easy. Matron wants a word with you. I'll go and fetch her."

The tall grey-haired woman leant over the bed; asked how she felt and then she said, "I have to tell you that you have had a miscarriage."

Her eyes went to Janet's ringless left hand. She had changed Bill's engagement ring to the right.

"I hope that perhaps the news will not distress you too much."

There were visiting hours every afternoon. Her mother sat by the bed the next day.

"It gave me quite a turn. They were very good about letting me know. Some woman officer rang me from your HQ. I caught the eleven o'clock this morning, terribly crowded. I had to stand in the corridor all the way, with a first-class ticket too. Oh dear, I do hope that your nose is going to be all right. It will be dreadful if you have to go through life with it crooked.

"I was quite shocked driving through the streets in the taxi from Liverpool Street to see so much destruction. How long can we go on like this? They say that the prime minister cried when he went to look and the people who had been bombed out cheered him. I'm really very proud of you doing that job right in the middle of the worst part of London."

"It was nice of you to come, Mummy, and lovely to see you. Where are you staying?"

"I'm staying at Aunt Kitty's. I couldn't get in touch with her. She's still somewhere in Scotland, but she said that she had a bed for me at any time."

"How very improper, when she told Uncle Neville the same thing and he's already there."

She laughed.

"Uncle Neville's over sixty, and I'm not much younger. I'll be glad of his company though. I shall stay in London till you're better. Perhaps they'll give you some convalescent leave and you can come back to Brandon with me for a while. The country is looking lovely with all the lilac and laburnum and hawthorn out."

Janet was swept by a wave of nostalgia. She thought of the lilac, laburnum and hawthorn, blue skies and the country air of her childhood. For those she could exchange the grey London streets, the sour smelling rubble, the reek of smoke and ashes, the sight of blood on pavements and of the wide black river into which the unscreened sewage had gone when the outfall works had been bombed.

"It sounds very nice," she said and smiled.

"Well I'm sure it can be arranged. I shan't be able to stay in London very long. Most of the evacuees came back to us in September, along with some new ones as well and I'm on two new committees. It would be wonderful to have you at home for a little while, especially after you've had such a beastly winter."

"It wasn't really such a beastly winter. Not until March."

There were tears in the swollen eyes. Her mother took her hand.

"Now, my darling, I've told you in my letters, you've got to put it out of your mind. If you have lovely memories treasure them, as I did, and still do, but face life all the time."

Jim Cartwright called the next day.

"Blue watch is on leave," he said, dropping a pile of magazines onto her feet. "Well, well, you look just like the panda in the zoo, only your black eyes are bigger."

"Jim, how nice of you to come, but I don't think that is a very complimentary remark."

"Why not? I think the panda is a very beautiful animal and a very sweet little animal, also very rare. Someone told me it's been evacuated. You ought to be too. How about going down to Sunningdale for a spot of convalescence when they let you out of here? Mother and father both think it would be a good thing."

"How kind of them. Are they all right?"

"Yes, they're fine. Father works in the office all day

and does home guard duty most of the night. Mama stays in London to keep an eye on him. They generally go to Sunningdale for the weekend."

"And what about you, Jim? It's such a long time since I saw you."

"Well that wasn't my fault. I'm all right and a very experienced fireman. We usually get sent to the city on the worst nights. Do you remember Tom Blake?"

"Yes, I remember him."

"I was with him the night he was hit. We all thought he had had his chips, but he came back on duty this week. He is a sub-officer now under the unification scheme. If it goes on much longer there won't be any firemen's round caps left in the LFB. Well anyway, the nearest shave I ever had, was on the night that Tom Blake was hit, I mean.

"One of the same bomb's splinters hit me in the leg. I remember a rubber boot full of blood; a visit to a first-aid post where they found it had only gone through the calf; seven stitches; and four days off. That's about all that happened to Auxiliary Fireman J. Cartwright, except the most appalling conjunctivitis that made me think once or twice that I was going blind; but what about you, Janet? I heard that you were driving one of F district's petrol lorries. I thought that the C class men usually did that."

"You know what happened to me?"

"Yes, I'm terribly sorry. Did you get my letter?"

"Yes, thank you, Jim. It was a very nice letter, one of the nicest. I'm sorry that I didn't answer it. I must answer the others. I'll say thank you to you now."

"That's all right, old girl. I just wondered — well, I

didn't mean to bring it up today. Now he's gone is there any chance for me? I do love you, you know."

"Oh Jim, not here and not now. You're very kind and I'm very fond of you, but don't talk about that. I don't think that anyone could be in love twice in a lifetime. Not in love as I was."

"I'm sorry. I'm a tactless fool. I shouldn't have mentioned it. Well I'll go now. Can I call again next leave day?"

"Yes, of course. Goodbye Jim, it was good of you to come."

The days passed with visits from her mother, from Colonel Boyd, Mollie Breaks and Charlie Pierce. She had been there for over a week when a nurse announced.

"A visitor for you."

She saw a tall figure in double breasted blue suit, stiff white collar and black-tie walking down the ward. She sat up straight in bed.

"For God's sake, relax," he said. "You're not on parade now. Well how's Firewoman Finch? Brought you something to read," he said, laying *Punch* and *The Tattler* on the bedside table. "How are the ribs?"

"Getting on fine, thank you, sir. Still hurting a bit if I cough."

"I'm afraid I owe you an apology. I was a bit harassed on the night of May 10th and it doesn't improve the temper to have a hundred pumps and five hundred firemen at your disposal without a drop of water. Of course, I had no idea that you were injured or I wouldn't have been so curt. Took it just as another bit of equipment arriving late. You did very well to deliver it at all under the circumstances and it made all the difference. I'm very grateful."

Janet saw her mother walk up.

"Oh, hello Mummy. This is Lieutenant Commander Stephens, one of our principal officers."

"How do you do, Mrs Finch?"

"The name is Carew-Finch," she said, smiling.

"Oh, I'm sorry. Your daughter is always known as Finch, even in her personal record card, which I read before coming here. Auxiliary Firewoman J.M. Finch, but I happen to know that she is referred to locally as Dicky, which I assume is not correct either."

"No, it's Janet. How kind of you to call on her, Commander Stephens, especially when you must be so busy."

"Not at all. All part of the job and today is a particularly pleasant part. However, I'll leave her with you. I've got two more visits in the men's wards here. Good afternoon. Goodbye Finch. Hurry up and get better."

"Who is he?"

"One of what they call the principal officers; direct entry, which means they come straight in at the top. A divisional officer actually."

"He seems very young."

"Yes, I suppose so, but he's one of the big shots. Even a chief superintendent has to salute him."

"Well, it's what I have been saying for the past eighteen months, my darling. If only you would put in for transfer to HQ and for promotion you could be mixing with those sorts of people which would be far more suitable for you than living in a substation in Bermondsey. Why don't you do it?"

"I should be taken off driving and have to go to a training school and learn mobilising and how to boss people about and I'd have to leave substation 69Y and all my friends there. Besides, nearly all the women officers are people who joined before the war."

"Oh dear, I suppose I'll never persuade you. I had a word with the sister before I came in. I told her I thought that broken ribs, once they were securely strapped, mended very quickly and that it was time they let you take a little walk around the ward. She said no, and that you must remain lying down a bit longer. It's very peculiar."

She was back the next day.

"Well my dear, what a charming man your Commander Stephens is. I met him again yesterday afternoon after I left you. I stood outside the hospital trying desperately to get a taxi. Of course, I might have known that the AFS had requisitioned most of them.

"He came up to me wearing a peaked cap with black oak leaves on the peak, which did look a bit incongruous with a blue suit and he asked if he could give me a lift. Of course, I said yes, and he took me all the way to Kensington. We sat in the back and chatted. You know he seems to know quite a lot about you, and he is terribly pleased with you. He said that you were one of the best types in the service. There were a few more like you but not enough. I've asked him to dinner."

"Oh Mummy, you shouldn't have done that."

"Why ever not. We got on famously. I've arranged to

ring him up when you're out of hospital and he's coming to dinner with us. I'm sure that Neville will like him."

Edith Brown was one of the last visitors just before Janet left the hospital.

"'Ullo Dicky, 'ow are you now? They told me you was getting on fine. Coming out the day after tomorrow aren't you. I brought the book from your locker you asked for 'Tess of the D'Urbervilles. A Pure Woman'. I don't know 'ow you plough through all this sort of stuff. I stick to Peg's Paper and the Mirror. What's it about?"

"Thanks for bringing it. I just wanted to finish it while I was here. It's about a poor country girl in Dorset. She was seduced by one of the gentry, and she had a baby by him that died. Later, she married an artist called Angel Clare who she loved very much. Then she told him about the baby, and he just walked out and left her. Then she met the other man again and she murdered him; stabbed him with a knife. That's as far as I got, but I know that she gets hanged in the end."

"Cor! It's quite sexy then and murder too. I didn't think those sorts of books were like that. Still I don't go much on the title. She wasn't a very pure woman if she got in the pod before she got married was, she? More like you and me, I should think."

The last remark was accompanied by a huge wink.

Janet sat up sharply.

"Who told you?"

"Oh, don't look so upset. Nobody told me, not really. All the girls in the dormitory knew you was getting morning sickness. Then when I came back from sick leave

Mollie Breaks asks me for the address I went to, over my little bit of trouble. Wanted it for an acquaintance she said, just in case she changed 'er mind.

"Do you mean you want it for Dicky Finch," I said. "She flared up straight away and asked me what I knew about it, so I told 'er. She isn't 'alf getting bossy since she 'as a couple of stripes on 'er shoulders."

"I suppose that everybody on the substation knows by now?"

"Well not everybody. I don't reckon all the men know. Any 'ow Dicky, we all want to 'elp. We'll all stand by you. I've brought the address. You want to get cracking as soon as you're out of 'ere. It's worse if you leave it too long."

"It's very kind of you Edith, but it won't be necessary. I've had a miscarriage. I told Mollie when she visited me here."

"Cor, that was lucky wasn't it? Where did you 'ave it?"

"Lying in the road at Five Ways, on the night of May 10th."

"Well stuff me!"

Chapter 10

Her mother brought the Alvis to fetch her from the hospital.

"I found the garage all right, but I don't know how I found my way around these south London streets. Aren't they a maze? You've got nearly three quarters of a tank full of petrol. Isn't that lucky?

"Some people in Brandon would give their eye teeth for it. Petrol rationing does hit us hard in the country you know. I hear there's talk of banning private motoring altogether. Well, you can tell me on the way from here to Kensington, can't you?"

She drove under Janet's expert directions to Kitty Farrow's house.

"Let me carry your case in. Your same bedroom is all ready for you."

"I can manage perfectly well, Mummy."

She took the case and she went upstairs where Alice greeted her.

"Oh, I was so sorry to hear you had been hurt, Miss Janet. What could it have been like that terrible night? Much the worst raid of all they say, and parliament bombed out too. I've only been back from Wiltshire a week but I'm not sorry to be back; especially as there hasn't been a proper raid since; just the sirens and a few distant bangs.

"You soon get tired of the country when you're used to London, you know. It's nice to be back and have the colonel and your mother here to be looked after. I should think the mistress will be back as well soon. I don't think Scotland really suits her and she doesn't see much of Mr Claude. Now you just let me unpack your bag and I'll be down to make a pot of tea in a few minutes."

Her mother put the telephone down as Janet walked downstairs.

"I've just been phoning your headquarters. It's such a pity, Commander Stephens is engaged every evening this week and I must go back to Brandon on Sunday. He was most apologetic, and I could tell from his voice that he really meant it. He made me promise to ring the very next time I'm in London, though heaven knows when that will be.

"He said that he was very disappointed at being unable to accept my invitation to dinner but would be even more so if I didn't ask him again. He asked after you and I told him that you were fully recovered. Of course, if I had thought of it in time, I should have said that you needed some rest in the country. I'm sure that he would have granted it straight away. It's quite ridiculous that you are reporting back for duty at that awful substation only two days after coming out of hospital."

"Well, that's what the doctor says, Mother, and since he won't sign a certificate for more sick leave I'm sure that the divisional officer wouldn't interfere with his ruling."

"Well, I think that it's very unfair. There hasn't been

a proper raid since May the10th so they can't need you all that badly. I wonder what the Germans are up to, leaving us alone for so long?"

Two days later Janet reported at substation 69Y with the Blue watch.

"Well, if it isn't little old Dicky Finch come back to us," said Bert Foster. "'Ow are you, my old duck?"

They crowded around her, shook her hand and patted her on the back.

"You did all right, that night," said Davies. "You were a credit to my substation."

The general-purpose lorry stood in the yard, repaired and with two new front tyres.

"I've booked you in," said Mollie Breaks, "and there's a job waiting for you, so you might as well get cracking. Lorry to Olaf Street depot. Pick up stores for delivery to station 69."

They walked out into the yard together.

"How are you feeling?"

"I'm feeling all right, thanks. I'm glad to be back."

"That's right, girl. Keep going and come and talk to your old Mollie if you ever feel down."

Drawn by her curiosity, Janet made a detour by Five Ways and she pulled the lorry out of the thin stream of traffic to park it between two piles of bricks. They were neatly stacked by the kerb, charred and re-baked by the fire, and they had been taken from the piles of rubble.

The five roads joined in a great circle of ruins, only the hotel stood more than two stories high and the burnt-out roof was sheeted over with tarpaulins. She got down from the cab to look around; then she walked along the pavement. The place was almost unrecognisable. A low brick wall, part newly built ran along on the left. She looked over it into a large basement. It had been cleared of rubble and a gang of firemen were rendering the walls with cement. She returned their waves and one of them mounted the ladder that led to the top of the wall.

"You want any of us, Miss?"

"No thank you. I just stopped to have a look. I was here on May the 10th. What are you all doing here?"

"You were here on May the 10th? Were you one of the girls with the canteen van? That was a rough old night, wasn't it? Well, we're just rendering this basement to make it watertight. When we've finished, we'll be able to pump about half a million gallons of water into it. Then on the next raid, it'll be handy for any fires around 'ere. Not that there's much left to burn, is there?

"We saved most of the pub though, didn't we? That's what some of the public say. 'You firemen always seem to manage to save the pub even if you let everything else burn'. Pity it's not opening time yet. You and I might nip in for a quick one.

"I like this job, you know. It's better than drilling all morning and more useful. Those silly little steel tanks they put in before weren't much cop, were they? My crew set a large trailer pump in here one night and it was empty in five minutes. Then where did we go for water; half a mile away, we've heard today that we've got to come off this work. The unions say it's got to be done by tradesmen, bricklayers and the like; reckon they don't know that there's a war on.

"You hang around or better still come back at eleven o'clock. It'll be stand easy time and opening time and I'll nip into the pub with you and buy you one."

"It's very kind of you but I've got to get on my way or I shall be in trouble."

"Ah, I bet there's one or two who wouldn't mind getting you in trouble. What watch are you?"

"Blue."

"Pity, I'm White. What's your station?"

"It's substation 69Y."

"Some stations have all the luck. There's lucky stations and unlucky stations. Station 69 wasn't so lucky though. They lost a whole crew with one bomb last March. I expect that you heard about it; of course, you would, being on one of their substations."

"Yes, I heard about it. I must go now."

She walked quickly back to the lorry and drove away. On this bright June morning Bill's death had been out of her mind. Always something or somebody brought it back. Keep working they had said to her. Keep driving. You could think all the time you were driving in the sparse traffic of wartime London that nightmares might become bad daydreams.

Her worst was looking again at Fred Mason's charred and blasted face, with bone showing around the empty eye socket. The wispy white hair changed to thick brown and the undamaged left-hand side became Bill's face.

Her hand went to her pocket and she pulled out a packet of cigarettes and a box of matches. Holding box and steering wheel in one hand she struck a match and lit up as she drove along.

'If I'd swung the lead a bit, I could have had that week of convalescent leave at Brandon,' she mused. 'I wonder if it would have been any better.'

An hour later she drove into Piper Place and through the gates of station 69's yard.

"'Ullo Dicky, what 'ave you brought us?" said Ernie Cliffe.

"Stores from Olaf Street. Where do you want them?"

"Leave it to me. I'll get it unloaded. You all right again? Good. They've been expecting you. There's a message in the watch-room for you to report to Mrs Bridger."

She went to the office.

"Good morning Finch. How are you feeling? I wanted to see you as soon as you got back. You did very well the night I last saw you, though if you hadn't been driving quite so fast, you might have got the dam to Five Ways quicker and without getting hurt. Still, that's partly my fault. I told you to hurry. That's the nice part of this interview. The other part isn't so nice. I've had a telephone call from HQ. You were seen smoking while on duty and driving a Brigade vehicle this morning. Do you admit it?"

"Yes Ma'am."

"You know perfectly well that it isn't allowed. I thought that you were one of the women who hadn't succumbed to that silly habit."

"I started it in March."

"Yes, I do understand. You had a very sad experience.

Well I'm not going to make an issue of it. Just a caution and not an official one that will be put on your record card, but don't do it again."

Janet slipped back into the substation's routine. The mess room chairs were brought out into the yard again in the long summer evenings.

"Well I can't fuckin' see 'ow we're going to win this 'ere fuckin' war. They slung us out of Norway, they fuckin' slung us out of France, then Greece, then Crete and now fuckin' Rommel's slung us out of most of North Africa that we captured from the Eyeties. Every fuckin' time we come into contact, we fuckin' get slung out. Where's it going to end? 'Ere we are all on our lonesome and little old 'Itler's got Italy and Russia and most of fuckin' Europe on 'is side."

"Ah but 'e 'asn't got the Empire."

"What the fuck can they do? Their soldiers get fuckin' slung out along with ours."

"Well, we sunk the *Bismarck*."

"Ah, we did an' all, and I'll tell you another thing. Ol' 'Itler isn't all that 'appy neither. 'Ardly a raid since May the 10th and I'll tell you for why. 'E lost over thirty planes that night. That's the record for nights, ain't it? We've got new night fighters with special pilots what get fed on carrots, so they can see in the dark. 'E 'ad to give up the big daylight raids last September because we shot so many down. Like as not that 'e'll 'ave to give up the big night raids for the same reason. 'Ess didn't fly to Scotland for no reason. I reckon 'e brought peace terms."

"It's not only night fuckin' fighters, the fuckin' ack-

ack's getting better. You seen these new Z fuckers like they've got in 'Yde Park. They fire rockets, not fuckin' shells and loose off ninety-six fuckers in one go. Unrotating projectiles they call 'em. Talk about a Brock's benefit."

"Oh, fuck the ack-ack They're fuckin' bloody dangerous. I 'ate it when their fuckin' splinters come showering down round a fuckin' fire. They're as bad as the bombs."

"We're improving too. They've delivered the new auxiliary towing vehicles to Southwark's grounds. Davies says we'll be getting ours next week. I've seen one. They're all right. Lots of room for the crew and the hose and a bit of guts under the bonnet. They really will tow a trailer pump. It'll be a bit different from these old taxis."

"Ah, I shan't be sorry to see the backs of those fuckers. Cor, do you remember the beginning of the fuckin' war when they didn't even 'ave fuckin' tow bars on them and we lashed the trailer pumps to the bumpers with fuckin' bits of rope? If there'd been a fuckin' raid, then 'alf the fuckers would never 'ave got to a fire."

"They were fun to drive though," said Janet. "I'll miss them. They had such a lovely lock."

"Yes, but you didn't 'ave to drive 'em with a crew and all that fuckin' 'ose on board and a trailer pump be'ind. Bottom fuckin' gear for the smallest fuckin' 'ill and even that pulling the fuckin' guts out of 'em."

"I think that all this water they're sticking into the bombed basements is much more important than the auxiliary towing vehicles. Just think what we could 'ave done with that some nights, instead of all that relaying from pump to pump for miles and miles."

"Well we couldn't 'ave 'ad that at the start 'cos there wasn't no bombed fuckin' basements."

"No, but they're going to stick great big bore hole pumps under all the bridges that'll pump thousands of gallons a minute of water ashore at low tide. They could have done that before."

"And per'aps saved me getting stuck in the fuckin' mud."

"Well, you know what they're going to do now. They're going to nationalise us. Make a National Fire Service instead of AFS and LFB and all the municipal brigades. It said so in the papers."

"What fuckin' difference will that make? Will they give us service rations?"

"You, you're always thinking of your guts. I don't know what difference it'll make. They said up at station 69 that nothing would happen until August, but we'd come under the Home Office instead of the London County fuckin' Council."

"Can't see that making any difference. I was always told it was the government that wouldn't let us have a second fire tunic until last January."

"Well, I don't know. How many more summers 'ave we got to sit 'ere talking about the war? I'm not looking forward to next winter and the old blackout starting again round about five o'clock."

The next day was Sunday. Janet came in at lunchtime from a journey to HQ.

"You heard the news?" said Cissie Spence.

"No what is it?"

"It was on the wireless. The Germans have invaded Russia."

The mess room table buzzed with conversation.

"It won't 'elp much. 'Itler will roll 'em up in a blitzkrieg in a fortnight."

"'Ow do you know?"

"Well if a little country like Finland could stand up to 'em all that time, what good will they be against the Germans. Besides they shot all their best generals back in 1938."

"Cor, but what a turn up for the book, eh. Non-aggression Pact, dividing up Poland with the Jerry, supplying 'im with corn and things and now fuckin' invaded by 'im. Teach 'em a lesson I should think."

"It doesn't matter about teaching anybody a lesson. What matters is that we've got somebody on our side now."

"Yes, but what fuckin' good will they be? That's what matters."

"It said that Winnie is going to speak on the nine o'clock news. 'E'll tell us."

"I don't fuckin' care what Winnie says. What I say is, if the Russians only kill ten of the fuckers that'll be ten of the fuckers less for us to kill."

Through the rest of June and through July, they studied the news and the maps as the German column pushed deep into Russia.

"What did I fuckin' tell you? They're just getting

rolled up like I said."

"Ah, but they've lasted more than a fortnight and they're keeping the Jerries busy. There's 'ardly been a raid worth speaking of since May the 10th."

Mabel Smith came out of the watch-room.

"Message for you, Dicky. You're to go up to station 69 to see Mrs Bridger at two o'clock. What've you been up to? Smoking on duty again?"

Mrs Bridger saw Janet in her office.

"There's a message for you Finch. You are to report to the divisional officer at headquarters at three o'clock. I haven't the slightest idea what it is about. Have you?" she added, after a pause during which her curiosity overcame her reluctance to show it.

"No Ma'am."

"Well, see that you're there on time. Good heavens. Just look at that uniform of yours. It's so shiny I can almost see my face in it. Still what can one do when there's only been one issue since 1938."

At five minutes to three, Janet reported to the divisional officer's secretary. A pleasant faced dark-haired girl in AFS uniform.

"What are you doing here at this time? Your interview is for four o'clock."

"I was told to be here at three."

"Oh well. That's the usual form. Nobody must ever be late. I should take a walk for an hour."

She walked along the embankment in the hot summer sun, a vague anxiety troubling her as she tried to think of a reason for this unexpected summons. Across the river, she could see charred beams sticking out from the damaged roof of the House of Commons and behind, the pigmy figures of men working high up on the roof of the damaged Abbey. She turned left at St Thomas's Hospital, walking around the shattered north entrance that was shored up by great bulks of timber and she went over Westminster Bridge and past Westminster Hall.

Richard the Lion Heart sat on his splinter pierced horse, holding a blast bent sword aloft. She remembered people saying that it was a good omen that the sword had not broken. She returned over Lambeth Bridge where the roadway, pierced by a bomb that had not exploded, showed a small area of new tarmac where the hole had been repaired. The minutes ticked slowly by until four o'clock and she was shown in as Big Ben struck the hour.

He was sitting behind a large desk, but he got up as she entered.

"Good afternoon. Please sit down. I've got some news for you. Congratulations on being awarded the British Empire Medal. The London Gazette will be out this afternoon. I expect the press have already got it and it may be in the late editions of the evening papers. We like to give recipients a little bit of warning. Would you like to see a copy of the citation?"

He picked up a sheet of paper from his desk and he handed it to her.

She looked, unbelievingly, at the typewritten words: 'Auxiliary Firewoman Janet Mary Carew-Finch, substation 69Y, Bermondsey. On the night of May, the 10th 1941, this firewoman was ordered to take a lorry carrying a portable dam to the fire at Five Ways'. She felt embarrassment as she sat under his gaze and skimmed over the words, 'drove into a new bomb crater — severely injured — four broken ribs — drove on with great persistence and gallantry — badly needed equipment — served throughout the raids — driver of petrol lorry — always showed devotion to duty'.

She put the paper on her knee and looked up

He was smiling.

"Finished already? You're a quick reader. It was a very stout effort. Wish that we could have made it a George Medal. I think that it was worth it, but our standards are rather high you know. Congratulations again."

He held out his hand.

"I expect that your mother will be very pleased. Give her my regards and tell her that I really was sorry that I couldn't accept her invitation. You'll be getting your own invitation in a few weeks' time to Buck House. In the meantime, you can put the ribbon up straight away."

He went back to his desk. He sat down and nodded.

She took it as a form of dismissal and went out. His secretary was outside the door.

"Congratulations, well done!" she said.

She walked all the way back to Bermondsey, with a lighter step than she had used since March and she thought of the September day in 1939 when she had driven from Brandon to London. The divisional officer's hand had lingered longer than necessary for a formal handshake of congratulations. She did not mind. She liked him. If only

Bill had been there to share her pleasure.

The announcement was among others in the evening papers, with a short extract from the citation. She warmed to the obvious pleasure of her colleagues at substation 69Y, as they pumped her arm and slapped her back.

"This'll mean a party, Dicky. We'll 'ave a real good un."

"Yes, of course, and it will be on me."

"Well, I didn't mean it like that."

"No, of course you didn't, but that's the form anyhow."

Telegrams came from Colonel Boyd, Mrs Farrow, her mother and Jim Cartwright. Mrs Bridger came around with her congratulations and she brought with her a small pink and grey edged ribbon for Janet's uniform.

She went to bed tired and she felt slightly muzzy from a preliminary and surreptitious celebration at the Carpenter's Arms with a small party of her particular friends from the station.

The next morning, she fell out from the nine o'clock parade and made her way to Kensington. Kitty Farrow came to the door as her key turned in the lock.

"Here's our little heroine," she cried. "Claude will be pleased when he hears and such a lovely surprise for you. Look who's here."

Her mother came forward from the shadows in the hall and kissed her.

"I simply couldn't resist it, darling. I caught the night train. I thought that we must have a little celebration right away. I'm so proud of you. It was in the Evening Standard, not that I'd ever see it, but Neville saw it and he rang me. He seemed surprised to hear that I knew nothing about it until then. When did you hear?"

"The divisional officer told me yesterday afternoon at the same time as the Gazette was published."

"Well, wasn't that nice of him. Now, don't think I've been a designing mama but he's coming to our celebration dinner. He said yes straight away, and he will be here at seven. I didn't think it right for Neville Boyd to be the only man there with three women."

"It will be someone for him to talk to. I've brought two chickens with me and on the strength of a twenty-five-year custom I have been able to wring a couple of bottles out of the wine merchant. Neville is bringing a bottle of sherry. He says he can sometimes get one as a favour through his old mess secretary."

Lieutenant Commander Stephens arrived punctually. Janet felt relaxed and at ease out of uniform and in the atmosphere of Mrs Farrow's well-furnished home.

The conversation followed the trend of most of the dinner table talk of the day: the war, the blitz and rationing.

"I believe that the German advance is slowing down," said Colonel Boyd. "If only the Russians can hang on until the winter, it's going to make a tremendous difference to us. Remember Napoleon."

"Well it's made a difference already," said Lieutenant Commander Stephens. "There hasn't been a serious raid since May the 10th. If they had kept it up on that scale as they did last autumn, we'd have been in serious difficulties. They put five hundred and fifty planes over

London that night and we are told that some of them made two journeys flying back to France, refuelling and reloading."

"I see from the papers that the fire service is going to be reorganised and come directly under the government instead of the local authorities," said Colonel Boyd. "Do you know anything about it or is it all highly confidential?"

"No, it's not confidential. It's all been in the papers. We are going to be nationalised and the appointed day is August the 18th, in just a fortnight's time. I do happen to know quite a lot about it because some of my colleagues and I have been pressing for it since last autumn.

"Our experiences in taking the London columns to the raided provincial cities were an eye opener, you know. They just didn't stand a chance. London was fine in comparison. We had all the best equipment available and when we needed to call reinforcements in from outside, they were only a fraction of our own resources and we could generally absorb them and get them to work in the right places."

"The chief officer of a provincial city would probably have to call reinforcements that outnumbered his own establishment four or five times over and they would be sent in from about twenty neighbouring towns and rural district councils. Some would send one pump; others might send up to twenty. Lots of them came without officers. The regulars, if they did come, had all sorts of different ranks and all sorts of different uniforms.

"A lot of town councils were very naughty. They wouldn't send their regulars but only their AFS, who were paid by the government anyhow. If they did send an experienced officer, he had no powers in the assisted town but had to take orders from its most junior fireman. We found that out when we took a column of one hundred pumps in as reinforcements. It was chaotic and we thought that the fire damage was very much greater than it need have been. We put reports in and we were told that they were interesting. We suggested nationalisation and we were told that it was impossible. We kept plugging away and were then more or less told to mind our own business. Then we were very naughty and we went elsewhere."

"Where was elsewhere?"

"Certain MPs and one very senior civil servant. Well, it's happened now but I'm afraid that we are not very popular in high up Home Office circles. It's going to be one service instead of over one thousand, four hundred different local authority brigades. There will be one standard uniform, a countrywide hierarchy of ranks, so that if a senior officer from, say, Plymouth goes to, say, Liverpool, the junior officers there will have to obey him. Most important of all, the AFS and the regulars are going to be completely amalgamated.

"You know that the AFS have had a pretty raw deal. What would the army have done, Colonel, if the government had told them that they were to fight a war with all the volunteers, territorials and conscripts worse paid and worse equipped than the regular army and with no chance of promotion beyond lance-corporal?" Lieutenant Commander Stephens said.

"Well it would have been quite impossible. It seems

madness to me. I'm glad it's been sorted out. How do you come out of it?" Colonel Boyd replied.

"I'm leaving London for a time. It's not official of course until August the 18th but I'm going to be given a command in the North, among those dark satanic mills. There are also hundreds of square miles of very pleasant countryside. It's a region of five counties and all they contain, including a large number of county boroughs. It's going to be interesting welding them altogether into one fire brigade," Lieutenant Commander Stephens said.

"Won't you be sorry to leave London?"

"In some ways, of course. I would like to see what we could do in a heavy raid with all the new big water basins dotted around. They should make a big difference."

"Will the Women's Service be altered at all?" asked Mrs Carew-Finch.

"Oh yes, in just the same way. A complete hierarchy of new ranks for women right up to the women staff officers at a Chief Regional Fire Officer's headquarters."

"There you are, you see, Janet. You really should take the opportunity. She's so stubborn, Commander Stephens. She just won't try for promotion because she doesn't want to be taken off driving. She got a very good school certificate and she has the brains, if only she would use them. She ought to put in for promotion, don't you agree?"

"What do you think, Janet?" he said.

It was the first time he had used her Christian name.

"I don't think that I'd make a very good officer and I'd hate to be stuck in a watch-room or control room all day and all night."

"There's a transport pool at HQ with a couple of women officers. There might be a vacancy there in the shake-up that's coming."

"Couldn't you find her a vacancy in your new command? I think that she's been in Bermondsey long enough."

"That would give me the greatest pleasure, but I don't think that it would work. It's awkward you know offering promotions to friends," he said. He hurriedly added, "or acquaintances. It seems to be rather a question of 'Who doth ambition shun and loves lie in the sun,'* though when the sun does shine in Bermondsey it's apt to be a bit obscured by the atmosphere. To please your mother, why don't you put in for a transfer to one of the West End stations?"

"Because I should have to leave my friends at substation 69Y. They're wonderful people you know."

"Yes, I do know."

The evening passed pleasantly, and it was ten thirty p.m. before their guest looked at his watch and said that he must be going. They made their farewells.

"Janet will see you out," said Mrs Carew Finch.

"I'd better switch the hall light out before I open the door or we'll have all the policemen and wardens in Kensington around. Is your car there?"

"It should be."

She flicked the switch up and fumbled for the latch.

---

* *From As You Like It — William Shakespeare*

His hand went to her shoulder and he turned her towards him. He kissed her on the mouth.

"Oh sir!" she said in mock terror.

"I'm sorry. I've wanted to do that since a year ago last September. You looked such a forlorn little thing standing to attention in a smelly tannery yard. Instead, I could only give you a surreptitious wink."

"Perhaps it was as good as a nod to a blind horse. No, it's the other way around isn't it?"

"Yes, it is, but that's got nothing to do with it. Will you meet me again? Come and have dinner with me."

"I thought that you were leaving London."

"Exactly. That's why we can meet again if you'll agree. It would have been awkward if you had still been one of my firewomen. You know what it is in this service. Several junior officers have been in trouble for having affairs with their AFS women."

"You're not expecting that sort of affair, are you?"

"No, of course not. It was not very well put. But there would be a lot of silly talk if a senior officer was known to be taking a firewoman out. I should be in London at least once a month for meetings at the Home Office and I shall have to stay the night. I just hoped that you might join me for dinner one evening when Blue watch is on leave."

"Am I to understand that you would like to take me out to dinner but dare not do so because I'm only a firewoman. However, you will be brave enough to do so when you have taken up an appointment in a different part of the country?"

"I'm sorry. It did sound rather like that. All right, will

you come out to dinner with me on your next leave day?"

"Yes, I think I will."

"Fine. Shall I pick you up here at seven o'clock?"

"That will do very nicely. I'll look forward to seeing you."

"Sorry about the unprovoked assault just now."

"That's all right. You can do it again if you like."

A moment later, she opened the door and he walked out to the waiting car.

"What have you been doing?" asked Mrs Farrow. "It took a long time to see a visitor out."

"We were discussing a service matter."

They dined three days later at a West End hotel on brown Windsor soup, rabbit and pink blancmange. He asked for wine, and the waiter could only offer them a bottle of Algerian. She noticed him counting out notes when the bill was presented.

"It seems an awful lot. I thought that you weren't allowed to spend more than five shillings on a restaurant meal now?"

"Yes, but the big hotels can charge five shillings each guest extra for house charge and five shillings for the band. What did you think of the wine?"

"I'd rather have a pint of bitter."

"They won't serve it, I'm afraid. Would you like a drink in a pub?"

"Yes. Let's try the Wallace Head."

"God forbid. It'll be full of people from station number two slipping out for a sly one, while the officers' backs are turned."

"Perhaps they wouldn't recognise you if you didn't always wear that blue suit and black tie."

"Sorry. You just don't think of changing. Nobody recognises it outside the service, though people on railway stations think they do. They always ask you the time of the next train. Next week, we shall all have to wear a real uniform. I've seen the patterns."

"What shall I be wearing?"

"Just the same, I'm afraid, except that your cap badge will have NFS on it instead of AFS and there'll be a crown on top of the star. Come on. I'll take you somewhere where you can have that pint."

The next evening the first conscript firemen arrived at substation 69Y carrying their awkward bundles of kit bags, boots and gear. An additional trailer pump stood in the yard for them to man. The taxis had gone, and each pump was attached to the new towing vehicles, purpose built and sturdy.

Davies met the newcomers at the door, told them to put their gear on their beds and follow him into an empty classroom.

"Now this 'ere's a 'appy ship and that's the way we're going to keep it."

The door closed on the opening remarks and the men and women in the mess room looked at one another and grinned.

"Giving them 'is pep talk," said Arthur Clayton. "Now they'll 'ave to learn that a floor is a deck and a kitchen is a galley and all his other naval palaver. Well they've 'ad a fortnight at training school to learn some of it. Not like the sixty hours basic we 'ad."

"Did you notice that long lanky one?" said Harry Booth. "Well 'e's a fuckin' conchie*. One of the blokes up at station 69 'ood been instructing at the training school told me. We got a nice old lot to mix up with now, 'aven't we?"

"They'll be all right," said Charlie Pierce. "I'd rather 'ave some conchies than some bloke what puts on a uniform and finds a safe number and then makes sure 'e sticks to it. Conchies must 'ave a bit of guts to stand up to all the ribbing they get."

The door opened and Davies walked out into the watch-room. His audience followed, looking around awkwardly like new boys at school.

Harry Booth walked to the piano, threw up the lid and played the opening bars of 'Onward Christian Soldiers'.

He then sang, "Onward conscript firemen, marching as to war. You would not be conscripts if you'd marched before"

"Now then, cut it out, 'Arry," said Charlie Pierce.

"Well don't you remember way back in 1917 that was what we sang to the first conscripts when they turned up in France?"

"Yes, but there's no cause to sing it 'ere. Come on, you lads. Sit down and make yourselves at 'ome. My name's Charlie Pierce. What's yours?"

"Peter Grafton," said the tall young man who stood in

---

* *conscientious objector (pacifist)*

front of the group, who he then introduced.

"Well, sit down then and tell us all about yourselves. Don't take no notice of 'Arry Booth there. 'E's got a 'eart of gold really but 'e likes to show off 'is piano playing and with good cause 'cause 'e really can tickle the ivories. 'E'll be giving us a song one of these nights won't you, 'Arry."

"Ah, that's right, if you want it. You whistle it, I'll play it."

"I like the look of the tall one," whispered Edith Brown to Mabel Smith, "even if 'e is a conchie. Speaks lah di dah, don't 'e? What do you bet 'e makes a pass at Dicky?"

"Don't know but they say like to like, don't they?"

A week later, Janet drove the general-purpose lorry into the yard, looked into the watch-room and returned with a bucket of water to wash the vehicle down. Peter Grafton stood by the radiator.

"Hello. Can I give you a hand with that?"

"It's very kind of you but it's part of my job. You'll only make both of us look rather silly."

"I don't mind. Have you got another leather?"

"No, I haven't. They're issued very sparingly. You get a new one when the old one is too slimy to use. What's the idea anyhow?"

"Just that I want a bit of civilised company."

"There's plenty of civilised company in the mess room."

"Do you really think so? God, I think they're awful. Do they ever use any adjectives other than the copulative one?"

"Yes. They sometimes use the perverted one. If you're so refined, you can say fornicating. You'll find that they understand."

"I should have thought that you'd be shocked by it all."

"I wasn't at first because I didn't know what it all meant. I thought that it was just part of the local argot. Then the girls told me what it meant. They use it too you know. But after a time, I just took no notice. It doesn't mean anything. It's only an expletive. The dangerous stage is when you start using it yourself at moments of exasperation. You have to watch your step and your company."

"Well, I must say, I think that you're a remarkable person. How long have you been here?"

"Two years at the beginning of next month."

"Why did you come here in the first place?"

"For the same reason as you. I was posted here, and I stay here because I like it here, but I don't like people who infer that my chinas are uncivilised. So now will you kindly bugger off and let me get on with my work."

He winced and walked away.

She finished washing down the truck and walked to the mess room and sat down.

"You 'eard old Taff Davies is up before a board next week for NFS officer rank. 'E's started polishing 'is shoes, belt and medals already."

"Well, good luck to 'im. 'E ain't a bad old boy, really. I reckon 'e did fuckin' well in the raids. What's 'e in for?"

"Company officer."

"What's that?"

"Blimey, don't you ever read the fuckin' orders? It's the same as station officer. They've altered all the names of the ranks just to make it more confusing. A sub-officer's going to be called a section leader and they're going to make lots of leading firemen. Every pump and trailer pump is going to 'ave one in charge of the crew."

"Chance for some of us, then?"

"Ought to be. It'll be a few bob a week extra for some."

"Don't we all get a bit extra? I thought that it was all going to be one service and that we'd get the same pay as the regulars."

"Well, you've got another fuckin' think coming," said Newton. "We're all going to be plain firemen, no more auxiliary fuckin' firemen but the rate of pay's going to be the fuckin' same and the regular fuckers that don't get a fuckin' rank and there won't be many of them, have got a non-worsening clause so they can keep their old pay."

"It's the same fuckin' pay, the same fuckin' hours, the same fuckin' uniform for the likes of us, except the fuckin' buttons and badges will be fuckin' different. But the regulars are going to get one hell of a fuckin' shock. There are twenty-five thousand of us and only two thousand of them fuckers. Well they couldn't change twenty-five thousand uniforms could they now? So, the regular fuckers 'ave got to wear the same as us. No more round caps and no more blue civvy suits for the top brass. They're 'aving a special issue, of course. I'll tell you one difference it's going to make to us though. You might find yourself ordered up to Liverpool or Glasgow after next week."

Davies was made a company officer. A fortnight later he appeared on the station in a smart dark blue belted uniform with silver buttons and a white metal rank marking on each shoulder strap.

Janet overheard Newton's comments made to Peter Grafton.

"'Asn't got an aitch to 'is name, over twenty years in and passed over for promotion a dozen times in that period and now they make him an officer — white collar, black tie and everything. I was fuckin' holding down twice as responsible a job as 'e did in peacetime and what consideration do I get. I tell you we AFS fuckers get nothing but the dirty end of the stick. There's no fuckin' future for us."

The appointments boards sat on to review junior ranks and finally the new leading firemen were appointed. Both Charlie Pierce's and Alf Newton's names were in the list. Newton was given the command of number five trailer pump with a crew composed entirely of conscript newcomers and the soon earned the reputation of a martinet and as an instructor whose main technique was sarcasm.

"Those red stripes don't 'arf weigh 'eavy on Alf's shoulders," said Jack Adams.

"'E's as snotty as a new made lance-corporal," replied Harry Booth.

Janet received her summons to the palace at the end of October. A week before the investiture Molly Breaks handed her a docket for a new uniform.

"There you are. Go and get yourself fixed up. Well,

that's one way of getting a new set of kit, but we can't all be given medals."

"No, but lots of you deserved them more than I did."

"Oh, don't be so modest. Lucky it didn't fall on your leave day. They'd have given you the whole afternoon off. Who are you taking with you? You're allowed two."

"My mother and Aunt Kitty."

Well, it'll be a nice day for them. I bet that they'll be proud of you."

The evening of the day after the ceremony Janet stood in the yard watching the sun setting over the roofs of Rampton Road. Bert Foster joined her.

"So, you've been to see the little old King, Dicky. That must 'ave been very nice."

"Yes, it was, Bert and very impressive."

"Ah, I'd like to see 'im. 'E's a good boy. 'E's got three or four places in the country what 'e could 'ave gone to when the Blitz was on but 'e didn't did 'e? Stayed in London even when 'is own 'ouse was bombed. I saw 'im in the distance once after the big April raid and 'e was walking round the damaged area. I wanted to drop the branch and go nearer and give 'im a cheer but you couldn't do that now could you. Did 'e talk to you?"

"Yes, a few words and he shook my hand."

Bert held out his. "Well, you shake mine, Dicky. That's the nearest I'll ever get to it."

They shook hands solemnly and he looked up at the sky.

"Evenings are drawing in, ain't they? Soon be winter, the third winter. 'Ope it won't be as boring as the first or as lively as the second. We ain't doing so well, are we,

Dicky? Makes you a bit anxious, when you think about things. 'Ow's it all going to end and when's it all going to end? The Germans are only twenty miles from Moscow. You 'eard that song on the wireless, 'There'll be blue birds over the white cliffs of Dover tomorrow not so far way' and it goes on something about 'Jonny will go to sleep in 'is own little room again'. Good ain't it? 'Arry Booth can play it. Those are the ones that must 'ave the biggest worries, the ones with kids.

"Both my girls are grown up, but it must be 'ard for those with youngsters' round 'em, sweets going on the ration and all. My neighbour's boy's been killed in Africa and now this 'ere Rommel's pushed us right out of all what we won there in the spring. Now, you're an educated person, Dicky, 'ow are we going to win and when are we going to?"

"I don't know, Bert. I just know that we're going to."

"Ah, it's good to 'ear you say that. You get a bit anxious at times."

Chapter 11

"Well, there's the first week of December gone and the Ruskies are still in the war," said Jack Adams. "Who said they wouldn't last a fortnight? The Germans are further away from Moscow than they were a month ago and that Rundstedt bloke has been pushed out of Rostov."

"Yes, but they already got a fuck of a lot of Russia."

"What does that matter? The paper says that this is the first failure of a German blitzkrieg."

"My paper says that the two best Russian generals are General January and General February."

"I thought that their best general was Timo fuckin' Shenko. Seems funny to have two generals both called after a month."

"Don't be so fuckin' daft. It means the Russian winter 'elps 'em more than their fuckin' generals do. What a laugh ain't it? The Jerries are appealing for warm clothes for their troops and all the old frau's are 'anding in their fur coats. Fancy going to war in a fur coat."

"Well, I 'appen to know the Germans are in real trouble. They've got strung out with bad communications and are about to suffer a real defeat."

"'Ow do you know?"

"A bloke what's in the army told me."

"'Oos that?"

"My brother-in-law."

"Well, what is 'e in the army?"

"'E's a corporal in the ASC*."

"Well then, 'e must be a real military expert. Thank you very much for the information. We'll keep it very dark 'cos it wouldn't do for your brother-in-law to get into trouble for passing on vital information, would it now?"

Charlie Pierce walked into the room.

"Now stop being sarcastic and forget about the Russians for a bit and switch on the news at nine o'clock. I've just been up to Southwark. The Japanese 'ave bombed Pearl 'arbour."

"Pearl 'arbour. Where the fuck is that?"

"It's the main base of the American Pacific fleet and it's reckoned they've sunk most of it, battleships an' all. We've got the Yanks on our side now, same as 'appened in 1917."

Janet went on leave the next day. Colonel Boyd was in the hall of Kitty Farrow's house when she arrived.

"Hello, my dear. Is this what you were looking for?"

He handed her a letter from the silver tray on the hall table.

"Quite a regular correspondent, isn't he? How's he getting on among the dark satanic mills as he calls them?"

"Very well, I think." She slit the envelope. "Oh good, he's coming to London a week on Thursday. No, is that right? Blue watch is on leave today. On duty two days."

---

* *Army Service Corps*

She counted the days on her fingers. "Yes, Blue watch is on leave a week on Thursday."

"Getting fond of him?"

"Oh, I don't know about that, Uncle Neville. He's very good company and really rather erudite. Yes, perhaps I am a little bit."

"Well I am pleased. I thought him a jolly good type. Well, I suppose you know I'm off today, out of here. They've patched my old place up and put all the window glass back. Kitty asked me to stay on, but I must admit she gets on my nerves a bit. However, please be particularly nice to her today. She's worrying about Claude. Just heard he's got an overseas posting, Singapore. I've told her she's got nothing to worry about; biggest fortress in the east. We sank millions of pounds into it in the nineteen thirties. Glad we're sending some more ack-ack though.

"I was talking to an air commodore at the club last night; he says that the Japanese air force is not to be sniffed at. Americans found that out at the weekend anyhow. Well, must be on my way. Bring Stephens to dinner with me at the club when he's up."

Janet walked upstairs to bath and change but she first sat on the bed to read her letter. Ten minutes later, she lay thinking in the comfort of the hot water. He had said that she was always in his thoughts. She would write back and tell him that she thought of him often, too.

'Oh dear, it was less than ten months since Bill had been killed. Was it terribly disloyal to his memory to be almost happy again?' she thought.

She had twenty-four hours leave, and a dull dark

December day stretched ahead of her. How eagerly she had looked forward to each leave day last winter. Now she found the hours hung heavily. A week on Thursday, the fifth leave day from today, she had that to look forward to. He would arrive on the afternoon train. They would spend the evening together. She smiled at her fond fancies of the previous year. Perhaps after all she would one day be the mistress of the big flat at headquarters.

"Oh, Bill darling, forgive me," she said aloud.

The water was getting cold and she stepped out of the bath. She heard the telephone ringing. Aunt Kitty knocked on the bathroom door.

"It's for you, Janet."

She wrapped a towel around her and went to the phone. Jim Cartwright's voice answered her greeting.

"Hello Janet. The theatres are opening again. How about coming to a show with me this evening?"

She thanked him and accepted, half regretting that she had done so a few moments later. She stood thinking.

'He's a very nice person and a very persistent one but the impossible has happened and I seem to be falling in love again. I mustn't encourage him only to disappoint him again.'

"Janet, what are you doing, standing there like that and so near the window too? Surely you could have put a dressing gown on. Really, I think it is quite brazen. People can see in from the windows opposite."

"I'm sorry Aunt Kitty. I'll go and get dressed."

"Yes, please do. I'd like to have a little talk with you."

A quarter of an hour later Janet went into the drawing

room.

"Come and sit down my dear. I'm so worried about Claude. I heard Neville Boyd telling you in the hall that he'd been posted to Singapore. He doesn't want to go, and I don't think that he's temperamentally suited. He's got embarkation leave next week and he's coming to stay here. Now, you will be nice to him Janet dear, won't you?"

"Of course, I'll be nice to him, Aunt Kitty. Why shouldn't I be?"

"Well, you haven't always been as nice to him as you could have been. You know how fond he is of you."

She looked out of the window and dabbed her eyes with her handkerchief.

"They're not sending some of the married officers."

"Well, if Claude thinks he could get out of an overseas posting by getting married he's left it rather late, hasn't he?"

"I don't know what you mean by that. You know that he would have married you in 1938 if you had given him the slightest bit of encouragement. I thought that perhaps after..." she paused, "...well, after what happened in March, you might perhaps think things over again."

Janet clenched her hands in anger that soon turned to pity as she looked at the pathetic figure seated opposite her. Deserted but, despite her own ample means, well endowed by a wealthy husband when their only child was an infant, she had lavished on Claude all her affection and much of her resources.

"I'm sorry, Aunt Kitty. I can't fall in love with Claude to order, you know, but I'll be very glad to see him next week. In fact, I shall look forward to seeing him. As for being nice to him, well of course I shall be. We'll make his leave a very happy one for all of us. The theatres are opening again. Would you like me to get some tickets? Oh, by the way, I'm going out tonight. I shan't be in for dinner."

"Are you going with the Cartwright boy? It was him asking for you on the phone wasn't it?"

"Yes, I am going with him, but don't worry about that. He's just good company and we're just good friends."

"Saw you in the West End last night," said Mollie Breaks the next morning, "but you didn't see me. Have a good time?"

"Yes, thank you. Where did you see me?"

"Outside the Palladium. Was it a good show?"

"Yes, I enjoyed it."

"We nearly went ourselves, but Eric Price wanted cheering up a bit. Being ex-Navy, he couldn't get over the loss of the Prince of Wales and the Repulse. He seemed to feel personally responsible. I must say that the news shook me when I heard it — our two best battleships sunk by those little yellow bastards."

"Yes, I think that it's too awful, but what's all this about Eric Price?"

"You know him, don't you?"

"Do you mean the station officer at Southwark who used to be in charge of transport?"

"Yes, station officer that was, column officer that is now. I'm like you, I still can't get used to these new NFS ranks. Anyhow Eric got a promotion on nationalisation."

"Good, I liked him. He once gave me an hour's instruction on lorry driving. So, were you out with him yesterday evening?"

"Yes, and most evenings when our leave times fit. I thought that you knew. Most of them here seem to. You can't keep anything dark in this mob, can you? Not that we want to. It's made a big difference to me, Dicky, these past few weeks.

"When you're widowed, and in your twenties, you can't live with the dead all the rest of your life. There's no disrespect in saying that. That's why I was glad to see you out with someone last night. It was the young bloke from Manchester Square wasn't it?"

"Yes, that's who it was."

"Well I'm glad that you're out and about again. You couldn't have spent all your life moping, you know. Are you keen on him?"

"No. I like him that's all. I think that I'm really keen on somebody else."

"Who's that?"

"Well it's really a secret and if I tell you, you mustn't let anyone else on the station know."

"Cross my heart."

Mollie made the gesture as she spoke the words.

"It's Commander Stephens."

"Crikey! And is he keen on you?"

"I think so. I hope so anyway but he's very funny about things. He seems quite terrified to think that the service and his colleagues might find out that he's friendly with someone of the opposite sex who is so lowly in the

329

service."

"Well, perhaps you can't altogether blame him. After all, there've been one or two juicy old scandals haven't there? And the officer always gets broken when they get found out. Surprised that you haven't put in for a transfer up north to be near him."

"He won't hear of it. Says it wouldn't do at all. But when will it end? The Japs seem to be pushing us all the way down Malaya. I'm glad I've got nobody close to me involved in that affair.

"I've got a sort of second cousin. Well, it's Aunt Kitty's son, who's been posted to Singapore."

"Oh, he'll be all right there. That's a bloody great fortress. The paper says that it's impregnable," Mollie said.

Janet went on leave a week later, expecting to find Claude Farrow at home. The house seemed empty, but she found Alice in the kitchen.

"Where's Mrs Farrow? Has Master Claude arrived yet?"

"Oh No, Miss Janet. He's not coming. He's ill. Mrs Farrow went off to Scotland yesterday."

"Mrs Farrow said that it was nervous debility. He's missed going abroad with all his friends. He will be disappointed."

Christmas passed and the New Year came with its ill tidings. Minor intermittent air raids brought some action to substation 69Y, an antidote to stress caused by the country's unbroken record of defeat.

The news of Singapore's fall followed the news of the

loss of Benghazi in North Africa. The U-boats inflicted the most grievous losses of the war and rationing became tighter.

Agnes Jenkins had tears in her eyes as she faced Company Officer Davies across his office table.

"I can't do it, Mr Davies. It's not possible to provide thirty dinners out of that."

She waved the small joint of mutton before his eyes.

"Well, you'll 'ave to do your best. You'll 'ave to eke it out with gravy and potatoes. It's no good coming to me and complaining. It says in the papers that land girls and government farm workers 'ave been sent out to 'ard manual work with nothing but beetroot sandwiches for their dinners. Well, we 'aven't come down to beetroot sandwiches yet."

"No, because we 'aven't got any bloody beetroot. Thirty dinners of this, I ask you!" exclaimed Agnes Jenkins.

"Well, stop waving it about and go and get on with it. Make it into a stew or something. Mrs Breaks, will you kindly take her out of my office and let me get on with these returns," said Company Officer Davies.

"Off you go Jenkins. I'll come and see you in the kitchen in a minute. We'll work something out. I've got trouble with Firewoman Brown, Mr Davies. She refused to hand in her clothing coupons."

"Well, you're meant to deal with that."

"I think that you'd better see her. She's used them all and has none left to hand in. It may involve a discipline charge and you'll have to make the charge sheet out."

Edith Brown looking surly and dishevelled, stood before the company officer a few minutes later.

"Now, Firewoman Brown, what's this all about not 'anding in twenty clothing coupons in lieu," Company Officer Davies said.

"I can't 'and 'em in. I've used them," Edith Brown replied.

"What do you mean, used them? You wasn't allowed to use them," Davies said.

"Well I 'ave done. They don't provide no underclothes and mine was worn out. Cor, four coupons for a bra they wanted and six for a pair of knickers, blooming utility ones."

She ran one hand over her ample bosoms and another down her thigh as she spoke.

"Well I'm not 'ere to discuss intimate matters of ladies underwear. I'm 'ere to collect twenty clothing coupons in accordance with Brigade orders. There, it's up to you."

He rose from his chair, picked up a paper from the table and walked out to the notice board where he pinned it up.

"There you are, my lucky lads. 'Ow to get out of fire service despite the Police and the Firemen's Employment Order."

Some of the men waiting for dinner crowded around the notice board.

"What does it say?" said Arthur Clayton, who remained sitting over the newspapers.

"It says that any man who has had previous

experience at sea with the Merchant Navy will be released to re-join it."

"Blimey, and the best of British luck to them. Anybody 'ere ever been in the old MN?"

"No. Nobody been further than Southend Pier, I should think."

"God, I pity those poor fuckers. No one can say that they don't earn their fuckin' money."

Edith Brown was duly charged with disobedience to orders and she was punished by a stoppage of pay of two pounds.

"Well, that puts the fuckin' tin lid on it," said Jack Adams. "Poor little Edie, a whole week's money gone. If we'd known, we could 'ave subbed up twenty coupons for her. What a palaver; sent for to Southwark and the fire force commander and the woman officer and the whole fuckin' lot there. The old LFB would never 'ave done that to 'er. If the NFS is going to carry on like that they can stuff the NFS as far as I'm concerned. What do you think, Dicky?"

"I think that it's ridiculous; a caution or a stoppage of five shillings would have been enough."

"Too true, my old duck. You're going up to Southwark to fetch the new pipe lorry this afternoon, aren't you? They aren't 'alf dishing out some equipment now. Pity we didn't 'ave it in 1940."

Janet walked to Southwark. It was a March day of cold wind and fitful sunshine as the grey clouds scurried across the sky. This time last year Bill had been alive. It was the day that he had been promoted. He had another seven hours of life.

She passed a bombed block of working-class flats where there had been heavy casualties that night. On the concrete ledge that supported battered railings were three jam jars that contained spring flowers. One stood on the edge of a slip of paper. She bent down to read the writing on it.

'From friends and neighbours in sad memory'.

The hole in the road at New Cross had been filled in and new tarmac laid. There was no ledge in the street that could accommodate a little vase of flowers. Was she so unfeeling? Only a year had passed. She hadn't believed them when they said that time would heal, but her pleasure at the thought that Peter Stephens' next visit to London would coincide with a leave day now seemed a guilty pleasure. She walked on with her thoughts.

Claude was on leave and making his first visit to London since his posting to Scotland. He would arrive today, and Aunt Kitty was twittering with pleasure. She would be on leave the day after tomorrow. Perhaps she would ring Uncle Neville and ask herself to lunch. No, that wouldn't do. It would upset Aunt Kitty.

Kitty Farrow heard the taxi draw up and she hurried downstairs to meet her son. She hugged him on the doorstep.

"Well, was it a dreadful journey, darling? Tea is ready. As soon as you've unpacked and had a wash we can have a lovely chat."

A quarter of an hour later they sat on the comfortable drawing room chairs.

"Well, you know that Janet will be here the day after tomorrow. She'll have the whole day off. I think that we'll have lunch here and you can take her out in the evening. Now, you must make the most of the opportunity. I'm afraid that she has become rather hard. It's the environment, you know. Nothing wrong with her really but she smokes non-stop and sometimes comes out with terrible bad language.

"Of course, you've heard all about that affair with an ordinary fireman. It seems dreadful to say, but perhaps it was just as well he was killed. I could never understand Betty's attitude. She condoned the whole business and then she had him to stay at Brandon. She was completely resigned to their getting married.

"I never saw him, but apparently he was absurdly good looking and I suppose that had a lot to do with it. If Janet was a bit distant with you last time you met, it was because the affair was at its height then. I'm sure that you'll find her different now. Incidentally, she has struck up a friendship with one of the very senior fire officers. Betty asked him to dinner here the evening after her medal was announced.

"I thought him rather smooth and ridiculously young for the position that he held. I believe that she's seen him once or twice since but there's nothing in it. She's more in love with his position than with him. It's quite ridiculous the way that the fire service seems to have got right inside her as she says. Anyhow he's not interested. I'm pretty sure of that.

"Betty tells me that he gets quite embarrassed over

having a friendship with someone in his service of such junior rank. Now, you just go right ahead and put yourself over to her. I think it's quite disgraceful that they haven't made you a Captain yet. I'm sure that would have helped."

Claude took Janet out to dinner on the evening of her next leave day.

"Well, it's two years since we last went out together, old girl. Quite a lot has happened since then."

"Yes, quite a lot has happened since then."

"You were very cross with me because I was rude to some of your officers in the Criterion bar. Do you remember?"

"Yes, I remember."

"Look, old girl, I feel a bit shy about saying this, perhaps I should have written at the time, but I was terribly sorry about your fiancé's death, rotten luck."

"Thank you, Claude. I was terribly upset. I thought that I would never get over it."

"Well, I don't want to rush things, but you do know don't you that I'm very much in love with you and I want to marry you if you'll only say yes."

"That is rather rushing things. Perhaps you wouldn't want to anymore if you knew everything that has happened. Whoever I marry will have to know it all and love me enough to still want to marry me."

"Well, I love you enough to want to marry you despite whatever has happened. What was it?"

She smiled and patted his hand across the table.

"I said that you were rushing things. I was thinking of something else. We'll change the subject. Tell me about

Scotland. I hear that you are stationed in a wonderful country house with a squash court and tennis courts and a park with fishing. No wonder you didn't want to leave it."

The meal passed with small talk until the waiter presented the bill.

Claude put the money on top of it and said, "If our officers' mess manager had served us a meal like that, he'd have got the sack."

"I thought that it was very good for wartime," said Janet.

The sirens sounded as she finished speaking. Claude sat straight up looking tense.

"Hello, a raid," he said. "Where do we go?"

"What do you mean, where do we go? We'd just stay here normally, but someone will want the table. If we go outside, we'll probably get a taxi and you can take us home. They're only little raids nowadays. The all clear will probably sound soon."

"Are you sure that it's all right? Are there not regulations about taking cover?"

"No there are no regulations. Look, everyone else is walking about normally."

They went towards the park, Janet finding it hard to keep up with Claude who was half running. Three, almost simultaneous, explosions thumped in the night air. He sprang into a doorway.

"Come on, silly, that was only guns."

"That was bombs. I know what guns sound like."

"Well come on anyway. You can't stand there all night."

He emerged and they hurried on.

"Don't go so fast. I can't keep up with you," said Janet.

They were passing a tube station and a trickle of people, some carrying bedding, were walking towards the entrance at which a short queue had formed. There was another explosion, preceded by a faint long whine of a distant bomb. He took her arm and he began to push her across the road towards the tube station.

"What are you doing? We can't get a train from there. It's the wrong line."

"We must take cover. It's most irresponsible behaviour not to. People get hurt or killed through irresponsible bravado and then they take up the time of the casualty services."

"People get buried alive in those places and they die a lingering death."

"You can't put me off like that. I'm going if you won't."

He joined the queue.

Janet shrugged her shoulders and walked on. It was not so far to Kensington and she could walk across the park.

The all clear sounded as she let herself in to Aunt Kitty's house forty minutes later.

"Janet my dear, you are alone? Where's Claude?"

"He's taking cover in the underground."

"Have you left him there?"

"Yes, I'm afraid I have, Aunt Kitty. Did you expect me to stay and hold his hand?"

"Oh, I don't think that was very kind of you. After all he's not used to air raids like you and I are."

The siren sounded again in the night. Janet stirred and then she pricked her ears to a thumping in the corridor outside her room. She switched on the light and opened the door to see Claude struggling to move his half rolled up mattress down the passage.

"Whatever are you doing?"

"I'm taking my bed down to the cellar of course."

"Crikey, you're not one to take risks, are you?"

Aunt Kitty's door opened, and she appeared in dressing gown and curling pins.

"I don't think that the cellar is really necessary, dear. Put your mattress down in the passage. They say that it's almost as safe if you're between interior walls. Janet I must speak to you. Can I come into your room?"

She followed Janet in, shutting the door behind her.

"Really! Haven't you got a dressing gown? I do think that it's disgraceful standing there in a nylon nightie in front of Claude with the light on behind you. Whatever will he think of you?"

"I don't suppose he'll think anything. He wasn't the slightest bit interested. He had other things on his mind, his own precious skin being the first."

"Oh, I think that you're impossible and so unfair. We can't all go winning medals for bravery. I don't know why I have kept open house for you all this time."

She went out slamming the door behind her, but her voice was still audible.

"I think that you're being a little bit over cautious,

dear; after all, whatever would you do if ever you had to go to the front."

Janet left the house to report for duty the next morning when only Alice was up and about.

During the next two days she wondered what she should do about her leave day accommodation. Could she impose on Aunt Kitty anymore? She loved the house in Kensington with its comforts, especially the big bathroom and Alice's care for her. Oh, damn Claude. If it wasn't for him everything would be all right, there.

Mrs Cartwright would put her up. No, that wouldn't be fair. Jim was still pressing her to marry him and almost every leave day she made her excuses in answer to his invitations to meals, the theatre or to Sunningdale.

She sat on her bed, mulling over the problem on the evening of the second duty day.

"I suppose I'd better go and find a room somewhere," she said to herself as Cissie Spence walked in.

"Ullo Dicky. I saw that you'd booked in. A message came for you while you were out with the store's lorry. Your mum's in London. She says will you please call at Colonel Boyd's flat before going to Kensington tomorrow morning. 'Ere it is. I wrote it down on a message slip."

Janet arrived at the flat at nine thirty a.m. and she responded affectionately to her mother's greeting.

"You didn't come up specially, did you?"

"No. I'm going to see Sylvia Henshaw, but I think it just as well I did have the appointment. Kitty Farrow rang me at Brandon, and I went and saw her yesterday afternoon. She's very upset with you. She says first of all you were rude to Claude and the next moment you were flaunting your charms before him and making him very upset.

"I do think that you should try and behave a bit better. After all you've been staying there for two and a half years and she's always refused to take a penny. I did suggest ages ago that you should be a paying guest, but she wouldn't hear of it.

"I gather that Claude had proposed to you and that you turned him down. Well, that was to be expected, but you don't seem to have been very kind. Anyway, tell me all about it. I know that I've only heard one side of the story."

Janet told her mother about the dinner and the air raid.

"Oh well," she said. "It all seems to be a fuss over nothing. I told Kitty about Peter Stephens. She seemed surprised and a little bit huffy, but she must realise now that Claude is out as far as you are concerned.

"Poor Kitty, it seems to have been almost a lifelong ambition of hers that you and Claude should marry. She used to talk about it when you played together as children. There's nothing that can't be put right by your taking her a big bunch of flowers and saying that you're sorry.

"I do want you to stay there, you know, because I feel less anxious about you staying there on your leave days. Of course, as I keep saying, the best thing would be for you to resign now. The real raids seem to be over and there's so much other war work. I met Mrs Wilson in Norwich last week. She said that her two girls are having a simply marvellous time in the Wrens. Deirdre had told her that the food was absolutely gorgeous."

"She would; don't you remember that she always used to make herself sick at children's parties," Janet said.

"Yes, but that's not the point. I know that Peter thinks that you ought to leave the service now. He feels that it would be so much better from his point of view and he told me a transfer to the Wrens could be quite easily arranged. How is he by the way? When are you going to see him?"

"Next week. He's coming up on the five o'clock train. We're going to spend the evening together. He has a meeting at the Home Office tomorrow."

"Well, that will be nice for you. Are you going to get some proper leave this year or is it only going to be one week again?"

"No. I've heard that they're going to give us a fortnight."

"Perhaps you could arrange it to coincide with his. I thought that he might like to come to Brandon with you."

"It's very kind of you, Mummy. I think that he would like to. I hope so anyway."

Chapter 12

The chairs came into the yard under the mess room windows again as the summer evenings lengthened.

"Well, what do you think of that?" said Bert Foster, "A thousand bomber raid on Cologne. Blimey, that should make 'Itler sit up and take notice."

"It should and all. I wouldn't 'ave liked to 'ave been there when that load of shit was dropping. 'Ow many did they used to send over London?"

"May the 10th last year was the worst. That was five hundred and fifty planes, but this lot was dropped all in the one hour."

"Well, perhaps that's not as bad as them dropping for six or seven hours like we 'ad it. At least most of the time you could be fighting fires without wondering if you was going to be blown sky fuckin' 'igh any minute."

"Well, they sowed the wind and they're reaping the whirlwind," said Charlie Pierce. "What worries me is the way that the news bulletins keep saying so many of our bombers failed to return. It must be 'ard for those lads in air force blue."

"You could 'ave a go yourself, Charlie boy. It's on the notice board."

"What's on the notice board?" asked Bert Foster.

"You wouldn't know. You never fuckin' read it. It

says that you can be released from the fire service if you volunteer for aircrew duties. Why don't you 'ave a go?"

"Don't talk so fuckin' daft," said Charlie Pierce. "If you read it all, it says that you've got to be under thirty so they won't get very many of us lot. Not like the Merchant Navy releases. They took them up to my age."

"One or two of 'em's been drowned already. I'd stay on dry land any time. What's for tea?"

"It's spam again. Dicky Finch's has gone up to stores to collect some more, only she isn't back yet."

"Expect she's called in at station 69, trying to get one of the women drivers there to swop leave days with 'er. She's forever swapping leave days now. What's she got lined up?"

"'Oos got 'er lined up, you mean. One of 'er own class I suppose. Nobody we'd know anything about. Cor, I'd like to 'ave a crack at 'er. She'd make a lovely lay."

"Do you reckon that old Brusher White ever got 'is oats off with 'er?"

"I know 'e did."

"Well, 'e was lucky even if 'e did get blown to bits."

"You lot cut that out," said Charlie Pierce. "That's no way to talk about a decent girl. You don't know what you're saying."

"I know what I'm saying when I say that I know that Brusher White fuckin' 'ad 'er."

"No, you don't. You don't know fuck nothing. Cut it out. I'm telling you."

"Are you becoming the leading fuckin' fireman during standby hours, Charlie?"

"Yes I am. Now let's 'ear no more of it."

"Silly old bugger, 'e doesn't even know the facts of life!" whispered Harry Booth behind his hand. "You want to 'ave a talk with Edie Brown after she's 'ad a beer or two. She'll tell you a thing or two about Brusher and Dicky."

"Well, she seems to 'ave got over it. Cor, wasn't she down for months afterwards?"

"Yes, but she's as bright as a fuckin' cricket again now. You get over these things when you're young. It'd be nice to be young again."

"Especially if the old Blitz was to start up again. Been quiet, 'asn't it these past few months."

It stayed quiet in London and the years of defeat were followed by the years of victory. El-Alamein, Stalingrad, Guadalcanal, the surrender of Italy, the series of good news that came as regularly as the bad news had come before.

Nineteen forty-four came in with the little Blitz, a series of short raids with new German techniques which included phosphorous bombs, anti-personnel bombs and a high proportion of explosive incendiaries. Substation 69Y was busy, and the mess room talk turned again to fire experiences and to service casualties but it always came back to the impending invasion of Europe.

There was tenseness still, but it was a confident tenseness. The smell of victory was in the air and, as the summer carne, elaborate security precautions failed to prevent the news reaching them that over a thousand firemen from the north were driving their pumps to the built-up areas along the south coast. They came to protect the great mass of stores, petrol and explosives that lay in dumps around the ports.

Janet heard the news of D-Day at the substation. The wireless was switched on for every news bulletin and in a battered atlas the coastline of France was studied and marked with pencils.

At nine o'clock the next morning the dismissed White watch stayed in the yard to talk to the arriving Red watch in case, in their twenty-four hours of freedom, they had heard some news that had not reached the substation.

"Saw you and your missus in the street last night when I was taking the lamps round," said Janet to Charlie Pierce. "What were you doing wearing your uniform on your leave day?"

"I'd been to Church, my old duck. Little evening service that our vicar laid on special to put a word in for the lads out there. Nice idea, I thought. The missus asked me to wear me uniform. We went with neighbours what've got two boys what've been shut up in camp without being allowed to send letters for a fortnight so it's certain that they're there. Bit 'ard, isn't it, the two only boys from one family. Well, the wireless this morning says that we're established on the beaches and inland. If things go right, we'll soon 'ave those French airfields and I reckon that our job'll be finished. They'll be cancelling this old Firemen's Employment Order soon and I can go back to Stevedoring and you can go back to Norfolk. You won't forget your old Charlie boy, will you?"

"No, I'll never forget you Charlie."

"There's a good old girl."

Eight days later, Janet stood in the yard enjoying the June sunshine. She looked up into the sky.

"Look, there's a little plane," she said to Cissie Spence, who stood beside her. "It must be quite low. You can hear the engine plainly."

"There's another over there," said Cissie. "Looks as if it's on fire. It's coming down. The engine's stopped"

They saw a cloud of smoke and a burst of flame over the rooftops. Company Officer Davies pressed the switch of Bert Foster's home-made bell system and switched on the light for the self-propelled pump. The men ran out of the station, dressing as they jumped onto the vehicle. In the watch-room Mabel Smith picked up the phone and reported to station 69.

"'Ullo substation 69Y 'ere, SP out to an explosion and fire beyond Augur Street. Locality not yet certain."

In a quarter of an hour the pump and its crew were back, the men arguing as they got down from the vehicle.

"It was a little plane I keep telling you. It 'as little wings. There was quite big pieces of it left and a tail fin."

"Well it fuckin' well wasn't one of ours."

"Of course, the fucker wasn't."

"Well there wasn't no fuckin' pilot."

"'Ow do you know there wasn't no pilot?"

"'E'd have been blown to buggery in that lot. Seven 'ouses gone for a burton. It's left the fuckin' first aid parties busy even if there wasn't no fuckin' fire to deal with. Come on Taffy, what do you think it was?"

"Maybe I know and maybe I don't. I've got to get on

to station 69 about it."

He walked away to the watch-room.

Five minutes later Mr Sutton arrived in his car.

"Fall them all in," he said, "except for one woman who is to stay in the watch-room."

They gathered together in the recreation room.

"Now what some of you have just seen and what I expect you've all been talking about is confidential and it is not to be talked about to the public. It's the same thing that fell in Bethnal Green three nights ago. It won't be confidential long because they're dropping one after the other this minute, but it's Hitler's secret weapon that he's been talking about for so long. It's a pilotless aircraft or a flying bomb."

A distant explosion punctuated his words.

"It's only a biggish HE and we shouldn't expect many fires from them but you'll all be expected to help in rescue work when needed. Some special training has already been laid on and this substation is going to take part in it."

The Home Secretary announced the arrival of the new weapon that afternoon.

"Well that didn't stay confidential long," said Charlie Pierce. "If that's all there was to 'Itler's secret weapon it wasn't much to worry about."

They burst in London all through the summer. At substation 69Y they watched them from the yard or from the roof and they were sometimes called to help in rescue or sheeting up damaged buildings, rarely a fire.

"I 'ate these doodlebugs," said Agnes Jenkins. "I don't mind when they're buzzing, but when the engine cuts out and they start to dive, 'specially when they're pointing in your direction, it makes my old knees go quite shaky."

A belt of barrage balloons and AA guns were set up around the south east coast to intercept them and in July Claude Farrow was posted south to join it.

"Well, he's really in the thick of things now," said Aunt Kitty on one of Janet's leave days. "Isn't he wonderful? Do you know that last week one of those things flying low dived right towards his gun sight? He simply flung himself into a hole, tearing his Mac in the process. Fortunately, it went over their heads and burst about a mile away. I suppose that you'll be going to Brandon for your summer leave and that Peter Stephens will be there. When is it?"

"Not until September. He can't get away before then."

"Well, I should have thought that it would have been easy enough for him. There can't be much happening up there."

The implied criticism irked her, and she got up and left the room. She went to her bedroom and took out the bundle of his letters to re-read them, smiling to note how the early ones had opened 'Dear Janet' changing to 'My Dear Janet' mutating to the 'Darling' of the one she had received the day before. It would not be long before September came.

"You want to 'itch 'ike," said Mollie Breaks. "The trains are bloody awful. You'll be standing all the way. There's a lot of army and air force traffic on the roads and quite a few essential car users. Wear your uniform. When they see you standing by the road with your old BEM up somebody will be bound to stop."

Janet took her advice and she arrived at Brandon on a golden afternoon of late September.

"I don't think it was a very correct thing for a young lady to do," said her mother. "I don't think that Peter will be very pleased to hear about it."

"Oh, nonsense Mummy. Everybody does it nowadays. It was much quicker than the train and pleasanter and cheaper. I did it in three lifts right to the door. You never know. You may find that Peter has done the same thing when he arrives on Thursday."

"I don't think so. It doesn't sound like him at all. Will you take the bus into Norwich and meet him at the station? It does seem dreadful not to be able to meet your guest's train with the car.

"Dr Harris, who has been worked to death running a large practice single-handed, took his car to the golf club on Sunday. A policeman saw it there and he was heavily fined. He could easily have said that the golf club was on the way to a patient, but of course he is too honest to do that.

"It's a good job that the bus service fits in fairly well with the four thirty train. I won't come with you. I expect you'd rather meet him alone. How is everything going?"

"Oh, everything's going fine. We've decided not to leave it until the end of the war. You know that he never went into quarters after leaving London. Being a bachelor, he didn't think it necessary, as it's only a wartime and temporary posting. Anyhow they've started reducing the service already in the north and there is a very nice house available. He's entitled to quarters of course, so he's going to take it.

"Do you mind if we get married towards the end of next month? We don't want anything elaborate in the way of a wedding."

"Of course, I don't mind, darling. I'm very happy about it and I'm sure that you will be."

They met on the station platform and took the bus back to Brandon.

"Mother's out but she'll be back for dinner. Now you can give me a proper kiss, not one of your railway station pecks."

"That's what I've been looking forward to for weeks."

A moment later he felt in his pocket and he handed her a small package.

"I got it in London. I do hope that you like it."

The ring was a cluster of diamonds. She looked at it with pleasure, briefly remembering the one with the little single diamond she no longer wore on her right hand.

"I think it's lovely. Oh, you're so good to me, Peter."

"Am I? Let me put it on. There's a snag about the house but there's another one almost as good."

"What was the snag?"

"The owner is a solicitor, but he left it empty when he joined the army in 1939 and it was requisitioned by the NFS for quarters. Well the owner has heard that the present occupant is leaving and apparently, he's had a good offer and he wants to sell. Of course, while requisitioning powers last, we could hang on to it, but he has written a very strong letter to the regional commissioner all about the scandal of an officer serving his country in His Majesty's forces having his house requisitioned for the benefit of a mere fire officer.

"The regional commissioner is inclined to give it up and I wouldn't press him not to. The other one is almost as good and anyhow we'll be back in London soon. The war can't last much longer."

"No. Anyhow what does it matter? Let the poor man have his house back. Is he a commando or something?"

"No, he's a major in the Judge Advocate's department. He runs the courts martial in Cornwall. He's been there all the war."

They both laughed and he hugged her to him.

"Well, we'll make it October then. They'll let you resign. Any of the women can go now. They've taken all the ex-building workers already, to repair flying bomb damage. Please name the day. I think that is the correct form isn't it?"

"Just unhand me a moment Peter. Sit down. There's one thing that I've got to tell you."

He sat in an easy chair and she took the one opposite him.

"Well, what are you looking so serious about?"

"I'm not a virgin. Perhaps I should have told you before. I wanted you to know and I'm sure that you love me enough for it not to make any difference."

She noticed that he had flushed, and his hands gripped the arms of the chair.

"I must say that you surprise me. Somehow, I'd never

have thought it of you. It won't make any difference but am I entitled to ask who it was? Not presumably anyone I know."

"I was coming to that. I'm afraid that I haven't finished. I've been pregnant."

"Good God! What happened?"

"I had a miscarriage at between two and three months."

"I suppose that was just as well. You haven't answered my question yet."

"It was an LFB sub-officer. No, a station officer. He was made up the day that he was killed."

He got up suddenly and he walked to the window and looked out while she gazed anxiously at his back.

"What name?"

"White. W.B. White."

"I remember him from station 69. He was in for accelerated promotion; very good looking. I suppose that was the attraction."

"Darling, don't be angry with me. You're very good looking too, but that isn't the only attraction. It all seems so long ago. Does it make such a difference? We were going to be married."

"I should think from what you've told me that it was about time that you were. Does it make such a difference? It wouldn't, if it hadn't been an LFB man. How many people know about it?"

"Even my mother doesn't know."

"I don't mean your family. I mean in the Service."

"Some of them knew on the substation."

"Well, that means most of the district and most of the division. You know the LFB; long duty hours and long standby hours every station interconnected by direct line telephone. Gossip passing to and fro all through the night. You make it pretty impossible for me."

The words chilled her and her voice quivered.

"Why is it pretty impossible for you?"

"It would never be forgotten all my service. You'd have to attend service functions. At the annual review you'd sit beside me on the platform — the divisional officer's wife, perhaps one day the chief officer's wife. Can't you imagine them saying out of the corner of their mouths — 'There she is. During the war she was put in the family way by a sub-officer'. They'd assume that I never knew.

"Are you necessarily going back to the LFB? There are other big fire brigades and when the NFS is wound up at the end of the war there will be people who have got their foot in London.

"That's out of the question. The London County Council is famous for its integrity. When the LFB was formally handed over to the Home Office the chairman of the county council himself told us that our work in the Blitz would never be forgotten."

She got up, walked to the window and laid her hand on his arm.

"What are you going to do, Peter? Are you going to reject me?"

He drew away from her.

"Oh, for God's sake. Give me time to think, Janet."

"How long do you want to think?"

"I don't know. This has been a shock to me. I want to think it out alone."

"Do you mean that you want to go? Your bags are still in the hall. There's a bus to Norwich in ten minutes time."

She waited hopefully for a negative answer.

"Yes, I think I'd better go," he said.

"You'd better take this with you."

She pulled the ring off her finger and she held it out.

"Keep it as a souvenir de la guerre; another souvenir de la guerre."

He was walking towards the door.

"Will you write to me?" she asked.

"Yes, I'll write to you when I've sorted it out. Goodbye Janet."

She did not answer but she followed him to the porch and stood there watching the tall figure walking up the drive, suitcase in hand. He turned the corner and she sat down on a chair in the hall. She was still there when her mother came home.

"Why Janet, what's the matter? You look as if you'd seen a ghost. Where's Peter?"

"He's gone."

"Gone? But he was only arriving this afternoon. Now don't tell me you've had some silly tiff. If you have, it'll soon be made up. You must be patient. Men aren't angels you know."

She got up and she stared at her mother.

"He's an angel. A bloody Angel Clare."

She sat down and burst into laughter mixed with sobs.

"Pull yourself together, Janet. If there's one thing I can't stand, it's hysteria. Now pull yourself together and tell me what's happened."

At the end of her leave, Janet returned to London and reported to substation 69Y at nine o'clock the next morning.

"You look a bit down, Dicky," said Mollie Breaks that evening. "I should have thought that the country air would have done you a bit of good. It's been bang, bang, crump, crump all day and all night but they haven't started many fires. I hear that some V2s have been dropped around Norwich."

"Yes, we heard one or two. They didn't do any damage. They nearly all fell in the country."

She sat in the spare watch-room chair and lit a cigarette from the stub end of the one she had just finished.

"Well, come on, tell me all about it," said Mollie. "You've had a face as long as a wet week all day and been smoking like a chimney. Is something wrong? How was his nibs?"

"I only saw his nibs for about an hour. I told him about Bill and about me expecting a baby. He left straight away promising to write. I met the postman every morning, waiting in the road for him. There hasn't been a letter yet."

"Well, I'll be dammed, the dirty great big self-satisfied twicer. I'd bet that he isn't a bull virgin himself. Did you have to tell him?"

"Yes, I had to. Don't say things like that about him Mollie. You must see his point of view. If I marry him — and we were going to be married in October, when he comes back to London people will look at his wife and say she was poked by a sub. It wouldn't be so hot for him or for me either."

"They wouldn't say it out loud and these things get forgotten. Anyhow hardly anybody knows except for a few on this substation. That bloody little Edith Brown started talking until I threatened to box her ears, but I'll lay odds it hasn't spread very far. Anyhow, all I can say, if that's his attitude then he's not good enough for you.

"You want to give him the old song, Dicky. 'Let him go, let him tarry, let him sink or let him swim. He doesn't care for me and I don't care for him'. Cheer up we'll have a pint and get Harry Booth to play it."

"I'm not in a singing mood Mollie and the trouble is I do care for him."

"Well, we'll have a pint anyway. I've got to see Mrs Bridger at station 69 at half past eight. I was going to walk up. You can come with me. Come on. Cissie Spence is going to take over the watch-room. The Carpenter's Arms is on our way. If we just slip in and try a couple of Mrs Barnacles' lousy bitters, it won't lose the war, or my stripes.

Janet returned to the substation at nine o'clock. She stood at the watch-room door holding a quart bottle in each hand.

"Book me returned."

Cissie Spence looked up from the table.

"Book you returned? You haven't even been booked out."

"Doesn't matter. Have they had supper?"

"Of course, they have. Aggie's got yours in the kitchen for you."

"Doesn't matter."

She walked into the mess room and she stopped opposite Harry Booth.

"Harry, do you know a song called, 'Let him go, let him tarry'?"

"Yes, I know it."

"Well. Play it and that's yours."

She dropped one of the quart bottles into his lap.

"That's very civil of you, my old duck. I'd 'ave played it for you for nothing."

"What are you doing with the other bottle, Dicky?" asked Arthur Clayton.

She threw it to him.

"I could only carry two. Anyone game to make a quick dash to the Carpenter's and back? Here's a quid. Bring back as much as you can carry."

"What's this in aid of, Dicky?"

"Just a little celebration. The end of my leave."

They filled the glasses and gathered around the piano.

"Let him go, let him tarry, let him sink or let him swim.

He doesn't care for me and I don't care for him.

He can go and get another who I hope he will enjoy.

I'm going to marry a far nicer boy."

"Anybody know the verses?"

"Yes, I do."

"Come on then, sing the next one."

"That was very nice of Dicky Finch, wasn't it? She's

a rum'un. I reckon she was 'alf pissed when she came in. Your very good 'ealth, Dicky. Eh, where's Dicky gone?"

She was sitting on her bed in the women's dormitory, elbows on her knees, her chin in her hands.

"I don't mean it, Peter. You know that I don't mean it," she said to herself.

"Go and look for 'er, Edith."

Edith Brown did as she was told, and she returned a few minutes later.

"She's sitting on 'er bed. I asked why she'd left the party."

"What did she say?"

"She said 'oh bugger off'."

"She's a rum'un. Come on 'Arry, give us 'Bless 'em all'."

The weeks passed and the months passed, and no letter came from Peter Stephens. The German offensive in the Ardennes opened on December the 16th and it flickered out at the end of the month. On January the 1st the Luftwaffe made a last despairing fling in a low-level attack on allied airfields in France, catching many planes on the ground and destroying them. A few more ack-ack batteries were sent across the channel to strengthen aerodrome defences and Claude Farrow's unit was among them.

Janet went to Kensington on a leave day morning and she met Colonel Boyd leaving the house.

"Hello, my dear, such goings on. Claude went off last night and Kitty's in a dreadful flap. She's quite convinced that he'll be going by aeroplane and that he will parachute, and she has asked us all to pray for him. I've told her not to worry and that I'll lay odds that he'll be further from the German lines than she is; Cherbourg probably. However, be kind to her.

"And how are you getting on? Had any trouble with the flying bombs? They are persistent, aren't they? I thought that when we overran the French launching sites in September that it would be the end of them, but it's these sites in Holland we can't get hold of and they're launching them from planes too. I hear that they had quite a few falling up in the north, launched from planes off the east coast.

"Well, it looks as if it's nearly over. Can't be long once the spring comes. You'll be getting demobbed soon. Then what are you going to do?"

"I don't know Uncle Neville. I'll go back to Brandon I suppose and live a quiet country life."

He looked at her quizzically.

"I'm sorry about what happened, my dear. It was tough. You forget about him. He can't be worth remembering to have behaved like that."

"He had his reasons. I don't blame him."

"Oh well. You know best. Must be on my way. Don't forget to be particularly nice to Kitty."

The winter leave days seemed interminable and Janet was glad when they ended, and she could go back to the substation and drive her lorry and sit in the warm mess room playing solo and discussing the triumphant progress of the war.

Changing out of uniform on a March morning she put on her blue suit and she pinned Jim Cartwright's brooch to it. On impulse, she went to the phone and dialled the number of his parents' house. There was no reply. She tried again at intervals during the day and in the evening, she walked to Manchester Square Fire Station.

"Is Cartwright on duty?" she asked a fireman in the yard.

"Don't know 'im. 'E's not on this station. Not this watch any'ow. There's an officer in there. 'E might know."

Janet saw Tom Blake, standing by the notice board in the passage.

"Hello Tom. How are you? Congratulations on the officer rank. I saw it in orders last year and I was very pleased."

"Why hello, Janet. How nice to see you after all this time? Still visiting stations on your leave day. Can't keep you away?"

"I've come for a purpose. I wanted to contact Jim Cartwright. Is he still Blue watch and on leave today? If so, I'll leave a message for him."

He looked hard at her.

"No, he's not been here for two years. He used to be very sweet on you, didn't he? Haven't you heard?"

"No. I haven't heard of him for a long time."

"Not since you gave him the brush off?"

"No, not since then."

He pointed to the top of the notice board where, looking old and yellowed was the foolscap sheet headed 'Police and Firemen's Employment Order. Release of Personnel for Air Crew Duties'.

"He was one of those. He's had the chop."

"Had the chop?"

"Well, that's what the RAF boys say. Shot down. Dead. We heard here at the beginning of the month. It was the raid on Dresden. He was a squadron leader with the DFC by then."

She walked slowly back to Kensington and she wrote a letter of condolence to Mr and Mrs Cartwright. Her tears splashed on the envelope as she sealed it.

The last rocket fell on March the 27th. Six weeks later the war in Europe was over. Janet was on leave for VE Day.

"Isn't it wonderful?" said Aunt Kitty. "I think that we ought to have a little celebration but I've no idea where we should go. I suppose that everywhere will be dreadfully overcrowded. If only Claude was at home, he would take us somewhere. Never mind. Let's put it off until he is. It can't be long now. Perhaps your mother will come up and join us.

"Claude said in his last letter that they would be going forward into Germany as part of the occupation troops. I think that is a very good thing. I was afraid at one time that they might send him to the Far East."

Mollie Breaks rang up at six o'clock.

"Hello Dicky, isn't it lovely? What are you doing?"

"I'm just sitting here reading a book."

"Well, you can't do that today. I've got short leave. Eric's getting three hours short leave from eight o'clock. Come and meet up with us. Come and meet me now, and Eric can join us later."

"Wouldn't you like to be alone with him?"

"No, of course not. You can't sit there brooding."

They met in a pub in Borough High Street. It was crowded and noisy with singing. Outside in the street, fireworks banged and fizzed.

"I don't think much of this," said Mollie. "I feel like going somewhere quiet and just resting and thinking and being thankful. I keep thinking of Johnny and Norway. It doesn't seem as if it all happened five years ago. It's been a long time. Eric says when we're married, we'll have a little boy and we'll call him Johnny. That was nice of him wasn't it? When he comes, let's get out of here and go somewhere quiet, if there is anywhere quiet."

"When are you going to get married?"

"This summer. Just a quiet little wedding in the church over the road. The fire force commander has given permission for the reception to be held in the gym at Southwark. You'll come won't you, Dicky?"

"Yes, of course I'll come."

Column Officer Price arrived punctually.

"Dicky and I don't think much of this place, Eric. Let's go somewhere quiet. I somehow don't feel like dancing in the street and those sorts of capers."

"There isn't anywhere quiet tonight."

He stood thinking.

"I know. There's a little bit of green at the back of Pageants Wharf's yard. There's a seat there looking over the river. It's a lovely evening and it won't be dark till ten with double summertime. They'll let us have some beer from their canteen and we can sit there and watch the river."

They took the tube to Surrey Docks Station and walked down Rotherhithe Street to the fire station. Eric Price went in while his two companions walked to the riverside seat. He joined them a few minutes later, carrying a tray loaded with bottles and glasses. They sat and looked across the wide, sluggish river to the Limehouse side with its jagged ruins of warehouses silhouetted against the evening sky.

"Do you remember when all this lot round here was on fire, Dicky?"

"That was a night. September the 7th wasn't it?"

"And now I suppose that tomorrow we can all give a week's notice and walk out."

"You women can. Most of the AFS men think they're going to be able to but they've got another think coming. I've been at an officers' meeting this evening. The Government is going to insist on an orderly and graded demobilisation. They're not going to allow a sudden and complete exodus from the NFS so that conscript firemen can pick up the best jobs before the troops get home. And there's all the steel piping to be lifted from the streets and the emergency water supplies to be drained and the substations to be handed back."

"Well, that'll cause a bit of bother at substation 69Y," said Mollie. "Most of them are chafing to get out and back to their old jobs."

Darkness fell and the air became chilly. Janet shivered. Her companions had moved closer together on the seat and were holding hands. She felt lonely and unwanted and she was glad when Eric said that he must report back to duty.

Mr Sutton sent for her the next day.

"You know they won't be insisting on you women staying in the service, though the Police and the Firemen's Employment Order will probably stay in force for another year. We're going to be short of drivers with all the clearing up that's got to be done. Will you stay on with us for a bit, Miss Finch?"

She agreed willingly, thinking that if she stayed in the service that there would be a chance of at least hearing news of Peter Stephens.

The school children came back and substation 69Y was returned to the education department.

"Quite a joke, isn't it?" said Charlie Price. "They've been evacuated to North Wales and now they all speak Welsh. The teacher was here yesterday talking to Taff Davies and she said that some of the parents were very cross about it. They've got a secret language that they speak to one another in front of their mums and dads who don't understand a word of what they're saying."

The remainder of the men who had not been released to key industrial jobs moved to station 69 and they occupied the huts in the yard that had been the women's quarters. The control room had reverted to a station watch-room and it was now manned by firemen. Janet shared a small bedroom partitioned off from the main hut with the only other remaining woman, who was a driver like herself.

August came and VJ Day. Only Charlie Pierce, Jack

Adams, Harry Booth and Bert Foster remained of the original strength of substation 69Y.

"Pity there isn't a piano up here, Harry, you could give us a tune. Just our luck to be on duty, today of all days."

"Well, they must let us go now. The war's over properly, isn't it? They can't keep us 'ere for fuckin' ever. There's some big money being offered in the docks to fuckers like us who know our way about there."

"You got nothing to fuckin' worry about since they put us on twenty-four hours on and twenty-four hours off like civil defence was always on. You can fuckin' earn good fuckin' money on your leave day and pick up your pay packet 'ere."

"Ah maybe, but I'm tired of this old blue uniform. What do you think was special about them bombs that they dropped on the Japs?"

"Well they was just big bombs I suppose. Bigger than any they'd dropped before. It's all over now, so I don't suppose that we shall 'ear anything more about 'em."

"You 'eard, poor old Taff Davies 'as 'ad the result of the reassessment board? They've reduced the poor fucker to section leader."

"Well what did 'e expect. That's the same as a pre-war sub officer, isn't it and 'e was only a plain fuckin' fireman before the war. Did all the regulars expect to go on 'olding their wartime ranks now that the service is only a quarter of the size?"

"Ah, but 'e took it 'ard. I was there when 'e 'eard and 'e said 'I knew that you lot would get me broken'."

"Poor old Taff. 'E did used to worry. Still, 'e's near

the end of 'is time. 'E can take a pension soon."

"They were talking about the fire service staying national, but now they say that it won't and that the local authorities will be taking over again soon."

"'Ere, 'ave you seen the order that's come out? Anyone what's done three years can go and get a form from the post office and fill it in and get it signed and they'll get a fuckin' medal. It's called the defence medal."

"I've seen it and you know what they can do with their medal? Every fucker's being given it, even part time fuckin' firewatchers in Blackpool."

"You've already got a medal, Dicky. You going to put in for it?"

"I don't know. I haven't thought about it."

"Fancy you 'anging on with us 'ere, Dicky. Why do you do it? I bet you don't need the money."

"I don't know why. I promised Mr Sutton that I'd stay on for a bit until we'd got all the steel piping driven down to the docks."

"Well it's very nice to 'ave you with us still, my old duck."

In the late autumn Janet heard that a senior officers' meeting was to be held in London. That evening Mr Sutton walked into the yard where she was washing down the general-purpose lorry.

"You're wanted on the phone, Miss Finch. You can take it in my office."

Her heart beat fast as she hurried to take the call. He was in London. She had often thought that he would contact her at the station.

"Janet Finch here."

Kitty Farrow's voice dashed her hopes.

"Janet dear, I know that I shouldn't phone you at the station but it's so exciting. Claude is home. I wasn't expecting him till next week but he's just walked in. He's wearing his medal ribbons. He's got four. He'll be demobbed next month. You will hurry straight home in the morning, won't you? He's simply longing to see you."

Claude was tactful and attentive. He went back to work in the city. He proposed and she turned him down again.

Three months later Janet was lonely and despondent, and she had started to wonder whether life with Claude, might have been better than the emptiness that she now felt. One thing she was sure of was that she did not love him and the thought of a loveless marriage frightened her.

The more she thought about this, the more certain she was that she had made the right decision. She still yearned for Peter, in spite of resenting him for his inability to accept her earlier affair and for his snobbery and his insensitivity.

Sitting in the bath late one morning, she turned her anger with him onto herself. It was ridiculous for her to go on hoping that some miracle would occur and fantasising that he might relent and come back to her. She told herself to forget him and to be grateful for the invitation to go to a job in Sydney and escape all her longing.

She got out of the bath and had just finished drying herself when the doorbell rang. Holding the towel in front of her she walked to the window and looked out. The caller stood on the porch and she could not see him. She put on a housecoat that buttoned to the chin, put her feet in her slippers, walked downstairs and opened the door.

"Hello Janet," said Peter Stephens.

"Peter, what are you doing in London, and in uniform too?"

"Just been to County Hall to the appointments board for the new chief officer of the about to be resuscitated London Fire Brigade."

"Did you get it?"

He shook his head and smiled.

"One of the others of the old principal officers then?"

He shook his head again.

"I want to talk to you, Janet. I can't do so standing on the doorstep."

"Come in then, but you can't stay long."

She walked in front of him to the drawing room.

"So, they turned you all down. I'm sorry. Did they give any reason? I suppose that there was lots of handshaking and thanks and talk about the Blitz."

"There were formal five-minute interviews and at the end, a uniformed porter walked into the room and said, 'You can go now'. It was a charade and it has obviously been fixed. However, not to worry it's going to be exciting running one of the big new county brigades and I've had the offer of one already; more formal interviews of course to comply with the regulations, but they're keen for me to take it and they say that it's mine if I'll accept.

"They're nice people, Janet and it's a nice part of the country. You'd be happy there. I'll make you happy. I've never forgotten you for one moment. I've been a fool and I must have hurt you. Please forgive me."

"Are you asking me again to marry you?"

"Yes of course. Please say you will."

"I think that you've got the bloodiest awful effrontery. You couldn't marry the former mistress; I suppose that's the accepted term, of an LFB sub-officer, because you'd be worrying about the LFB knowing and about what they would say. Now that the LFB have turned you down, you'll graciously condescend to do so."

"That isn't true, Janet. I'd already made up my mind whichever way it went. I wrote and I sent the letter to Brandon two days ago. You'll find it there when you go home. Yesterday evening when I got to London, I tried to ring you there. Your mother's housekeeper said, 'Miss Janet is in London' and she put the receiver down. Oh, I know that I should have done it months ago. Please forgive me, darling."

She put out a hand and she touched his left breast.

"Yes, I forgive you Peter. Only the Defence Medal? And after fifty-seven nights of continuous duty running the Blitz."

The touch of her hand inflamed him. His arms went around her, and he drew her to him, and he kissed her on the mouth. She responded avidly.

His hand ran down her back.

"Nothing on under this Janet? You must have got up late."

She pushed him from her with both hands.

"No, I was changing. You must go, Peter. Go quickly.

My mother and Aunt Kitty will be here in a minute. They mustn't find you here. You've left it too late. I am finalising my plans with them to go to Australia where I have been offered a job and a place to live with distant cousins."

"Why Janet? I would like to see your mother and Aunt Kitty. I owe them an apology too. You have forgiven me. Won't they?"

She became calmer.

"No, I don't suppose they will because they hated you for hurting me so much."

"For God's sake, you mustn't go to the other side of the world where you know nobody. You can't do that."

"I must assure you that I can. Everything has been fixed for some time. I have bought my ticket and it will be hard to cancel everything now."

She sat clenching and unclenching her hands on her knees fighting back her tears. He sat down next to her and he took her hands in his.

"I love you. Please trust me and believe me. I will never forsake you again. I was trapped in my own senseless pride and I regret what I did in abandoning you, more than I have ever done. Let me make amends. Forget Australia and come with me. I believe that you still love me, and I want you to marry me."

She sobbed. He let her weep until she was able to look at him.

"I have never stopped loving you. I still do and I always will."

They were married four weeks later.

WELSH
FOOTBALL
QUIZ BOOK

Dedicated to all those who have endured these heartaches, traumas and shattered dreams

THE
WELSH
FOOTBALL
QUIZ BOOK

DAVID COLLINS

y Lolfa

ISBN: 978 1 78461 241 2

Published and printed in Wales
on paper from well-maintained forests by
Y Lolfa Cyf., Talybont, Ceredigion SY24 5HE
e-mail ylolfa@ylolfa.com
website www.ylolfa.com
tel 01970 832 304
fax 832 782

Contents

Contents

Introduction

Before we start – this book is not what you think it is.

Oh sure, it's a quiz book alright. And it's definitely about Welsh football. That is beyond debate. There are questions, and answers. That's the easy bit.

But as I settled down to my task, I soon realised that this book was becoming so much more. I found my life unfolding through its pages: games I could barely recall, names I would hear no more, friends and family who were no longer with us, trips to lands which no longer existed.

I found myself distracted over the minutiae of each question. I rang lifelong friends to check answers and corroborate facts. Inevitably, we digressed from our task on a wave of nostalgia: penalties which crashed against the bar, day glow kits and sideburns, injustice at the hands of a Scotsman, droolings over the feats of a Galáctico.

I wanted this book to be a time capsule; a set-in-stone tribute to my dashed hopes and shattered dreams.

But no, this book is more of a time traveller.

Like the TARDIS itself, its pages disclose much more on the inside than might possibly appear likely from the outside. It will take you to foreign lands; it will span the eras of your mind. Its pages reveal a world that is past, present, and one, which may not even come at all...

Enjoy the book. It's been a long time coming.

David Collins

Round 1
I read the news today, oh boy...

Oh boy, indeed.

What heady times we live through, eh?

Wales stars at the top of the Premier League; our very own real live European superstar and, of course, the icing on the cake, Wales in the finals of a major tournament for the first time in many a long year. This is the modern world, for sure.

But how much attention did you really pay to all this? Are you packing a case for France in a blur of excitement, or even looking back over it all months later thinking... did all this really happen?

Here a few gentle reminders...

1. Current Wales stars Joe Ledley and Wayne Hennessy took Crystal Palace to the FA Cup final in May 2016. Which team did they beat in the semi-final?

2. During 2016, Gareth Bale became the highest scoring British player ever in La Liga. Whose record did he beat?

3. For which club side did Chris Coleman make his league debut as a player?

4. Against which club did Danny Ward make his Premier League debut towards the end of the 2015/16 season?

5. Which of our current squad sat on the bench during the 2016 Capital One Cup final?

6. Can you name the recipient of a prestigious PFA Merit Award in 2016?

7. Simon Church enjoyed a reasonably successful spell on loan at Aberdeen as 2015/16 drew to a close... but on loan from whom?

8. Which tiny Welsh striker announced his retirement from football during 2015/16?

9. 'I signed for my current club as a 16 year old in 2004, and have played over 300 times for them since. I have over 30 Welsh caps.' Who am I?

10. 'Shaun Macdonald Had a Farm, E-I-E-I-O.' But for which current Premier League side has the former Swansea City star made over 100 appearances in total?

I say, I say, I say...

What was Chris Coleman discussing when he told a packed hall of Wales fans, 'It's OK to get excited', in April 2016?

Picture this...

Can you name the first club side managed by Chris Coleman?

Round 2
The Bale Factor

Toshack, Rush, Giggs? Maybe even Charles?

Sure, over the years, we have boasted the odd superstar. That 'first name you look for', the bums-on-seats guy, the one player who we hoped would be fit for the big game. The sort of name you would toss into a conversation on holiday abroad to help explain where, or even what, Wales is.

But this thing with Bale – this is something else.

Never before in my experience has a player carried the hopes of a people so single-handedly. His value to the team, his commitment to the cause, and the effect he has on the opposition, make him a talisman not so much for the team but for the nation itself. It's hard to overstate his role in the story.

Many, many awards have come his way: Champions League winner, European Super Cup, BBC Wales Sports Personality of the Year. But now, Gareth, you have the ultimate accolade: your very own round in my quiz book. See how you do with these:

1. Gareth became the youngest player to represent Wales at 16 years and 315 days. But who subsequently broke that record?
2. How many appearances did Bale make for Spurs? Go on, I'll give you, say, five either way.
3. Who is taller: Bale or Ashley Williams?
4. Bale won the League Cup while at Spurs. True or false?
5. In 2014, Bale became only the fourth Welshman to win a Champions' League / European Cup winners' medal. Tell me the other three.
6. Can you name Gareth's slightly less famous footballing uncle?

7. On 12 October 2012, Bale scored two goals in a 2–1 victory over which country in a 2014 World Cup qualifier?

8. What is the connection between Bale's daughter and a certain ex-Spurs boss?

9. Before our hero's move to Spain, who held the title of the world's most expensive player?

10. Who did Real Madrid beat to win the European Super Cup in Cardiff in 2014?

I say, I say, I say…

As if to underline my opening comments, who has described Bale as 'a key part of the bid to create a legacy in this country'?

Picture this…

Against which team did this comic strip hero grab four goals for his club side in 2015?

Round 3
We are Premier League!

Over the many years since I began following Wales, the squad has often had something of 'home-made' look about it. Or even a charity shop.

Oh we have had our big names of course, your Rushies, Giggs, and Toshacks. But often such names have been supplemented by a cast of lower division hopefuls and fringe players. We even saw a League of Wales player drafted into the squad by Bobby Gould in the '90s.

Not these days, mind. These days we can virtually boast an entire XI of Premier League regulars… and one Galáctico.

So how much have you taken in as you tune into the Monday night Premier League action? Or up the pub for Super Sunday? Try these out:

1. During season 2015/16, which Premier League Wales star had his name on the front *and* back of his shirt?

2. How many times did Ryan Giggs win a Premier League winners' medal?

3. Craig Bellamy achieved a record by becoming the first player to score for seven different Premier League teams. How many can you name?

4. Which was the first Premier League game to be played outside England?

5. At the start of the 2015/16 season, how many Premier League clubs had Welsh managers?

6. How much did Liverpool pay Swansea City for Joe Allen?

7. Which often criticised Welsh international actually has 346 Premier League appearances on his CV?

8. Which goalie became the oldest player to make his debut for Liverpool since the war, in 2003?

9. Which Championship club did Aaron Ramsey join on loan in 2010 from Premiership big guns Arsenal to regain his fitness after he broke his leg?

10. Go on then, I know you want to. Can you name that League of Wales player called up by Bobby Gould in 1997? It was Belgium away, if that helps.

I Say, I Say, I Say...

These quotes are all from the same Welsh player who graced [*sic*] the Premier League for many years. But can you name him:

'I am not Pelé or Maradona.'

'I'm upset. There was nothing like putting on the red shirt.'

'John Toshack hates me.'

Picture this...

Which former Wales boss once managed these Premier League superstars. (Man City that is, not Cardiff City!)

Barclays Premier League
Manchester City FC vs Cardiff City FC
Sat 18 January 2014
Kick Off: 15:00

Stand: South Stand Level 1
Entrance: M
Block: 113　　Aisle: 114
Row: H　　Seat: 341

Price: £47.00

0161 444 1894 MCFC.CO.UK　　4600183

ADULT

Round 4
Bad Boys

Many aspects of this book celebrate the good times: the star names, famous goals or great games.

But oh, there have been darker moments.

For not always do things go to plan. A red card can change a game, while a missed penalty can blot an entire career. Just ask Paul Bodin.

So this round may be painful for you, as we recall years of heartache and some unfortunate moments for our lads. Dark Nights… and Dark Knights, so to speak. Let the heartaches begin:

1. Whose last international game for Wales, a 2–0 defeat to USA in May 2003, ended with a red card, during his 13th appearance? Unlucky for some?

2. In 1985 Dave Phillips was judged to have handled the ball against Scotland at a packed Ninian Park, to give Jock Stein's men a chance to drive a firm nail through our World Cup qualification hopes. Can you name the Scottish star that sent the tartan hoards into ecstasy from the spot that night?

3. And the Scotsman who ensured that Joe Jordan's handiwork paid dividends at Anfield in 1977? Another dubious penalty, to say the least.

4. That game officially counted as a home match for Wales, though you would never have guessed had you been stood on the Kop as I was. But the away leg also went badly. Which former Swansea City manager scored an own goal to give the Scots a 1–0 victory in Glasgow in 1976?

5. That terrible night against Romania in 1993 ended the career of Terry Yorath as manager of Wales. The next match didn't go so well either, as we lost 3–1 to Norway at Ninian Park, in a game featured elsewhere in these pages.

Can you name the future manager of Wales who scored our goal that night?

6. Welsh fortunes seemed to go from bad to worse in the mid '90s. We'll skip past the 5–0 defeat in Georgia in 1994, but I expect you to be able the name the Welshman [*sic*] who saw red as the mighty Georgians beat us 1–0 in Cardiff in June 1995.

7. Twenty-three goals in 38 international appearances is the impressive record of this star of the '40s and '50s, but after leaving Cardiff City in 1955 to join PSV Eindhoven, he was banned *sine die* by the Football League for revelations about his spell at Sunderland. Who was that then?

8. Talking of things Dutch, how many times have Wales beaten The Netherlands? I will give you five either way.

9. How many of you remember this palaver. In 1969 which Welsh player had to give up his seat on the plane to Dresden ahead of a World Cup qualifier in East Germany? The plane was overbooked and he was forced to take a later flight the next day.

10. Ryan Giggs was never sent off for Manchester United, but was dismissed once for Wales in 2002. Can you name the Scandinavian opponents on that unfortunate occasion?

I Say, I Say, I Say...

Who once said, 'As far as I am concerned, people in the Welsh TV game are not fit to lace Sparky's boots.' (Sparky being manager Mark Hughes, of course.)

Picture this...

Who is the Wales striker beneath the Stetson?

Round 5
In the Dugout

The hot seat – the managerial merry-go-round, 'From the Dugout'. There can be few aspects of modern football so riddled with clichés and analysis than the role of the manager. These days there is so much focus on the comments, opinions and decisions of the men in charge that sometimes I feel I could name more top managers than I could players.

But was it ever thus?

How much do you recall about the fortunes of those men in grey suits (or is Men in Tracksuits?) who have been given responsibility by the FAW for picking our teams down the years. Do you recall the distant days of Dave Bowen, or the one match of John Toshack? Try your luck with these teasers:

1. 'Bobby Gould Must Go'? Well he did, of course, famously resigning after a 4–0 defeat at the hands of which major footballing nation in 1999?

2. Go on then, easy one next. That single Tosh game at the helm at Ninian Park in March 1994. Can you name the opponents?

3. Where is Chris Coleman from?

4. Where is Mike England from?

5. These days the managerial set-up with Wales is pretty professional. Good habits introduced by Hughes, Speed and others. But in days gone by? Hmmm… For example, Dave Bowen split his time in the Welsh dugout between 1964 and 1974 by also looking after the affairs of which other major soccer power?

6. Can you name the controversial figure who was approached to be manager of the Welsh national team in 1987, but his club refused permission for him to speak to the Welsh FA?

7. Who was the manager of Wales for our one and only victory at Wembley, in 1977?

8. And who was in the hot seat in Sweden 1958?

9. For which German side did Mark Hughes make 18 appearances back in 1987/88? Way before his time as Wales boss, of course.

10. Which former Wales boss can count Coventry City, Spurs and Vancouver Whitecaps amongst his former clubs?

I Say, I Say, I Say...

Allegedly, which former Wales boss once instructed Mark Hughes 'not to tackle the Italians as they'll only dive'?

Picture this...

Who manages the Welsh women's team?

Round 6
The Road to France

Now, I should confess here that I had high hopes for this round. I planned to construct it carefully as the campaign unfurled.

'Who scored Wales' fifth goal in their stunning victory in Andorra?'

'Who scored a last-minute winner to seal qualification at home to Israel?'

'Which restaurant in Brussels gave us free beer all night?'

Like so many of my ideas which are centered on football though, things didn't quite go according to plan. The scruffy Andorran pitch and an uncooperative Belgian landlord combined with many other developments to totally scupper my dream of crafting a cunning chronology of curious questions.

So, it was a case of resorting to plan B: cheat.

These questions are therefore stolen from a hastily-arranged brain-storming session held amongst other Wales fans gathered before the friendly against the Dutch. My thanks to the bar staff of the City Arms, Cardiff, for their inevitable contribution to ensuring the flow of wisdom.

1. Which Bosnian striker scored a hat-trick against Andorra in March 2015? (Blimey Dan, that's a hard one!)
2. Can you name the Cwmbrân-born defender who retired during the campaign on 49 caps?
3. Andorra has the fifth smallest population of any UEFA country. Can you name the others?
4. Two Scottish clubs were represented in our squads during the campaign. Can you name either?
5. Against which team did Wales kick off their home fixtures in this campaign?

6. Who scored our winner in Cyprus?
7. Who won his 50th cap in the home tie against Belgium?
8. For which club does Chris Gunter play?
9. Can you name the midfielder who was sent off against Cyprus at the Cardiff City Stadium?
10. Wales played an away game at the King Baudouin Stadium on the way to qualifying. Can you name the hosts?

I Say, I Say, I Say...

During this famous campaign, Chris Coleman buried the hatchet with which tough-tackling defender? They went for a coffee in St David's Centre 'so it could not kick off' Coleman later disclosed!

Picture this...

What was the half-time score in this game?

Round 7
The Euros!

Well I had to, didn't I? How could I write a book like this and *not* include a section on the Euros? Whether you are reading this on the plane to France, or sat in a Moscow bar ahead of the 2018 World Cup final, 2016 is the year when finally, finally, we did it. Wales at a major finals.

At last… our turn.

At last.

So let's go with the bug shall we? After all, we may not get the chance again.

1. Easy one to open proceedings. But take care, you don't want to slip up in the opening game and leave yourself a mountain to climb do you? Against which team would Wales open their fixtures on 11 June 2016?

2. Next up, the big one. The one nobody wanted but for which tickets were like gold dust. England in Lens. Tell me, who is the record goal scorer for England in international football?

3. Talking of Moscow. Can you name the Wales manager when we blew it against Russia in the play-offs in 2003?

4. Penalties – we can't contemplate a major tournament without the drama of penalties. Hey, here's one for you. Who missed a penalty in Craig Bellamy's last home appearance for Wales?

5. And you can never write off the Germans. Who scored a famous goal the last time Wales beat Germany, for instance?

6. Tell me the venues for the 2016 European Championship semi-finals.

7. Tell me the name of the trophy!

8.   When was the first time Wales competed in the Euros?
9.   Which unusual venue was used for two Welsh home games in the 2000 qualifying campaign?
10. Where will the 2020 finals take place?

I Say, I Say, I Say...

Who said, 'Between 12 and 14, I shot up a ridiculous amount. The muscles were struggling to stretch and grow at the rate my bones were growing. It gave me problems with my back and my hamstrings.'

Picture this...

We may have faced Denmark in this Euro qualifier in 1987, but are Wales likely to face the Danes in France?

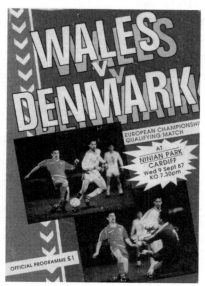

Round 8
Just a Minute

Ha-ha, this is a good round. Slightly different format here. It's ten questions but you only have 60 seconds to answer, OK? Quick-fire fun. I must accept your first answer.

I couldn't include a buzzer though sorry, so you'll have to make that 'eh-eh' noise yourself.

1. Who is Wales' most capped player of all time?
2. In what part of Manchester was Ryan Giggs born?
3. What is the motto on the FAW crest?
4. What is the English translation of these words?
5. In which year was Aaron Ramsey born?
6. In what year was the FAW formed?
7. Who was the last non-Welshman to manage Wales?
8. From which club did Spurs sign Gareth Bale?
9. What is Jazz Richards' real name?
10. Who is Jessica Fishlock?

Round 9
1976 and all that

There are two schools of thought about the summer of '76. For in 1976, Wales reached the quarter-finals of the European Championships. Yes, you read that right. The last eight. Now one view – particularly amongst the players who featured at the time – is that this achievement has been somewhat airbrushed from history, swept aside amidst stories of how Pelé broke our hearts back in 1958.

In 1976 the eight group winners from the qualifying stages included Wales. A forgotten success. But the elite eight were then required to play two-legged quarter-finals in order to reach the tournament itself. In other words, only four semi-finalists reached the 'finals' tournament. This changed for the 1980 tournament and, these days, 24 teams qualify for the finals. In 2015 Wales reached the finals by finishing in the last 24, but in 1976, we reached the last eight, even though, strictly speaking, we didn't make 'the finals' that year. History can be cruel sometimes, eh?

Of course, all this is only half the story. The home leg of that quarter-final, played at Ninian Park on 22 May 1976, has entered football folklore. Arguably it began the tale of mishaps, failures and self-destruction that has characterised Welsh football ever since.

See how much you recall about this unbelievable day. I will try and tell the story chronologically through the questions:

1. A Wales team featuring the likes of Brian Flynn, John Mahoney and Dai Davies finished top of Group 2, losing only one game, with over 27,000 squeezing into The Racecourse, Wrexham, for the final qualifier against Austria. Who scored the Welsh winner that night?
2. Who did Wales come up against in that two-legged quarter-final?

3. What was the result in the away leg?

4. Right, the game itself then. Things started badly when the East German referee threatened to abandon the game because the East German flag was not flying at the ground. Who was that infamous official?

5. It is fair to say that that referee 'irritated' the home crowd of 30,306 with a series of unpopular decisions. For example, whose 'goal' was disallowed after 63 minutes?

6. Who missed a penalty for Wales?

7. As beer cans, sticks and bottles rained onto the pitch from an angry crowd, for how long was the game stopped as the ref threatened to abandon proceedings once more?

8. Come here, there's more. How did the opposition player Jurica Jerković add his own contribution to the day?

9. And what unusual item was thrown at a linesman as fans invaded the pitch after the game?

10. Finally, the actual football match. What was the final score?

I Say, I Say, I Say...

Some critics argued that Wales were their own worst enemies this day, taking an over-physical attitude in an attempt to knock the silky Slavs out of their stride. For example, can you name the BBC commentator who suggested during his commentary that Wales were 'allowing their fire to get in the way of their football'?

Picture this...

Which Welsh team did both of the guys pictured here manage?

Round 10
Dad or Chips

So, how have you been doing so far? Still ploughing through the questions, or are you just cherry-picking to look good by choosing rounds that you think you know most about? No matter, as long as you are enjoying it.

Anyway, we have reached the midpoint of the book know. Time for a break? A half-time break, even? Yeah, let's give your grey matter a rest then, as I invite you to indulge me with a stroll back through the mists of time.

Try yourself with these little memory-jerkers. It's a mini interview. There are no right or wrong answers; just imagine that you are on a chat show with me as Michael Parkinson, or Mrs Merton if you prefer.

I have included my own answers for fun. After all, it is my show.

1. **What was the first ever Wales game you went to?**

   Wales vs England at Ninian Park in 1972. Lost 1–0 to a goal by Colin Bell.

2. **And the first away game?**

   England vs Wales, 1977.

3. **Favourite current Wales player?**

   Joe Ledley. Never a fan of that beard, though.

4. **Fave player, all-time?**

   In terms of real excitement and entertainment provided in matches I was actually at, I am going to say… Leighton James.

5. **Best goal?**

   That winner against Italy at the Millennium in 2002. Bellissimo!

6. **High?**

Leighton James' penalty to beat England back in 1977. I was only 18. Life was good.

7. **Low?**

Romania '93. Or maybe Anfield '77. Or Russia, or Iceland or…

8. **Favourite kit?**

No surprises here. That red, yellow and green ensemble from the '70s.

9. **Favourite song/chant?**

'Can't Take My Eyes Off Of You' (du ruh du ruh…)

10. **Finally, one current player who you wish was Welsh…**

Yaya Touré

Round 11
140 Not Out

One of the joys of producing a book such as this is that I have occasionally unearthed facts and figures of which I may have previously been unaware.

We can all recall famous incidents, players and goals down the years. We all have our own special 'I was there' moments too. But from time to time, well, the odd fact has sprung up which has either surprised me or which I just simply had not appreciated before.

Had you realised, for example, that in tracing its origins back to 1876, the Football Association of Wales is older than the Welsh Rugby Union? Did you know that Wales played their early games in white, only switching to red in 1883? Did you know that Alan Curtis had trials with Manchester United when he was a lad?

See how much you never quite knew from the last 140 years of pain and suffering, with this intriguing mix of the trivial yet true.

1. Wales have always had a dragon on their shirts, haven't they? Haven't they?
2. Nothing is new in this world. In 1895 Manchester City withdrew superstar Billy Meredith from a Wales squad assembled to face Scotland, yet still picked him to play against Lincoln City. What feat did Meredith perform against Lincoln to suggest that, d'you know, he may have been fit enough to turn out for us after all?
3. How many of Cardiff City's famous FA Cup winning side of 1927 were actually Welsh?
4. How many of Swansea City's 2013 Carling Cup winning side were actually Welsh?
5. How old was Pelé when he 'broke our hearts' in 1958?
6. What 'feat' was achieved by Gary Speed, Ryan Giggs,

Robbie Savage and Robert Earnshaw? It wouldn't have been possible for Billy Meredith to do this. Speed did it first in 1993. Joe Calzaghe did it in 1998. I have never done it, though there is still time.

7. Who was in goal for Wales when they drew 0–0 with the USSR at The Racecourse in 1981?

8. Who is the patron of the Football Association of Wales?

9. Where is Dragon Park?

10. What 'first' took place at the Millennium Stadium in 2000? Brazil were the illustrious opposition.

I Say, I Say, I Say...

Who is David Giles describing here: 'There can be no doubt that _____ made me a better player. His coaching methods were light years ahead of his peers.'

Picture this...

WELSH SCHOOLS' FOOTBALL ASSOCIATION

N° 0460

VICTORY SHIELD COMPETITION

ENGLAND

VERSUS

WALES

at

Ninian Park, Cardiff
(by kind permission of Cardiff City A.F.C.)

on

Saturday, 29th March, 1969
Kick off 3 p.m.

SOUVENIR PROGRAMME   •   SIXPENCE

A toughie here, when was the Welsh Schools FA formed?

Round 12
Easy Peasy Round!

Now I'm aware that this book may stretch you here and there. Some questions are hard, even obscure.

But I am a broad church, if nothing else. I realise that not everyone grew up in the '70s, or has travelled the far corners of Europe following Wales.

So, just for you, here are what you might call some straightforward questions that I hope you enjoy. This may appeal to youngsters, new fans… or even rugby supporters.

1. From which club did Real Madrid sign Gareth Bale?
2. Who missed a penalty against The Netherlands in November 2015?
3. Which sports giant manufactures the current Wales kit (2016)?
4. In what year did Wales reach the quarter-finals of the World Cup?
5. Who was manager of Wales immediately before Chris Coleman?
6. Which Scottish club sold Joe Ledley to Crystal Palace?
7. At which club ground do Wales mostly play their home games these days (2016)?
8. Which of these countries is *not* in Wales' group for the forthcoming World Cup qualifiers: Austria, Slovenia or Serbia?
9. At whose club ground did Wales lose to Scotland in 1977?
10. In which city was Joe Ledley born?

I Say, I Say, I Say...

Can you name the record-breaking keeper who greeted Euro qualification with the line, 'Now go and try to win it'?

Picture this...

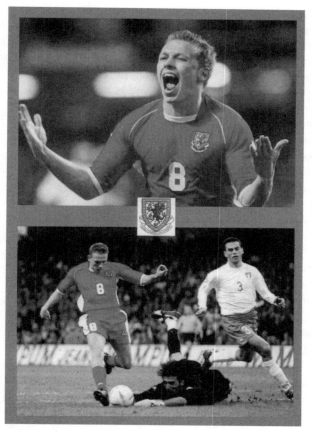

Who is this?

Round 13
The Gentle Giant

There are a handful of players who could lay claim to the title of the greatest ever Welsh footballer.

Ryan Giggs may have been in with a shout, but for a tendency to miss out on so many friendly appearances. Ian Rush would have his backers, I suppose. Like Giggs, his career at club level was a glittering one and his availability for Wales always gave grounds for optimism. Neville Southall was a giant for Wales and I would always throw Craig Bellamy into this kind of debate. Older fans would point to Ivor Allchurch, even Billy Meredith. Gareth Bale would have much support from the modern fan.

But few would argue with the choice of John Charles as the greatest ever Welsh footballer. Indeed, to those who saw him play, he is in with a shout as the greatest player ever, bar none.

We won't use these pages to develop that particular argument, but there is no doubt that Charles' standing in the game merits, at the very least, a special place in a book such as this. So here goes:

1. How many Welsh international caps did John Charles earn?

2. How many goals did he score for Wales?

3. Can you name either of the Italian teams for whom Charles played?

4. What relation was John to Mel Charles, who also starred for Wales in the 1958 World Cup?

5. For which team did John Charles play against Cardiff City in the 1968 Welsh Cup final at Ninian Park?

6. There is little doubt that the big man's contribution to the national cause was immense. But he was also a major figure at club level. Can you tell me the nickname applied

to Leeds United when Charles was a dominant figure there during the 1956/57 season?

7. Talking of nicknames, how's your Italian? What did the Italians nickname John Charles?

8. What can you tell me about Jake Charles?

9. Here's a nasty one. Can you name the Canadian club where John Charles had a spell as chief coach in 1987/88?

10. Finally, in which city would you find the street 'John Charles Way'? Worth a guess, maybe.

I Say, I Say, I Say...

Can you name the slightly controversial Welsh football figure who said, 'If you had 22 players of John's calibre, there would be no need for referees – only time-keepers.'

Picture this...

A National Memorial Service and
Celebration of the life of

John Charles

The Gentle Giant

John Charles
1931 - 2004

Brangwyn Hall, Swansea, 19th April 2004

Which song did John Charles once record?

Round 14
With My Can of Wrexham Lager...

Wrexham AFC is the oldest club in Wales. In fact it's the third oldest professional football team in the world, formed way back in 1864.

The first international fixture at The Racecourse was held almost 140 years ago, in 1877, between Wales and Scotland (a 2–0 victory for the away side) and, even though it is a less frequent international venue these days, it remains the world's oldest international stadium that still continues to host international games.

A long and glorious history then, memorable nights stood on the Kop or toasting success in The Turf. A host of famous names have swapped Wrexham's Crys Coch for the full national version. A gift to writers of quiz books on Welsh football, eh?

1. Which Wrexham-born midfielder notched two goals in a 3–0 home win over Norway at The Racecourse in 2008?

2. How many full international caps did Joey Jones win in total?

3. On 17 May 1980 Wales battered England 4–1 at Wrexham. Can you name the Welsh goal scorers that great day?

4. One for the even older fans next. Can you name the son of a Wrexham director who won 33 of his 43 caps while playing for West Bromwich Albion? He played in all Wales' group stage matches at the 1958 FIFA World Cup in Sweden, including the defeat to Brazil. Pelé later described his 'excellent play' in that famous match.

5. As I said, The Racecourse is a less frequent venue for home games these days, but back in the '70s and '80s it was very much the venue of choice. Hardly surprising when you recall some of the great results

Wales achieved there. For example, can you name the opponents when Wales won 7–0 there in a European qualifier in 1978?

6. Which future Wales manager headed the winner past England's Peter Shilton at The Racecourse on his debut in 1984?

7. Whose life story, *Football Wizard*, was described by the *Border Counties Advertiser* as 'A fascinating biography of a controversial but brilliant career'? His crowning achievement came when Wales beat England 2–1 at Highbury in 1920 on the last of his 48 appearances.

8. According to a banner at the 1977 European Cup final, who 'Ate the Frogs Legs', 'Made the Swiss Role' and was now 'Munching Gladbach'?

9. Which former Wrexham boss can count Cardiff City, Benfica and Galatasaray amongst his former clubs?

10. Which Welsh international striker once scored five goals in a single game for Wrexham in 2002 to equal a record that had stood for 68 years?

I say I say I say...

Who recently said 'I'd kept diaries at the start of a number of previous qualification campaigns but had to abandon them as Wales crashed out of contention after just a few games.'

Picture this...

Which son of Wrexham scored a cracker in this game?

Round 15
From a Jack to a... Dragon

In recent times, the story of Swansea City FC has been little short of remarkable.

From that dramatic 'I was there' moment against Hull City on the final day of the 2003 season, to the heights of the Premier League. Silverware, Wembley showpieces, European adventures. Just how high can these boys go?

Not surprisingly, such success has crossed over into the national side. Swans captain Ashley Williams leads both teams with such grit and dignity that, frankly, it would be hard to imagine anyone else doing either job. Even when the Swans have unloaded some of their talent for whatever reason, former Liberty favourites such as Joe Allen, Ben Davies or even Jazz Richards have come back to perform heroics for Chris Coleman's lads.

But was it always like this? Or do some of us recall darker days, so to speak.

Did you stand on the North Bank as the Welsh faced the Irish in 1979? Do you still shake with fear as you recall Alan Knill's debut against Marco Van Basten in a World Cup qualifier in Amsterdam back in 1988? Sure you do. This round should be no trouble for you then.

1. Easy one to start. We all know that Ash qualifies for Wales through his maternal grandfather, but do you know which Black Country town is named as his birthplace?

2. That famous (?) Alan Knill debut, can you remember the result?

3. Do we recall the darker days then? That infamous night against Iceland when the floodlights failed, did the shadows clear long enough for you to recollect the names of the two Welsh goal scorers from that eventful evening back in 1981?

4. Another great favourite of the old Vetch, keeper Roger Freestone spent many years waiting for a drop in form which never came from Neville Southall, but was finally rewarded to join Alan Knill in the 'one cap' club in 2000 against which country at the Millennium Stadium?

5. Right then, let's take you back a bit now shall we? Can you tell me Wales' opponents in the first ever international in Swansea? And tell me the venue?

6. From which fellow Welsh club did the Swans sign current Wales star Neil Taylor?

7. Another player who played for the same two Welsh clubs scored the winner against Czechoslovakia at Ninian Park in November 1980. Can you name him?

8. How many goals did Alan Curtis score for Wales?

9. Where was Joe Allen born?

10. Which former Swansea City striker once managed Macedonia?

I say, I say, I say...

A bit of a gimme here perhaps. Who was Matt Busby describing when he said 'Ivor didn't need a number on his back? His polish and class could not be missed'?

Picture this...

What was significant about this game, in terms of Swansea City?

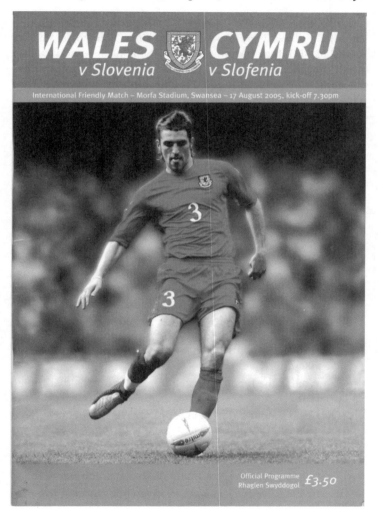

Round 16
Born Under a Grange End Star

Cardiff City have been around a long time. Formed in 1899 as Riverside AFC, they became Cardiff City in 1908. Famously, they are the only non-English team to have won the FA Cup. They have played in the Premier League. They have played in Europe. They have played in the Fourth Division.

Not surprisingly then, during this long, if fluctuating history, the Bluebirds have provided many players for the national side. Fred Keenor, John Toshack, Phil Dwyer – many sons of the city have gone on to earn Welsh caps. Over the years Cardiff City have also signed many a big name from the Welsh team to add sparkle to the side: Allchurch, Charles, Bellamy and many, many more.

So, surely you know all about these guys don't you? Don't you??

1. Let's go back a bit for the first one shall we? In a 1924 home international game between Wales and Scotland at Ninian Park, what was unusual about the two captains?

2. Who were the two Wales colleagues that Craig Bellamy teamed up with when he joined Blackburn Rovers in 2005?

3. What is the record attendance for a match held at Ninian Park?

4. Kevin Ratcliffe won many caps for Wales, but only one as a Cardiff City player. Can you name the opponents? It was in the 1992/93 season, if that helps.

5. Phil Dwyer made over 500 appearances for Cardiff City but do you know how many Wales caps 'Joe' earned?

6. In 1983, five players were involved in a startling five-man

swap deal between Cardiff City and Newport County. All five players were Welsh but only one earned full international honours. Which one was that then?

7. John Toshack had a spell as manager of Cardiff City. True or false?

8. We have somehow wandered into connections with both Newport and Swansea in this round. May as well go the whole hog, eh? Which Wrexham-born midfielder won 34 caps for Wales and enjoyed two spells as a Bluebird between 2005/06 and 2010/11?

9. Can you name the two Cardiff City favourites who made their debuts for Wales in a 3–1 defeat to Norway at Ninian Park in 1994?

10. Name the Cardiff-born winger who gained 29 Welsh caps between 1966 and 1975. I always associate him most closely with Sheffield United, though he also scored 35 goals in 114 games for The Bluebirds before joining Swansea City on loan in 1976. He also turned out for Ton Pentre, Pembroke Borough and Newport County. But, as I say, think Sheffield United.

I Say, I Say, I Say...

In discussing the improved preparations for international games after Mark Hughes replaced Bobby Gould in 1999, which unreserved Cardiff-born international wrote, 'We weren't in chaos... We didn't play charades any more. Sparky didn't have wrestling matches with the centre forward.' Ninety appearances for Cardiff City feature on his CV.

Picture this…

Against which side did this famous Kaairdiff Kiddy make his final appearance for Wales?

Round 17
County Set

If Swansea City, the national team and Gareth Bale have made many of the headlines in recent year, the lads down at Newport County have also enjoyed an eventful few years.

After years in the wilderness, 'the Exiles' eventually enjoyed improved fortunes, culminating in Wembley glory and a return to the Football League.

This is yet to manifest itself in any real representation in the national side and you might not necessarily put Newport County and international football together in your mind. But you would be wrong, for over the years 'the Port' have had their share of the international spotlight, as we shall demonstrate. See how the lads in the Ivy Bush get on with these, eh?

1   Which former County manager scored against Wales in 1983?

2   In September 2014, who became the youngest ever player to appear for Newport County, passing Steve Aizlewood's record of 1969?

3   Which north Wales club did former Welsh international midfielder John Mahoney manage before and after managing Newport County?

4   To which London club did Newport sell Cwmbrân product Steve Lowndes in August 1983?

5   Can you name the former Cardiff City manager who, when manager at Newport County, gave Nigel Vaughan his professional debut?

6   To which club did Mark Aizlewood move when he left Somerton Park in 1978?

7   The last few questions have featured players who began their careers at County, before going on to enjoy greater

success elsewhere. Over the years though, a number of star names from Welsh football have also moved to Newport towards the end of their playing days. For example, Rod Thomas won 50 Welsh caps and the 1974 league title with Derby County. But can you name the West Country side for whom he made nearly 300 appearances between 1964 and 1973?

8   Same sort of era perhaps. Flying winger Leighton James spent a spell as player-coach with Newport towards the end of his career before returning for another stint with Burnley. How many goals did James score in his 54 appearances for Wales?

9   Which former Wales international captained Aston Villa at Wembley in the 1970/71 League Cup final and joined Newport County for £10,000 in June 1973 from Bristol Rovers?

10   Trevor Ford became the leading Welsh goal scorer of all time in 1952, ending his international career with 23 goals in a glittering and 'colourful' career with many leading British clubs of the day. But from which Dutch club did Newport County sign Trevor Ford in 1960? There are clues elsewhere in these pages…

I say, I say, I say…

Who said this about who? 'It doesn't matter which country you are in, or where you are in the world, when Manchester United come calling you have to answer.'

Picture this...

Check out the Cewnty shirt on the cover here. Can you name the Welsh football fans' charity who undertake visits like the one shown in this picture?

Round 18
Eric Young is a Welshman!

One of the most popular chants amongst the faithful at Swansea's Liberty Stadium is a serenade to the skipper with the accolade 'Ashley Williams, he's captain of Wales.' Yes, for a non-Welshman, the Swansea captain has certainly cemented his place in the hearts of Welsh football fans.

But have all 'Anglo' Welsh players been as popular? For every Robert Earnshaw or Hal Robson-Kanu, do we also find a George Berry or an Alan Neilson? Try your hand at these questions to see how much you recall from these 'instant' Welshmen.

1. The 'Eric Young is a Welshman' line appeared on a fan's banner at the old Arms Park during the Palace stopper's spell in the red shirt back in the early '90s. Eric wasn't really Welsh of course, so can you tell me the land of *his* fathers?

2. Which Watford-born son of a Caerphilly father won 31 caps in the '80s and later managed Swansea City?

3. Funny how lots of the players in this round seem to be defenders? Can you recall the Gosport-born center-half who is probably best remembered for his role in the infamous Joe Jordan handball incident of 1977?

4. Where was James Chester born? And no, it's not Chester.

5. Of course, probably the most famous, or is that 'infamous', beneficiary of Welsh ancestry in this respect, was one Vincent Peter Jones, whose grandparents earned him nine caps between 1995 and 1997. Jones became a movie star when he hung up his boots. What was his debut film?

6. Who scored a hat-trick at the Millennium Stadium in 2004?

7. Let's go back a bit now. Which Keighley-born hard man was the first player to be sent off for Wales?

8. Sometimes these guys surprise you, mind. Dick Krzywicki doesn't sound like a native Welshman does he? But this scorer of a famous goal against England in 1970 is actually from which village in north Wales?

9. Jeremy Goss won 9 caps for Wales during the 1990s. In which land was he born?

10. Acton-born Hal Robson-Kanu is one of the more popular 'Anglos' of modern times. What's his proper name, though?

I Say, I Say, I Say...

'It's been emotional.' Says who?

Picture this...

Who is pictured here? Another not born in Wales.

Round 19
Pot Luck, or Pot 1?

Well? Like me, did you sit glued to the TV in July 2015 as the names were drawn? Was your remote control in one hand and your travel brochures in the other as you anticipated Mediterranean trips full of cold beer and hot nights?

Wales' run of recent form had, amazingly, seen us shoot up the infamous FIFA rankings to the dizzy heights of tenth. This put us at the very head of the queue when it came to drawing the names out of the hat for the 'race to Russia'. For once, we rubbed shoulders with the high and mighty of world football. And England.

Seems a long time ago doesn't it now though? For the time being, we may have parked the World Cup as we contemplate other goals, but it won't be long. And you will need to know your stuff ready for the next quiz book! Here's a taster for you to see how much of the draw you remember, just to whet your appetite.

1. As I said, Wales entered the draw for the World Cup as one of the top seeds, 'Pot 1' if you remember. But can you name the other teams that shared top billing with us in Pot 1 for the draw?

2. And then, the following day, the fixtures themselves were announced. Dublin on a Friday night! But against which opponent will Wales kick off their qualifying campaign?

3. Wales will face on or two old friends in these matches. Some of us still bear the scars. Which of the sides will we face beat us 5–0 as we battled to reach Euro '96?

4. And who scored our only goal as we slumped 6–1 away in Novi Sad during the last World Cup qualifiers?

5. Republic of Ireland boss Martin O'Neill played for Northern Ireland. True or False?

6. What is the capital of Moldova?

7. What group are we in? I mean, is it Group 1? 2? A? The Group of Death?

8. Which Wales legend scored an own goal 'for' Ireland at the Vetch in 1979?

9. In 1975 Wales famously beat Austria by a single goal at Wrexham to qualify for the quarter-finals of the European Championships. Who was the manager of Wales back then?

10. Wales look set for yet another trip to Belgrade to face the Serbs then. Can you name the two club sides that are mighty rivals in Belgrade?

I say, I say, I say...

What trip is this *Daily Telegraph* reporter describing here? 'I can remember flying in and thinking what a beautiful place it looked with all its vineyards. On the ground it was a different matter. Everything seemed as though it was black and white, like a 1950s Ealing Comedy.'

Picture this...

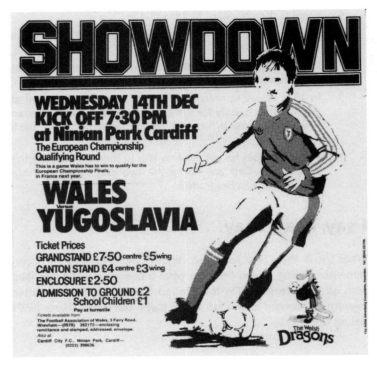

Many years ago, Serbia was part of Yugoslavia. Half of modern-day Europe seemed to be part of Yugoslavia then, and they were always just that bit too strong for us. This was yet another 'nearly night' for Wales. But what was the year?

Round 20
Gary Speed

To finish then, by way of a tribute, a round devoted to Gary Speed – a man who sowed the seeds for so much of what was to follow.

1. Gary Speed played for Wrexham for a spell. True or False?
2. For which of his league clubs did Speed score the most goals?
3. Here is a good one. Can you name the only player to be managed by Speed at both club and international level?
4. How old was Gary Speed when he eventually finished playing?
5. What was Gary Speed's role in THAT penalty against Romania in 1993?
6. Against which country did Wales play in the first game after Gary Speed's death?
7. Whose record did Speed pass for the most Welsh caps by an outfield player in 2003?
8. Which England striker attended the same school as Gary Speed?
9. How old was Gary when he died?
10. Sky reporter Bryn Law has used book signing sessions to help raise awareness of the Gary Speed Foundation. Can you tell me the name of his 2015 book?

I say, I say, I say...

Upon his death in 2011, which world football figure described Speed as 'a model professional and a fantastic ambassador for the game'.

Picture this...

Well, were Jamaica up to Speed?

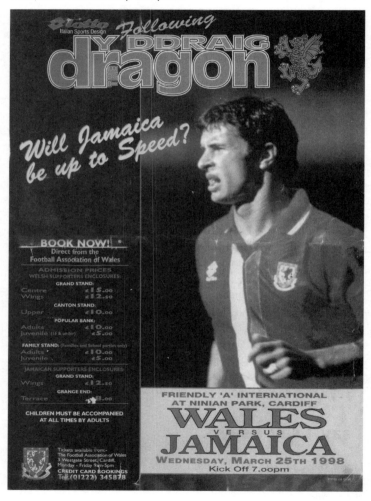

The Answers

Round 1
I read the news today, oh boy...

1. Watford.
2. Gary Lineker.
3. Swansea City, in 1987.
4. AFC Bournemouth.
5. Joe Allen watched his Liverpool team mates lose on penalties to Manchester City.
6. Ryan Giggs. The award is given for 'meritorious service to football'. Giggs picked up his special honour to complete a unique hat-trick of PFA prizes following his previous Young Player of the Year (1992) and Player of the Year (2009) successes.
7. Milton Keynes Dons.
8. Robert Earnshaw.
9. Andy King; 2016 was quite a year for him!
10. AFC Bournemouth.

I say, I say, I say...

France.

Picture this...

Fulham.

Round 2
The Bale Factor

1. Harry Wilson of Liverpool.

2. 203.

3. They are exactly the same height. Honest. Google it.

4. False. Spurs qualified for the Europa League via their league form during Bale's stint at the 'Lane'.

5. Joey Jones, Ian Rush and Ryan Giggs.

6. Chris Pike. Pike scored over 50 goals for Cardiff City in the '80s and '90s. His list of other Welsh clubs include: Cwmbrân Town, Llanelli and Rhayader Town.

7. Scotland.

8. The young lady is called Alba Violet Bale – a tribute to his former manager André Villas-Boas. (Does anyone else find that slightly weird?)

9. The deal for Bale easily beat the previous record set when Real Madrid acquired Cristiano Ronaldo for £80 million from Manchester United in 2009.

10. Seville.

I say, I say, I say...

FAW Chief Executive Jonathan Ford.

Picture this...

Rayo Vallecano.

Round 3
We are Premier League!

1. Andy King plays for Leicester City, who are sponsored by King Power.

2. 13.

3. When he netted against Norwich City on 1 February 2014, Bellamy set the record for having scored for seven different clubs in the Barclays Premier League: Cardiff City, Liverpool, Manchester City, West Ham United, Blackburn Rovers, Newcastle United and Coventry City.

4. It was Swansea City's home game with Wigan Athletic on 20 August 2011.

5. Two. West Bromwich Albion were managed by Newport-born Tony Pullis and Mark Hughes was in charge at Stoke. (Ryan Giggs was assistant manager too, of course. And don't forget Alan Curtis' role at Swansea.)

6. £15 million.

7. Robbie Savage (more than many who criticise!).

8. Paul Jones. The Chirk-born stopper went to Anfield on emergency loan. (By the way, some sources quote the year as 2004.)

9. Nottingham Forest. Wrong if you said Cardiff! Though he did have a spell on loan with the Bluebirds in 2011.

10. Gary Lloyd of Barry Town. Didn't win a cap though.

I Say, I Say, I Say…

Robbie Savage (again!).

Picture this…

Mark Hughes.

Round 4
Bad Boys

1. Matt Jones.
2. Davie Cooper.
3. Don Masson blasted the penalty past Dai Davies.
4. Ian Evans.
5. Chris Coleman.
6. Vinnie Jones.
7. Trevor Ford.
8. Never. Played eight, lost eight, including a 7–1 defeat in Eindhoven in 1996. Shame Trevor Ford wasn't still in Eindhoven that night!
9. Gil Reece.
10. Norway.

I Say, I Say, I Say...

The notorious Robbie Savage in 2001.

Picture this...

Christian Roberts, a man who knew some troubles in his time.

Round 5
In the Dugout

1. Italy.
2. Norway.
3. He was born in Swansea.
4. Holywell in Flintshire.
5. Northampton Town.
6. Brian Clough. Honest.
7. Mike Smith.
8. Jimmy Murphy.
9. Bayern Munich, on loan from Barcelona.
10. Terry Yorath.

I Say, I Say, I Say...

Well, it has to be, doesn't it? R. Gould Esq.

Picture this...

Jayne Ludlow.

Round 6
The Road to France

1. Edin Džeko.
2. Danny Gabbidon.
3. San Marino, Liechtenstein, Gibraltar, and the Faroe Islands.
4. Well, you can have Inverness Caledonian Thistle, where Owain Fôn Williams keeps goal; or Aberdeen, where Danny Ward spent time on loan.
5. Bosnia-Herzegovina, 0–0. Seems an age ago.
6. Some chap Bale.
7. This Bale chap again.
8. Reading.
9. Andy King.
10. Belgium. The stadium is on the site of the old Heysel Stadium.

I Say, I Say, I Say...

James Collins.

Picture this...

1–1.

Round 7
The Euros!

1. Slovakia. Course it is. But was there a touch of nerves there? Did you almost stumble and say Slovenia? Or even Czechoslovakia?
2. Wayne Rooney, of course. He passed Bobby Charlton's record in 2015. By the way, did you know that Peter Crouch has scored more goals for England than Kevin Keegan? Hard to imagine isn't it?
3. Mark Hughes. It ended in agonising defeat as we stood on the brink of further progress.
4. Aaron Ramsey. It was against Macedonia.
5. Ian Rush.
6. Lyon and Marseille.
7. The Henri Delaunay trophy.
8. None of the home nations took part until 1962.
9. Anfield.
10. They will be held in 13 cities in 13 different European countries.

I Say, I Say, I Say…

Gareth Bale. God, I hope these words don't come back to haunt us.

Picture this…

Nope. Denmark failed to qualify.

Round 8
Just a Minute

1. Neville Southall tops the list with 92 caps.
2. Cardiff!
3. Gorau Chwarae Cyd Chwarae.
4. Team Play is the Best Play. The 'Together.Stronger' tag is a modern adaptation of this.
5. He was born on Boxing Day 1990.
6. The FAW was formed on 2 February 1876.
7. Bobby Gould.
8. Southampton.
9. Ashley Darel Jazz Richards.
10. Jessica Fishlock is one of the leading lights of Welsh women's football. The Cardiff-born midfield dynamo has over 80 international caps and has captained the side on many occasions.

Round 9
1976 and all that

1. Arfon Griffiths.
2. Yugoslavia. A land which history and conflict subsequently divided into half-a-dozen different countries.
3. Yugoslavia 2 Wales 0. The tie was played in Zagreb, which is now the capital of Croatia.
4. Rudi Glöckner. He had also refereed the 1970 World Cup final, a wholly different occasion I promise you.
5. John Toshack's goal. Flynn, Philips and Mahoney were also booked by Mr Glöckner.
6. Terry Yorath.
7. A full four minutes.
8. He punched a home fan on the way down the tunnel! The mayhem that day was such that Wales were banned from competing in the next tournament, though this was overturned on appeal, to be replaced by a near £40,000 fine and an order that no home match in the next championship could be played within 125 miles of Cardiff.
9. A corner flag. But police arrested the wrong guy afterwards. I swear I am not making any of this up.
10. It was 1–1. Ian Evans scored for Wales after 38 minutes. Josip Katalinski had given the away side the lead with, inevitably, a penalty.

I Say, I Say, I Say...

Barry Davies.

Picture this...

Swansea City.

Round 11
140 Not Out

1. Nope. In their early fixtures the Welsh team's white shirts sported the three feathers, later to become so associated with rugby union.

2. He scored five goals! Meredith went on to miss six of the next 18 games for Wales.

3. Just three: Len Davies, Fred Keenor and Earnie Curtis.

4. Just two: Ashley Williams and Ben Davies.

5. 17.

6. They all appeared on *A Question of Sport*.

7. Dai Davies. Dai was the club keeper at Wrexham in those days so appeared on his home ground for this fixture. But the point about this game was that it was Wales' fifth clean sheet in five World Cup qualifiers at the start of the campaign. But did they qualify? Did they heck as like.

8. HM The Queen.

9. It's the FAW's Development and Training Centre at Newport International Sports Village.

10. In 2000, Wales played Brazil at the Millennium Stadium with the roof closed, thus making it the first international staged indoors in Britain.

I Say, I Say, I Say...

John Toshack.

Picture this...

1912.

Round 12
Easy Peasy Round!

1. Spurs.
2. Joe Allen.
3. Adidas.
4. 1958.
5. Gary Speed.
6. Celtic.
7. Cardiff City.
8. Slovenia.
9. Liverpool (I won't accept 'Anfield'. Read the question!)
10. Cardiff.

I Say, I Say, I Say...

Neville Southall.

Picture this...

Craig Bellamy.

Round 13
The Gentle Giant

1. 38, between 1950 and 1965.

2. 15.

3. Juventus or AS Roma.

4. John was Mel's older brother.

5. Hereford United. First match I ever went to!

6. Charles United.

7. Charles was never sent off or even booked throughout his career and was dubbed 'Il Gigante Buono' (The Gentle Giant) during his five years at Juventus. The respect Charles earned from Juventus fans was displayed when, in 1997, they voted him the best-ever foreign player to play for the team.

8. He is the grandson of John Charles and has represented Wales at various levels. He plays for Huddersfield Town.

9. The Hamilton Steelers! No, me neither.

10. Leeds. It's not far from Leeds' home ground at Elland Road.

I Say, I Say, I Say...

Referee Clive Thomas.

Picture this...

'Sixteen Tons'. Honest, it's even on YouTube.

Round 14
With My Can of Wrexham Lager...

1. Jason Koumas. By my reckoning this was the most recent full international played at Wrexham, though there have been under-21 games since.

2. 72.

3. Wrexham legend Micky Thomas grabbed one for Wales along with Ian Walsh and Leighton James. David Giles produced the last goal by shrugging off Kenny Sansom's challenge, forcing England's Phil Thompson to turn the ball into his own net. Gilo is a Wrexham old boy though, and he tells me he is claiming it! It was £1.50 to stand on The Kop that day by the way. Worth every penny.

4. Stuart Williams. The Wrexham-born defender made five appearances for his home town club before leaving for West Bromwich Albion.

5. Malta. Four goals for Ian Edwards that night.

6. Ruabon-born Mark Hughes.

7. Billy Meredith of Chirk.

8. Joey Jones! Rumour has it that he now has the actual banner in his garage.

9. Dean Saunders. One of a rare breed loaned to Cardiff City by Swansea City!

10. Lee Jones. Another locally-born product, who scored his five goals against Cambridge United on the day Wrexham were relegated.

I say I say I say...

Wexham fan and Sky Sports reporter Bryn Law (I can't tell you the title of the book until after Round 20!).

Picture this...

Mark Hughes.

Round 15
From a Jack to a... Dragon

1. Wolverhampton.
2. Amazingly, Wales did pretty well, losing only 1–0 to a late Ruud Gullit goal. Knill was never capped again.
3. Swans legend Robbie James gave Wales the lead while another, Alan Curtis, equalised to make it 2–2. Six Swansea players in the home line-up that night, by the way.
4. Brazil.
5. Wales beat Ireland 4–1 on 24 February 1894 at St Helen's.
6. Wrexham.
7. David Giles. Gilo also played for Cardiff and Newport. A unique feat.
8. 6.
9. Carmarthen, in 1990.
10. John Toshack. He also managed Swansea City too, as you may be aware.

I say, I say, I say...

Why, local golden boy Ivor Allchurch, of course; 68 caps for Wales, the last of which was earned when he was 37 years old.

Picture this...

This was the first international at what we now know as the Liberty Stadium. This game was before that name was even in use though, as the front of the programme confirms. It was the first game staged at the 'new' stadium.

Round 16
Born Under a Grange End Star

1. Both played for Cardiff City. Fred Keenor skippered the Welsh and the Scots were led by Jimmy Blair. You probably could have guessed that, but did you know that, according to the custom of the time, they both wore their club socks in the game?

2. Manager Mark Hughes and Robbie Savage.

3. On 14 October 1961, a record attendance of 61,566 saw Wales draw 1–1 with England at Ninian Park.

4. Belgium.

5. 10 (he was called Joe due a likeness with the Everton star Joe Royle, apparently).

6. Nigel Vaughan. He and Karl Elsey left Somerton Park for Ninian Park with Linden Jones, Tarki Micallef and Linden Jones travelling in the opposite direction. Nigel Vaughan won ten caps for Wales, the first of which he won as a County player, against Yugoslavia.

7. False. Cardiff-born Toshack famously managed Swansea City of course, but never his home town club. Big Tosh did have a one-game spell in the Ninian Park dugout as manager of Wales against Norway in 1994. Tosh resigned after 44 days but was reappointed in 2004.

8. Jason Koumas.

9. Nathan Blake and Jason Perry (John Toshack's 'one-game reign').

10. Gil Reece.

I Say, I Say, I Say…

Craig Bellamy.

Picture this…

Belgium 2013.

Round 17
County Set

1   Terry Butcher equalised for England after Ian Rush had given Wales the lead. England ran out 2–1 winners.

2   Welshman Regan Poole. Regan was born as recently as, wait for it, 18 June 1998. I have socks older than that!

3   Bangor City.

4   Millwall.

5   Jimmy Scoular. Like Lowndes, Vaughan won ten full caps for Wales.

6   Luton Town. Aizlewood's career started at County as a 16 year old, before earning 39 caps alongside the likes of Rush, Hughes and Southall.

7   Swindon Town. The Wiltshire outfit also won the League Cup in 1969. Thomas made a handful of appearances for County at the end of his playing days.

8   10.

9   Brian Godfrey.

10 PSV Einhoven.

I say, I say, I say...

Terry Butcher said this when describing Regan Poole's astonishing move to Manchester United in 2015.

Picture this...

Gôl.

Round 18
Eric Young is a Welshman!

1. Eric Young is one of a number of players who qualify for any of the four home countries by virtue of being a UK passport holder. Pat Van Den Hauwe is another. Young was born in Singapore of West Indian parents.

2. Kenny Jacket. Kenny the Jack, even.

3. Dave Jones.

4. Warrington. His mother is from Rhyl.

5. *Lock, Stock and Two Smoking Barrels*. A 1998 box office hit.

6. Robert Earnshaw. Earnie was born in Zambia.

7. Trevor Hockey. Nine caps in the early '70s.

8. Penley, which is near Wrexham. His father, a soldier from Poland, was serving there at the time.

9. Cyprus.

10. Henry Alex Robson-Kanu.

I Say, I Say, I Say...

Big Chris (Vinnie Jones' character in *Lock, Stock and Two Smoking Barrels*).

Picture this...

Boston-born John Oster.

Round 19
Pot Luck, or Pot 1

1. A toughie, I agree. Well, you could have had Belgium, Croatia, England, Germany, The Netherlands, Portugal, Romania and Spain.
2. Moldova, 5 September 2016.
3. Georgia, away in Tbilisi.
4. Gareth Bale. A Serbian stuffing.
5. True. He won 64 caps. He also played Gaelic Football with distinction.
6. Chişinău – and you have to include all those little accents in your answer.
7. Group D.
8. Joey Jones.
9. Mike Smith.
10. Red Star Belgrade and Partizan Belgrade.

I say, I say, I say...

This colourful account refers to Wales' journey to Moldova in 1994. Still fancy the trip lads?

Picture this...

It was 1983. Wales would have qualified for Euro '84 with a victory but the Slavs equalised ten minutes from time.

Round 20
Gary Speed

1. Sadly, it's untrue. He was born in Mancot, Flint, but never played for Wrexham.
2. Between 1988 and 1996 Gary Speed appeared for Leeds United 248 times, and scored 39 times.
3. Ched Evans. Sheffield United was the club.
4. He played his last game aged 39 but announced his retirement at the age of 41.
5. He was brought down for the penalty.
6. Costa Rica. Speed's first appearance had come against the same opposition in 1990 at Ninian Park.
7. Speed broke the record held by Dean Saunders when he won his 76th cap against Finland.
8. Michael Owen. The school in question was Hawarden High School.
9. 42.
10. *Zombie Nation Awakes*.

I say, I say, I say...

Sepp Blatter.

Picture this...

Not so much. The game finished without a goal.

Acknowledgements

Bibliography, References
and ideas stolen from other people

It's hard to construct an accurate list of reference sources for a book like this. Most of the questions have been produced from nothing more authoritative than the faded pages of my own imagination.

For example, the Andy King shirt sponsorship question came to me one morning in Llandudno whilst watching *Match of the Day*. I didn't look it up, it just came to me. You can check it out of course, but it works.

Other facts have more reliable sources. Joe Allen's birthplace is a matter of public record, for instance. And I knew Roger Freestone played against Brazil, simply because I was at the match.

OK, I probably checked the odd fact here and there to confirm who-scored-in-which-game-and-in-what-year, but to try and list, or even remember, each time I did that would be virtually impossible.

Nevertheless I am obliged to quote any specific sources upon which I have relied. So we'll have a go...

Some sources stick more in the mind, of course. There are some great quotes from Robbie Savage on the 'Expert Football' website for instance. I should also record my appreciation for the plethora of facts churned out by Sky Sports, BBC Radio Wales, the Cardiff City Message Board, various Facebook and Twitter accounts run by Wales fans, the *Western Mail*, *South Wales Echo*, *South Wales Evening Post*, *South Wales Argus* and Wales Online. The FAW's website was also a great source of corroboration and knowledge, especially this bit www.faw.org.uk/history.

Individual publications have also played their part. My

Philip's Modern School Atlas, for example, from 1973 was vital in researching the geography of Yugoslavia, while Lonely Planet's *Europe on a Shoestring* has navigated me around many continental excursions which have informed questions in this book.

Here are some other sources, listed loosely in chronological order, which I have found to be especially reliable:

Neil Dymock's excellent fanzine *The Dragon Has Landed* has been going for over ten years now. Its engaging mix of opinion, stories, facts and figures has been a well of useful information. Rhys Lewis' contributions were especially helpful here and there.

When Pelé Broke Our Hearts, Mario Risoli's account of the Welsh national football team's 1958 World Cup campaign, published by St David's Press, includes a foreword by John Charles, with the 2001 edition also including a preface by Manic Street Preacher's Nicky Wire.

Born Under a Grange End Star (Sigma, 2002). Author, Yours Truly. Read the bit about the Draig Goch.

Hard Man, Hard Knocks by Terry Yorath (Celluloid, 2004), is an incisive insight into the life of a former Wales captain who played in the last eight of the European Championships.

Wales: The Complete Who's Who of Footballers since 1946 (Sutton Publishing, 2004), the definitive guide to those lucky enough to have pulled on the red jersey. A very useful bedside companion.

Swans and Dragons, John Burgum's 2005 recollections from his days as the *South Wales Evening Post* football correspondent between 1974 and 1999.

The Who's Who of Cardiff City (Breedon Books, 2006), Dean Hayes' encyclopaedia was a vital reference book for me. I might have had a sneaky look back through the *Never Mind the Bluebirds Quiz Books* too, I guess. Published by the History Press in 2012 and 2013. Authors? Me and Gareth Bennett.

Shine on Swansea City, Keith Haynes' emotional tale of just one season in the life of his beloved Swans. Published by my friends at the History Press in 2012.

A Question of Sport Quiz Book, David Gymer and David Ball, published by BBC Books in 2011.

GoodFella, Craig Bellamy's frank autobiography, published by Trinity Mirror Sport Media in 2013.

More recent works of authority include Phil Stead's excellent *Red Dragons: The Story of Welsh Football* (Y Lolfa, 2015). Huw Richards from *When Saturday Comes* described Phil's chronicles as a better contribution to Welsh football than many who have actually played the game.

Zombie Nation Awakes (St David's Press, 2015), Bryn Law's evocative account of the life of a Wales fan; the book we all wish we were clever enough to write.

A number of individuals have also been supportive of this book, offering encouragement, titbits, critical assessment, help with foreign travel and alcoholic sustenance throughout its development. Special mention to Karen Robinson, Tim Hartley, Duncan Jardine, Tim Williams, David Giles, Gareth Bennett, Corky, Vince Alm, Mal Pope, Dan Collins, Rhys Collins, the bar staff at the City Arms, the Hollybush, Pentwyn, and New Quay FC clubhouse. Diolch hefyd i bawb at Y Lolfa for believing that I could actually deliver this book in time.

I should also record my thanks to the many people who have endured and shared my pain watching Wales over the years. My father who took me to my first Wales game, Kevin Davies, Gary Stockford, Cwmislwyn, Mark Watkins and Irene, Andrew Gibraltar, SO58, Tommy Collins, DOG, Alyson Rees and Gwilym. The Gogs who drove me to Macedonia. That mad bird in a bar in Andorra. The 4 on Tour. Everyone at Gôl. You all played your part.

Finally, I must acknowledge the contribution to this book made by those whose work is now housed in my attic. For there, you will find 60 years of football programmes, many produced by the hard-working FAW. Credit also to the numerous publications produced by the various associations against whose teams we have crossed swords down the years. Toss in around three generations of personal memorabilia and sack-loads of assorted debris from matches I barely remember, and you have quite a body of work. Forget the national library, if you are thinking of writing a book, just look in my attic!

David Collins
2016

Gôl is the Welsh football supporters' charity which aims to help underprivileged children, both home and abroad, whenever the Welsh national football team play. Formed in 2002, Gôl has helped over 30 orphanages, children's hospitals and schools in over 30 countries. On our drive to the Bosnia game in 2015 we also visited a Syrian refugee camp in Koblenz, Germany, with gifts of clothes and sports equipment. Will you help us help them? 'Together Stronger.'

https://www.facebook.com/golcymru

"Hartley writes with wisdom and passion as he shares his world in these thoroughly entertaining travel diaries."

Huw Edwards

KICKING OFF IN NORTH KOREA

Football and Friendship in Foreign Lands

TIM HARTLEY

y Lolfa

£9.99

'An excellent contribution to Welsh football literature.'
Chris Coleman

The Dragon
Roars Again

WALES' JOURNEY
TO EURO 2016

#TogetherStronger
FRANCE 2016

JAMIE THOMAS

y Lolfa

£9.99

"This truly is one of the greatest football titles that I have ever read."
—International Soccer Network

Red Dragons

THE STORY OF WELSH FOOTBALL

Phil Stead

Includes the road to France

£9.99

The Welsh Football Quiz Book is just one
of a whole range of publications from Y Lolfa.
For a full list of books currently in print, send
now for your free copy of our new full-colour
catalogue. Or simply surf into our website

www.ylolfa.com

for secure on-line ordering.

TALYBONT CEREDIGION CYMRU SY24 5HE
e-mail ylolfa@ylolfa.com
website www.ylolfa.com
phone (01970) 832 304
fax 832 782